CW01497724

The Waterfall

Also by Gareth Rubin

Holmes and Moriarty
The Turnglass
The Winter Agent
Liberation Square

The Waterfall

Gareth Rubin

**SIMON &
SCHUSTER**

London · New York · Amsterdam/Antwerp · Sydney/Melbourne · Toronto · New Delhi

First published in Great Britain by Simon & Schuster UK Ltd, 2025

Copyright © Gareth Rubin, 2025

The right of Gareth Rubin to be identified as author of this work has been asserted in accordance with the Copyright, Designs and Patents Act, 1988.

1 3 5 7 9 10 8 6 4 2

Simon & Schuster UK Ltd, 1st Floor
222 Gray's Inn Road, London WC1X 8HB

For more than 100 years, Simon & Schuster has championed authors and the stories they create. By respecting the copyright of an author's intellectual property, you enable Simon & Schuster and the author to continue publishing exceptional books for years to come. We thank you for supporting the author's copyright by purchasing an authorised edition of this book.

Simon & Schuster Australia, Sydney
Simon & Schuster India, New Delhi

www.simonandschuster.co.uk
www.simonandschuster.com.au
www.simonandschuster.co.in

The authorised representative in the EEA is Simon & Schuster Netherlands BV, Herculesplein 96, 3584 AA Utrecht, Netherlands. info@simonandschuster.nl

Simon & Schuster strongly believes in freedom of expression and stands against censorship in all its forms. For more information, visit BooksBelong.com

A CIP catalogue record for this book is available from the British Library

Hardback ISBN: 978-1-3985-3538-1
Trade Paperback ISBN: 978-1-3985-3539-8
eBook ISBN: 978-1-3985-3540-4
Audio ISBN: 978-1-3985-3542-8

This book is a work of fiction. Names, characters, places and incidents are either a product of the author's imagination or are used fictitiously. Any resemblance to actual people living or dead, events or locales is entirely coincidental.

Typeset in the UK by Palimpsest Book Production Limited, Falkirk, Stirlingshire

Printed and Bound in the UK using 100% Renewable Electricity
at CPI Group (UK) Ltd

To Penelope and Aldrich,
for your years of friendship.
Matthew Wetherby, 10 December 1925

The Waterfall

A Testament

The First Part

It is now the spring of the year of our Lord one thousand five hundred and ninety-three. I scratch these letters onto whatever scraps of paper remain to me. I dare not stop writing lest another hand stops mine before I am done.

I must begin with a thread of recollection.

It was Ascension-eve, the nineteenth day of May under the new calendar, and a Saturday, too, so a merry day. The proud sun was warming us like a blanket while Alicette and I rode from Canterbury to London on the great Watling Street that the Romans had laid.

I was on an especially lazy white cob, with Alicette on a dun pony at my side. Along the way, we had eaten well of the bounty of Kent – England's Garden, as the portly King Henry named it. Apples, plums, a little mutton. Oh yes, our bellies were straining at the girdles.

I had been to Kent with Lord Strange's Men to play my *Shrew* at a few inns and churchyards, the London stages being all closed. Canterbury has been spared the horror of our age, and I fancy it is the spirit of the great martyr St Thomas that keeps the Pestilence at bay.

The tomb of that holy man is a fine sight to behold. And no less is the patient, wending line of gentlemen, paupers, women and servants to kneel before it. The cathedral, a seat that points to the Heavens, is built of yellow stones and joyful pilgrim tears, such that I felt affected by their quiet piety. Even the stalls within the great church selling beer and capons and the 'doctors' selling their patent cures for corns of the toes showed a modicum of respect, so that they held their tongues while the archdeacon made the Eucharist.

Alicette and I – oh, writing the letters of her name affects me in a way that writing Anne's never did, for which I feel at once joyful and ashamed – took a turn in the cathedral precincts aftertime. There I set eyes on the Lord of Canterbury, the Archbishop himself, John Whitgift – a walnut-skinned fellow a little shorter than myself and of a strongly built stature, with small dark eyes that flicked about. He was deep in conversation with one of his minions, a beautiful-faced young man, perhaps five-and-twenty, with hair like white silk. They were walking and chuckling at some jest, I fancied. Whitgift is not a gentleman known as a great rollicker – indeed, better known for his jealousy of ecclesiastical riches and having his enemies within the Church broken to pieces – so the jest must have been an excellent one.

We passed them as we went out to enjoy the city. Canterbury would do well to have a playhouse as grand as our Rose. The burghers seem less dim-witted than most, and I did wish that we could play again in a true theatre. My feet have had enough of stomping on cobblestones in inn yards. (I am not the hardiest creature, I confess – I am of a middling height, with genial features and thinning ginger hair. And my delicate fingers would have suited a girl, I was told at school in Warwickshire.)

But on that Saturday, we were gone, and it was as we reached the Thames-side village of Greenwich, some three miles from London, that we passed the Palace of Placentia, where our gracious Queen had been brought into this world. It is a fine red-brick dwelling, built long on the riverbank to watch the boats pass by. Made for pleasure, and pleasure only, it pleases the eye as well as the heart of any Englishman who takes pride in the repute that his country has for merriment.

We trotted happily another hour through the fields and lanes that took us to the city where we had made our home; but by and by, the day began to darken a little. The sun still shone, the birds still tweeted, but the mood around us had changed.

'Do you feel that, Will?' Alicette asked me.

'I do.' It was a cold wind. Its fingers were creeping inside my doublet and wringing at my heart. Sometimes nature herself will send us missives in disguise.

Forsooth, the spirit of London had come upon us. Suspicion in every casement, every doorway, watchful for what foulness we might bring with us. More eyes than the cornfields followed us as we rode through the streets. My fingers went to the poniard in my boot, to tell myself that it was there still. Oh, the idol of our age is a barred door; and all the angels are turned to guardsmen.

As our hooves entered the great city and fell as fours on the great bridge arching over the Thames, I heard a tell-tale sound: the ringing of a bell. With more hope than belief, I looked to the chapel of St Thomas in the centre of the bridge, asking that the noise be coming from the bell-loft there. But those rings have been gone for fifty years, since the old king crushed the Catholic religion.

No, this sound was a handbell, and it walked palm-in-palm with the terrible words: *bring out your dead*. We halted in front of the chapel. One of those dread doctors, encased in a wool cloak sealed with wax, his bird-beak leather mask over his face to ward off the sick-making miasma with a mush of peppermint and cloves, stood before me. His arms were up to the Heavens as he recited those words over and over. Behind him was his handcart loaded with the dead. I know not how he came to be but five yards from me, for I swear by Christ's wounds that he had not been a moment before. My cob whinnied and bucked. Animals have senses men cannot conceive, and he could tell that this creature was not of the sanctified earth. Time and again, these bird-men enter a putrid house and push away the clawed hands imploring them for cure, for medicine. But they cure nothing.

They only remove and record. The body goes on the bier, the score goes on the slate.

He stood still, with his arms and face raised up as if welcoming me to Hell.

'What do you want?' I demanded, angered by his presence thrust into my life.

He said nothing, but I saw his eyes moving behind the dusty glass lenses in his mask. They roved over me and Alicette. Then, without a word, he turned, pushed his handcart to the edge of the bridge and lifted the handles. At first, the three naked corpses upon it did not move. Then they shook. They began to roll and tumble, and over the stone edge they fell. A great ring of water rose up as they dropped through the chill surface, down to the reeds that would entangle them and never let go.

'Are there no pits?' Alicette asked me, shocked.

'There are. But it takes him time to get to them,' I told her. She shivered, and I did the same. Death is nothing but the currency of the age. The theatres are shut, the apprentices make no mayday riots, all is sad. But to see what had once been bonny young lives disposed of as trash left me heart-sick as we walked to the house that I rent close by the Aldersgate. I should have felt cheerier, for it is a fine new place, built well, cool in the summer and warm in the winter. And it has little problem with rats.

I was upon the threshold and about to call up to my servant, Marcel, who is cheap, when Alicette pointed to a big heap of old clothes that someone had cast down at the corner of the building.

'Be wary, Will,' she said.

I did not need her to recall to me what danger lurked in old clothes. The Pestilence is always on our shoulders in London. With a great care, I drew the poniard from my boot and made to shog the heap away from my home.

'Hold your hand!' the pile growled. And I suddenly beheld within it two eyes, livid as brimstone, staring at me. I knew them even before their owner had dragged himself to his feet and pulled the hood from his scalp.

'For the love of Heaven, Kit!' I said. 'You smell like a goat.'

He opened his doublet and sniffed. 'I cannot forswear you, Will. I do. I have been living like one for the past three days. It was without chance that I would not smell like a farmyard.'

'Oh, come in.' I sighed wearily. 'I will have Marcel pour some rose water over you. It might disguise the reek for a short while.'

'Thank you kindly.'

'Who is he?' Alicette whispered as Marcel opened the house and stood back to let my friend and collaborator enter.

'Kit Marlowe. Sometime playmaker, sometime gentleman, sometime pigsty.'

'Yet always a gentleman,' he insisted, having earwigged. He bowed low. And there was a slight malevolence in his eye-cast. To describe him, Kit was a tall and broad-built man and Roister Doister pugnacious. His features were boyishly pointed, which made him look untrustworthy, when most of the time he was simply bored. His staccato vowels denoted Kent as his origin, and he rarely wore ruffs, preferring collars because he said ruffs itched at his neck. He never mentioned the truth that he attended the university at Cambridge, allowing him the title of 'gentleman', while I did not; but he many times very noisily did not mention it. It so happens that our beginnings were remarkably similar: both born in the year 1564 in the provinces. His father made shoes, while mine made gloves, and we were both schooled in the grammars. Had fate and fatherhood not decreed that I should be forced to marry Anne at the age of eighteen years, we might even have met and begun composing works together then. Perhaps I could have diverted him from the path of self-destruction.

'Do gentlemen often dress like dung-heaps?' Alicette replied.

'Take care,' I told her. 'He bites.'

'Bite, kick . . .'

'. . . steal?' I proposed.

'On occasion.' And he broke into a wide smile. He had, at least, a handsome smile, Kit. And good teeth, a pleasing shade of yellow.

My parlour was comfortably appointed, with rush matting that covered the beaten-earth floor and two good-quality benches that I had bought from the Earl of Leicester's man when the old gentleman decided he wished to reside in Wales with his mistress. I am all for residing with one's mistress, but not if it means Wales. Alicette arranged herself most comely on one bench as I held my arms open for Kit.

'Come, then,' I said. He embraced me and did a little sailor's jig as he did so. 'Sit and tell me why you have not bathed for a month.'

He sat and peeped around at my home. The man who built my house had begun to deck the walls with oak panelling, but seems to have run out of gold, for the panelling also runs out, about halfway across the room, leaving only the whitewashed plaster. He had also been unable to afford glass for the windows, so they are constructed of oiled cloth instead and let little light in. Marcel therefore lit a half-dozen tallow candles, filling the room with the smell of burning pig fat. To oppose this stink, he subsequently went around wafting dried lavender.

'What the devil is he doing?' Kit asked.

'Wasting his legs. Marcel, leave be and fetch us some wine.'

'Aye, master,' he said, ambling back to the kitchen.

I took note of Kit staring at a tapestry I had hung. It was a rough depiction of sinners standing before St Peter to be judged. Some were being lifted by angels to the clouds overhead, while others were being dragged down by horned devils to the underworld.

'What do you think of it?' I asked.

'I think it scares me right to Hell.'

'Then it has achieved the weaver's intent.'

'I hope he gets gut-ache!' He shivered. 'I am in danger, Will.'

'Your everlasting soul?'

'My more fragile body.'

Marcel brought us three pewter cups of Rhenish

wine. It was stale and tasted so. Alicette grimaced and I nearly spat mine on the floor, but Kit threw his back and asked for more.

'You are not jesting,' I said.

'I am not.'

In the few years I had known Kit, he had rarely been out of danger. He had a nose for it.

'What is it this time? Have you been selling saints' bones? Is it a jealous husband? A jealous wife? Murder?'

'Murder is closest,' he said grimly.

I caught Alicette's glance. She had known him for three minutes and already she could tell that anything sinful was within Kit Marlowe's scope.

'Will you tell me?'

He licked his lips. It was his habit when he was uncertain whether to reveal himself or not. 'You are not my confessor.'

'I hope, Kit, that you do not *have* a confessor. If you have, they will hang you.'

He jumped up and began pacing. 'Ach!' he cried. 'You think that is the danger? You think I have gone back to the old religion? Oh, Will, if only you—' He caught his tongue and stared at Alicette.

'She is my companion, Kit, and I trust her to play mum far more than I trust you for it.'

He grumbled under his breath.

'I shall leave if you wish it,' she said, rising.

I held up my hand. This was my house, and I would choose who could or could not haunt it. I was irritated by Kit's unfriendly actions. 'No,' I said. 'Kit can go or stay, but I have invited you and not him. Few people ever invite Kit, he just appears.'

'This is no game, Will,' he said.

Alicette could see the determination on his countenance. 'I shall leave,' she said firmly. I accepted, though I had been relishing our evening together. I kissed her hand, she curtsied and left.

'What is the affair?' I asked sharply as her gown rustled up the staircase.

'Your man?'

I sighed.

'Marcel!' He came. 'Bring the rest of the bottle, then you may retire for the night.' He nodded happily, fetched the rest of the Rhenish and betook himself to the loft at the rear of the house, where he had a comfortable cot lined with fresh straw.

'*Marcel*,' Kit muttered to himself.

'Aye.'

'French, is he?'

'Piedmontese. Why?'

'Can't trust the French right now.'

'Piedmontese. And a Huguenot.'

'Pah! So he says.'

'Do you think he has been sent by the French king to spy on my kitchen? Mayhap he is sending back intelligence on how I like my hens cooked.'

'Mayhap he is!' He jumped up as if bitten by ants and strode around the room. 'There are stranger things in this life, Will. Five miles stranger.'

'What has gotten into you? And what do you mean "murder is closest" to what makes you so nervy?' He stopped by the window, tried to penetrate the oily cover with his sight, gave up and opened the door to peep out. 'Calm yourself. No spies.'

'So you think.'

'Aye, so I think.' His histrionics were beginning to itch upon me. He was a master playmaker but a grating player.

'Elizabeth has signed a warrant for my arrest.'

That jolted me. He had been taken by the constables for brawling many a time, but that his riots had reached the ears of the Queen was a surprise. 'Upon what grounds?'

He turned and showed me his teeth again. 'Atheism.'

'Oh, Kit, for the love of . . . How?'

'They took Kyd on the same charge last week. The little adder gave me to them in return. He handed them some of my writing that I had left in our rooms.'

'What did it say?'

He leant his back to the wall and gave way to a crooked smile, as if it were a summer's morn in Kew. 'I believe it was my claim that Christ used John the Evangelist as a boy of Sodom.'

I shook my head. Kit was a preening child at times. 'How clever of you. So clever that they may tie a noose around your neck and snap it. You may die laughing. It is no wonder you are frightened.'

'Frightened? Of that? Pish.' He fluttered his hands. 'Whitgift will stay that order.'

'Whitgift?'

'My Lord of Canterbury, aye.'

My first thought was that he was boasting. My

second, which carried more danger, was that he was not. If the prelate of all England was like to prevent Kit's persecution for such a calumny on Christ, the reason was a dark one. I was uncertain that I wanted an answer to my following question.

'Why should he do that?'

'Why should he do anything?' He chuckled to himself and none other. 'Because he wants something.' I knew he was expecting me to guess a black deed. 'He wants knowledge that I possess.'

'Will you give it to him?'

He drummed his palms on the wall. It quivered a little. 'I have not yet determined that. There are reasons to do so, reasons not to do so.'

'If the reason to give it is that he stays the Queen's hand and keeps you from dancing the Tyburn jig at the end of a rope, I should say that would out-strong any argument to the contrary.'

'Yes, you would think so, would you not? And yet . . .' He stopped his tongue and peered hard through the oil cloth. 'The church clock strikes.'

'It is St Botolph's.'

'St Botolph's,' he said thoughtfully. 'Was that eight chimes?'

'It was.'

'Then I must go. I am late already.'

I was tiring of his mood and did not want to enquire where he was expected. 'Go, then.'

'May I return tomorrow?'

'Tomorrow eve. Sup with us.'

'I shall.'

Without another word, he threw his black cloak over himself, studied the street, up and down, and hurried in the direction of the river. I watched him leave, startling a constable of the watch, who shone his lamp in Kit's face and shrank into a crevice, his lavender nosegay pressed to his face to keep the Pestilence at bay.

I betook myself to our sleeping chamber. Alicette was warm and soft after a hard journey.

The morning arrived, and I made my way to the Rose. That fine playhouse is most certainly the best of our theatres. Oh, it may not have the luxury of those on the north side of the Thames, but Southwark does well for it, and there are both a bear pit and a bordello within twenty paces, so all a man's entertainment is on hand with great convenience.

I spent the day working on my new play about a moneylender of Venice. George Bryan, who was to play the character of Shylock, was uncertain about a speech that he said would make the groundlings cry, which was out of sorts for a comedy. 'Ah, but George, they cry so that they can later laugh,' I told him. He took the thought, and we worked on how best to present the speech. Afterwards I spent some hours writing more, but I had trouble with a scene in a courthouse, wherein Shylock is bested by an old lawyer's clever words that call first for mercy and then for its very opposite. I could find not the spirit of the scene, and my mind went to a time more than a year beforehand, when Kit had been struggling with his *Faustus* play in the same way.

We had only been braced together as friends for a few months then – I had come from my home in Stratford-upon-Avon to seek a life more vivid than that of a glovemaker's son with three mewing children and a wife already turning her eye upon others. I had found work as a player, oftentimes taking the role of the faithful retainer or a comic porter. I would never play the young lover or king, I knew. But I felt it strongly that the playmakers of the day were too poetical in their minds and failing in the drama. Give me tragedy, give me comedy, but do not give me page after page of flowers.

And then I saw Kit's *Tamburlaine*. A tale of nations at war, and of a man who controlled them. And his *Jew of Malta*, where the Hebrew is wicked, but beneath his skin you can see a human heart beat. The sheer danger of *The Massacre at Paris* as it depicted the killing of our fellow Protestants and agitated for the murder of those across the waters who would undermine England, all watched by an English agent who warns of what is to come. The people of our country, from the lowest drudge to the highest duke, were flocking to his dizzying plays, and with fine reason. Christopher Marlowe's stages held swathes of history but populated the eye and ear with human lives. Such a blaze of talent he had, such soaring ambition. What I had not realized, until I met the man, was just how much of an arse he could be in person. And I write that as one of his closest friends. Forsooth, I write that as possibly his only remaining friend after what appeared to have been his long campaign to make all the others look upon him as they would an especially careless bullock that had suddenly appeared in their bed chambers.

By the autumn of the year of our Lord one thousand five hundred and ninety, Kit was composing what he said would be his highest glory, *The Tragical History of the Life and Death of Doctor Faustus*, the man who dared to grasp the genius of the Heavens and was dragged down to the fiery pit for it. But after Kit's pen ran dry of words and we had spent two full days attempting to wet it in the taverns of Cheapside and Southwark, I told him to go home and sleep it off.

'We must act it out!' he burbled like an ape, upending the dregs of a flagon of ale upon his crown.

'What do you mean?' I answered him – or at least, I thought I did. I was so drunk I might have been addressing a stool.

'On the morrow. At midnight. Not a minute too soon, not a minute too late. The hour of the witch. Then my Mephistopheles will come!'

I thought he was talking out of his hose, of course.

Aye, I thought that right up until I was freezing my stones off beneath the clock of St John's Church in Farringdon in the pitch dark.

'There should be rain. Thunder. Bugger it, there should be lightning!' That was Kit, yelling his head off against the lack of strong weather flashing about us. 'Did you hear what—'

'Yes, I heard.' That was me, huddling myself and wishing I had not come.

'And you two. Do something.' He jabbed a finger at the others on the scene. 'Don't make me come over and do it for you.'

A boy aged perhaps fifteen and a girl ten years older than him were lying on the rough earth. A few sprigs of grass poked into their flesh.

'Oh, get on with it,' the girl muttered. 'I have to be out of my bed in five hours.'

'You are being well paid.'

'Thruppence? That won't even pay the wherry to Chelsea.'

'Oh, does milady wish for more? Perhaps a barge and chair to remove her to her bawdy house?'

The girl sneezed. 'The grass does this,' she said.

Around them were a ring of six torches stuck in the ground.

'Kit,' I tried.

'I can send for a cart, if you want.'

'I *do* want!' She started to push the boy off her.

'Kit!'

Marlowe took three paces at speed, about to hoof the boy back down. 'I've paid for this debauchery. We're going to see it through.'

'Kit! For God's sake.'

He relented and knelt to the girl. 'But dearie, we are creating a history. A tragical history. For a few hours, you will be Joan of Arc.' She blinked in golden ignorance. 'We must summon a friend to be our audience. His part in the story is as central as the wizard's.'

'Another one?' the girl said. 'I'm not—'

'He will do nothing but watch.'

'Who is he?'

Kit's crooked smile stretched to the back of his head. 'The Devil. Beg him for mercy when he comes.'

And that was the end of the night. The two youths upped and ran as much as if Kit had sprouted horns himself. I blamed them not one inch. 'Run, then!' he had yelled at their behinds.

Strangely, the memory helped me to write the trial scene with which I had struggled, for it made me wonder: were those who spoke of mercy, but did not grant it, more wicked than those they accused? Yes, I thought they were.

Within a minute of the clock of St Botolph's striking eight that night, there was a hammering on my door.

'For once, Kit comes in good time,' I said, and Alicette laughed. And when I opened up, there he was. But he had a curious expression upon his face.

'Can we dine elsewhere?' he burst out.

'Where?' I asked, surprised, though why I should have been surprised by anything he did was itself a strangeness.

'Bermondsey. I am meeting . . . some people.' I noticed that he had something tucked under his arm, a bundle wrapped in what seemed to be sealskin. He followed my gaze and thrust it into my hands. 'Take it. It is for you.' I felt a roughness on the surface – grains of sea salt, I thought.

'Bermondsey?' After a full day's working, I was not

keen to leave my comfortable home. To delay my decision, I opened the package. Inside were a scroll and a silver coin. The coin was a guilder of the Low Countries. The traders at the docks often used these pieces, and they were well known and commanded respect. 'What is—'

'The manuscript,' he said impatiently.

I unrolled the paper. It was new and had kept dry in the sealskin. Curiously, it was topped with a cartoon of two outstretched hands. Each digit bore a word written in uneven letters up its length.

If I eat, I live. If I drink, I die.

But below the picture were the lines that were the meat of the meal.

I, Christopher Marlowe, born in Canterbury in the sixth year of our splendid Queen's reign, do bequeath all my worldly goods to my friend Will Shakespere. He may dispose of all said chattels as he wishes. He may burn them if the mood takes him. He may throw them in the sea to stun the fish. He may . . .

'Were you in an idle humour when you composed this?'

'I was, yes.'

I read the rest of the lines. They continued in the same ironical vein.

'Thank you for the gift, if that is what it is meant to be,' I said.

'That is not *quite* what it is meant to be.'

'And this?' I flicked the coin in the air and caught it.

'Neither is that.'

'Oh-so-many secrets, Kit.' I looked again at the inked cartoon. *If I eat, I live. If I drink, I die.* 'And what does this mean?'

'When the time comes, you will know,' he replied.

'Heaven's tears, Kit, it is like talking to the Sphinx.'

'This is my last will, Will.' And even in his impatient humour, he could not stop himself laughing at his own jest, as if it were the first time I had ever heard it in my life. 'Ah, and it might soon be all that is left of me.'

'Why so?' I asked, exasperated with his evasion.

'Come to Bermondsey.'

I had had my fill of him by then. 'I will not.'

His face fell, all jest gone from it. 'Will, I know not what to do. Tell me my path.'

'Your path? How would *I* know?'

'You will know if you come to Bermondsey.'

God save me, against my better judgement, I took pity on something within his expression. 'Bah!' I said. 'I will come.'

He clapped his hands to my shoulders. 'I thank you.'

I betook myself to the scullery and, taking a dry biscuit with cheese, slipped the sealskin package behind the trunk that contained our dishes. 'I am ready,' I said, wearily.

*

At the edge of the water, by the huge and foreboding Bridewell Hospital for wayward women, where the Fleet flows into the Thames, we found a wherryman huddled into his cloak. He seemed aggrieved that we should employ him in his trade and huffed and puffed like the north wind when we scrambled aboard his boat.

'Penny a man to Bermondsey,' mumbled this Charon. I pointed at Kit.

'Aye, yes,' he grumbled, fishing in his purse for a pair of coins, and we set in for the half-hour's journey downstream to the southern shore of our great artery. The many swans that dabbled on the water were white ghosts in black times. As we passed through the shadow of the Tower, the great stone keep that William of Normandy built, it seemed to glower down upon us, and I wondered which souls condemned to the gallows were watching us through bars and wishing they had just five minutes of our years outside those heavy doors. A fool is the man who lives for tomorrow, never seeing today.

'You have not told me whom we are to meet,' I said. Kit glanced my way, then set his sight back on the dark horizon. 'Tell me.'

'Men.'

'I did not think it would be apes. What men?'

'Scoundrels.'

I was beginning to think I should depart and leave him to his own affairs. 'More, Kit, or I return to my pipe and Alicette.'

'Ach,' he muttered. 'Men with intelligence of affairs into which I would pry.'

It was his evasion that bolstered my interest. 'Boatman, turn about. We go back to Bridewell.'

'Penny a man to Bridewell,' he said with little concern.

'A cheap price. He will pay.'

'Ach!' Kit muttered once more. 'Very well. Keep your bearing.' He sat closer to me and lowered his voice. 'I have taken on work. Work of a secret nature. I have done it before.'

He was not speaking of playmaking, I knew that. 'What work?'

'It began long before you and I met. When I was at Cambridge.' He watched Charon closely, but the boatman seemed deaf to our speech.

'Continue.'

'There was a club of radicals. Young men with heretical thoughts on political and religious life. One of my tutors asked me to tell him what they said. I kept him informed, and he paid my fees through the university.'

'Who was he?'

He turned his face to me. It was more shadow than flesh. 'John Whitgift.'

I was taken aback. I knew not that the Archbishop dealt in such matters, though the royal court is surely a nest of spies. 'He sends you on your errand this night?'

'My errand this night is part of my duty. Though when all is said and done, it is not the Lord of Canterbury that I serve.'

'Who is it, then?'

'England, Will. England.' And even in the dark, I saw his eyes glitter then. 'Well, England and Kit Marlowe.'

We followed the river, passing a few merchant ships coming or going with the tide, and tied up at St Saviour's Dock in Bermondsey, once owned by the warrior Knights Templar. Lolling against a battered carriage with a driver was a thin, beardless fellow in cheap garb, smoking a pipe. 'Nicholas,' Kit said with an obvious foul taste in his mouth. 'Who let you out of the Clink?'

The fellow grinned to show not a single tooth in his head. 'Mashter Marlowe,' he slavered, his tongue twisting about like a dying snake. 'I have not been in that plaish for yearsh.'

'More's the pity.'

'Oh, a-ha-ha-ha,' cried the thin one with as much true mirth as a hyena. 'Yesh, yesh, it ish a pity. Yesh, it ish. I have been ashked to take you to meet shome gentlemen.'

'Have you?'

'Aye, aye, I have.' He waved his arm at the carriage, which was fully enclosed and had grille windows. 'And who ish your friend?'

'Master Will Shakespere. A playmaker of growing repute.'

'Ish he now, ish he now?' He stroked his beardless chin.

'Aye,' I said. 'I am.' A revulsion against this creature was growing in my stomach.

The man smiled genially. 'Come then, let ush be on

our way.' We all climbed into the carriage. Its benches were wet even though it was a dry night.

We set off, the two horses clipping on the cobbles of the wharf. We rounded a large, tumbledown building that might have been an abandoned store, and steered out onto a high road, passing a few late sailors and the women who serve their wants. All the while, the creature Nicholas was burbling to himself. Eventually his sounds resolved into human words.

'Ah, but I regret that the gentlemen we are meeting will be deshiroush of a degree of shecrecy.'

'What are you babbling?' I demanded.

He reached to the windows and folded shutters across them, blocking entirely our view of the outside world. My hand went to the poniard in my boot, but Kit stayed me.

'All will be well,' he said, though I was not of his mind.

'We do but travel, shirrah. No more than that.'

'Will, for my sake.'

I relented.

We travelled for hours through what felt to my rump to be city streets, then country lanes. Expensive beeswax candles gave us light inside, but we had little use for it, for we spoke not a single word during that time, until the wheels seemed to turn from rural mud onto stones once more and the coachman pulled his beasts up.

'We are arrived,' said our little Mephistopheles.

'I had guessed that,' I replied.

'Mashter Shakeshpere will have his jesht.' He opened

the door. The moon was fully overhead, so we must
have been on the roads for three or four hours, and
its light fell on a country cottage. It looked shut and
dark to me. 'After you, Mashter Shakeshpere.'

I was tired and pained by the journey such that
my limbs barely worked, but I was able to stumble
out onto the pitted highway. I stretched my stiff back
and thought that I would betake myself to the roadside to empty my bladder. I was turning to tell my
companions so, when two burly shadows seemed to
rise from the ground itself. Sensing danger like a
dog, I started to yell a warning, but at the very
moment the sound formed in my throat something
heavy and wooden cracked onto my crown. My knees
gave way, and I found myself in the muddy ruts. I
tried to lift my head, but another hard swipe of the
weapon to my skull and a guttural 'Stay down' kept
me in my place as the two shadows flew into the
coach. Despite their order, I tried to stand and shout,
but neither my legs nor my voice lifted. And all I
saw was the coachman hie the horses away into the
gloom.

I lay there groaning until my brain came to itself
and I could stand and walk. Knowing nothing of
where I was, I chose the direction that the coach
had gone. Yet it was hard and very slow going in
the total dark, such that I gave up after less than
an hour and rolled myself into a ball by the roadside, there to rest until the dawn when I might make
better progress.

*

Thus it was that my eyes blinked open to find myself on a bed of daisies and cowslip. For a full minute, I was at beautiful peace in that bucolic natural garden. But then my memory began to return. 'Kit?' I said, lifting my head. There was no one on the road, which stretched as far as I could see in each direction. I heard sheep somewhere, but they were not in sight. At least I could walk well enough.

I knew not even which county I was in, so choosing a direction of travel was like throwing dice. I chose to go north, for that was more like to be towards London, unless we had crossed the Thames without my knowledge.

I found blackberries along the way and drank from a cool stream, which aided my head. And I gained luck when a shepherd in a field pointed my way to the village of Sidcup. When there, I begged a little bread from a young wife sitting in her cottage window. I asked if she knew of any coach that had passed by late at night. She had no idea of what I spoke, and I thanked her. I tried to sell my boots for a cart-ride to London, but was met with only laughter. They told me it was eight hours' stride, and I resolved myself to the walk, passing the grand old Eltham Palace, another of the fat king's homes, on the way. The sound of boys gaily practising tilting on horseback drifted out from its gardens.

When I finally reached the streets of London, pestilent as they were, and my feet so sore I would have walked on my hands had I been able, I felt my heart lift.

Yet I was greatly afeared for Kit and knew not where he was lodging or any other way to find him. So as soon as I crossed my threshold, I sent notes to all our friends asking urgently for news of him. All I could do in the waiting time was betake myself to bed for the rest that I needed. My mind and body were so ruined that as soon as I fell upon my bed, I was dead to all the world.

The next day some replies had come but only saying that they had not heard of Kit for months. I went then between all our remaining acquaintances, to the theatres north and south of the river, to every tavern and stew that I knew he frequented. Nothing.

Hungry and thirsty, I sat upon the bankside and bought a pie and ale. Neither was even of middling quality, but I cared not. I wolfed them down and pondered. There was one avenue that I had yet to walk. I had of recent times gained a patron, and a rich one at that. My Lord of Southampton was, at twenty years, younger than myself, yet had vast estates and wealth with which to play. And play he did, bestowing it on any poet, musician or dauber who took his fancy. His youth was enamoured with the court and its painted game birds – those of both branches – and I guessed I would find him there rather than at Southampton House. So to Whitehall I trod.

My footfall took me close to St Paul's churchyard, where I have spent many joyful hours browsing the books for sale. The yells of the costermongers are music to mine ears there – and yet, as I drew close

this while, the cries were of a different and less son-
orous ilk. A crowd was milling and swirling itself
around in the churchyard. I could not penetrate it
with my eyes, but there were words.

'Tear him, tear his Papist heart out!'

'What happens?' I asked, astonied, of a young appren-
tice, who was smartly drawing down the screens before
his master's hosiery shop.

'A Jesuit!' the boy gasped, as if I had presented the
malefactor right before him. 'Caught! They caught
him right there. His books, his books!'

'Papist villain!' the long-shanked hosier added,
bursting out with a bar of iron in his grasp. 'Books
from Rome and Madrid. All murder!' He sawed the
iron up and down in the air, as if breaking open the
man's head.

'Into the Hound's Ditch with him!' screeched an
old straggle-haired maid. 'Dogs know dogs.'

And then I saw the one they had laid hands upon.
He was a timid fellow who I knew well enough. He
was of the German lands, and his foreign way of
speaking must have marked him out to the simpletons
who were forcing his jowls to the ground. I started
forward, but the hosier grabbed my doublet and
wagged his finger. I should not entertain such an
idea, it said, as to get between the *mobile vulgus* and
the supposed Catholic spy it had most heroically
apprehended.

What to do? It was only seven years since we had
beheaded the Papist Mary, Queen of Scots, for her
part in the plot to murder Queen Elizabeth and seize

the throne. Had we not uncovered the plot, Mary would have invited the Spanish armies to arrive and burn Protestants in the market squares. There was no doubt, we were at war.

To the side, I saw an old woman in a window watching the scene with fright and I for sure witnessed her forefingers trace a rough cross on her apron of brown hemp. She met my eyes and, in terror that I had witnessed her popery, drew back from the window.

I did not wait to watch the man's fate. I hoped that the ward constables would soon call some sort of order and the truth be made plain. If the truth can ever be made plain.

It was an hour later that I hove across the dirt before the Whitehall. I must say that it is not my favourite of the Queen's palaces. Greenwich for pleasure, Windsor for power, say I. Still, there is a quiet majesty about the place. The Thames licks at the edges of its gardens, while the palace itself winds through a labyrinth of rooms, connected harum-scarum by a bees' nest of arched galleries and courtyards humming with courtly manners.

The guards agreed, with only a little grumbling, to convey a message to my patron begging speech; or, if not, if he could tell me if he had heard any of Kit Marlowe.

It was not long before my heart leapt to see Southampton stride towards me, beckoning. The guards allowed me entry, and we walked to the rose garden, where no intelligencer could eavesdrop.

'Will, I am glad you came to me privately,' he said,

embracing me. He wore a very fine silver doublet and black pearl earrings on both sides. His equal-black hair was swept to the back in a daring style.

'You know where Kit is?'

'No, but I am glad he is not with you. He is a danger now. Have you not heard? Her supreme majesty has issued a writ for his arrest. He is as good as hanged. You have not been speaking atheist calumnies as he, have you?' He sounded worried – pained, even.

'No! Even if I believed in them, I would not be such a fool as to let others know.'

He relaxed and set himself upon a bench with his calf displayed to its best. 'That is better. Affairs at court have been so very fraught of late.'

'Kit said something about Whitgift.' Southampton looked to the ground. I knew something was upon his mind. 'What of him?'

'The Archbishop has assumed a new role at court.'

'That being?'

'You know that my bent is not for intrigue, Will.'

'I do, my lord.'

'I wish that all could be plays and music.'

I gave him a moment to pity himself. Then prompted. 'Whitgift, my lord?'

He sighed like a mild wind. 'I am no intriguer. But I hear that the Archbishop is one.'

'He desires power?'

'I know not what he wants, but I do not think it is power.'

What, then, could it be? I stared at the palace

windows. 'Will you ask if any have knowledge of Kit?'
I asked.

'I shall do so.' He looked to the sides as if peering
at his pearl earrings. 'In a soft voice.' He rubbed his
hands. 'But to better news. Your play of the Venice
merchant. It goes well?'

I was in no humour for idle chat, but since he was
my patron and I could maintain a house in London
and in Stratford for my chicks only with his aid, I
did my best to extemporize the tale for half an hour,
during which he sat rapt at the comings and goings
of Shylock and his rivals.

When my lord dismissed me to attend upon an
evening of musical revels, I hard-footed back to my
lodging in the hope that more news might have reached
me there. Yet all that I found was Alicette, worried.
We said little for the rest of the night, chewing on
spatchcock but tasting not one mouthful of it.

I woke the next morn to an urgent hammering on my
door. Elated at the thought that my friend had
returned, I hurried to open it.

But when I pulled back the timber, it was not to
Kit Marlowe, but to another face – the face of an
adder in Kit's own words.

'Thomas!' I said, with surprise. Although Kit had
been incensed that Thomas Kyd, his former friend
and bedfellow, had informed the Queen's men that
Kit had espoused atheism and a calumny about Christ,
I was more circumspect. Elizabeth's inquisitors had
methods of extracting any information they desired

from a prisoner, and I did not blame him for his deed. In truth, there were fresh welts on his face that he had tried to disguise with soot, and I was sure I knew how he had come by them. 'I was expecting Kit.'

His eyes fell to the muddy ground. 'No, you have not heard. I had hoped you had, and that this would already be a house of sorrow.'

I felt a thumping in my chest. 'Tell me.' He pushed past, closed the door himself and sat on a bench. He did not need to speak. I could write that it was a shock, and yet it was not. There was something in Kit that had starred him for a young death from the very day he was born. 'How was it done?'

'I do not know. There is to be an inquest today.'

'Will you go?'

'No. At the end, we were not friends.'

'Then I will. One of us must. Where?'

'An inn in Deptford. The sign of the crossed keys at two.'

'Deptford? Why Deptford?'

'That is where he died. He was in another tavern with some men the night before last.'

'Deptford? Surely Kent.'

'Kent?' He looked bemused.

My mind het up. There was falsehood afoot, of that I was sure. 'What men were they?'

'Drinking fellows. There was a brawl, they say.'

My blistered feet would hardly bear my standing weight, yet I knew I had to attend. 'I will go.'

'Will you send word to me after, to tell what was discovered?' He looked sheepish, and I knew he felt

shame for his betrayal of Kit, no matter how enforced
it had been.

'I shall.'

He bade me goodbye and departed.

On the Deptford quay, I was directed to the inn of
the Cross Keys, where the air inside was thick with
tobacco smoke and the smell of bad beer. A serving
boy was being pushed around by a fellow with a great
deal of flesh hanging below his chin, and the lad was
relieved to tell me that the inquest was being held in
the upper room. I climbed a set of stairs more like a
ladder into what had surely been the hayloft before
the landlord decided that he could make a few angels
selling it as a meeting place.

'Atheism, let me remind you gentles, is but a path to
Hell,' a doddering fool was prattling from the bench,
a tankard of ale at his hand. 'And't seems to have
caught this enemy of God, good'n'proper.' He supped
his drink hard. The ten or twelve men in that loft
muttered in agreement. 'Always would, y'see. The Lord
does not miss!' He supped again and scratched his
ballocks. The men muttered again. 'This Deptford is a
foul spot. His death here comes from his wickedness.'
He caught sight of me. 'You! Who are you?'

'Will Shakespere,' I said.

'What are you?'

'Playmaker. You said Christopher Marlowe died
here?'

'Ah. *Playmaker.*' He said it like it was a spider in
his mouth. 'Like this Marlowe.'

'Like Marlowe, aye.' It was clear that his sympathies did not lie with my friend.

'And why are you here?'

'Is this inquest open to all?'

He sneered his mouth. 'If I say it is.'

'Then I shall stay. You said he died here,' I repeated. I still did not credit the claim with so much as a germ of truth.

I could see that the man was considering having me cast out on my buttocks, but the effort seemed too much. 'You may do so. Well, this Marlowe was a godless beast, so he is no loss. And yes, he died here. In the house of Mistress . . .' He looked to a young man at his side who was acting as clerk.

'Bull, Doctor Gadd.'

'Bull. Mistress Bull.'

'When did it happen?'

He narrowed his eyes. 'I am not accustomed to answering questions. I *ask* questions.'

I could have wrung the man's blubbery neck but had to honey my tongue. 'I offer my *apologia*.'

He wafted his hand graciously. 'But to state: your bosom consort, this Marlowe, died the day before last in the tavern house of this Mistress Bull. He had been there with friends for the whole day.'

'That . . . cannot be right.'

He looked angry at my dispute. 'It is. They had been in their cups, and a disagreement about the reckoning led to an unfortunate struggle, in which this Marlowe was the aggressor party. He drew his dagger and went at one of his companions. The others bravely held

him off, but the knife ended his life.' He blinked and
twitched a smile at his poor rhyme. 'It seems he is
not the only poet, what?'

'It is not true!' I growled.

'I have heard the witnesses testify with mine own
ears.'

'Who?'

He lifted his chin and called to someone in the
corner behind me. 'You! Tell this *playmaker* what you
told me.'

As I turned, I heard a voice I recognized in an
instant.

'Your worship tellsh all sho well.'

And then I was face to face with the creature who
had pulled us all into his hellish schemes.

'I know this man,' I told the coroner. 'He is lying
to you.'

'I am lying?' Nicholas replied. 'How?'

'He led me and Marlowe into a trap. I was beaten,
and Marlowe was taken.'

'Nonshenshe!' The imp laughed. 'I have never sheen
you before, shirrah.'

'Lying!' I appealed to all those present.

'You have evidence to back your claim? This man
has a half-dozen witnesses. You are a playmaker. And
not a good one, I presume, if this is the best fantasy
you can design.' He chuckled at his jest.

'His name is Nicholas,' I said. 'If I have never met
him, how do I know of that?'

'Umm,' the coroner warbled for a second, his brow

clouding over with what must have been the first hard thinking he had done that day.

'Ah, shirrah. He heard it while he shtayed below and you ashked me my teshtimony.'

'That! That is it. A simple answer. You thought you could cozen us, playmaker? This man is a loyal servant of Sir Thomas Walsingham!'

'What did you do with Marlowe's body? Is he buried?' I demanded.

'Dropped in a pauper's pit in the churchyard of St Nicholas,' the coroner declared. 'You may root there for him if you will. Now begone or I shall have my bailiff eject you.'

He would have done it in a twinkle, I could see, and that would have played me no good.

Angrily, I descended the ladder and went straight to the pot boy, taking from his hand a tankard of ale, throwing him a groat and chucking the drink down my throat. The foul brew almost made me retch, but I cared not and barged out.

'Picture of the killing, sirrah?' I spun around. A fat oaf was selling quarto sheets emblazoned with *Horrible Death of Playmaker Christofer Marlow*. 'But one angel, sirrah.'

I took a noble from my purse, pressed it into his ink-stained palm and took the uppermost leaf.

Below the title was a poorly made woodcut print of the murder scene as described. Within an inn, a man labelled 'Marlow' was on his back on a settle, while another had an arm wrapped serpent-like around his throat, one had his waist and a third was plunging a knife into his forehead. I was about to crush the page in my fist and throw it in the Thames when a voice stopped me.

'I believe you.' It was sweetly toned, male but melodic. The speaker had near-white hair and a face as charming as his voice. I recognized him, but it took me a few moments to place him. Then I knew: he was the young man who had been with Archbishop Whitgift when I had seen him in the precincts of Canterbury Cathedral.

'Do you? Why?'

'Walk with me, will you?'

I folded the quarto and placed it inside my doublet. It would be a talisman to remind me of what had befallen my friend. Then Whitgift's man slipped his arm through mine, and we paraded like two lovers. 'I work for His Worship Lord Canterbury.'

'I know.'

'You do?'

'I saw you with him recently. I was visiting the cathedral.'

'Ah.' He stopped. 'His Worship is a very busy man.'

'I have no doubt of that.'

'And yet I believe he would like to speak to you.'

This was outwith all expectation. 'Why would he wish to meet a lowly playmaker?'

'More than that, Master Shakespere. A poet. Would you come with me to the Lambeth Palace?'

Like all who walk the London lanes, I had often looked up at the walls of the Archbishop's palace and wondered at the power therein. Temporal power moved hither and thither: Chiswick, Greenwich, St James, Windsor. The whims of the monarch meant it was a flighty thing, never to be trusted. But the men who wielded the power spiritual, they remained steadfast.

'I would, most certainly.'

'Then I shall take you to him.' He turned and lifted a palm. It was then that I noted we had been followed by four footmen carrying a gilded sedan chair built for two men.

'You never told me your name,' I said as the servants set the box down and opened it for us.

'No, forgive me. I am Gabriel Cullen, secretary to His Worship.'

Upon his order, we turned and trotted to the wharf, where we hailed a wherry that took us upstream to the Archbishop's private stone jetty on a stretch of riverfront planted with roses and marjoram. It was as if the Lord of Canterbury already trod in Heaven and we mortals walked in his wake.

The palace looks like nothing so much as a guild hall, if I am to give my opinion. Long and low, with the antique Lollards' tower – part of which functions as an occasional prison for those found guilty of lewd conduct in the Archbishop's Commissary Court – at one end, it would have been no shock if a phalanx of rioting apprentices had burst out in pursuit of the May Fair and wenches. Instead, there was an odd little stall, where three porters waited with bowls of warm water and clean napkins to wash our hands before we entered the hallowed building. I was given a sprig of liquorice to rub on my teeth in order to make my breath sweet, and a paste of treasured nutmeg from the East Indies to protect against the Pestilence.

'Where is His Worship?'

'The chapel, sir.'

'Do you truly mean to disturb him at prayers?' I asked as we trod towards the chapel.

'He will be eager to meet you.'

Ahead of us stood a great red-brick gatehouse. Two or three score bedraggled examples of humanity were lolling around the front of it. 'They are waiting for the Dole,' Cullen said.

'What is that?'

'Daily bread and broth. A few groats, too. It began in the time of the first King Edward, and here we continue it three centuries on.' To prove his words, two servants emerged from the gatehouse with a cart of victuals. The crowd surged forward, grabbing at the food, until the servants reached into a leather purse and threw coins over their heads, causing them to turn and scrabble for the money, fighting each other for the coins, then running back to the bread when all the coins had been stashed in shoes and mouths.

We passed around them to the Archbishop's private chapel, where six guards with armour and spears gave us entry to a modest church. There were but two pews on either side of the nave, which was attractively decked in black-and-white tiles. 'It is so we can play chequers if we bore,' Cullen whispered to me with a wicked smile. The stained-glass windows told the story of Man from his creation to his Day of Judgement. But they had in many places had sections replaced and patched, as if children had been playing at tennis and broken a dozen panes.

My sight was drawn to a curiosity: upon the altar was a painted and richly gilded wooden icon of the infant Jesus in the arms of his mother, which had been smashed by a fist or hammer. What it was doing on the altar I could but guess. It looked like something the corrupt monasteries and priories had held before Henry deprived them of their rubied riches. Before that altar, a man was on his knees, muttering prayers, so we waited with patience until he stood to face us with a kindly expression. The last time I had seen him, he had been laughing merrily.

'This is?' He spoke, like me, as a man of the north.

'Master Shakespere. A playmaker.'

'A playmaker?' His eyebrows lifted as if Cullen had said I could swallow my own feet. And I noticed something a little odd when he spoke. A click-clacking sound like a twig stuck within the spokes of a cart-wheel.

'A friend of Marlowe.'

'*Ah.*' And in that one sound, there were a hundred thoughts. He walked away, and we followed, through a low door that opened to a very narrow staircase. We squeezed up the steps to find ourselves in a close little room, with a balcony overlooking the altar. 'Cranmer composed the *Book of Common Prayer* in here forty years ago. For that reason, some call it the Chapterhouse. I like the name,' Whitgift said. 'It is the most private place in this palace, for there is nowhere for a spy to hide and eavesdrop.' There was that clicking again. I looked close and understood the cause: the Archbishop's teeth were made of white-stained wood, the natural ivory having rotted away, I presumed. Perhaps he had a fondness for sugar.

'It is only for the most important guests,' Cullen muttered in my ear, as if it were a private thought.

Whitgift sat on a short pew and gazed at me thoughtfully. 'Tell.'

I told him. I told him how Kit had come to me, had said that Whitgift would protect him from certain accusations – the Archbishop's eyebrow nearly lifted off his head at that, but he said nothing – how the man I knew only as 'Nicholas' had born false witness at the inquest.

'Nicholas Skeres.'

'You have the advantage of me, my lord.'

He gazed down at the altar. 'Master Shakespere, who is your enemy?' *Click-clack-click*.

Well, I had rivals such as Ben Jonson, whom I should have enjoyed seeing dropped in a pit of dung, but I would not have described him so much as an enemy. 'None that I should like to nominate.'

'A wise fellow. A politic fellow, no?' He looked to Cullen.

'Yes, Your Worship.'

'But you are incorrect. Your enemy is the Pope.'

'Of course, my lord.'

'And his minions. The Spaniard, his Infanta. I could go on. Do you know who is your friend?'

'I suspect, my lord, I am about to be informed.'

A sly smile pulled his mouth to one side. 'A very politic fellow indeed! Your friend is the Turk. For he is the enemy of the Pope. Now, should the Pope turn Turk and follow the infidel Prophet, or the Turk turn his sight unto Rome, we should be left friendless. A pretty game, no?'

'Pretty as a daffodil.'

He cleared his throat. 'Her Majesty plays the game well. For a woman. She is sending the Turk sultan a gift to remind him how we of the true Church and they of their . . . cult are equally opposed to the idolatry of Rome.'

'What gift is that?' It was a little insubordinate of me to ask, but I was curious.

He paused, then pointed to the altar and the smashed icon upon it. 'A picture paints a thousand words, does it not?' He rose and walked to the balcony, which was opposite one of the stained windows. It depicted the building of the Temple of Solomon in Jerusalem. 'Marlowe was in my employ.' I made no answer. I was not of the mind to let on just how much Kit had told me. 'Did he speak to you of his mission?'

'He did not.'

'Mention a name or place?'

'Who is Nicholas Skeres?'

He returned to the pew. 'He is in Walsingham's employ.' I had heard as much during the inquest. Yet there was more to delve in that well, that was a certainty.

'Walsingham is a traitor,' muttered Cullen. Oho, there was enmity between these sons of England. Then I would have to be on my guard, too – for it ill befits a man to nail his colours to a mast before he knows which ship is the quickest.

'Come, Gabriel, come. We do not know that for certain. Not yet.'

'He takes the Pope's gold, I know it. For a box of treasure, he would sell us all to Spain. If only the Queen could see it, too! The Spanish every day plot another Armada to set the Infanta upon the throne. Our throne, a Protestant throne!'

I had no doubt that the Archbishop feared a Spanish invasion more than any other in our land. If they were to succeed, he would be one of those tied to a stake and burned.

'Kit was your spy on the Catholics of Holland, was he not?' I suggested, thinking of the Dutch guilder he had bequeathed me within the sealskin package. 'To infiltrate their bands and watch for Spanish schemes.' He did not reply, but I knew that the answer was yes. 'Then I should say the evidence against Walsingham is not so weak.'

'I have seen weaker,' Whitgift allowed. 'Did Marlowe tell you anything? Give you anything?' I made no answer, but my eyes betrayed me. 'Ah, so he did.' There was a pause. 'Have you ever taken bread with an Archbishop of Canterbury?' he asked with a twinkle in his eye and a clicking in his mouth.

'You would, perhaps, care to dine with us this eve?' Cullen suggested.

'It would be the honour of my life.'

'Oh, I am sure you will find it a more humble occasion than that,' Whitgift replied. 'I am to visit the Queen now. But if you return at the hour of eight, perhaps with something that Marlowe gave you, you will be most welcome.' It was an order doused in honey.

'I will, and gladly,' I said. I bent my knee and walked backwards to the stairs and out of the chapel, leaving the two men to discuss what I had told them.

And yet, despite my words, whatever Kit had discovered of this plot, information for which he had been slain, I baulked at handing it to Whitgift. For there were wheels within wheels.

Outside, I hurried along the rose-lined Bishop's Walk and out to the streets of Lambeth itself. I know not if it was decreed by God or a more mortal power, but the second I left the precinct of the palace the stench of death was once again in my nostrils. To my left, I saw a house with a plank nailed across the door and the tell-tale red cross painted upon it.

I hastened home. Marcel was sweeping the earth floor and looked surprised by my entry. Down the stairs came Alicette.

'My dear?' she said. 'What befell you?'

'I am sorry, I cannot tell you now.' I took her in my arms and kissed her hard. 'You should stay a while at your parents' house. Get out of London. I do not trust this city.'

'The Pestilence has reached Guildford, too.'

'I talk not of the Pestilence.'

She looked at me queer. 'What are you saying, Will? Is this to do with Kit? What happened to him?'

'It is to do with him. But what happened to him I cannot say. There are designs at work that I cannot fathom.' At that, I went to the kitchen, where I had stashed the package that Kit had entrusted to me. I carefully unwrapped it and unfurled the scroll, his final testament with the curious cartoon at the top of a pair of hands with the motto *If I eat, I live. If I drink, I die* inscribed finger by finger.

I stared at them. And the goddess Reason chose that moment to breathe into my mind. *If I eat, I live. If I drink, I die.* It was no rallying cry, it was a riddle. Oh, Kit, you knew well to whom you left this parchment. I never could resist a riddle, and you knew I would unpick it soon enough. For what lives if provisioned with dry victuals, but dies if provisioned with water?

Why, fire.

I called Marcel to build one and be quick to it. He looked at me as if my brains had already roasted.

'But Master Shakespere, it is a hot day!'

I set him right and, though he grumbled, he soon built the fire and departed. Then, taking the paper, I held it before the hopping flames.

Sure as oaks stand strong, within a blink more writing appeared on the page. Written with lemon juice! Between the sardonic lines bequeathing me his worldly chattels, I beheld words as if set down by a brown spider.

Will. That you read this means danger or the worse has fallen upon me. Whitgift sent me to Aemsterdam to enter into secret Catholic circles. You may know the truth of my peril – and my death, if that has come – if you find Leon of Prague, who resides there. He will tell you of the Two Houses, which will shake our world to the very core. You must take up my mission with him, for it is of such import that failure will cast a pall on all our land – and other lands, too, no doubt. Will, I am sorry: by telling you this, I put you in danger. Be wary. But if ever I have been friend to you, find Leon of Prague.

What might shake our world to its core? Was this madness? Or had Kit knowledge of something quite diabolical? My heart beat hard. I knew not where this would or could lead. But I knew that I was for Aemsterdam in place of the Archbishop's dinner. Kit had been murdered, and the truth lay in that city. Yet there was, that last testament of his whispered, something of far greater moment there, too, that I must witness.

I would seek out this Leon of Prague.

I walked along Deptford Strand, the puddles of river spray on the quay wetting my boots as the sun sank into the earth.

'Constable?' I made him jump in alarm.

'Who goes there?'

'But a stranger.'

'State your business.'

Deptford was not a friendly place at night, it appeared. 'I seek St Nicholas's Church.'

He relented and pointed me in the correct direction, cautioning me to speak to no one on the way, lest I find a poniard at my throat and my purse in another's hand.

With my lantern, a tallow candle shining within, I picked my way. The church was a big square edifice, strong-faced like a Roman regiment, with a bell tower whence a brace of bats flew in pursuit of some luckless morsel. I circled the building to the rear, where the graves were, and shone the lamplight on the stones. Some of the occupants should have been in the school-room, not the boneyard, and I thought of my own dear three chicks. When my heart grew pallid for Stratford, it was for them, and my annual return was like all the Holy Days at one.

Something stirred, a shadow rising at my side. I whirled and brandished my lantern, to find a degenerate, a man covered in the pox of the French disease. Seeing him, I took a step back – I was not desirous of weeks in a sweating tub with my sores lanced and then covered in searing quicksilver.

'Spare a noble, sirrah?' he huffed, his lungs working like burst bellows.

I kept my place. A beggar can quickly turn cutpurse.

'I may. Know you where the grave of Christopher Marlowe lies?'

'The playmaker?' he said, holding his hand to shade his eyes.

'Aye.'

He pointed to a spot at the foot of the bell tower. 'Pauper's grave there, sirrah. Saw him tipped in myself, so save me. I saw him before, too, when alive.'

'When?'

'Before I was . . . reduced, sirrah, I was a carpenter. Some of the struts in The Theatre are my own hands' work. I saw him then, when the Admiral's Men played *Doctor Faustus*. Ah, it was a pity to see him chucked into the ground like that. I did enjoy the play.'

I glanced back. There was a heap of fresh earth piled up. I tossed the pock-marked vagabond a noble. He picked it from the grass and bit it as I sidled to the rough grave.

'Oh, Kit,' I said. 'You should have seen a better end. We have all been robbed of the worlds you would have made.' I said a silent prayer for him and made to leave.

'Sirrah?' It was the rogue's hoarse voice.

'Aye.'

His voice became quite low, like the breeze through the headstones. 'For another noble, I shall tell you something.'

I paused. I liked not his tone of hidden knowledge. But a noble I could spare for the right intelligence. I held the coin before my lamp beam. 'Speak it.'

'You are not the first to come.'

'No?'

'Yesternight. Two men.'

'What men?'

'The coin.'

I threw it to him. He grabbed it in the air and bit this one, too. He seemed satisfied. 'They had spades.'

Spades? 'For what purpose?' He said nothing but pointed to the heap of earth. I caught his meaning. 'Were they graverobbing?' It seemed improbable – a man who robs graves does not choose a pauper's pit.

'I did not see. I betook myself elsewhere. I did not want it to be *my* grave, too.'

Before my final destination that night, I had one last call to make.

Thomas Kyd lived within a set of well-appointed rooms that he rented from a rich poulterer – perhaps the constant babble of geese from the yard below had been soothing to Kit's quick brain when he lived here, too.

The rooms were well swept by a chambermaid who was straightening her skirt as I arrived, leaving Kyd at his writing board with a pen in hand.

'Will!' he said, surprised.

'I have news of the inquest.' I told him all that I had heard. 'Of course, not a word of it is the truth.'

He slumped over his desk and tossed the quill aside. 'There never was much of that when Kit was around.'

'There is something even stranger.' He perked up his head. 'Did he travel overseas?'

'Oh, you mean his spying visits?' Kit was not kin to discretion! I shook my head in disbelief at his idiotic loose tongue. 'Yes, yes. Back and forth to France, Spain.'

'Did he speak of what occurred?'

'Only in his cups. He credited himself as the greatest

discoverer of Papist plots in Albion. To hear him tell it, he alone had saved the life of the Queen and half the court from being blasted to pieces, stabbed in the heart or spirited away to Rome in a wicker basket.'

'Then it seems churlish for her to have him arrested for his calumnies against the Son of God.'

'Just so. But of course, Kit probably thinks not that they were calumnies. Christ using John the Evangelist as a Ganymede? Kit would say it was a fine way to pass the time. "All they that love not tobacco and boys are fools!" That was his frequent refrain. And his self-condemnation. But . . .' He stopped and looked at me shiftily.

'Continue.'

'I think his arrest was not for that offence.'

'What do you mean?'

'I wonder if one in the court was unhappy with his intelligencing and had him taken for that instead. The charge of atheism meant that our rooms could be searched and something deeper found.'

'Who would have such influence over the Queen?'

He lifted his empty hands. 'I am a playmaker, Will, no intelligencer. But Kit claimed the Whitehall is as riddled with spies as with mouseholes; and Elizabeth enjoys setting one lord against another, so to maintain position they must traffic in intelligence, scandal or ridicule. Kit offered up all three. You know that it was Kit himself who put it about that he and Walter Raleigh were found together by Sir Walter's manservant? Kit said he had been paid well to make the rumour.' It did not surprise me for one moment that

Kit would whore out his reputation in that manner – he would consider it a fine jest, and the golden angels he would no doubt be paid would be but sugar on the cake. Who had paid Kit for such work was a mystery – I could not see Whitgift indulging such a scheme.

'Has the spying taken him to Aemsterdam?'

'Most recent, it has. I knew he had been there, for he had excellent Chinese silks to sell.'

'What did he tell you of it?'

He pondered. 'He was elated, as if all his ships had docked at once. And spoke of a great coming together.'

'A coming together of what?'

'He would not say. But he did tell me that it would render thrones toys and armies boys' games.' He shrugged his shoulders. 'You may make of that what you will.' It was indeed cryptic. 'Kit found an excitement in these duties that he took nowhere else. Not even watching his plays mount for the first time and hearing the roar of applause.' I knew no playmaker who could remain untouched by that sound. Kyd's voice softened. 'Will, I never betrayed him. He betrayed himself. When our rooms were searched and the beadles found his blasphemic papers, what was I to say? That they were mine? Then I should hang for his offence.'

He spoke true. Kit had none to blame but himself. I gazed at the writing board. There were papers there, rolls of script, that Kyd was working upon. But beneath them there were others, and I recognized Kit's hand. 'What is that?' I asked.

'Oh, fragments of a play that Kit was writing when they came for him. I rescued the pages in case he should want them again.' I picked them up. In his spider-like letters, the title leaf read *Romeo and Juliet. A tragedie of family*. I looked through. There were enough scenes for perhaps half a play. Some of the poetry was grand, some lacking in any finesse. 'Take them if you wish. He has no more need of them.' I rolled them and placed them within my doublet.

The Second Part

For once, I had good fortune when I came to the dock-side. A vessel trading Hampshire wool was destined for Holland within the hour, and the captain was happy to take a paying passenger, asking no further questions.

The crossing lasted the night and a morning, and was a mild one apart from the time a fast ship crossed right before us and nearly turned us over in its wake. A figure on its deck laughed like a madman and waved his hat in mockery. But still, it was no distraction from my task. I spent most of the time looking into the white waves that we left behind us and considering just what Kit Marlowe was to me. He was a rose with thorns. Perhaps my closest friend when I was setting out on my road of playmaker – a confidante, a mentor, a traveller on the same road. But he could be a drain of good humour, too – a Narcissus, a squall always ready to become a storm. Still, take him all in all, he was a good man, though God's blood it could be hard discovering that fact.

The port of Aemsterdam is a rich one, its trade with the Orient drawing in spices and silk and sending cloth and blue pottery in return; so that we had to fight for space coming in. On the quayside, merchants in fine woollen coats and broad-brimmed hats haggled over prices, their eyes glittering with the anticipation of profit, but I noted how their gloved hands rested on the pommels of their swords, too, so as to warn off the cutpurse.

I had seen no town quite like it. A warren of narrow streets, and the houses all so thin and lanky like the giraffe of Africa, because the lack of land – the sea laps almost at one's feet – has forced the burghers to build higher and higher while jostling at each other's shanks all around their famous canals.

Setting foot on the portside and kicking rats from my path, it became clear how hard my task to find the true agent of Kit's murder and know the truth of the great plot to which he had alluded in obscure terms, was to be. All I had to follow was the name of Leon of Prague. But where I might find this Bohemian was beyond my ken. I began my search with the knowledge that he was the sort of man with whom Kit would consort for the purpose of his mission for Whitgift. A man, therefore, connected to Catholic groups with hugger-mugger plans against England.

The Dutch had driven the Church of Rome underground, as we had, twenty years earlier. All their churches had turned Protestant by the force of law. But just as recusants lived in the English shadows, flitting between priest holes and secret sayings of Latin mass, so, too, in the Low Countries. I therefore designed a stratagem to make me appear one of them.

I looked for lodgings. Many were offered to me, but I made my choice of a landlord with a Spanish name. He was a red-nosed man of at least fifty years, not the sort to easily convert to a new religion as the tide changed. He wore a tattered and yellowed ruff, too, as if trying to regain better days.

I paid for my room with English angels, with which the landlord was quite content – gold is gold, and he no doubt saw many English merchants come and go, for he spoke the language well – and I made sure that he saw I had many of them. In return, I was shown to a room in the upper part of the house, next to my host's.

For the first day, so as not to excite any suspicion on the part of him or any watching agents of the Crown, I was content to walk the streets of the town, enjoying the new sights. It is a well-kept burgh with excellent guild halls. In the evening, I returned and paid my host for victuals, a stew of lamb and carrots that was well spiced. For certain, the trade with the Indies was to the good of the townsfolk. I then retired to my bed chamber, where, hearing the floorboards outside my room creak, I began to recite the Luminous Mysteries of the Rosary as if I were halfway through it already. At that, I heard the creaks pause, as if the walker had stopped to listen.

In the morning, I observed the landlord watching me from a distance and whispered a Latin grace as he served herrings for my breakfast. He pretended not to hear, and I struck up conversation under pretext of seeking good food during the day. He asked my business in the town. I said that I was seeking trade opportunities, my mother being of Sicily and we having family there still. He nodded sagely.

'In truth, England is not a friendly realm in these harsh times, and I wish to leave while I am still able,' I said *sotto voce*.

He looked to his left and right. 'There is a tavern, at the sign of the white lamb, by St Anthony's Gate. You might find friends there.' At that, he left off, having decided he had said enough. I thanked him, ate and departed.

An inn looks the same in London, Bristol, Aemsterdam or Seville. The same shabby menfolk, the same beer in tankards. I placed myself in a corner of the room and when the bar wench offered me drink, I understood her meaning without knowing a word she spoke. I handed her a noble and, like my host, she accepted English metal as any other.

I tried to begin talk with those who looked like they might know of the secret groups that Kit had touched upon: men with clothes of foreign cuts and secrets in their eyes. But my approach was too brazen. They shut their mouths until I moved to another bench. I remained there for three or four hours and gained no companions, no germane knowledge. I had fooled myself that I was a born intelligencer. I was not.

Finally, when I could stomach no more bad ale, I asked the maid for some bread and cheese to take thence so I could eat without a score of suspicious gazes upon me.

She brought what I asked for and, having worn down my stock of English coin, I handed her the Dutch guilder that Kit had left me to ease my progress. She bit into it to test it.

The next thing I knew, she had flung it back in my face and was ranting in her natural tongue. She grabbed my purse, plucked out a couple of the remaining nobles and took them away, still cursing me. A few men around us stared. One, a gaunt fellow with fluff where his beard should sit and ears like an elephant, was laughing enough to die. I wished that he would.

'Englishman,' he said in a local voice. 'Let me see.' And he took the guilder from the table, where it had come to rest in a pool of ale, and examined it with care. Then he slid it back to me, looked me up and down and sat back with his arms folded. And then it was all clear. Kit had not given me the silver to pay for my lodgings, it was a fingerpost to point me on the path. I had heard that the Catholic circles forged coins to pay for their plots. Kit and my unknowing host had led me into their orbit.

The gaunt man rubbed his left ear and subtly pointed outside before leaving in that direction. I waited a few moments, then followed.

'Sssssst!' I heard from the lane to the side of the inn. Elephant ears was there, resting against the wall, looking at his nails as if considering paring them. I joined him, and he stared at me.

It was certain he had something to impart. I thought

a bluff would be in order. 'I have no time for games,' I said.

'The guilder. It is a good one.'

'I know.' Kit's thread was silver, and he had laid it well.

'You want more?' he offered. 'I can get them.'

'Pah! Not as good as this one.'

'Oh, you think so? What if I tell you that I can get more from the same place? I know the master who made that coin.'

Oh, Kit, you have been clever, I thought.

I remained quiet for a while, as if in thought. 'If what you say is true – and I am not assured that it is – I will pay well for more of these. And I will pay you for the introduction.'

He smiled. It was the smile of a true villain, but that was what told me I had struck the bull. He said nothing but looked all around and, seeing none observing, walked away. I went in his wake.

We crossed the city, circling here and there – I believe to make it harder for me to remember the path – and in and out of taverns to confuse anyone on our heels.

After an hour, we came to a low part of town. At the end of a lane that abutted one of the city's canals stood a dusty apothecary's shop wherein a few cakes of roses and a tortoise shell hung. We betook ourselves to the yard behind the shop and down a ladder into its cellar. I could smell the brimstone even before we entered.

My guide knocked hard on a door, and a panel slid back to see who approached. No words were exchanged, but we were given entry into a small depiction of

Vulcan's forge. Flames billowed, molten lead cascaded from crucibles into sand moulds to become coins painted with silver leaf. That leaf was being harvested in one corner of the room, as a Moor with handsome features shook a bag of silver coins to sweat silver dust from them, ready to paint onto the lead.

It was all overseen by a white-haired woman, who recognized my companion but gave me the harshest of stares, full of threat. She was dressed in something approximating a nun's habit, and the jarring effect gave me pause.

'*Wie is hij?*' she demanded of my guide.

He glanced at me and spoke in English, so as to reassure me, I thought. 'A man who would buy from you. He has one of your guilders.'

I proffered the coin. She took and weighed it in her palm, then went to a box and lifted the lid. Inside, I saw enough coins to make the Royal Mint envious. She plucked one out, took a glass lens from her bosom and examined the two coins side by side. She seemed satisfied.

'I not know you.'

'You know my friend. Christopher Marlowe. You may know him as "Kit".'

The Moor in the corner dropped his bag of coins with a metal crash. His mouth was agape, then he looked shamefaced at the floor. The woman did not falter. 'I know him not. I not know you. Go.' The man pouring the lead into the moulds moved towards me, with the crucible of molten metal before him as a weapon most threatening. My guide had badly misjudged.

I knew this was not the way. I lifted my hands in supplication. 'I offer my apology. I mistook.' I backed out of the cellar.

Outside, I heard raised voices and a clattering, as if my companion was being taught never to take such action again.

But I was not prepared to let my one opening to the truth close. I therefore slipped into the shop of the apothecary, who jumped up from a rug whereon he had been sleeping and, yawning, offered to aid me in any request. My only request, supported by the last noble in my purse, was to let me stay and watch out the window. The man was befuddled, but in dire times, and accepted the money.

I waited for hours on a stool by the window, near hidden by an empty trunk. Finally, I saw my quarry. It was the fine-looking Moor, aged perhaps eighteen or twenty years. He ambled slow as a snail, like a schoolboy creeping to school, watching his feet. Happily, he was alone, and I stepped out to stand in his path.

His eyes met mine and widened.

'*Wie* . . .'

'I think you can speak English.' He shook his head. 'You must. Because Kit could speak no Netherlandish, and there must have been a way for him to draw you to him.'

And what I had seen in his face hours earlier, when I had uttered Kit's name, was real and deep. He looked sadly up at the sky. That look assured me that the boy was genuine.

'You know where he is?' he asked.

I placed my hand on his shoulder. 'I am sorry, but I must tell you that Kit is dead.'

He let out a cry of pain and fell to his knees, as if I had struck him hard in the chest. His hands wrapped over his head, and he stayed there a while whispering something to himself. When he became quiet, I helped him to stand once more.

'How?'

I felt sorrow for the boy and told him the bare bones of what I knew. But I was there to collect knowledge. 'Did he ever speak of Leon of Prague?'

He blinked hard. 'But yes, I heard that name. Who is he? One day, Kit and I did a fight. He went. I asked him that night where he went. He said with Leon of Prague.'

'How did he seem then?'

'I thought he did not look to me. He looked far away. I asked him what he wanted. He said it mattered not. The world was to change. All was to change.'

'Kit said that this man, Leon of Prague, would tell me of the Two Houses. Did he say anything of that to you?'

He looked puzzled. 'Yes,' he said slowly. 'Two Houses at war would become one.'

'Did he explain?'

'No.'

It was all riddles within riddles. 'I want to speak to Leon,' I said. 'Did Kit say where he is to be found?'

He shook his head. 'I asked him again and again.'

I thought a moment. 'What are you called?'

'Jalid.'

'My name is Will. I must have your aid. To find who killed Kit, and why it was done.' A look of terror flicked like lightning across his features. Then, just as quick, it became an acceptance.

'I will.'

'Discover what you can from those with whom you work.'

'It was there that I met him for the first. He wanted to buy false coin.' He was wistful.

'Meet me tomorrow at the hour of one in the afternoon,' I told him. It would give him the morning to press his confederates for intelligence.

'Where?'

'I am a stranger to this city. Tell me the place.'

He looked to the sky. 'Come to my lodging. I have a room in a bawdy house. I work there for my keep.' He caught my look. 'As a guard, to keep the safety of the girls.'

'It is your life to lead.'

'It is on the New Dike, at the sign of the golden calf.'

That eve, I ate in my room. I was changing my shirt when something fell from my baggage. It was the play-roll that Kyd had found among Kit's papers. *Romeo and Juliet*. I sat down and read it through.

It was good. Some parts were very good. Some were dross, but that was the way of a playmaker: to plant and harvest all, then sort the wheat from the chaff. The girl was sweet and faithful, the boy a gentleman throughout – and there was the trouble, I felt. The hero needed some fire within his belly. Their ill fortune must come from his hot head. And he was too old, at thirty. He needs be younger, before manners are beaten into a man . . .

I would think on it another time.

I spent the next morn in a fruitless pursuit of Leon of Prague. Any question that I put to my landlord, or to any stranger in an alehouse, paid me only blank looks.

I tried the city's markets, too. In the New Market, the Weighing House stood over all, as if trying to escape the smell of gutted fish, while the wealthier merchants within held sprigs of flowers and mint to keep the reek from their nostrils. Gulls circled over-head, ready to swoop for a piece of fish-meat, telling me that the River Amstel was never far. Again, I learnt nothing. And at the Old Church, I made the most subtle enquiries that I could, but they looked upon me as if I were a Bedlam child.

After some herrings to fill my belly, I went my way to the New Dike. It was a bustling street of shops – verily, the commerce and the liveliness of the city presented like one of its tulips in spring: quite ready to bloom. I watched a trader lay cloths of royal blue or blood red to prick the fancy of the ladies walking past, inviting the dames to touch and feel the quality. The anvil-clanging blacksmith in the next building invited those same ladies to feel something else, and they laughed as good sports and went on their way.

Soon I spied the house with the sign of the golden

calf, crushed between a man who sold swaddling and a maker of coffins: thus the beginning, middle and end of life were represented in but five paces.

Upon knocking, the house opened to me, and I was beckoned in by a woman well past the time of life suited to her profession. I made it as clear to her as I could without speaking a word of her language that I was not there to present her with custom. When I asked for her guard, Jalid the Moor, she sniffed and cast her chin towards a dirty curtain, which covered the threshold to a side-chamber.

It was a monkish cell that I found within, with a few discarded pieces of poor clothing, a spoon and plate of wood, a straw mattress and no more. My suspicion aroused, I asked where the resident was. The madam had me understand in Netherlandish that she was as amazed by the Moor's absence as I was.

Amazed, yes, I was. But I was also angry. Either he had fled me or someone had taken him away – and I thought the latter explanation had the greater chance.

With that idea, I was then about to leave when something caught my eye. Something on the floor, half of it under the straw mattress, half of it in the open to be seen: a coin. I stooped and plucked it up.

A guilder. But one made of lead and not yet painted with a silver coat to fool the unwary. It was a missive to me, I was certain. Quick, I flipped the mattress to the wall, ignoring the protestations of the lady bawd, and was instantly rewarded. For on the floor, written in white chalk, was a message. *Seek the humblest merchant in the Weighing House.* The hostess blinked at the sight and started yelling at me, as if this were a message from Satan. I rubbed it away with my foot lest any try to follow me, and hurried away, for I had no more business in that house.

But I had some elsewhere.

The boy was in trouble, I thought, and before I would fulfil his instruction to seek a humble merchant, I would see about his own being.

The weather turned foul as I ran to the coiners' forge. The rain was coming down as the flood on Noah, so that I was wet through when betimes I reached the place. I was given admittance by the woman chief, who was there with the mangle-headed oaf who had stood to me before with the crucible of molten metal. As wheezing bellows wafted the flames of the forge, she huffed at my entry. Why, she had never even met a Moor, let alone made one her servant!

'A brown man here? You are hot in your head.' She knocked a jug against her skull.

My thoughts, in truth, were quite cold. I might have taken her false coins and forced her to swallow them along with her lie. But through the fumes from the charcoal fire emerged the sweat-pouring oaf, hot tongs in his hands as he barked mutt-like words at me. 'Bark again, hound, and I will stop your cat-chasing,' I snapped, drawing my poniard from my boot. He stopped momentarily, then let out a roar and charged, swiping with the tongs. A pretty pass this was.

Nimbly, I stepped to my left around an anvil, breaking his stride. He swiped again with the tongs at my face, but I was beyond his reach and, in return, thrust with my dagger. I found the flesh of his hand, the sharp tooth of my blade hitting hard against the bone. The mongrel screeched and dropped his weapon.

I did not wish to press my luck, however, and backed out of the house, scrambling up the ladder to the street and catching my breath.

I had hoped he would remain in his lair, but a murderous yell from below told me that he still sought my blood. The rain was washing down my face, almost blinding me, as he bounded up in pursuit. He had fetched his hammer, which whipped back and forth in front of him. Upon the street he charged again, and I feared for my life, but I spun on my heel and got my arm under his shoulder, thrusting him against the wall of the apothecary's shop and breaking his grip on the hammer. He managed to get his elbow to my temple, though, knocking me back, and the blow and the rain blurred all as I stumbled close to the canal. Seeing his advantage, he ran at me and threw his oafish arms around me, attempting to choke the air from my lungs. I felt lightheaded but could not get loose of his blacksmith's grip. I saw but one risk-filled way to break my bonds. I sank low on my knees, tilting him, and then thrust with all my strength to my side, bringing us both to the edge of the canal, and then hard towards the flowing water, dragging him over the lip so that we both fell into the stream.

Immediately, my whole world was murk-brown and the last of the air in my body escaped in a silent cry up to the surface. The horror of death crept into my soul, but now there were no arms around me, and I could climb, bursting through and able to breathe once more. With all that I had, I clawed for the stone bank, grabbing at a steel ring set therein for boats to moor.

Yet, terribly, just as my fingers closed upon the metal, they were snatched away. I had not been the only one to break the surface, it seemed.

I knocked the blacksmith's meaty hands away, but they pulled again and again at my clothing, taking hold and dragging me back down. I had no strength left in my body and I thought this time I was lost, quite lost. I resolved myself finally to sinking forever into the brown depths . . . until suddenly something came into my vision, something crushing down on his face. I stared up as a brown-booted foot stamped down from the street. My assailant cried in pain and tried to fend it away, but it betook itself to press him down under the water. Feeling the blessing of life regained, I did not attend to see the outcome, but dragged myself up, with the aid of the steel ring, onto the street, to collapse, staring at the sky, feeling the rain pour into my mouth and the air into my lungs.

'Guid efternuin, Master Shakespere.' I looked about me. ''Tis an honour tae mak yer acquaintance.' There were two men. One was on the canalside, attempting to drown, or nearly so, the man who had attacked me. I could see only his back. The other was standing above me. He had a long blond moustachio and was speaking to me in what I knew to be Lowland Scots.

'Is it?' I spluttered.

'Och aye. We dinna meet mony playwrichts here.' He spoke to his underling. 'Let him sweem awa noo.'

The man on the canalside allowed the blacksmith to break the surface, breathe deeply and escape across the canal and away.

I got unsteadily to my feet. 'You have the advantage of me, sirrah.' I was grateful, but also still dazed.

'Aye, ah hae.' He lifted his wide hat, bedecked with a peacock feather, and swept it low. 'Jamie MacIntosh o' Glasgow.' His lackey turned and ambled to us with a rolling gait. 'Somebody is lookin' fir ye. They speir'd me tae fin' ye.'

'Did they?'

'Aye.'

I took a moment to recover my breath. 'And tell me, how does a Scot end up in Aemsterdam?'

'Ah speir masel the same question! Come this wey an' ye micht learn some things.'

He led the way, his mute companion at my heels, as we squelched through the drenched streets. 'The Jordaan,' my man said as we reached a plush part of the city where gents no doubt walked with their ladies in better weather. Our destination proved to be a tall red-brick house with stepped gables reaching skyward, adorned with delicate flourishes of sculpted stone that drew the eye upwards, as if beckoning one to enter a world of secrets and grandeur.

The front entrance opened to us, and I smelled rich spices wafting from a kitchen hidden somewhere at the rear. Looking up, the vestibule ceiling was high and richly decorated with a painting of the Heavens surrounded by images of commerce: weavers, traders, growers of spices. Truly, Aemsterdam knew its destiny.

I trailed water up the gleaming stairs to a parlour where red silken drapes hung at the windows and excellent tapestries were displayed upon the walls. Most striking of all was in the centre of the room: a model of the city, carved from wood, and with true water trickling through tiny canals. Behind it, examining in his palm a set of gentlemanly figures, was a man I could only conclude was a city elder. His doublet was of the finest indigo velvet, adorned with delicate gold embroidery, while his ruff was a masterpiece of lace and starch, framing his face with deliberate elegance. Deep lines upon the latter were like the canals of the city itself. A wig lay discarded on a gilded side table. He appeared to be of the Biblical threescore years and ten.

'Heer Shakespere,' the man said quietly, placing the figurines in the Butter Market. 'Do you enjoy your time in our city?'

My Scottish chaperone ambled to the far wall.

'It is one of the finest cities I have seen.'

He made a sound of satisfaction in his throat. 'You search for something.' He waited, but I did not reply. 'I know that you do,' he said finally, then walked slowly and dropped heavily onto a chair behind a desk with a crystal top. There were a number of other figurines upon the desk.

'I search for my friend. Perhaps you have heard of him.'

'Perhaps.' His teeth were stained mahogany brown, as the sugar trade had turned most of the wealthy Netherlandish teeth.

'Christopher Marlowe. Sometimes known as "Kit".'

'Sometimes known as "Kit".' He sighed. 'Heer Shakespere, as Burgomaster of Aemsterdam, it was my duty to have Heer Marlowe arrested for trading bad guilders.'

'I am sure you fulfilled your duty.'

'I did.' He picked up another figurine, of a chestnut horse, and drew it close to his face. He smiled at it and placed it back down. 'I had him whipped, then told him to leave our city and not to return.'

'I think he did as you asked.'

'Mayhap, mayhap. And now I think I must ask you to do the same. I hope I do not have to have you whipped, too?' I did not reply. 'I will believe that is an answer that I do not.'

'Kit was murdered.'

The Burgomaster shrugged. 'Heer Shakespere, I do not care.'

'I think he was murdered regarding his business in this city. And I do not mean coining.'

'No?'

I threw all caution to the ground. After all, the Protestant Netherlanders were our allies. 'No. He was discovering a plot by Catholics to kill our Queen and place a Catholic on the throne.'

'There are no Catholics in Aemsterdam.'

'None?' I said, without credulity.

'None. We have a law.' He said it as if he believed it.

'Then your law has failed.'

A dark look crossed his wrinkled brow. MacIntosh pressed himself away from the wall and took a pace towards me. His master waved him back. 'You are not correct.'

'Do you know of Leon of Prague?'

His eyes opened wide, then narrowed. 'I do not know that name.'

'I think you do.'

'And what do you know of this *person*?' He spat the last word from his mouth as if it were poison.

I grinned and opened my hands, continuing to drip water onto a Chinese rug that probably cost more than I had earned in a twelvemonth. 'His name and that he must be a danger to you. And that Kit had meetings with him. No more than that.'

MacIntosh bent low and whispered in his master's ear.

'*In het kanaal?!*' said the Burgomaster with some disbelief. His servant nodded. The old man broke into a chuckle. 'Mayhap Heer MacIntosh should have let you sink.'

'Mayhap.'

He returned to his staid demeanour as if the whole interview had been of little interest. 'There are many boats to London. Please be aboard one by midday tomorrow.' And he plucked up the inch-high steed to examine it carefully.

The Scotsman showed me from the house.

'It's been a pleisure meetin' ye, but it wid be best if ye were tae gang on yer way,' he told me on the doorstep.

'Is that an invitation to leave?'

'A wee bit mair than that,' he said.

*

In my room, I stripped off my sopping hose and mulled the Burgomaster's warning. My mood was low. I had learned little of use and had been near-murdered myself. What good would it do Kit if I stayed and lost my own life alongside his? And with the Burgomaster and his hounds watching, I could discover little more.

No, as I lay on my bed in my nightshirt, it seemed to me that Jamie MacIntosh was correct: it would be best if I were to go on my way.

Sullenly, I packed my bag. I had brought little with me, so it was the work of seconds. In the morn, I would pay my host and make my way to the port, there to find the first ship calling at London. With good luck, I would be back in my own bed with Alicette two days thence.

I went to the window to draw the curtain across. The roofs of Aemsterdam were pretty with their many crenelations and carvings, it must be said, and a tabby cat was prancing across one on the opposite side of the lane. It stopped to clean its face, then, on a whim, dashed away, perhaps in pursuit of quarry. Music and chatter were lifting from the tavern below. The rain had washed away most of the smell of the street, so all seemed fresh.

I began to pull the drape, until something caught my eye. On the street, in a doorway to a bakery, something moved in the shade. A figure.

'Go home, MacIntosh,' I shouted down, quite angry.

I prickled at his insolence. And it turned my mind

once more. *If you are so keen for my departure, there must be good reason*, I thought to myself. *So I shall discover it.*

The next day I was still angry, so that I rose, washed and left the inn before the hour of eight. The events of the previous afternoon had prevented me from following Jalid's direction to attend the Weighing House in the New Market and to find the 'humblest merchant' there.

I made my way via the Butter Market, where linen canopies covered the stalls. Servants and a few ruff-bedecked masters and mistresses were already picking from the stacks of eggs, pails of milk, paper-wrapped pats of butter and huge wheels of wax-covered golden cheese. The morning sun had dried the rain quite away, and some young apprentices were making merry with the dairy maids. I bought a little cheese to fill my stomach as I walked on.

The Weighing House is mostly square, with romantic roundel towers topped with peaked hats at each corner. As such, it had the appearance of a squat creature about to pounce. But its prey was not flesh, but money, for this beast lived on commerce. A constant traffic of well-to-do gentlemen flowed in and out, haggling, agreeing and threatening, as I presented myself at the front door and was granted admittance.

I discovered the building's nature to be more general than I had thought. It was a wide meeting-house for the city's guilds and men of status. As I stepped inside, I noted the high hammer beam ceiling decorated with the arms of many families and, in the centre, the enormously wealthy Dutch East Indies Company. In one corner, scales were clinking as spices were traded, but in another I was quite amazed to see the public dissection of a body, performed by the local barber-surgeons for the education of their apprentices and the entertainment of the gentry. I presumed the cadaver was that of an executed criminal, as in our own custom. A maid was selling oranges from a basket as the black-robed gentlemen looked on, nodding sagely. In another corner, a minstrel was playing songs for the amusement of three younger gents.

For an hour I circled the room, attempting to discover the humblest merchant among a hundred dealing in all sorts of goods, engaging them in what conversation I could to discern their humility. And while the replies I received were for the most part courteous, they were also devoid of information. Frustration overtook me as I watched yet another of their number place a bag of red spice upon the scales to have its value confirmed. I paused and spun my gaze across the whole room.

And then I saw, and I laughed.

For I realized that for the last hour I had been watching the humblest merchant in the Weighing House walking to and fro. *Oh, Will,* I said to myself, *you must remember your own simple roots.* And I pushed myself from the wall and approached the hessian-clad young maid selling oranges, who was surely the humblest trader in that great room.

I motioned for her to come to the side of the hall with me. 'You speak English?'

She nodded, watching me beadily. 'My mother is from Dover.'

'A friend told me to speak to you.' She made no reaction. 'I seek Leon of Prague.' She stiffened, ready to dash like game. I grabbed her arm, and she relented. 'You know of him?' She stared at me. I looked about, then led her behind a carved oak screen. 'My friend told me I must find him.'

'Your . . . friend?'

'Aye, my friend.'

'What is he called?' she asked slowly, as if she had an answer in mind.

'Christopher Marlowe.' I looked for recognition, but there was none in her face. 'An Englishman?' At this, the light of knowing glowed in her. Kit had like presented himself under a different name, but he would have been hard pressed to claim himself a Netherlander even if he had learned some of the language. 'You *did* know him.' She looked at the floor.

I cannot say why, but a question that was not germane was in my head, and I could not dismiss it. 'What did you think of Kit?'

She met my gaze, as if it were something she had wanted to say for half her life. 'He is . . .' She searched for the word. 'Beautiful.'

This girl was one of the unfortunates born to be fascinated by others. I could see how Kit could whisper in her ear and slip into her thoughts, there to live. And he would not think twice of doing so. I could never tell what Kit possessed that allowed him to possess others in that way. A chalice, it was, but one that contained poison.

'Leon of Prague. Who is he?'

'He is a . . . He tells us many things. Things we did not know. He has a . . . church.'

'A church?'

'The Church of the Waterfall.'

An entire Catholic church hidden from the sight of the authorities? It was possible. But there was something else, I could tell. Something she would not or could not describe. 'I wish to attend. I wish to meet this man.'

Two merchants walked close by us, muttering. We waited until they were out of hearing.

'He is more than a man.'

'Then I wish to meet him even more.'

She looked over her shoulders, then pulled me quickly out of the room and into a side-chamber. She peered around again to make certain there were no eavesdroppers. 'Beside the Hook Tower, there is a door in the city wall. At midnight, not before, knock thrice, then once, then thrice.'

'How do you know of it?'

'My father.'

'He attends, too?'

With no warning, her eyes poured tears down her cheeks. 'He did. He has died.'

'I am sorry.'

Her eyes lifted, shining, to mine. 'I will see him again. With new life.'

And she ran back to the hall, where she began serving her custom in earnest and casting not one glance at me. I trusted this girl as I trusted no one else I had met in Aemsterdam or London in the past sevenday.

*

I called in at my lodging. My host was in the pot-room. As many were making merry and turning themselves sot, he sat alone on a bench, staring into his own cup. I have often seen how strong drink turns a man to joy and then very quick to sorrow. I had nothing to do but wait then, so I sat beside him on the bench, and we remained in silent communion for hours, until his work called him away and I retired to my chamber, there to ponder what the evening would hold.

The Third Part

As night settled, I dressed in dark clothing, the better to hide if so needed, for I knew that there would be a danger to my actions and a hero who takes no precautions is better called a fool. My poniard was in its usual place in my boot. I thought of taking another, but that seemed an excess – if I were set upon by an army, two daggers would be of little aid.

I passed the Old Church, standing mighty as the moon shone silver light onto its spire and intricate carvings. Their shadows stretched down towards me and to the graveyard around it, whose stones were eerie grey in the noiseless night.

The air was thick with the smell of wet earth as I paced towards the Hook Tower. My way was the towing path of the Oudezijds Kolk canal, ground down by countless ponies' hooves and navigators' feet.

The scent of the river took over as I neared the tower, seeing here and there the city walls that lined the Amstel as it took the Netherlandish merchant fleet to the sea. The sugar, spices and silks it brought back would gorge the city's coffers 'til they burst.

I halted hard, thinking I heard a padding foot. I listened, straining my ears, but there was nothing. I went on.

The city walls were solid stone, yards thick, built up with an earthen skin so that it would take a thousand cannonballs launched by any Spanish navy to crack them. And then there was the tower: round and brown, that guarded a sharp bend in the Amstel. A light was burning in one of the upper windows: doubtless the guards on constant watch for invasion by water.

The buildings around were of the docks: a harbourmaster's house with a fine front, a few stores, one with pictures of barrels, candles and compasses painted on the sign overhead.

I approached, wary – for the guards might be suspicious of a midnight visitor – stealing forward, myself a-watch, looking for a doorway in the wall beside the tower. Then, in a little yellow light spilling from the window above, I saw it. It was low and made of solid iron, set deep in the stone.

A skidding sound: a stone kicked. I was sure that was what it was. I peered back, my fingers itching for the blade in my boot. But nothing. It must have been my nerves stretched like a yew bow. I set my feet apace once more.

'Will!'

I spun around. It had come from my left.

'Jalid?' I called, loud enough to be heard by whomsoever had hailed me, soft enough that it would not be detected by those in the harbour houses.

'Will!' This time, it was from the right. Had it echoed or had the speaker moved quickly and silently, one man surrounding me like a hundred?

'Where are you?'

'Will!'

It came from further away now, muffled by distance and perhaps by walls and buildings.

I started towards it at high pace, throwing the caution of the night down a well. 'Jalid! I am coming for you!' I hissed.

'Will!' And it was further away again, but this time accompanied by the sound of boots running on the earth and stones back towards the Old Church.

I gave chase, charging along the edge of the canal, past the great basilica of St Nicholas, quiet as the grave now that the monks had been driven to Rome. The wind whistling through its bell tower seemed to repeat their old names, their old psalter chants and liturgies.

And then I caught sight of my quarry for the first time. There was a great barge moored on the canal, with the navigators sitting on its roof carousing with flaming torches and a shoal of empty bottles in the water around it. He leapt through the yellow pool of light, showing me only the soles of his shoes. The navigators cheered at his escape.

I ran after, my lungs fit to burst. I could see the great church itself a hundred yards beyond, its coloured windows lit as if with a service, though what service would take place at the witching hour defied my knowledge.

Another shaft of light, this one from a tall merchant's house, wherein the master must have been counting his guilders late.

Then my game bird was vaulting over the low railings surrounding the church's boneyard and dashing between the headstones. I pursued him still, keeping pace, until of a sudden I realized I had lost sight of him. I turned this way and that, but to my anger all I could see were the stones of a thousand dead. I cursed and kicked one.

'Will.'

It was spoken soft, as to a lover.

I turned my head. And there, in a patch of blue-and-gold light from the tall stained-glass windows of the Old Church, leaning upon a grave as if it were a Whitsun afternoon, he stood. And the face that greeted me was that of Kit Marlowe. A dead man up and walking.

'Hello, Will,' he said with the lightest crooked smile. 'Are you surprised?'

And I will tell you that no, I was not. For there was a spirit who walked with Kit in all his days. And that spirit was the Devil himself.

The bell in the great church tower above us struck.

'Did you die, Kit?' I asked. For if he had told me then that he had never even been born, it would have been as simple to believe.

He laughed.

'I see you read my message in chalk.'

'I thought it was from Jalid.' He glanced at the chiming bell, then met my gaze again. '*Did* you die?

Someone told me he saw your body fall into the pit at the churchyard in Deptford.'

'I am glad you came, Will. I was not at first, but now I am.'

I was not going to let my questions rest. 'Were you thrown into a pauper's grave?'

The bell struck for the sixth time, the seventh time, the eighth. He stared up at it, then his eyes slid down to mine. 'Aye. I did. Aye, I was.'

It was an answer as strange as could be, yet the one I had expected. 'And how stand you here?'

'How stand I here . . . Yes, that is the mystery, is it not?'

I felt cool, not hot, as if we spoke of the latest play on the stage. 'It is so.'

'But you saw me before. As you sailed to Aemsterdam.'

'It was you on the boat that passed mine.'

'It was.'

'You were laughing like a lunatic.'

'Why would I not, after what I had come through?' The wind whistled around us. For the twelfth time, the bell chimed. 'Look at all the houses, Will.' He gestured to the great merchant homes around the square – the greatest houses of the richest city in Europe. 'Look at all the people in them. They walk and they talk as if they know their own lives. They know nothing. They know not one tenth of what is coming.'

'And what is that?' His riddles were becoming stale. Now I wanted answers.

'When I left you that page in London to set you on

the path, it was because I thought that death would be the end, and you would come to avenge me.'

'What changed?'

'Why, I did not realize the power that Leon has.' He sat on a long mound of earth that marked the grave of a burgher long since departed.

'Tell me what is coming against us,' I demanded.

He looked to the tower, where the chimes of midnight had come and gone. 'Words have limits. They can convey only the conceits of men. What is coming needs more.'

'Tell me of the Catholics' plot!'

'The Catholics?' He stared at me as if I were mad. 'Fuck the Catholics! Come with me, and I will show you real power.'

We ran through the night, retracing our path along the canal, through the light thrown by the late carousers, to the lonely and hard-faced city wall.

'Whitgift sent you to spy upon the Catholics, did he not?' I asked, confusion wracking my brains.

'He did.'

'Did you betray him?'

'Not with intention.'

'Explain.'

'I found something else. Something far greater.'

'What?'

'Beyond this door, all your questions will find their answers,' Kit said, his breath quick and shallow.

My heart was beating hard in my chest and my ears. 'Leon of Prague?'

'He is there.'

'He will tell me of the Two Houses?'

He hesitated. 'If he believes you to be worthy of the knowledge. It is not for everyone.' He could tell from my look that I felt some insult. 'No, no, it is not a matter of raw cunning. Nor of subtlety of thought – your brain is as subtle as any man's. It is . . . spirit. Some have the right animation, some have not.'

'It is a question of moral being?' I said, the affront returning.

'No, nor that. You are a good man, Will.' And he looked at me sidelong. 'Perhaps even too good.'

'Too—' I started. But his hand reached out and grabbed my arm, and he put a finger to his lips. I harkened hard. There was the muffled sound of whispers, all coming from behind the iron door set into the wall.

We stepped close and put our ears to the metal. It was frosty. 'It is always cold down there,' Kit said, knowing my thoughts without my mouthing them.

The conspiracy of whispering seemed to grow. I made out a few words: 'the tablets', 'reborn', 'Jerusalem', 'he comes!' The last was uttered with a breath caught in the throat, as if the speaker had been grabbed.

Kit drew a dagger from his doublet. At that sign, I reached for my own, but he stayed my hand. 'No, there may be danger, but it comes not now.' And he used his knife only to tap thrice, then once, then thrice again on the metal, making it ring like the bell we had heard minutes earlier. Minutes that felt like hours. Oh, time can spread and shrink as it sees fit, and we must wear it.

'*Wie is daar?*' hissed a woman's voice from the other side.

'*De Engelsman.*'

More hissing on the other side, as if a coterie of snakes had turned sentry. I heard '*De Engelsman*' repeated, as if the serpent was considering these syllables.

We waited. Kit looked less certain now, as if he had calculated ill. I glanced at the poniard in his hand.

Then a steel clang resounded like a cannon, signalling a heavy bolt drawn back. And another. A squeal as the door swung on hinges that had seen no oil for a century, if seemings were true. Before us stood a woman holding a beeswax candle that lit hair as white as a blizzard and lips red as cherries.

She stood in a stone passage that ran within the thickness of the walls, though the glow from the candle dimmed within a yard or two and left only blackness beyond. Still, I could see that the floor sloped downwards, as if angling into the ground. There was a smell of wet earth.

Whomsoever she had been speaking to was concealed within the gloom.

'Madame Jaune,' Kit said.

'You return. We did not think you would.' Her accent was from France. She turned her sight upon me.

'Will is to be trusted.'

She stepped forward, her gaze drilling into my flesh and bones. 'He is not for us. Take him hence.'

I knew not what I was being refused, and yet I knew I desired it. I was seeing fragments of the truth and wanted to see all.

'Madame Jaune,' I said, 'I am a man of honour. All that I see I shall keep within my bosom.'

She snorted. 'You shall?' And she hissed, 'If you were to gain entry and see what we have, you would scream it in every marketplace.'

'I shall—'

'Silence,' she uttered. 'I choose who may join us.'

'No,' declared Kit. 'It is for Leon to choose. None other may do so.'

She tilted her head to peer at him. 'You say so?'

'I do.'

She paused in thought, then smiled sweetly as a girl. 'Then you may plead before him.'

And she stood back to give us entry. The triumph I felt was undercut with trepidation.

Kit walked first into the passage, and I followed, a moment later hearing the woman slam the door closed, sealing us within the tomb. I could see far enough before me to walk and no more. 'You must trust the path if you are to join us,' she said, and I could hear the satire in her voice.

The candle illuminated walls of heavy grey stone blocks, their surfaces glistening with water that dripped down to soften the earth under our feet as I followed Kit.

The decline was steep, and every few paces there would be a step down, too, so that we seemed to be treading into the very bowels of Aemsterdam. After thirty yards, I thought we must have been well below the ground. The walls began to run with water, and the smell of the river began to take over. From time to time, I heard footsteps before us but never saw the walkers.

Another twenty paces and the passage took a sharp turn to the left. Then the floor and ceiling became stone, too, as if we were walking through a church nave, until before us there was the glow of more candles through a wooden doorway, whose lintel was carved with a motif of three circles, one within the other.

'Are you certain?' the woman asked me in a whisper.

I snorted in derision. I had had enough of her theatrics and strode through the doorway.

I found that we were in the cellar of a large house – no, an inn, because there were barrels stacked in a corner. It was all lit by rings of candles in glass bottles set around the edge of the room to make the room ripple like a dream. Another doorway was set into the opposite wall.

There were people there standing, talking quietly among themselves. Four or five dozen of them, I should say, and from their clothing they were drawn from every walk of the city: rich and poor, young and old. There was a child of twelve and a man of ancient years leaning on a wheeled frame of wood, all mixed without class or caste. At our entry, they stopped to stare at us.

'*Een vriend van de Engelsman*,' Madame Jaune informed them. One or two mumbled to their neighbours.

'A friend of the Englishman?' The voice was deep as the sea, and I looked hard to see whence it had come.

The people parted. In that dank cellar, I had found what I had sought, almost at the cost of my own life. For sitting quite still on a chair of brilliant ivory carved like the spires of a great cathedral church, behind an equally ornate ivory table, was a bear of a man. He was dressed in black furs, and a grey beard that flowed to his chest added to his ursine look so strongly that if he had roared and shown claws, I should have counted it natural.

'Leon of Prague,' I said.

He swept his gaze around the room, bringing everyone into his being. 'I have that name. I have others.' His tongue had the sound of a German to me.

'By which should I address you?'

The corner of his mouth turned up a little, as if amusement had been sparked. 'In my own country, they call me Rabbi Loew. In your language, Loew means "lion". Hence Leon.'

'I understand.'

'You understand no more than a mouse.' He pushed himself from his chair. 'No more than a mouse.' In common days, it would have seemed an insult, but I felt it only as a setting down of a fact.

'My friend Kit told me I would see some acts of power here.'

'Power?' His back was to me as he walked through his acolytes. 'Power is the beggar neighbour of thought.' He said it as if sad that it had befallen him to instruct me. 'It flows not from me. It flows from *Ein Sof.*' I knew not that name but hazarded that we were speaking of God Almighty. And as he walked on, I noticed a face among the congregants that I had seen before: the maid who sold oranges at the Weighing

House, the one who had wound out the thread that I had followed to this place. She had said her deceased father had attended the church; and she now looked worried, perhaps that I should prove a spy or unfriendly and the guilt would be upon her. 'What brought you here?'

The answer sounded like the most absurd jest. 'I came because I believed my friend was murdered. I know now that he was never dead.'

At that, he stopped and turned square to me. 'Oh, but he *was*. He *was* dead. And buried, too.'

And I knew in my stomach that he spoke not in poetic fiction, but in plain language.

For a second, I reached for the right words, the right question. 'But he stands behind me now.'

'That, too, is true.'

'Yet both cannot be the case. One must be false.'

Kit, moving to my side, spoke. 'You must take my word for it, Will. I was dead, and yet here I am walking.' And he did a slow little jig on the spot, both to prove and poke fun. 'I told you there was more power here than have all the Catholics of Rome.'

At that, Leon of Prague knelt to the floor. And all around him followed. Only I remained standing. But they were not kneeling to me, for the man of Bohemia had seized an iron ring set in the floor. He lifted away a thin stone to reveal a small chamber below. Dark water rippled within.

I started forward, but he raised his hand to back me away and reached down into the hole. I saw the fur on his sleeves become wet. And when they lifted out, they held ten or twelve large black stone tablets, broken at the edges, as thin as writing slates. I made out that they were inscribed on both sides in an alphabet that I did not recognize. Leon stood, mirrored by all those around him, and carried the tablets to the ivory table, setting them down with all the reverence that the Jews afford their holy scrolls. He whispered a prayer to himself as he did.

'Do you believe yourself a good man?' he asked.

'Does not everyone?' I thought it a sharp answer.

'Oh, but no. That is a common falsity. Many men know they are not of the righteous. Many delight in it.'

He was right, of course. I wrote for the stage so often of wicked personae that I had quite forgot such men walked outside theatres as well. 'I believe myself good.'

'Do you wish the best for men?'

My mind went to my children, as a father's will. 'And for women, too.'

There was the shadow of a smile.

He raised his hand to the woman, Madame Jaune, who went to the door behind him and spoke a few words to someone I could not see. She returned with a large plain leather satchel in her hand, and in her wake staggered two young men bearing a heavy burden. It was a bier, laden with the body of a man. I knew him not but saw by the weeping of the orange seller that this was her father whom she had said had died so recently.

He was lain down to the ground, his funeral processionaries retreating in deference. Leon went to the pit of water as the woman handed him the satchel. He unfastened it and took a glass vial from within, which he used to scoop some of the water from the well.

Then he went to the body of the man and poured the water across his flesh. This was repeated six more times. Finally, from the satchel he took a large package, wrapped in paper and twine, and opened it. Within was a large ball of deep grey clay, which I found quite the most unexpected sight.

Leon closed his eyes and muttered what I took to be a silent prayer of blessing. When they opened again, he took a large pat of the clay in his hands, working it soft and smearing it all over the man laid before him. It was a funereal rite that I had never seen before nor could recall from any Gospel, but it perhaps made sense to those who had studied the ancient Israelites. All the while, the other denizens of that room made not a sound. They could have halted breathing for all the noise they made.

After covering the body in a thin layer of the clay, Leon took a pen and a short slip of parchment from the bag. From where I stood, I saw him write a few letters of Hebrew – a language that I cannot read – on the paper. With another prayer, the note was pushed into the man's mouth. Was it so that the dead man would have a prayer on his lips as he was judged by the Almighty? Next, Leon dipped his finger in the water and drew it through the clay on the man to form more Israelite letters, before reaching for the last time into the satchel to take out a vial of liquid of the lightest blue appearance. He unstoppered it, spread a little on his lips and then bent to the man before him. He touched his lips to the other's and lifted away, pouring the rest of the bottle into the man's mouth, wetting the paper with the writing upon it.

At that, everyone in the room muttered a low prayer, and Leon slowly returned to his ivory chair.

We waited in silence for him to speak.

'Have you heard the parable of the Two Houses alike in dignity?'

At last, one of the mysteries I had not delved was being laid before me.

'No.'

He gazed skyward, as if recalling a sight he had seen. 'In old Israel, there was a house in a river valley. It had two sons. One day, the father of the house became ill and died, his wife having passed over some years before. When the sons looked in their father's strongbox, they found it empty. The elder son, having reached the age of a man, set forth to create his own life. He swam across the river, for it was summer and the water was slow. On the other side of the valley, he built his own house. But his younger brother was incensed, saying, "Why have you left our parents' home? It is not just." The elder son replied in anger, "It was my calling. No more, no less."

'For twenty years, their houses grew. But hatred between them grew, too, and their servants would fight in the marketplace. One day, a fire broke out at the older house, collapsing a great wall. The flames could be seen across the valley. And though there had been loathing in his heart for many years, the elder son rushed to aid his brother. Between them, they doused the fire. And in the ashes, they found the riches that their father had hidden. "It is your house, so they are yours," said the elder. "But," said the younger, "you are the older son. So they are yours." "Then we shall share and build a better house for both our families," said the older.'

Silence enveloped the room again. 'I think I understand,' I said after a while. 'The Two Houses – your house and mine.'

He nodded gently. 'So much enmity flows from the river of ignorance.'

'Do you—'

But I was interrupted by a sound: a croaking sort of moan, like wind through broken trees. I looked to my side. It was coming from the throat of the man on the bier. The man who was dead.

'He cannot . . .' I attempted to say, turning white. But I held my tongue, as his slipped from his mouth, across his lips, licking life into them. The girl cried out and burst into tears, trying to run to him but held back by another, who told her, I thought, that she needs must wait for the ritual to complete. Perhaps it was the sound of her voice, surely familiar as her face, that lifted the man's eyelids. The spark of life behind them was dim, but it was there for all and any to witness.

'But how can . . .' I started to Leon.

'The Book of Philip,' he said, touching the tablets. 'Found a hundred years ago in the silt of the Dead Sea. It describes this ritual, a ritual it calls "The Waterfall"; and its power.' He knitted his fingers and watched me.

'But this is not the first time you have seen or heard of the sacrament I performed. You have heard of its effect all your life.'

'I have?'

'Every year, when you attend your Easter feasts.'

And they were the most dangerous words that I had ever heard.

I did not want to believe him. I did not want a war that would tear England, Europe and all the world to pieces. The two divided houses would unite once more? No, they would break each other to the ground, and ten hundred thousand would be burned as heretics. The smell of fired flesh would never leave our cities.

As I contemplated this future with fear, Kit spoke to me. 'Whitgift sent you, did he not?'

I felt shame and anger. 'What of it?'

'It was upon his orders that I was attacked. Nicholas Skeres and the others are secretly in the pay of the Archbishop, controlled by his angel-faced devil boy, Gabriel Cullen. I had told Whitgift of what I had seen here, of what you have seen and what is to come. I was a fool to do it. Can you imagine the wealth he would give up if the Church's song of divine resurrection were drowned out by a song of a magic that common men can wield? What he would be reduced to?'

So that was why Whitgift had turned from Kit's employer to his killer. The churches would have emptied and crumbled if men had come to believe that Christ had risen not because he was God but because mortal men like Leon of Prague had the power to give life back to those who had lost it. But Kit and Whitgift were both fools for giving credence to such an idea.

'You did not rise from death; you were never dead! Nor was this man!' I insisted, pointing to the one at my feet.

'He *was* dead,' said Kit. 'As was I.'

'Men have seemed dead for days and been revived,' I insisted. 'That elixir is powerful.'

'It is,' replied Leon.

'It can revive the living, but it cannot resurrect the dead.'

'I know that you are wrong.'

'Kit, be honest,' I demanded. 'How did you die?'

'Whitgift's men poisoned my drink, then stabbed me.'

It seemed to me the most obvious thing in the world. 'Then the poison was too weak! It put you in a stupor but not death. The stab was but a flesh wound.'

'And buried?'

'For a day. Men have survived stranger things!'

'No.'

A fury began to rise within me. The danger of what these people believed and performed they did not see. They were blind to the waves of death they would invite to flood every land of men. I had to reach Kit. And I had to do so in private, away from the ears and mouths of those who had beguiled him.

'Kit, we must speak.'

'We are speaking now.'

'Outside of this room.'

'Go with your friend,' Leon said calmly. 'The truth will remain the truth.'

'Aye, 'tis so,' said Kit. He showed me to the doorway whence the bier had brought the man who was dead and not dead. We went through and up some rough stairs, finding ourselves in a shut-up and dark inn, only a few glowing embers remaining in the hearth.

My mind flitted here and there. I wanted to put aside these terrifying questions until I could grapple with them. So I fixed on another. 'Kit, you left me a parchment that told me to seek the truth, and then did all you could to hide from me until this night. Why?'

He spoke calmly. 'I left you the package because I felt danger close and wanted the truth to out if I met with murder. I knew not that Leon had a plan for me, that if someone were to take my life, he would give it back to me. But when he returned me from the land of the dead, he said that I had to leave my old life and friends behind. So I kept myself apart from you. Yet when you reached our door, we knew it was useless to ignore you; so out I came. And here we are.' As my mind pulsed with all it had heard, Kit was no more than his old self, and lifted a flagon of stale ale from a table. 'There is no godliness in waste,' he said, drinking. He raised the pot again, but as it was about to reach his lips, his hand stopped and he shouted. 'There!'

I spun around at the word, full of warning. A shape was flying from the shadows to my side. I pulled my poniard just as Kit threw himself forward, grabbing at the moving darkness. A blade flashed in the red light from the dying fire as Kit wrestled for it, and the last I saw was the Scotsman thrusting a dagger, then a gaping well of blood in my chest. And the face of Whitgift's white-haired angel, looking down at me with no pinch of concern.

Darkness then, nothing but darkness.

The Fourth Part

It was the pain in my chest like a volcano that woke
me.

My eyes stung as I opened them. As blurred shapes
and colours resolved into chairs, a bed, a chamber, I
slowly realized that they were the features of my cheap
lodgings in the inn. I lay for a few minutes groaning,
before the floorboards outside creaked and the
innkeeper came bustling in. He was surprised to see
me awake.

I tried to speak but my mouth was dry, so he held
a soaked cloth to my lips, wringing it to wet my tongue.

'What . . .'

'You were found on the river bank. Close to death,
they say. You have a wound here.' He touched my
breast. 'The barber-surgeon who sewed it said it was
as bad as any he had seen.'

'Oh.' I touched my chest. The pain seared again.

'He said you spoke of . . . mad things. Things that
cannot be.' He leant close and whispered. 'I paid him.
You are *among friends*.'

How much he mistook me and who I was.

'I . . . I . . . You will tell . . . me that I died, will you not?' I said. He looked at me with confusion, and I could not but laugh. Though it felt like I was being run through again, I laughed.

'No, you did not die. You are still alive.'

'But is that a proof? Not anymore.' And I laughed again. There was black under my fingernails, but I could not tell if it was river mud or clay.

'I shall fetch a doctor. You need him.'

I sat up sharp.

'I need no doctor.' The pain burned, but I took no heed. I looked down at the sewn wound. It was directly where my heart beat, I knew. But there are many old soldiers who will show you scars that should have sent them to their maker, but did not. I asked not for this mission from God, Whitgift, the Devil or Kit Marlowe, but I needed then to know what had happened to me.

'As you wish,' he said, though he looked doubtful. 'I paid, yet there is the . . . matter of your reckoning.' He was afeared that I would die without settling my account.

'Take your money,' I mumbled, pointing him to my baggage and bidding him look in the pocket sewn into the lining. He did so and extracted a handful of nobles. I cared less than nothing for them now.

Already my strength was ebbing, and I fell weakly back against the bolster, drifting into sleep.

As I slept, I dreamed. I dreamed of the Two Houses that become one. But then fire began. And it raged and spread further than man could see.

For two days more, I tried to stand. Every time I awoke, I felt that I would be able, but nature soon told me otherwise and I fell back upon the mattress. Yet I grew stronger.

On the third day, I could stand. And with hours of sweat and pain, I walked down the stairs to the inn. I tried to leave then but stumbled, and my host helped me back to my bed, shaking his head.

On the fourth day, I could stand. I could walk. I could seek out.

With the aid of a staff, I pushed my body through the Butter Market, where the sellers of cheese and milk still hawked their wares as they had before I had been led to a harrowing truth. Past the Old Church and along the canal, where Kit and I had run. And finally to the iron door set into the ancient and stern city wall. I caught my breath as I approached. The sky was grey, as if the clouds had formed a sheet right across the Heavens to obscure the sun. I took steps towards the door, listening for a cry of welcome or, more like, warning.

But sound came there none, and my footsteps resounded without interruption. Four, five, six, they tripped on the cobbles. And as I drew close, I noticed something new about the door. For it was covered in dirt and corrosion, as if it had been without the slightest movement for a tenyear. A padlock upon it that I had not seen before was rotten with rust and would not move when I tried to lift or twist it. Had I the right place? It must be right. I had gone straight there, knowing the path. But this door could not have been the one I had passed through the other night unless it had aged like the Sibyl.

'*Wat ben je aan het doen?*'

A pair of constables had padded close and were looking upon me with suspicion. I did my best to convey that I wanted to enter through the door, that it was urgent that I do so. They understood not a word and seemed to think me a madman babbling in no language. A couple of cuffs to my pate with their truncheons sent me on my way.

I stumbled off. That channel was dammed, but there were others to try.

Yet at the Weighing House, I found nothing but blank looks. None recognized my face, there was no girl selling oranges – yes, there were such maids from time to time, but none of the merchants knew their names or where they might be found. I knew that if I tried the coiners' forge my life would not be worth a groat. At the bawdy house, the madam who spoke no English seemed to remember my face, but what could I glean from her? Nothing.

All were dumb, still, there was one who could not be. I hurried as best I could to the house of the Burgomaster.

I was ready for Jamie MacIntosh of Glasgow as I rapped upon the door, ready for assault, though I did not fear actual murder – if that was his desire, it would not take place in his master's house.

It was an older retainer who answered, though. He spoke no English but returned with a younger one who did. 'My name is William Shakespere. An

Englishman. I had an interview with the Burgomaster days ago. I must speak to him again.'

They two went away to ask if I should be given speech with their master, returning quickly with a burly groom who made it clear that I was not to be admitted to the house. No reason was given and no apology. If I wanted that, it would have to be else-where.

'What of Christopher Marlowe?' I demanded.

'Of who?'

I stepped back into the street and looked up at the window that I knew to be the Burgomaster's parlour. I called at the height of my voice to the windows above, loud enough to shake the red silk drapes within.

'CHRISTOPHER MARLOWE! WHAT OF HE? WHAT OF HE?'

The outline of a man came to stand behind the hanging cloth, but I could not make him out. I shouted again. The beast anger was within me and eager for freedom.

And I knew then that Kit was dead. I could see it in the clouded sky.

The city was theirs, not mine. Surrounded by strangers, I might as well have been surrounded by enemies. They would close in now that they knew I was alive despite their attempts. And so I walked away. But it was not only to lick my wounds. I had one final deer to stalk.

My boat touched in at the dock in Deptford, where my quest had begun a week before. I had begged the captain to take me for what little money I had left in my purse, and he had relented, seeing that there was no more to be had from this injured, stumbling man.

I should have returned to my home, to Alicette, who would be anxious for news of me. I did not.

Instead, I ran with empty stomach along the Thames, the bloodline of London that washed our sins to the sea; past the wharfs; past the Bridge Gate; past St Thomas's hospital, where the sick became sicker, and the Clink, where the despondent lost all hope. All the while scheming.

I made no stop until I reached the Rose, the wooden O of my life as playmaker. There, I halted as I saw a cart piled with bodies and a man dressed in leather overcoat and bird-beak mask, calling on all to bring out their dead.

He passed, dolefully ringing his bell. I took to my heels once more.

To Lambeth, to the palace wherein John Whitgift, Lord Archbishop of Canterbury and prelate of all England, resided.

I reached the high red-brick tower that guarded the palace, its denizens and its riches. The green-liveried sentries on the gate, swords at their waists, scoffed at the dusty creature before them when I begged to see the Lord of Canterbury. I gave them my name and told them that I knew he would see me, but they drew their weapons and prodded them to my ribs. I readied myself to knock them aside, caring little for what punishment would come. But a voice sang out, staying my hand. A voice I had heard only on a single day but would know anywhere. It was Whitgift's angel-faced devil boy, as Kit had it. Gabriel's tightly gartered thigh rippled under silken hose as he ambled without hurry through the gateway.

'Put up your swords. He is welcome.'

In an instant, they turned from guard dogs to fat pups, waving me on my path, and I followed the white-haired youth once more, through the heavy doors of the palace chapel.

'*The Lord did everything in a mystery, a baptism and an unction and a eucharist and a redemption and a bridal chamber.*' The words echoed around the nave as if God himself were speaking, shivering and folding over each other, before drifting away into the clouds. But it was not the Great Father who spoke. It was one with less mercy in his breast. Whitgift sat in a gilded wooden throne beside the altar, behind a lectern carved into the form of an eagle. And his eyes bore into my own like mines under the walls of a besieged city. Then they lowered to the lectern. His right forefinger traced words on a large black stone tablet that peeped over the top of the golden wood. '*For this reason, he said, "I came to make the things below like the things above, and the things outside like those inside. I came to unite them in the place."*' I waited. 'The Gospel of Philip.' He lifted it from the reading stand, holding it away from him as if it were a rotten fruit. 'You may read it, if you like, Master Shakespere.' He paused. 'If you are able to read the Coptic language?' It was not a real question, and I had no desire to answer it for his sport. 'No, of course you are not.' He let the tablet fall to the floor and shatter into a score of pieces. 'Everything is a mystery,' he said to himself as he rose stiffly on old joints. He trod on the black fragments as he walked towards the pews. 'An absurd heretical text. Fit only for mockery.' He dropped his podgy body onto the foremost bench, a few yards before me. And I noticed for the first time – I know not why I did not see it before – how old he looked. How tired.

'Marlowe is dead, I presume,' I said.

He waved his hand dismissively, without turning to look at me. 'He is no longer in the claws of the heresiarch.'

'Leon of Prague.'

'Just so.'

'How charitable you are.' I gazed at him, as he gazed at the altar's white cloth. This time, I could tell, Kit was truly gone. 'I have never seen a man so afraid as you,' I said. A sharp shove in my back knocked me against the pew.

'Oh, leave him,' he muttered. I righted myself and he looked at me with curiosity. 'How dare you speak to me in that fashion?' It was an honest question. No fury, but clerical interest.

'Because it is the truth. I have never seen a man so afraid as you.'

I would be a liar if I said I felt no fear myself, knowing of what he and the angel-faced boy were capable.

'Afraid?' His lips trembled a little, as if trying to form words but each time deciding he had not the right ones. 'Fear is well. We worship Him because we fear Him. We are loyal to our Queen because we fear her.' He sat for a moment, lost in his thoughts, then stood and climbed up the narrow winding staircase to the gallery above, his Chapterhouse. He spoke over the rail. 'We love our fellow man because, deep within our soul, we fear him. Fear is well. Fear is good. If we do not fear, then havoc and Hell come upon us.'

'I do not believe that,' I insisted.

'Why, then, Master Shakespere,' he said with light laughter, 'you are wrong. If you do not fear the Lord's retribution, what is to stop you taking your neighbour's ox? Or his wife? You desire them – oh, do not say that you do not – and all that prevents you from following your impulse is the fear that the Lord will strike you down. What prevents a man turning from the Church is the knowledge that the Church can strike him down – or give him new life.'

'Then you are the one who fears.'

He looked surprised, as if a theological student had raised a strange point of dispute. 'You say that I . . . ?'

'You fear men's self-belief. If they believe they have as much power to give life as God, the walls of the Church will crumble. Is that not what you fear?'

He slid his finger thoughtfully along the stone balustrade.

'Playmaker, are you?'

'I am that.'

'And what good do you do?'

It was a fair question. And I had a fair answer that I believed. 'I entertain folk.'

'Nothing better than entertainments?'

'Nothing worse, neither.' He took that as a dig. Well, it was meant as one.

'Are you an atheist?'

'I am not. Tell me your fear.'

'Are you, mayhap, a traitor for pay?'

I kept my voice flat. I would not let him rile me. 'I am not.'

'In favour of massacre, of murder?'

'No.'

In an instant he turned. 'Then why *invite* them?' he growled, his hands gripping the air as if to crush it in his grasp.

It affected me not. 'And if what Leon of Prague says is true, that men can perform miracles as well as God?'

At that, he only snorted in derision, his fury having abated as quickly as it appeared. 'You think men have the power to raise the dead? I have studied long at the University, and the grace of God has placed me at the head of the Holy Church. Yet even *I* cannot make a corpse dance.'

'Have not saints performed miracles?'

'That they do so but once or twice in their lives is testament to the truth that it is not their power – it is the Lord using them only as a vessel.'

'I have read that Christina of Brustem raised herself from her own coffin and preached of how she had spoken to God while dead.'

'Papist absurdity! Only the Lord—'

'Tell me what you fear!' I demanded.

His fist crashed down onto the balustrade. 'I will tell you what I fear,' he snarled, his face as dark as thunder. 'You think the Catholics will swallow this nonsense, this Gospel of Philip? That the Turk will swallow it? Every infidel who covets our land and wealth? You think they will do anything but sweep across England, laughing at our divided and undefended nation, burning and thieving, dashing our heads against our walls? You think so?' White spittle flew from his mouth. 'You care nothing for the Church? Well, care for your *life*! For *all* our lives!' He threw his arms to the sky. 'If that is the outcome of this calumny being known, of Leon, Liar of Prague, spreading his falsehoods, of all the others behind him spreading a thousand more so that the common men of the street and marketplace know not what to think, what will you do then? *What will you do*?' His voice shook the very tiles beneath me. The boy with the angel face felt it, too.

As I stood there, I saw the coming times that he predicted: the common men filled with doubt or belief. Some filled with both. Some warring with themselves. A threat of invasion. A promise of rupture. An ebony box of terrible futures that could not be known.

'I will take my chance,' I said at last.

And for what were seconds but felt to be hours, we all stood, a holy trinity of belief, misbelief and doubt. Our very breaths in the air eschewed combination.

Where this would take us, I knew not.

The boy did not stand in my way as I went. The guards did not stop me. I walked home through the Pestilence that pervaded the air and the street.

Alicette was not at home. Marcel, my servant,

simply stood aside as I entered, footsore, knees creaking with much effort and little rest, and I went up to my bed chamber. He could see that I was not then for talk. As I stripped off my doublet, a roll of papers fell to the floorboards, Kit's unfinished play, his *Romeo and Juliet*. I left it there and placed myself in my bed, ready to give myself up to our first elixir, sleep. Then I would see which way the wind was blowing.

That sleep lasted no more than an hour. In it there were, I think, dreams again of houses and terrible dangers and knowledge that tainted the knower, but I do not remember them clearly. I woke in a sweat, my body wracked and my mind as awake as if I were in the midst of a bloody battle. I lay there another hour, heart beating, thoughts tumbling. I could no more sleep than fly. 'So be it!' I said to myself.

At least it was day, and warm.

I placed my bare feet back down on the hessian rug and stretched my neck and back. I took a step but kicked something on the way: Kit's play. And I knew my task.

I took the sheaf of papers to my writing board. They spoke of a perfect bond between two lovers – not innocents, both with sins on their brows, but with intentions well-meant. It seemed to me that Kit had been writing of Leon's Two Houses without knowing it. That there was beauty and tragedy at every turn, but that poor fortune, alone, stood in the way of the two uniting and creating serenity. Yet fortune, I think, is not fed. I hope it is not.

The sun fell westward, losing itself behind the chimneys and roofs and bathing them deep red. The city sounds were distant. I thought of the Waterfall and the torrent of power and rebirth that it promised.

I sharpened a quill. The ink in my well was still thick as I dipped the nib in, to set long strokes on the page.

Drawn by Kit's soul and my ink, the two lovers would entwine themselves, at the end, in each other's arms. May it be so.

The end of mine testament

THE
ANGEL

M. Wetherby

Chapter 1

Few men have ever walked within half a mile of the whale blubber boileries of Greenland Dock in East London without retching. The stink of fat turned liquid by a thousand furnaces spreads through the air, permeating Deptford and reaching as far as the Isle of Dogs. It was a foul wonder of man's machinations that the majestic fish should somehow be turned airborne and swallow a patch of London as the leviathan had swallowed Jonah.

In September 1892, Amos Sacher stood on the upper deck of the SS *Molly*, a recent addition to the White Star Line's fleet, and felt the fat in the air, thick and heavy enough to grab hold of, as the ship came in to dock. He looked down at the cream-coloured three-piece suit, silk cravat and brogues he wore, that had all been made for him in Simla. They were comfortable enough here, although they would have been stifling in the heat of Rajasthan, where he felt at home. From a distance, his skin, turned brown by a lifetime under the strong sun, and his thick black hair would sometimes have the Indians thinking he was one of their brethren, and only up close would they see blue eyes. If you were to look closely enough, you might even see some dust still caked into the creases of his skin. It would be there his whole life, regardless of how many shower-baths he took. He wanted it there.

When he was twenty-one years old, his father had inducted him into the family grain barony, and Amos had lasted precisely two years before he had handed in his cards and left to map the hitherto obscure parts of Rajasthan, sometimes spending weeks alone in the Thar Desert to chart the rises and falls in the sand dunes.

But it was in regal Udaipur, during a break in his work, that he had been dragged by his sister to meet a cousin on his mother's side, Jessica Delpont, who had come to India with a companion. From time to time, Amos had been introduced to eligible young ladies dispatched to India by their aristocratic-yet-poor parents to meet young men grown wealthy on the riches of the Raj. He found the whole idea faintly distasteful. It was only the fact that he was distantly related to this young lady that led him to consent to the meeting.

Miss Delpont, Amos's sister had informed him, was very beautiful and terribly sweet. So would he at least spend an afternoon with her and her companion, Cleo Woodleigh? After all, while, at the age of twenty-six, he was a little too young to marry, he might at least give love the time of day. The girl was five years younger than him, anyway, so it would be a little far-fetched to expect too much.

He had sighed and agreed to humour his sibling. As the afternoon sun shone and he eased himself into a teak seat at a hotel he couldn't name – pronouncing himself charmed by the décor and furniture, but in actual fact considering how deep the oasis he had discovered the previous week might plunge in the winter – he had indeed been struck by just how astonishingly attractive his cousin was. She could have been a Titian with her curling red hair and clear, symmetrical complexion. A perfect rosebud mouth bloomed pink, and white teeth flashed from time to time as she spoke in perfectly elocuted tones.

'Good afternoon, Mr Sacher,' she said, a slight blush of pink appearing on her cheek, when he introduced himself. 'The desert? That sounds terribly romantic.'

'I must confess I have become a little jaded by too much experience of it,' he replied.

'Yet you seem to have taken some of it as a souvenir,' her friend, Miss Woodleigh, a plainer creature with light brown hair cut short at her chin line, observed. He looked at his trousers, which had some of the oasis encrusted upon them.

He smiled. 'It seems I have.'

'How many nights did you spend there?' Miss Woodleigh asked.

'This time, ten.'

'Ten! Is there so much entertainment in the desert?'

'Not very much.'

'Oh well. Perhaps next time you could write some poetry? For Jessica, perhaps,' she said, with a glint in her otherwise soft green eyes.

'Oh, Mr Sacher, I apologize for Cleo. She can be a bear,' Miss Delpont said.

'But Mr Sacher says he has time on his hands. I only want him to put it to use.' She suppressed a smile.

He gazed at Miss Woodleigh. 'Perhaps I will,' he said.

At the end of the afternoon, his sister took his arm and led him away. 'I have invited Jessica and Cleo to the house on Thursday. I am sure you would like to join us,' she informed him. He did want to.

And so, for the next few weeks, he and they were regular companions. He cancelled another surveying trip into the desert in favour of croquet, which bored him, and sandwiches on plates, which were all right, but he would have preferred bully beef from a can.

One day, he suggested a boat trip to the perfect white marble Lake Palace, which sat on its own island in the serene waters of Lake Pichola. 'It was built by an eighteenth-century prince with a lot of money,' he told them.

'And time on his hands,' Miss Woodleigh replied.

'It sounds wonderful,' Miss Delpont said. 'I should like to see it very much.'

'It is unforgettable.' He had been more taken with it, the first time he had seen it, than with any other sight in the whole of India.

'And such lovely bright weather. Like it will never be winter again,' Miss Delpont had added.

'Shall we swim?' her friend asked.

'There are crocodiles.'

'Then we shall swim very quickly.'

'You might need more than that.'

'Perhaps a slow-moving companion to sacrifice?'

'Cleo!' Miss Delpont remonstrated with her friend. 'Don't be a bear.'

'Bears, too? What an afternoon.'

'I try to please,' Amos replied with a laugh.

'We should be delighted to join you, Mr Sacher,' Miss Delpont said kindly. 'I am looking forward to it very much.'

'You are falling for her,' his sister said at the end of the summer, the day before Miss Delpont and her companion sailed home.

He did not reply, because it was true that he had felt something fresh and new.

He spoke to his father, who was pleased with his son's decision to spend some time in London. Indeed, it seemed that Miss Delpont's father, Sir Elijah – whose sister was Amos's mother – was a doctor and sometime collector of historical curios, and was in need of a secretary. He had recently gained an astonishing new acquisition, and Amos could cut his teeth working on the selling of it.

He bought a ticket on the *SS Molly* to take him to London.

To follow Cleo Woodleigh.

Chapter 2

His hands gripped the rail of the ship as ropes were cast down to tie the iron giant to Britain.

He had been to school here – in Rugby, then Cambridge to study mechanical sciences – but had not set foot on the island since then. And he had not missed a single breeze of the Old Country; he was of the new one.

'No valet, sir?' the steward asked, as Amos lifted his own bags.

'No valet.' The steward offered to carry the luggage. 'Thank you, but there's no need.' He had little respect for the English toffs who would struggle under the weight of a hamper of food. He handed the man a coin, which was accepted with a tap to a white peaked cap, and strode down the metal gangplank onto the quayside.

He walked along the waterfront, watching the hawkers and loafers. There were buns for tuppence, beer for a penny. Cheaper to get drunk than fed. A Finnish seamen's mission looked lively as old shipmates met and swapped news. A new brick church was holding a service. Mutts sniffed at rotting vegetables in the gutter, the victuals having been rejected by ships' cooks. Dogs Amos liked. Most in India were starving street hounds, and he had once adopted a lopsided one that had trotted at his side for a few years until it succumbed to age.

A cab took him to King's Cross station, where he was just in time to catch a train going north. It carried him out of the capital and through countryside where the afternoon light glowed richer. Over bridges and aqueducts, through fields and tunnels. Past cities he had heard of and towns he had not. The sun travelled through the sky and dimmed, until the wheels stopped turning in the city of Newcastle, close to the border with Scotland.

This city was part of the new England: industrious and noisy. He jumped from the carriage onto a platform thronged with people, part of a huge cathedral of iron and glass that proclaimed the modern era. But he was not stopping there. He was transferring to a smaller branch line, a single carriage drawn by a muddy locomotive that chugged away, bouncing over points and whistling here and there, as the weather turned grey and autumnal.

Eventually, a painted sign for the stop of Kirchin loomed through the fine September mist. Amos stretched his legs, lifted his bags from the overhead rack and descended from the train.

He walked for the best part of a mile before he saw the inn, which announced itself as The Haywain. A fly stood outside, with a sullen driver huddled in a cloak.

'Are you for me?'

The man, who had a keen, hawk-like countenance that was set off by thin white hair and eyebrows, did not even reply, just took up his whip, waited for the weary traveller to clamber in and ordered the horse to trot on.

It was half an hour later that the nag slowed to a walk, and Amos saw their path wind towards a giant stone gatehouse, a dozen yards high, with two ancient crenelated turrets. It was a ghost now, and only the relics of the surrounding wall could be picked out, lying broken under mounds of earth and grass. As they passed through, Amos set eyes for the first time on the remains of the thousand-year-old Kirchin Priory, previously home of a Benedictine order and now home to his uncle, Sir Elijah Delpont, baronet and celebrated doctor. Elijah's brothers, Gabriel and Maurice, lived there, too, though he knew very little about them. He was curious, yes, but they were not the object of his true desire; that was a young woman in their house.

All through the voyage, he had played with mental plans for courtship – a game to which he was not well suited – so that by now, they all seemed torpid or ludicrous. But he was resolved to shoot as best he could.

The driver said nothing but halted the vehicle and jumped down, followed by Amos. Something slithered under his feet, and he pushed it away. He had seen enough snakes in his time to know that they rarely troubled humans. But he did wonder what else was lurking with gleaming eyes in the dark undergrowth.

They followed an invisible path through the ruins, past a thin tower three storeys high that must have been a campanile. There were four pillars on the top, which had once supported a canopy and the long-gone bell that summoned the monks to prayers or meals. Most of the stones on the near side of the tower were missing, so that its staircase was open to the wind and rain. Everywhere Amos looked, the sprawling buildings that had been raised up a thousand years before were abandoned.

Except for one.

He stopped and stared at the second storey of an ornate round building, held up by stone columns, whose ground floor was entirely missing. A twisting set of steps led up. And among all the dark and broken edifices around it, only this one had a glow in the windows, so that it looked like a lighthouse to guide in spectral ships. A low insectoid hum seemed to drift from it.

The driver ignored the building, walking straight past, and Amos had to speak.

'What is that?' he asked.

The man stopped but didn't turn. 'Chapterhouse.'

'It's occupied.' That was to be remarked on, surely. He expected an explanation, yet the man merely hesitated, then resumed his journey. Well, there was no need to pursue the point. Amos was already gaining an understanding that explanations were not necessarily forthcoming at Kirchin Priory. They passed through a break in a high wall and then a low brick doorway. And suddenly there was another sign of life.

'The Prior's House.'

It was a fine double-storeyed residence in the same old English style, but with less about it that suited a vision of the end of the world. An oriel bay window projected out over the frontage.

As they approached, Amos had an animal instinct that he was under observation. He halted and gazed up. For sure, he could see, through the oriel window, the face of a sitting man, silently gazing back down, his chin resting in his hands. The figure stood and stepped back out of sight. *Friendly sorts around here*, Amos thought to himself.

The driver opened the door with an absurdly large iron key that clunked as it turned, revealing a floor made of eggshell-blue geometric tiles. To one side, there was a rough little door that presumably led to the kitchen and servants' area, while an archway led to a fair-sized room that, Amos noted, contained a dining table, a few sticks of furniture and a couple of odd paintings on the walls. He had the feeling that this was not a house where the residents played happy games together on a Sunday after church. A dark wood staircase, formed of steps so steep that one would have to turn sideways to climb it, as if averting one's eyes from the face of God, rose to the upper level. There were temples like that in Mexico and Peru, he knew. He intended to visit them one day, to wonder at the ingenuity of the ancients. He had not expected the same in the north of England.

'Sir Elijah is at the chapterhouse,' the driver said.

'I am Higgins. The butler.' Driver and butler. It was not a very prosperous house.

The servant turned and began to climb the religiously steep stairs. Amos followed.

'What is he doing there?'

Higgins turned and glared.

'Tending to the patients.'

'I was not aware there were any patients here. Is this a hospital?'

'Of course not.' The bizarre spectacle of rudeness from the servant almost smothered the strangeness of his reply.

The stairs led to a gallery in the shape of a ring. At the rear of the house, where the staircase ended, were three doors apparently leading to bed chambers, and at the front were three more. Only one was open: the one in the centre of the front of the house, where the oriel window stood. Even ten yards away, Amos could smell the wine fumes spreading from that room. He was far from Temperance League teetotal, but men who used alcohol as a crutch were tiresome in his experience.

Higgins glanced at the open door and met Amos's eye. He broke from it to show him into the chamber behind them.

'Your room.'

It was cheerful enough, with gold- and ruby-striped wallpaper, a hung four-poster bed and a copper bed warmer ready. Amos went to the window, which looked out behind the house. He saw a bower or two, a sunken garden, a kitchen plot planted with herbs and fruit bushes, a fountain representing Poseidon with his trident and a curious, squat building right at the back with Graeco-Roman columns and a portico. He was about to enquire what the building was but, given the butler's attitude so far, thought it better to wait for his host to return.

'Higgins, do you know why I am here?' he asked, wondering about the reason for the cool reception.

'We all know why you are here.' It was an answer that said nothing, and Amos became even more suspicious of this creature. There was a long pause. 'Do you require anything?' the butler finally asked.

'Nothing.'

'Sir Elijah will be back at eight. Dinner will be served then.'

And he left the room.

It occurred to Amos that he had not been told if there was anyone else in the house. Perhaps the young woman whose presence had attracted him was there, perhaps she wasn't. He wanted to see her, especially after his long journey and months away from her, but it would be better to wait until he had rested and washed, he knew. After all, their last meetings had been on his ground, where he was the exotic element. But now they were on her turf; and her sardonic bent might just be unleashed if he were to give it a reason. He could wait.

He stepped out of his chamber and immediately found himself looking at a young man aged around thirty, leaning against the doorway opposite his own.

The man had fair hair down to his shoulders in an almost feminine style, piercing eyes of a colour that Amos could not tell and hands thrust into the pockets of pin-striped black trousers. He wore no jacket, only a shirt and cravat. He was strikingly handsome, but with such a dissolute air that the effect was blunted. They stood gazing at each other for a long while. Amos found it curious, but he was becoming used to that in this odd house.

'Be a good fellow and bring me some Champagne,' the other one drawled after a while.

'And why should I do that?'

The man shrugged. 'No one else will. I'll order Higgers to do it, and he'll just walk off, pretending not to hear.'

'Perhaps that would be for the best.'

'Oh, I'm *sure* it would be for the best!' the young man replied quite warmly. 'But sometimes . . .' He broke off, interrupted by a fit of coughing, which he tried to stifle with a hand over his mouth, followed by a light wheezing. 'Sorry, old man,' he apologized, rubbing his fist on his chest. 'I was saying that sometimes one doesn't want the best, does one? Sometimes one simply wants what one wants, and hang the rest.' He returned to leaning against the door jamb as if it were his natural pose and anything else would be quite uncomfortable.

Amos considered. Then he acted.

'Higgins!' His voice was strong enough to carry through the house. They both waited. Higgins appeared. 'Would you bring the gentleman a half-bottle . . .' The young man tutted and shook his head. 'A full bottle,' Amos corrected himself, 'of Champagne?'

Higgins glanced at the young man without a jacket, then went away, reappearing half a minute later with the required bottle. The young fellow took it, nodded to Amos in acknowledgement and drifted back into his room.

Amos, too, returned to his own chamber, where he washed in a basin, changed his clothes and began to unpack. He was placing his shirts in the press when the sound of the front door crashing open interrupted his menial task.

'Where the blazes is he?!'

The words were shouted from below, and Amos had the impression that Sir Elijah Delpont had arrived back from the chapterhouse.

'Where do you think?' the servant answered.

Seconds later, Sir Elijah, a big man with ginger moustaches and, right then, a visible air of wanting to break a man in two, was storming up to the gallery. He glared at Amos through his doorway but turned immediately to the room opposite and stomped in.

'Do you know what you have done?' he yelled.

'I think the point is that I have done precisely nothing,' came the drawled reply. 'Surely you should be demanding to know what I have *not* done. I have *not* attended the hustings for Lower Hinchester.'

'Blast you!' the older man snarled. 'I bought that seat to—'

'Oh, brother Elijah. In our nation, one cannot *buy* a place in Parliament. *Surely* you wouldn't want to suggest that we still have placemen and rotten boroughs? *Surely* you wouldn't want me to enter the Commons on anything but my skills as an orator?'

'Your skills as an orator are precisely why I want you in the House! Those sheep need a . . . a . . .'

'A ewe?'

'Exactly. A blasted ewe! But when it comes to the hustings, you're here getting tight and staring at the moon.'

'You can't see the moon from here. I have tried.'

There was the sound of a bottle smashing. Amos hoped he would not be called upon to resume his duties as wine waiter. 'Any fool knows that Gladstone is a disaster for this nation.'

'In that case, I wonder why you need me to speak against him. Indeed, I wonder how he could form a government, unless the entirety of Her Majesty's Parliament is made up of fools.'

'Which, sir, it is!' the older man snapped.

'Then you and I are better off out of it. The high regard in which I hold you forces my hand, brother Elijah. For the sake of your good name, I must keep us both out of that den of dunderheadedness.'

'I don't know what has got into you lately, Gabriel. But it cannot stand. I will not let it!'

'Well, that is a pity. Because I am sorry to report that it is out of my hands. And so we both suffer it.'

Sir Elijah banged his way back out of his junior brother's chamber, sending a flurry of dust up from the gallery carpet, and descended the stairs.

'Would you be so kind as to send for another bottle

of Champagne? An accident seems to have befallen the last.' Gabriel Delpont was once more in his doorway. But just a little bit lower down the frame. He lifted his palm to forestall any objection. 'I know, I know. You need not tell me. I, sir, am the one inside this body. I feel its ebbs and its flows. You merely observe it from the outside.' At that, he returned to his chamber.

The decision before Amos – whether to grant his young uncle his desire or to ignore it in what might be his relative's best interests – was forestalled by the butler striking a small gong to denote the commencement of dinner.

Amos, who was already dressed for it, strode over to the room opposite. Gabriel was in his oriel window seat, his hands on the sill and his forehead resting on them. Amos glanced around the room, spied a jug of water beside the washbowl and tipped the contents over the head of his relation. Gabriel did not move, but did breathe more heavily for a few seconds before lifting his face. 'Thank you,' he said.

Leaving him to it, Amos went down to the dining room to find Sir Elijah at the head of the table. At the other end was another man, closer to Sir Elijah's age than Gabriel's. This had to be the other brother, Maurice. He was a plump little man with thinning hair, a florid face that squeezed out over the top of a clerical collar and fat fingers that were gripping a tiny brown book with a devotional look about it. He was staring at an open page and silently, quickly, mouthing the words.

'Good evening,' Amos said.

Maurice evidently didn't hear, because, if anything, his lips sped faster through the miniature verses. The page was turned swiftly, urgently even, and the divine started afresh at the top of a new leaf. It had barely come to rest before it was turned again.

'He said good evening!' Sir Elijah barked.

At that, the priest looked up. 'Good evening,' he muttered as rapidly as he read. 'I will not . . . No.' His eyes began to dart around the room as if watching a bird flit hither and thither.

'There,' Sir Elijah stabbed his index finger at a chair, and Amos took a step towards it, ignoring the curtness of the instruction, just as his cousin Jessica and her companion, Cleo, entered the room.

Amos felt his body tense a little. He told himself that it had been just the same when he had stalked tigers in the jungle. He wanted to speak to her alone, of course, but the chance would not present itself for a while. He would need patience.

He stood, and his uncle made a half-gesture of doing so. Maurice's eyes and lips moved faster and faster until he fumbled the book, dropping it to the floor, where he immediately cast himself to scrabble about for it. Amos picked it from the thin carpet and handed it to the man, who waved his fingers as an expression of gratitude. It seemed to Amos that everyone in this house needed help in some form or another.

The young women were like fresh air into the house. Upon seeing Amos, Jessica lightly caught her breath, while her friend inclined her head a little.

'Mr Sacher,' Cleo said. 'Fancy meeting you here.'

Ah, the sardonic side was at play already. 'Fancy,' he replied.

'Perhaps you came for the weather?'

'It is something of a relief. Rajasthan at this time is very hot.'

'Indeed? That is most interesting.' She struggled against a smile. He wanted her to let it play out, but she mastered it and forced it away. The two young women shared a glance and took their seats. Higgins began to serve the soup. Sir Elijah began hungrily demolishing his, while Maurice waved it away.

'Perhaps you will return to India in time?' Amos said to both the young women so as not to favour either one.

'I did so like it there,' his cousin agreed readily. 'Everything is so different.'

'Oh, come, Jessica, some things are the same the world over,' said Cleo.

And again, the glint in her eye was unmistakable to Amos, who was looking for it. 'Such as?' he prompted, daring her to go further.

'Cows.'

'Cows? Yes, there are, indeed, cows in India.' He allowed himself a grin.

'I was surprised how they seem to just walk around with no one stopping them,' Jessica added.

'They are sacred to the Hindu people. Not to be molested.'

'How nice for them.'

'Quite.'

At that, there was another entry to the room as Gabriel drifted in. He had dressed properly but had made only the most cursory of attempts to dry his head, so that his long, fair hair dripped a constant stream of water onto his shoulders.

Given what had come before, it was no surprise to Amos that the ensuing meal was poorly made. As they ate, the younger members of the party took all conversation upon themselves.

'Will you walk out with us tomorrow?' Cleo asked. 'Gabriel is to join us. We intend to make fun of him.'

Amos was happy to be invited. But he gazed at his young uncle. The man could hardly stand, let alone walk. And yet there was something in his eye and speech that told Amos watching him would be worth the time.

'I am sure he can take the criticism.'

'Are you? I am not,' the blond man replied, swigging wine from a tumbler. 'Words can cut like knives, you know.' Amos moved a glass of water in front of his uncle, who promptly put the wine down. 'Quite right. Quite right.' He drank from the proffered glass.

'Would—'

'Had enough of this nonsense,' Sir Elijah said gruffly, chucking aside his napkin. 'Come to the library. Something to show you,' he informed Amos.

Well, it was disappointing that his first conversation with Cleo had been cut so short, but perhaps there was no harm in that, since he would be walking out with her tomorrow – at her invitation, no less – and any more chat overseen by the rest of the table could hardly have been very relaxed and personal. No, he would look forward to the next day. He rose and followed his host.

'Enjoy the Madman's Library,' Gabriel bade him. 'Ah, I see that moniker amuses you? Well, you shall understand.' He took a plum from a brass serving plate and bit into it.

Chapter 3

They left the warm, brightly lit house, the one part of the priory that seemed to exist in the nineteenth century, and wound their way through tumbling curtain walls and over mounds of dirt and stone, back to the chambers and towers of the Middle Ages.

They reached a single-storey building that appeared to be octagonal in shape. Along with the structure that Higgins had told him earlier was the chapter-house, the library was one of only three buildings that had not fallen to pieces, as far as Amos could tell. The air smelled fruity and musty.

'Why do you think this survived – and your house, too – when most of the rest was destroyed?' he asked.

'The Prior's house came through because it was a damn fine house, and when it was sold off after the Reformation, the new owner fancied living there during the summer. My family bought it in the last century,' Sir Elijah said, fiddling with a bunch of modern keys. 'The library – now, why that survived is uncertain. Act of God, some would say, no doubt. Superstitious clap-trap, of course.' For someone who lived in a former

Benedictine priory, Sir Elijah Delpont bore some animus towards religion, Amos noted.

'And there is the chapterhouse.'

Sir Elijah scowled. 'Who told you of that?'

'I passed it when I came in. Higgins told me what it was called. It is put to some use, I believe?'

His uncle narrowed his eyes as if staring at a dangerous dog. Then he fitted one of the keys into the door and turned it. Amos let the subject drop.

The door opened onto an unlit, oval-shaped vestibule. A wave of heat blasted out. Sir Elijah stood back, a grin spreading on his face as he watched his nephew enter and walk through a stone archway carved with a relief of Adam, Eve and the serpent in the Garden of Eden, into an octagonal room.

Above was a ceiling fresco of the Heavens, with Jesus sitting at the right hand of God at a golden table spread with fruits. The walls of the room were covered with paintings, stacks of books stood all around, and here and there were cabinets containing finely polished musical instruments – some Amos recognized; many, such as a huge item that looked like a harpsichord but had three keyboards arranged in a triangle so that the player must have sat in the middle and spun madly to play them all, he did not.

'These instruments are quite unusual,' he said.

'Unusual? More than that, young man,' Sir Elijah told him, dripping with satisfaction. 'You see before you the greatest collection of wicked instruments the world has ever seen!'

'Wicked?' he asked, glancing sidelong at his uncle.

'Indeed,' Sir Elijah confirmed. 'That violin.' He pointed to a copper-brown instrument suspended within a glass case by a golden thread. 'Played by Paganini himself, after he is said to have sold his soul to the Devil for his talent. The Trichord,' he moved on to the three-sided harpsichord, 'was the last instrument Charles I heard before he walked out to the scaffold at Whitehall Palace to be beheaded.' He pointed to a mandolin with a broken neck. 'The Italian composer Gesualdo calmly composed a song upon it as he watched his wife and her lover bleed to death after he had stabbed them both twenty times.'

'I understand why you call them wicked.'

'And now the books.' Sir Elijah moved to a desk, drew on a pair of silk gloves and shuffled through the maze of books, throwing some aside, toppling cliffs of papers, snatching one, scanning its cover, then shoving it back into a different pile without a moment's thought of where it might end up. Evidently, he was searching for one with a green cover, because all those he took up were leather-bound in emerald green. He found the one he wanted and laid it, like a precious object, on a walnut-wood side table. The electric light bulb overhead showed it to be a thick, cloth-bound volume. 'What do you see?' he asked.

'What should I see?'

'Death, sir.'

'That I do not see.' Amos reached to open the cover. His host grabbed his hand.

'Oh no, you do not see. This green colouring, do you know it?'

'I do not.'

'What if I told you it was arsenic?'

'I would believe you.'

'Well, don't lick your fingers after leafing through it!' The doctor chuckled gutturally. 'Now, this is something else of interest,' he said, grabbing from a stool a small brown leather volume with the title *Everlasting Love* in gold letters. 'What would you say it is bound in?' The answer was obviously not to be arsenic this time, so Amos awaited elucidation. 'This novel is a romance bound in the skin of the Countess of Galway. It was her dying wish to make a gift of herself to her lover before she died of the pox. He probably gave it to her, of course.'

Amos weighed the book in his hand. It was light. She had not warranted a long story. 'Not what I would choose as a keepsake.'

'No. No. But there it is.' Sir Elijah went to a display cabinet and gently extracted a huge red book. 'Late Renaissance. Origin unknown.' He placed it in Amos's hands. The cover folded back stiffly, and Amos was presented with a double page of vellum on which a large, colourful machine was drawn. It was shaped like some sort of fat beast – a bull, maybe. And it seemed to be a vehicle, because a tumbril full of naked women – one or two of whom were, for some reason, drawn upside-down – was attached to the rear. But there were no horses or oxen drawing it. Moreover, it was soaring through the clouds. He turned the leaf to find a page of figures asleep in their beds and having strange medical instruments inserted into their ears.

'That illustration is of particular interest to me for professional reasons.'

'May I ask how so?'

'You are aware of my medical specialism?'

'I am not, I am sorry.'

'There are no more than a dozen of us in the world,' Sir Elijah informed him. '"Lethargists" is the correct title: physicians who specialize in sleep and its disorders.'

Alongside the bright pictures were four blocks of text in faded, handwritten ink. The script was from the Latin alphabet, but Amos peered at the words and furrowed his brow. He could make neither head nor tail of them. 'What language is this?'

'Ah, that is the question, is it not?' his uncle replied with a near-demoniacal expression on his face. 'I and many others have been puzzling over just that problem for years. We have tried every European language we can find.'

'An Oriental language transliterated into Latin script?'

'Quite possible. But we have asked scholars of Chinese languages, of Farsi and Sanskrit. To say nothing of Hebrew and Aramaic.' To demonstrate, he walked to a writing desk overflowing with books and drew out dictionaries of those languages, tossing them back as their lack of advantage deserved. 'All our efforts have drawn nothing.' Amos examined the script with fascination.

Sir Elijah looked at him slyly.

'But these are nothing – nothing! – compared to

the great find. The greatest discovery of the century.'
He went to a box of black ebony, polished like a
mirror. It was chained to a steel stud in the floor to
prevent any but the most audacious thief. Sir Elijah
took a small brass key from his fob pocket and fitted
it into a lock on the front of the box. He lifted the
lid, glanced at Amos, then carefully around the room.
'Yes,' he said to himself. 'Here it is.' He lifted a slim
volume, bound, Amos could see, not in cloth or
leather, but what seemed to be faded deerskin. The
front cover had *The Waterfall, a Testament* scratched
upon it in black script of straight strokes and sharp
angles. The back cover was missing. Sir Elijah raised
it to the electric light, sliding his gloved fingers over
the surface. Then he wiped the top of the box and
very gently placed the book down on the ebony. He
pointed to the case whence he had taken his gloves.
There was another pair there waiting for Amos, who
pulled them on. Without a word, Sir Elijah pointed
to the book.

Amos held it as if it were a holy relic. He read it
from first to last. And all the while, his uncle sat
opposite him, staring at his face.

At the end, Amos returned the item to the ebony
box and sat thinking. Sir Elijah had claimed this as
the find of the century. He might have been correct.

'What do you want me to do?' he asked after a
while.

'Isn't that obvious? I want you to find out if it's true!
Do some digging. Check the facts – could Marlowe
have originated *Romeo and Juliet*? Was Shakespeare

in Holland at that time? What of Marlowe and Whitgift? "Leon of Prague" I have established is more properly named Judah Loew ben Bezalel, of Bohemia. You have heard legends of the Golem, a figure raised from clay by Hebrew mystics?'

'I have not.'

'No matter. It is a person or semi-human form that carries out the orders of the master who has animated it using prayers and certain letters, often to gain vengeance and justice. It is my contention that the stories grew out of this ritual as described.'

'I see.' Amos sat quiet for a full minute to puzzle it all out. 'My first question is how this astonishing manuscript has remained unknown?'

'Corruption!' Sir Elijah showed lupine teeth. 'Centuries of it. In the Church. They kept it from us.'

'And how did *you* come by it?'

'Fellow I know owns a bookshop in Cecil Court in London. Extraordinary cove. Former Catholic seminarian who discovered a unique talent for rooting out the most astonishing literary finds. Offers them to a rascally bunch of subscribers. How he came by it I don't know. And to answer your next question: when I am certain of the provenance, I will reveal its existence to the world at large.'

'And not before then, I presume.'

Sir Elijah grunted. 'Until then, you are to guard this secret with your life.' He stroked the deerskin cover. 'The find of the century.'

'The find of the century, Uncle.'

Chapter 4

After further discussing with Sir Elijah how to go about verifying the document as genuine or dismissing it as a forgery, Amos returned to the house with a bundle of books – biographies of Shakespeare and Marlowe, collected volumes of their writing – which would be the first step in his research.

Passing through the house, he saw Jessica and Cleo leafing through ladies' magazines. 'Will you join us, Mr Sacher?' his cousin asked. 'We are deciding where we may travel to. I do so want to see Paris. Cleo has promised me that she will take me there. Or to Venice. I want to get away.' It appeared to Amos that her eyes glistened a little with tears.

He was about to ask why she felt so strongly, when Cleo forestalled him, saying, 'Mr Sacher has a far greater task on his mind right now. Those books under his arm aren't easy bedtime reading.'

'They are not,' he confirmed, though he would have happily ditched them for an hour of talking about travel. And he was curious about Jessica's suggestion that it would be Cleo taking her away from Kirchin

Priory, rather than, say, a husband. 'I'm sure we will have time for leisure soon.'

'We will, though there is little entertainment in these parts,' Cleo told him.

'No balls or tea dances?'

'None.'

'Would I like to go to a ball?' Jessica asked her friend.

'No, darling, you wouldn't.'

It seemed an odd question to Amos – how could she not know? She must have at least read of such things – but the two young women treated it as a perfectly natural part of their conversation. 'Then we must make our own entertainment,' he said.

'Yes, we must.'

He bade them a good night and withdrew to his room.

By midnight, his mind was tired from the poetry of *Romeo and Juliet* and the bombast of Marlowe's *Tamburlaine*. So as to better order it all, he took a stroll outside to smoke, and soon found himself gazing at the lit windows of the chapterhouse. He was more than curious to know what it contained.

'Do you have one for a lady?' Cleo was standing just a few yards away. He had not expected this. Her approaching tread must have been as silent as the grave. She wore a pale pink day dress that had turned the colour of burnt ochre in the moonlight. 'What, are you taken aback to see a girl walking about at night?'

'You may find the company around here less than genteel.'

'You place yourself on that list?'

'I place myself at the top of it.'

She came closer and took a cigarette from a case that he opened. She offered it up to him, and he took it from her fingers, placed it in his mouth, lit it and gave it back to her. She took it between her lips and blew a line of smoke to the grey clouds overhead. They stayed there for the length of time it took for their cigarettes to burn away to nothing.

'Now, tell me, what of the great find, Mr Sacher? Do you think it will turn out to be genuine?'

It was a slight surprise to him to discover she knew of the manuscript, given Sir Elijah's apparent secrecy over it. But then, the household must live in each other's pockets. 'I can't say yet.'

'No, of course you would play your cards close to your chest. But tell me one thing: with whom in that story – that account, if we are to believe it is true – do you most identify? Is it good old Will, who is loyal to his chum, if a little naïve at times? Is it Kit, the mercurial genius? Is it perhaps the Archbishop, doing his best for his Church, Queen and country? Or even the mysterious teacher of the Kabbalah ritual, who wields either the power of the Almighty to breathe life into the lifeless or that of a most talented doctor to bring men out of the deepest sleep?'

When he had read the manuscript, it had been as a sort of police detective of artefacts, not as a man with child-like imagination and a desire to live in other times. So when called upon to make a choice, he knew without a doubt with whom he most empathized. 'I am a sceptic by my nature. If I see a man on stage shooting sparks from his fingers, I look for the black powder up his sleeve.'

'Ah, so you are for Will.'

'I am. That nonsense about Marlowe being brought back from the dead? Poppycock. If this manuscript is at all genuine and not some joke on the part of a dramatist noted for his comedies as much as his tragedies, then Marlowe was a gull and this man from Prague was a pharmacologist and talented conjuror. And I can tell you one more thing.'

'And what is that?'

'The Church of England still stands.'

'That is for certain,' she replied.

'Now, tell me, what is that building for?' He pointed towards the chapterhouse.

She paused. 'Every house has its secrets.'

'Of course.'

'Then let us not spoil a pleasant little interlude.'

She flicked the glowing end of her cigarette onto the dry ground.

There were no dreams as he slept, only a blanket of night. So when he was woken, in the perfect darkness, there was nothing to leave. But something had drawn him back to the world. It was the sound of one of the house's outside doors closing.

This was not his home, yet he felt some sort of duty for its security. There they were, isolated and at the mercy of any malcontent forces that wished to storm in. So he would stand sentry for all of them, even those, like Higgins, who seemed to wish the ground to open up and swallow him.

Amos looked out the window to the rear. Was that a spark of light in the garden? It could have been.

He pulled on some clothes and padded barefoot down to the hall. As he did so, it happened again: an outside door closing, but more distant this time. Stealing through the house, he peered into the dining room, finding it quite empty; the kitchen likewise, and the pantry. All dead to the world. He found the front door locked, which left him with only the rear door.

The back garden must have been a good forty yards long, and the unkempt grass under his feet bristled as he walked through it to stand in the middle of the large damp lawn. The broken carcass of a lawn mower lay on its side, just discernible in the moonlight. He felt no fear – there was no indication of danger – but there was curiosity as he checked all around.

Doing so, over the top of a clump of hedges he could make out the top of the squat building at the end of the garden that he had seen during the day, and he wished he had enquired about it before, because it now took on an ominous aspect. A very faint metallic ringing drifted through the air, echoing off the walls and trees around.

A little tenser now, he walked towards the building. Although it was night – a couple of hours after midnight, he guessed purely by how tired he felt – his skin was damp and his shirt was sticking to him.

The building became more solid as he came closer. It was about two yards tall and six yards square, solidly built of bricks and whitewashed. It had no windows, suggesting some sort of storehouse, though the fancy columns and portico looked out of place for a repository of garden implements. The door, which had no handle but a short piece of rope to pull it closed, was locked. There was a hook beside the door that looked like it was there to hold a key. Well, by now there was no danger in sight, and he had done his bit as unpaid watchman, he felt. He therefore gave the bricks a thoughtful thump and turned to retreat to the house.

Immediately he stopped. There was something out of place, something at the top edge of his vision. He lifted his eyes to stare at the roofline of the ruined Kirchin Priory. Past the darkly glinting windows of the house was the high bell tower that had once called ancient monks to their devotions. The moon, low behind it, was a murky cream disc, almost a full circle, visible between the pillars that had once supported the bell. But there was a dark mark crossing the moon: something moving between the pillars. Whatever it was, it stopped and seemed to turn to Amos, and he saw it clearer now. It was a silhouette of a figure, its arms outstretched – man or woman he couldn't tell, because it was too distant and its outline was shimmering against the lunar light. But he was sure it was looking dead at him. In a moment, it was gone, absorbed into the black of the tower.

Amos didn't stop to think. It could be one of the household, of course, but there was something about the way whoever it was had suddenly stopped, as if startled, that made him doubt they had licence to be roaming the grounds in the night's spying hours.

Dashing around toppling mounds of stone and through breaks in walls, Amos stumbled here and there as hidden pitfalls snatched at him. Sometimes the campanile would be in sight, lit whitish-grey by the moon, but at others it would be hidden by the bones of Kirchin Priory. He rounded a corner and suddenly found himself at the foot of the tower, on the side where the wall had broken apart to reveal the staircase within. He checked above him. There was no figure in sight on the staircase and no silhouette on top. But neither was there any sign on the ground level, so where they lurked was unknown. He would go up. Amos quelled his nerves, but only a fool would feel no tension at all. If the other one was there to do them harm, the stairs were a dangerous place for a struggle.

Quickly, his bare feet silent on the stones, he climbed the tower. Up three flights, then one more, through what had once been a trapdoor and was now just a bent iron hinge, and onto the platform.

He was alone, quite alone. There wasn't a single sign that anyone had been there for a hundred years. Had he imagined it? He had to ask himself that. It could have been a trick of the light, a bird flitting across at an angle that warped it in his vision.

He called himself an idiot for chasing spectres like a child. He should quietly take himself back to bed. He—

There! He saw it. A rippling mass of black below him, climbing the stairs to the chapterhouse.

He charged back down the steps, out onto the damp ground, looking all around him as he ran to the chapterhouse stairs. Twenty seconds later, he was at the door of the building, rattling the handle. It was locked, and the door was a solid oak one that must have been in place for five hundred years, bound with copper. There was no way he could force it.

A light inside was dim but even – an electric bulb, he thought. And there was still that insectoid hum from within.

He skirted the building to look for any sign that someone had entered, finding none; then returned to the front, where he stood for ten or twelve minutes, waiting for any movement or sound within. Still nothing. He swore under his breath and left.

As he returned to the house, he wondered who – or what – he had seen and whether to wake his employer to report it. No, he decided. He had not yet established himself as one whose impressions should be believed. He would wait until the morning to tell Sir Elijah.

Inside, he noticed that the doorway to Gabriel's room was open and the young man was dressed and sitting perfectly still in his oriel window seat, looking out, clearly having eschewed sleep for the night. There were times when Amos stayed up all night, but only when he had a purpose. He did not entirely trust a man who chose to wait out the dim hours before the dawn without good reason. There was something self-indulgent about it.

'I heard it, too,' Gabriel said, without turning around. 'Something moving out there.'

Amos was glad. Now he wouldn't be accused of seeing things. 'What is it?'

'Ghosts, I imagine.' Amos walked around the gallery and entered the room. 'The place is, oh, a thousand years old, you know. A thousand years of collecting ghosts.' He showed no sign of knowing that the source of the movement was more earthly than spectral.

'Have you seen any?' Amos asked.

'Oh, my dear man. I am one.'

And he turned and stretched his mouth out into a grin.

'You are a sot. There is a difference.'

'A shade of what I used to be. Is that such a difference?'

'Cease the self-pity.'

'Ah, but if *I* don't pity me, who will?' He turned back to look out at the night sky, in which stars peppered a dark sheet. And then Gabriel started coughing hard, this time more deeply and sounding more painful than when Amos had first witnessed it. 'Sorry, sorry. A touch of consumption in my youth. After-effects only – no need for you to worry for yourself.'

Amos was not worried for himself, but for the man who looked like he required the ministrations of a physician. 'Will you go to bed tonight?' he asked.

'What would I do there that I cannot do sat here?'

'Sleep.'

'That I can do neither there nor here.'

There was no reasoning with a man in that mood. 'Then goodnight.'

Gabriel had a sharp mind, anyone could see that. To throw it away on pity for his own being was tantamount to burning down a public building, Amos thought. He made to go, but his uncle's left hand shot out and grabbed his arm.

Gabriel opened his mouth, struggling to say something. He attempted it once, twice, and then finally words came. 'Would you leave the house? For my sake?' His face was drenched in shame.

'What do you mean?' Amos could tell this was no idle or drunken muttering. There was something solid at the bottom of it. But what?

'I . . . I . . .' He faltered and let go. 'I mean nothing. No, nothing. I bid you goodnight.' He attempted a thin smile.

It was the best part of a silent minute before Amos turned his gaze from the man. There would be time to search those depths.

In his room, he stripped off his shirt, wet with sweat and night-mist, and went to put it away in his portmanteau. He drew the bag from under his bed.

It was shut. But he knew he had left it open.

Chapter 5

The next morning, Amos washed his face as he looked out at the garden, which was now, in the morning warmth, a perfect picture of overgrown serenity. How strange, the tides that were moving below the surface in this house, he told himself. An unknown figure wandering the grounds at night, and an intruder – possibly the same one, possibly not – in his room and rooting through his possessions. Who? Well, burglars would have taken booty, so they had to be of the household.

He pondered, as he brushed his hair, what to do. He had little money and no immediate prospects for employment, which ruled out leaving the place – and he rather felt that that would be an excessive reaction anyway. If there were danger close by, it had not shown itself quite yet.

He placed the ivory brush back in his portmanteau and resolved that he would inform Sir Elijah of having seen a figure flitting about the grounds, but not that someone had been in his room, for which he had little evidence.

He then spent two hours reading *Romeo and Juliet*, searching for clues that its authorship was more complex than hundreds of years of scholars had surmised. He rather enjoyed the task.

As he passed through the hall on the way to breakfast afterwards, he peered into the kitchen and was surprised to see Cleo eating at a table with the butler. She had dined with the family the previous evening, so she was not relegated to the status of servant in the house. And quite who would find the sullen Higgins attractive company was beyond him. Yet the glasses by their plates unmistakably held gold-coloured beer. She noticed him passing and came to the doorway. 'The man is so terribly bored most of the time,' she said confidentially. 'I like to provide him with just a little company over an occasional meal.'

'Beer for breakfast?'

'Small beer, not the hard stuff.'

He laughed and strode to the dining room, where Maurice, dressed in his clerical garb, was reading from his pocket-sized book again, silently mouthing words in between mouthfuls of boiled egg and seeming to be in a state of nervous exhaustion. He looked up. 'Mr Sacher.'

'Vicar.'

Maurice looked uncertain. 'Yes. My calling. Yes.' He opened his eyes wide. 'Sometimes I struggle with it.'

'How so?'

'It seems so *settled*.' A look almost of incomprehension of his own words flitted across his face. 'Does it not?'

Amos gazed at his relation. The man was surely not having a crisis of faith over breakfast. 'Are not all things settled by God?'

Maurice caught his breath, as if in shame. 'Well, yes, quite. I . . .' And he lowered his eyes nervously to his little brown book.

Amos sat and helped himself to a plateful of what the British laughingly called 'curry'. It was a sweet, very thick stew, full of garden peas and quite unlike anything he had eaten in India. He pictured the bemusement Rajesh, his family's cook, would have exhibited if faced with the dish.

He had barely taken more than three forks of the food before he was presented with the image of the youngest of the three brothers in the house falling into, rather than sitting on, the nearest chair. If he had been in the final stages of a malarial nightmare, Gabriel Delpont could not have looked worse. His night-time vigil had never ended, it seemed, it had simply extended into the day. Amos was, in fact, reminded of the description of a dead man rising in the manuscript locked away in the library.

Gabriel slid back the cuff of his left sleeve and peered at a gold-faced wristwatch. 'Dear me,' he said. 'The time has flown. Wherever has it gone? Oh, you can leave off your dumb moralistic lecture on sleeping, brother. I quite appreciate your superiority in that regard.' He looked at Maurice thoughtfully. 'Oh dear, is it to be Juvenal?'

'*Orandum est ut sit mens sana in corpore sano*. He says that you must pray for a healthy . . .'

'. . . mind in a healthy body. Yes, yes. But Juvenal was not forced to live in Kirchin, Maurice.' Gabriel turned to his nephew. 'Oh, Amos,' he drawled. 'We're off to Newcastle tomorrow.'

'To see the sights?'

'The ladies would like a day out. Can't think why, when this place offers so many opportunities for entertainment. You will come?'

'I'll look forward to it.'

Breakfast proceeded, during which it began to rain lightly, pattering onto the roofs of the house, dripping through cracks in the ceilings and pooling on the floors in dank puddles. Higgins went around chucking a few rags down here and there in a defiant show of absent effort.

When the meal finished, Amos went to find Sir Elijah, encountering him in the library, studying again the Renaissance book in the mysterious language.

'Sir Elijah. I have something to inform you of,' Amos said.

'The manuscript?' Sir Elijah said, sounding hopeful.

'I'm afraid not. Something rather stranger.'

He described what had happened during the night, leaving out the possibility of a trespasser in his room. He waited for a reaction. It was an angry one.

'Absurd!' Sir Elijah growled, smacking the book down onto his desk. 'You dreamed it. That is all.'

'I assure you, I did not.' He remained calm, having been quite prepared for such a response, although the vehemence was more than he had expected. 'Someone was walking around your estate at night.'

'You say so, do you?'

Amos ignored the scoffing tone. 'Whoever it was, they either went into the chapterhouse or were trying to. May I ask what is in there?'

Sir Elijah was silent for a long while. Then a snort burst from his lips. 'Well then, my boy, perhaps you should know.'

Out they went, through the grounds to the round building, which was still resonating with a low hum. Romanesque columns that held it floating in the air made the whole thing look like a giant creature about to scuttle away. They climbed the steps to the door. Sir Elijah put his hand to a niche between the stones and drew out a brass key, which he fitted into the lock. Amos wished there had been light enough the previous night to have seen the key.

The door opened, and Sir Elijah stood back.

The sight inside made Amos stop with astonishment. It was a hexagonal room, and like the library, religious medieval art abounded on the walls; most notably above a blackened fireplace, where a fading image painted directly onto the stone depicted a leathery dragon with the face of a man, grabbing handfuls of pink humans – some of them attempting to escape, others simply lying down to accept their fate – and stuffing them into his maw. The dragon's tail stretched down into an underworld of flames.

But the shock that checked Amos's breath was not at the imagery of punishment and torment. It was that arranged in a circle in the centre were six wooden beds, and each one was occupied by an unmoving man, lying on his back with a heavy mask of black cotton over his face, hiding his identity, and a pencil-thin metal tube running under the mask, fed from a huge silver metal canister by his side.

'Who on earth are they?' Amos exclaimed, unable to contain his surprise.

'They are my patients. I would have thought that would be obvious.' Amos took a step towards the closest man. He seemed to be a young fellow, judging by his taut skin and good muscles. What could be wrong with him was anybody's guess. 'These men all suffer from sleep conditions. You may examine them. They will not wake.'

Amos lowered himself to peer at the young man, whose wispy blond beard was poking out from under the black mask. Suddenly he felt lightheaded. He stood up and shook his head to clear it. 'Ether!' he said. Sir Elijah came close. He dabbed a handkerchief in a cup of water at the bedside and held it over his nose and mouth. Then he lifted the cotton mask. Beneath it, the curved metal tube ended below the blond man's nose, hissing gas. Amos felt his head swim again and moved away. He was not happy with the trick his uncle had played. Sir Elijah replaced the mask. 'What is the purpose?'

Sir Elijah settled contentedly on a gilded Queen Anne chair. To his side was a black metal box, which must have been some kind of electric generator because it had a pair of lit dials on the front and was the source of the humming Amos had heard. A wooden case with a lock on its side was attached to the wall above.

'That man suffers from dreadful nightmares. He would wake up screaming three or four times per night, rousing his household.' He pointed to the next patient. 'He is a somnambulist – a sleepwalker to you. His habit was to get out of bed in the early hours of the morning and pace hard up and down the road where he lived, wearing only his night things.' He pointed to another. 'Before he came to me, he had not slept more than ten hours in the previous month. He was a breathing corpse.' The next men: 'A narcoleptic. He falls asleep fifteen times per day. Not healthy for a senior official in Hoare's Bank. That one is a wake-dreamer; hours after he has woken, he will find himself back in a dream, just as vivid and apparently real as when he was asleep. And him, he is a somnatic amnesiac – each time he sleeps, it destroys every memory he has made.'

Amos gazed around the room. He had seen some sights in his days, but these men in this strange place were something unnatural. 'What is the treatment? You etherize them?'

'Their bodies have to be forced back into the correct form of sleep. The best method is to keep them under for eight weeks at a bare minimum. During that period, their brains will re-learn the process. They are woken every twelve hours to eat, drink and perform any other necessary functions. But they are not allowed to speak or resume normal life in any way. Their brains must be kept to the minimal tasks.'

Amos was no doctor and had never professed a great interest in medicine, but his mind instinctively revolted against any practice that turned thinking men into little more than automata.

Just then, the man with the blond beard began to stir. His chest lifted a little. Sir Elijah went to the canister by his bedside and turned a knob. The patient sighed and fell back into place.

'Does it cure them?'

'The method has worked in all but a few cases.'

'What of the few?'

'State your meaning.'

'I mean, what of the cases where it failed?'

Sir Elijah looked darkly at him. 'Total submission to the procedure is necessary for success. But some individuals will not submit fully. Ergo some will fail. The outcomes in the cases of recalcitrants are not my concern.'

Sleep and revival. Amos stared around him and an astonishing connection formed in his mind, one between these men and the task for which he had ostensibly been employed. He took a moment to grasp it fully. He had been misled by his relative. Yes, something pertinent had been kept from him regarding the reason that he had been invited into the house. Now he saw it. 'The Shakespeare manuscript,' he said. 'You want me to go further than just verifying its authenticity, don't you?'

Sir Elijah looked perfectly satisfied with his nephew's sharp mind. 'Yes, I do, young man. The drug that Leon of Prague administered to bring men out of their stupor – it is quite plausible that it is genuine. There are a thousand forgotten medicines that one will not

find in a British physician's pharmacopeia. I want it
identified. Its effects as described would be invaluable
to my research on lethargic pathology.'

Amos already knew exactly what his uncle meant
by that. 'You want to try it on these men.'

For a second, there was silence. Then Sir Elijah
spoke. 'That is correct.'

'Do they know that?'

'They know some of it.'

He would think later about that answer, and just
how much these men knew. But for now, Amos had
a more practical question. 'And how do you expect
me to identify it?'

The older man smirked. 'You are a clever fellow.
Search the document for any indication. Then there
are his plays and poems. This was the great event of
his life – he must have left some clues, however small,
however inadvertent. What you discover may give
these men a new life.'

He was dressing it in the clothes of philanthropy,
but Amos was certain that his uncle's motivation was
self-interest. The drug, if it existed at all, would bring
him professional fame.

A sound behind them made them look around. Cleo
stood in the doorway. For a moment, Amos felt it
was strange how comfortable she seemed in that weird
room, with the etherized men and the visions of
Heaven and Hell around them. But he recognized that
she was an admirably unusual woman. 'Sir Elijah,
would you like me to return later?' she asked.

'No. Make your rounds.'

She nodded and proceeded, lifting, one by one, the masks of the sleeping men to examine their faces, before checking their pulse rates against a wristwatch that she wore and making notes within a small notebook. 'Patient five is showing signs of mild distress,' she said.

'Then proceed.' She nodded and adjusted the knob on the ether bottle. 'He may be developing some resistance to the formula,' Sir Elijah informed Amos. 'It happens from time to time.'

'If that is all, Sir Elijah?' said Cleo.

He grunted. 'No, that is not all.' He waved his hand towards the side of the room. 'Show Mr Sacher what you have been working on.'

'I am sure Mr Sacher won't be interested . . .'

In fact, he was most interested. Even putting aside the fact that it was *her* tending to the men, the whole arrangement interested him. There were strange new layers to it being revealed by the minute. Where it would go next intrigued him greatly.

'Show him.'

Obediently, she went to what appeared to be a picture easel covered with a cloth at the side of the room. She turned it and lifted away the fabric. There was, indeed, a painting underneath. Cleo moved back towards the entrance as they perused the picture. 'She has talent, no?' She had talent indeed. The picture, unfinished, was of the room in which they stood. Only five of its six beds were occupied, however, and the sixth man could be seen from the rear, walking about.

As he viewed the artwork, at the edge of his vision Amos caught sight of Cleo's face reflected in the front of a glass cabinet. Her eyes were narrowed as if she were squinting at the painting, but they were, in fact, fixed on Sir Elijah Delpont, and Amos had never seen a gaze more like a scalpel. It seemed to be efficiently taking the man apart, piece by piece. A talented surgeon could not have done better.

Then her eyes met Amos's and held them hard.

'You see that one of the patients is awake,' Sir Elijah said, oblivious to what was happening behind him.

Amos glanced momentarily at the figure on the canvas, the man pacing the room. When he looked back to Cleo, she had moved away and was straightening some medical instruments on a side table, her face showing nothing but concentration on the task before her, as if what had just occurred had been a figment of Amos's imagination.

'Did you paint this from life?' he asked, wanting to engage her in conversation, to explore what he had just fleetingly witnessed.

'Yes,' she said, going about her work.

'You sat here painting his picture while that man walked about?'

She finished what she was doing and turned her attention to him. 'Are you concerned for my safety, Mr Sacher?' She gave a wicked little grin.

Sir Elijah grunted. 'Thank you. Goodbye.' She took the instruction and left. 'Quite the girl, eh?'

'Yes, she is.' He meant it, though in a different way. He thought back to the ulterior reason for his presence in that house and briefly speculated on what would happen if his relationship with Cleo were to flourish

wildly and in time they were to announce their engagement – would Sir Elijah have had the slightest inkling
about such things happening under his roof? Most
likely not.

'An excellent wife she will make one day.' Amos
made no reply. 'Playful filly, too. Teases my brother
Maurice about the Shakespeare manuscript,' Sir Elijah
chuckled. 'Makes him fear the black magic in it. Now,
back to the issue of what you thought you saw last
night. You want me to believe that one of these men
got up and walked around? Hah!' he huffed. 'They
could not possibly. Ether keeps them in full coma.'
Amos had to admit that he had not actually seen
anyone come or go from the building, and it would
not have aided his position to suggest that one of the
residents of the house might have turned off the gas.
'Absurd nonsense.'

Amos worked steadily all that day. Was there evidence
in *Romeo and Juliet* of Marlowe's hand, which would
suggest that the Shakespeare manuscript was genuine?
And if so, could the play – or any other – point the
way to a drug that could aid Sir Elijah's work? He had
decided there was no strong moral objection to iden-
tifying the compound, so long as his uncle's patients
would be made aware; after all, an effective drug was
a gift to medicine, and he saw no reason to think that
Sir Elijah would not put it to good use.

He started with the drug that Friar Lawrence gave
Juliet to falsify her death, ready for her to return to
life in Romeo's arms.

And in this borrow'd likeness of shrunk death Thou shalt continue two and forty hours, And then awake as from a pleasant sleep.

If the manuscript locked away in the library was true, Shakespeare had remained utterly sceptical that Leon of Prague had resurrected a man using Kabbalah magic, putting Marlowe's apparent death and miraculous revival instead down to Leon's earthly drugs.

This passage in the play could well be a reference to what he had seen. But it gave no indication of what the drug contained. Neither could he find any indication elsewhere in the play: not in plain language nor hidden in the words or imagery.

Frustrated, he broke off late in the afternoon, sauntering downstairs to stretch his legs.

In the parlour, he found Jessica and Cleo eating ham sandwiches over a game of cards.

'Do you play whist, Mr Sacher?' his cousin asked.

'At times.'

'Then this is one of those times.' Cleo smiled, dealing him a hand. He sat and played for a few minutes; it was a welcome change from pounding his brain through Renaissance family feuds. But all the while, he was watching Cleo Woodleigh. Yes, a most remarkable girl.

'This is quite intolerable!'

They all looked up to see Maurice barging, flustered, into the room.

'Intolerable?' Amos prompted him.

'Someone – I shall not say who, because at present

I do not know – has removed my cassock from my bed chamber. It is theft! I laid it out, ready for—'

'I asked Higgins to wash and fold it,' Cleo said. 'There was mud on it, probably from the last time you walked back from church. It should be back with you within an hour. I hope I did not do wrong?'

'Oh!' he said, more flustered than ever. 'Oh. No, no, Miss Woodleigh. You did . . . That is . . . I apologize.' His hands flitted to and fro. 'Yes, I am . . . Oh.' He attempted to move his feet, but they seemed rooted to the floor. Amos wondered if he would have to help the man out of the room. But then the cleric managed to about-turn and head away. When he was out of earshot, Cleo burst into quiet laughter, with Jessica following her lead. Amos managed to keep a straight face for the sake of propriety, as a guest in the house, although it was not easy. It was the only entertainment he had that day, soon returning to work and nothing but work.

Chapter 6

He joined Cleo, Jessica and Gabriel in the fly the next morning for the promised day out in Newcastle, to which Sir Elijah had grudgingly given his consent. It was to be a two-hour journey and not a comfortable one. The ruts and holes in the road made for uneven going, and the fly's springs were old and worn; still, he had had much worse back home. The conversation was stilted as they all clung on to avoid being thrown bodily out of the vehicle, but Amos could not help but notice how lovely his cousin looked in a sun-yellow dress and bonnet tied with matching yellow ribbon. Cleo met his gaze and smirked. Amos let her.

When they reached the city, Amos saw it for the first time in the bustle of the day. The streets were teeming with humanity hurrying to or from shops and market stalls, yelling and bickering, while the traffic on the river running through the city was like an armada under no one's control.

In line with the girls' wishes, they called in at a few

dress shops and a milliner's store. Cleo marched Gabriel
to his tailor to be fitted for a new lounge suit. It was
in an enclosed mall of glass and brass, and after the
fitting they strolled between the perfumiers, chocolatiers
and knots of men in top hats bidding each other a
good morning.

'See that spot there?' Gabriel pointed languidly to
an unassuming flagstone. 'I saw a man shot there.
Family squabble about oats, as I recall. I think they've
cleaned it since then. Can't be certain, of course.'

Behind them, Amos heard someone mutter: 'Gabriel
Delpont. Probably onto his second bottle of brandy
already.'

Gabriel spun around in a fury. 'How dare you, sir!'
he snapped. 'I'll have you know that it is my second
bottle of *port*. I'm not an *animal*.' He turned his back
on the other man and marched away, followed by his
companions, to the other end of the mall, where he
dropped heavily onto a bench, sucking in air. 'Oh, don't
look at me like that. It's all very well for you to go
walking about at this time of day. You have slept in
the last two days.'

'You could, too, if you weren't so busy drinking,'
Amos retorted.

'Ah, but if I don't put away the bottles, who will?
They'll just stack up and up in the vintner's until they
spread out onto the road and trip the passing horses.
Now, I have an appointment; meanwhile, the ladies
would like you to accompany them, I believe.'

'We have an errand to run,' Cleo told Amos. 'Jessica
and I have gone through our presses and pulled out

some old clothes we never wear, so we're donating them to a church mission.'

'No doubt the poor of the parish are in need of whale-bone corsets,' Gabriel added. 'I shall meet you after.' He lifted his hat and walked away.

They walked out to find Higgins waiting by the fly. 'Hardwell Street,' Cleo instructed him and they trotted away.

A few minutes later, after passing through a large market square and then into the less salubrious lanes surrounding the docks, they stopped outside a narrow building beside a new church.

A steady stream of the destitute and dispossessed were tramping in and out, each face an identical image of grim despair. The three dressed in fine clothes caused a minor sensation, and the needy cleared a path for those with plenty.

Inside, they found a high-ceilinged hall, although the floor was narrow, so that the overall impression was of a man about to teeter off his feet and come crashing to the ground. A dozen or so trestle tables were arranged in the centre of the room, each overseen by a matriarch who would quiz the approaching poverty-stricken applicants about their level of destitution before jealously handing over a garment; or refusing to do so and bullishly pointing to the exit, not to be swayed by tears or pleas. There was a separate room off the main hall where donations were being taken in. This room had carpet underfoot and upholstered chairs readily available if the ladies should wish to stop for a while and take some tea.

Cleo, familiar with the arrangement, led the others into this room. At her instruction, Amos laid on a polished teak table a few skirts, blouses and stockings, all in an excellent state of repair. The church verger, who was in charge of the business, thanked the ladies profusely.

'What more can we do to help?' Cleo asked. 'Perhaps we could offer a few hours of our time.'

That was, replied the verger, a truly Christian offer, but he was delighted to say that the current roster of volunteers, drawn from the class that also made up the clientele, were perfectly adequate at that time.

'Well then, we shall be on our way.' She led them out through the main hall, chatting to Jessica about their plans for the rest of the day. Then she stopped. She was staring at a woman at one of the tables, who was looking back at her with an intense, almost fearful, open-mouthed gaze. Jessica caught sight of the woman, too, and a flicker of recognition seemed to pass across her face. The woman was probably around their age, but years of hard life had taken their toll in lank hair and jaundiced skin stretched across bones. Pockmarks right up the left-hand side of her face spoke of her desperate profession. She dropped a threadbare skirt – a poor offer among poor offers – that she had been examining, and it cascaded to the floor.

'Is that . . . ?' Jessica began.

'Yes,' her friend replied.

There was a moment without movement, and then Cleo began walking. The woman hastily looked left and right, but there was no escape. 'Hello, Annalise,' Cleo said gently, placing a hand on the woman's shoulder. 'I'm sorry to see times have been trying, but I hope you are well.' The woman's lips shivered as if she were attempting to speak, but they gave up and her eyes instead rose in an imploring way. Cleo picked up the skirt the woman had dropped. 'I think this will suit you. From what I remember of you.' She held it out and waited. 'Annalise?' After ten seconds, a jaundiced hand lifted to take it from her grasp. 'That's better. Will it remind you of our schooldays? Of you and me and the other girls? I hope it will.' It seemed to Amos that the woman did not desire any such reminders.

'Good morning, Annalise,' Jessica said brightly, as she, too, arrived.

'Good morning,' Annalise whispered.

'Are you well?'

'Just look at her, dear,' Cleo interjected. 'Does she *look* well to you?'

Annalise looked crushed by the statement. 'Quite well, thank you,' she managed to whisper.

Amos noted the accent. It was refined, like Cleo's and Jessica's, although the voice itself had been roughened, perhaps by hard drink and cheap tobacco.

'Are you living near here?' Cleo asked.

The woman hesitated, looking again to the exit. 'Sometimes.'

'Sometimes?'

'When I can . . . pay for it.'

'That is nice.' There was a long, painful silence. 'Well, it was a pleasure seeing you again. Goodbye.' And Cleo gently guided Jessica away.

They were about to leave the room when the cry came.

'Cleo!'

The room went quiet as they turned.

'Yes?'

The woman had lifted her hands in an imploring way and opened her mouth to speak, but the words would not come. Her hands fell back down, and her gaze followed. 'Please don't tell anyone.'

There was a moment's silence. 'Not your parents?'

Annalise winced and shook her head.

'We could find them. They would want to know, I'm sure.'

'Please, no. Please.' The girl was clearly adamant, afraid of her parents' shame, retribution or sadness at what their daughter had become.

'But what if they could help you? I *do* think they should be told.' It was surely time to drop the attempt at persuasion, Amos thought.

'Cleo,' Jessica said, placing her hand on her friend's arm. Cleo gently removed it and held it in her own.

'Of course, I'll say nothing if you ask me not to. If you are quite certain.'

'I don't want them to know.'

'I won't breathe a word, Annalise. I hope you can find some strength.' And she walked away.

'Did you know she would be here?' Jessica whispered as they reached the exit, followed by Amos.

'If I had known, I would have stayed well away.'

'Yes, of course.'

Chapter 7

They met Gabriel in a nearby street, swinging his walking stick outside a townhouse with a sign alerting passers-by to the legal chambers of 'Alfred Lees, solicitor'.

'It is done,' Amos heard him inform Cleo quietly, as he jumped into the fly.

'I do wish you hadn't,' she replied under her breath. 'I don't know what people will say.'

He patted her on the arm.

'Shall we have another outing? Perhaps to Heddon-on-the-Wall?' Gabriel suggested out loud as they clipped along the road home.

'Oh no, I would prefer to stay inside this afternoon,' Jessica answered.

'Well, if you wish.'

'I say a tea party! And let's have it outdoors,' Cleo announced, holding on to her hat as a breeze lifted.

'We're into autumn,' Amos said. 'The leaves are coming down.'

'Surely you can brush aside a few leaves,' she laughed. 'We shall declare it a fine day.'

'I've stalked tigers in less dense jungles than that back garden,' he replied. But he was quite conscious that this would be the first activity of pure pleasure that he had indulged in with Cleo Woodleigh. It could be the first of many, or it could equally be the last.

'Croquet and sandwiches.'

'Your wish is my command,' Gabriel announced.

'Are there any balls, tea dances or the like?' Amos asked his uncle surreptitiously, while the young ladies were pointing to some distant hills and discussing a walk there sometime.

'Around here? Claret cups and fruit cake? I shouldn't think so.'

'A pity.' He thought of the conversation he had had with Jessica and Cleo. 'A little entertainment is always pleasurable. We have them in India.'

'A fine place to spend time with a certain young lady, perhaps?' Gabriel whispered, with a grin. He had guessed, Amos told himself. Well, it was only a matter of time, perhaps.

They retired to change into looser clothing and then went out to the rear garden, where autumn gusts were bringing down light flurries of leaves. A few rustling sounds in the undergrowth suggested the presence of stalking creatures on the search for food.

Higgins, as directed, appeared with a tray of sand-wiches that he placed on an ironwork table beside the fountain in the form of Poseidon, then went off to drag some old croquet mallets, hoops and balls from an unknown cupboard. These in hand, they all moved to the more open far end of the garden, where Amos enjoyed seeing Cleo at play, cutting loose. The balls were inexpertly knocked about, rarely going anywhere near the hoops, sometimes coming to rest in small piles of damp, fallen leaves. Jessica's ended up in the middle of an impenetrable bush, while Cleo managed to hit one so solidly that it smacked Gabriel's right out of the playing arena, to bounce off the small white building. He laughed and strode over to retrieve it but stopped short.

'Odd,' he said, barely audibly.

'What is?' Amos called over.

'Door's open.' He pushed the faded oak door, and it moved in with a creak.

The squat little building looked as lifeless as ever. 'What is this thing?' Amos asked, coming close to it.

Gabriel looked at him quizzically. He was about to speak when he suddenly doubled up, wheezing. Amos tried to help him, expecting another fit of coughing, the gift of youthful consumption, but Gabriel waved him away. 'I'm fine, I'm fine.' He straightened up and slowly, carefully, took in a full chest of air. 'You don't know what this is? Well, why would you? It's our family mausoleum.'

'What are you boys chatting about?' Cleo called over.

'Yes, come on, it's your go, Gabriel,' Jessica added.

'Any idea why this would be open?' he replied over his shoulder. They had none.

'Go in,' Amos instructed his relation.

'It's not exactly a tea parlour in there. Boxes of my dead ancestors, you know.'

'They won't hurt you.'

'They might.' The young women came over to investigate. At that, Gabriel seemed to find his courage. 'Nothing to worry about,' he informed them.

Amos was not going to wait any longer. They were his dead relatives, too, he reasoned, so he had an equal right to enter.

The hinges complained as he pushed the door inward, allowing the sunlight in and the reek of decaying matter out.

'What's that smell?' Jessica blurted out, then turned pale as she realized what it must be.

Behind the door was a screen made of bricks, designed so that even when the door was open, the daylight would be blocked from entering. Amos moved around it, followed by the others, just able to make out the floor where he walked.

'Good God!' he heard someone cry out. At the edge of his vision, he saw Gabriel raise his hands to his face, twisting and stumbling as he attempted to defend himself from something attacking him.

'For God's sake, they're just birds,' Amos said, batting the creatures away. 'They must have flown in while the door was open.' They fluttered out, cawing noisily.

'Yes, yes. I apologize. Bravery's your bag, not mine.'

Amos's eyesight had not yet adjusted from the day outside to the dark within. But there was a glimmer of light at the far end.

His foot connected with something that skidded across the floor, a piece of fallen masonry, and his skin prickled as he made his way forward, beginning to make out a room with two levels of shelves on each wall, each of them carrying a burden: coffins, some ancient, some newer, some covered in grime and others rotted almost wholly away. Rusted iron hooks stuck out here and there between them.

The glimmer of light was dripping down from a dusty glass panel in the roof. Amos rubbed away some of the dirt with his sleeve, and immediately a silver beam fell onto a wooden altar no more than a yard before him. A brass candelabra upon it seemed to glow in the dusty air.

The light revealed a new sight, too. There was something on the walls: a strange series of marks smeared on the bricks in soot and mud above the coffins of the dead. The mud looked fresh.

'How did. . . ?' Jessica began.

She was interrupted by a sound. A human sound of moaned suffering.

'*My God!*' exclaimed Cleo. '*There!*'

Amos spun to look where she was pointing. And he saw it. Huddled in the darkest corner, slumped on the damp stone floor, was the figure of a man. The silver light showed him strange: naked, curled under a coat of earth with his arms wrapped around his head so that his face couldn't be seen. Tentatively, Amos took a step towards him. The man shivered but didn't move. Another step – not fearful, but careful of this earthen creature. He crouched down to see who it could be.

As his eyes adjusted to the struggling light, it was

the black mask on the man's face that told Amos who he was, although he had never known the man's name.

'It's Sir Elijah's patient. The one who sleepwalks. I think he's sleepwalking now,' he said quietly, so as not to wake the man, whose arms pulled his head in tighter to his chest, as if trying to crawl away from the world.

'What on earth is he doing here?' Jessica whispered hoarsely.

'I have no idea. I'll wake him.'

'Is that wise?' Gabriel questioned.

Amos did not answer but reached out and gently shook the man's arm. There was no response. He tried again more forcefully, but the earth-covered man's breaths remained long and deep.

Why would he not wake? The supply of ether was nowhere close, and Sir Elijah had not said that the patient remained asleep when the gas was removed. Amos resolved to look deeper. He eased the cotton mask, fixed around the man's head, away from his face.

And then he understood. For it was stuffed with wool that gave off a sweet smell. Lifting it made his head swim and the dark creep into him, so that he could see nothing. Holding his breath, he quickly screwed it up and tossed it towards the opposite corner.

'It's ether. Soaked into the mask,' he said, sucking in the unpoisoned air.

'In the mask?' he heard Cleo say. 'But we don't do that. It comes to the patients from a pipe.'

Amos's vision became sharper again. He shook his head to clear it and tried gently waking the man. Still no reaction. 'I suppose it will take time for the ether to leave his lungs,' he said. They all waited silently for a while, just watching the huddled man. Then Amos tried again. And this time the breathing changed. It became shorter, shallower. The man's knitted fingers twitched on his skull. A rasp formed in his throat, which became words. 'I . . . please . . .' Then his whole body began to unfurl, his hands planting on the wet floor, his torso pushing up. Amos stood back as the somnambulist lifted his arms, threw back his head and opened his eyes. The sight of them made Amos stop hard. For precious blood streamed from the sockets, down mud-smeared cheeks, to drip onto the stone floor. A moan escaped the man's lips, growing and deepening into a cry of suffering.

And in the next moment, it became clear how those eyes had become such travesties, as the kneeling figure drew his hands to his face, his fingers roving over it until they found the red springs of blood and clawed at them.

Amos seized his wrists, prising them away as the man fought desperately to scrape at his own bleeding eyes. Gabriel rushed to help. Their shadows struggled and all the while the man's mouth was open like a river and screaming to God or Lucifer. His fingers thrust then into his mouth, and Amos grabbed them too, but the kneeling figure wrenched away and probed deep into his throat. Amos tried again to stop him, but the fingers slid back up and out of the dark maw with something pinched between them. The sleep-walker fell to his side, silently shivering and shaking. Amos discreetly removed from the man's grasp what had been in his throat.

'He's still asleep!' Cleo said, with astonishment in her voice. They all gazed at each other and at the wracked face below them.

Gabriel picked up the ether-soaked mask, keeping it balled tightly in his fist and at arm's length.

'Someone brought him here and used that to control him,' Amos commented.

'Someone did this to him?' Jessica gasped. 'Couldn't he have done it himself?'

'No. Not at all,' Cleo answered.

Amos spoke out. 'No, someone else arranged all this. To enact this scene.'

'Are they insane?'

'Perhaps.'

'I feel . . . quite unwell,' Jessica said faintly, grabbing hold of her friend's arm.

'Can you take her to her room?' Amos asked Cleo.

'Yes, of course.' She led the other young woman away. As they departed, Jessica began to sob. 'Now, there's no need to be dramatic, Jessica. All will turn out well and fine. Just put your faith in me.'

It seemed to Amos rather cold as a reaction, but perhaps that was their relationship: Cleo was the bedrock that kept her friend stable.

The two men were left with the earth- and blood-caked figure. 'Good God,' Gabriel said under his breath.

Amos examined the object that the sleepwalker had drawn from his throat. It was a small strip of paper, torn at the edges. Something had been scrawled upon it, but the light was too low to see. He moved into the vertical beam of solid light so he could trace its form.

The paper showed two rough symbols drawn by a finger dipped in soot. One was squarish, the other three-pronged.

'What *is* this?' Gabriel asked.

'I have no idea.' He folded it and put it in his pocket. 'Stay here. I will go for your brother.'

'I can do it. I just need to fortify myself first.'

Amos could guess what that meant and had no intention of waiting half an hour for Sir Elijah to be informed by his drunken brother of what had happened.

'No, I will go.'

As he walked quickly to the house, he turned the events over in his mind. What he had seen last night was obviously connected to the strange event that had taken place in the mausoleum. He realized that when he had gone out to the garden to investigate the sound and tried the mausoleum door only to find it locked and the key not on the hook, the perpetrator of this bizarre, seemingly aimless crime had probably been on the other side of the wood.

Outside Sir Elijah's chamber, Amos straightened his clothes. He had left a thin trail of soil up the staircase.

Sir Elijah and Maurice were bent over a volume, deep in discussion, as he knocked and entered.

'It is hardly worthy of our effort. No, the Willis pamphlet . . .' Maurice was insisting.

'Sir Elijah,' Amos interrupted.

'Please wait,' the vicar remonstrated with him. 'This is important. The Willis pamphlet—'

'Sir Elijah!' They turned, struck by his tone. 'Something has occurred.'

The senior of the two glared at him. 'Spit it out, then!'

He spat it out in an ordered fashion and waited.

Sir Elijah went to the window, pulled back the curtain and looked out, as if he would be able to see through the walls of the mausoleum. Then he went to a closet and grabbed a black leather doctor's bag. He hunted for something else behind it.

Maurice, meanwhile, stared at Amos, then slumped into a chair, his jaw falling open. He blinked rapidly and began to babble. 'The Willis pamphlet, it came to light in America, where a man says he conversed with an angel and he said that the angel would, would—'

'Calm yourself,' Amos said.

'No, no. But the, yes, we have bought a copy that . . .' He held up a blue pamphlet in quarto size. 'It would . . .' And his jaw continued to move, but no words came out.

Amos walked to a tray in the corner, poured a glass of water and handed it to Maurice, who drank it with a shaking hand, spilling half its contents down his shirt. He peered at his chest as if unable to comprehend how it came to be there.

The eldest brother turned back to the room. He was holding something: a strait-waistcoat. 'I don't think you'll need that,' Amos informed him.

'Leave those opinions to me. I know the man. He is my patient.'

'I am aware.' He decided not to press the point and went with his employer back to the mausoleum. Maurice followed at their heels.

Gabriel glanced at them as they arrived. 'He hasn't moved,' he said.

'What . . . Oh!' Maurice exclaimed as he saw the figure curled at their feet.

'Good God, his eyes!' Sir Elijah burst out as he reached the man shivering on the ground. Maurice took an audible breath as he, too, saw the streams of blood and the mutilated sockets. He had been warned, but his stomach was not strong enough for the sight, it seemed. 'What the Devil happened?'

'He did it to himself, with his hands.'

Sir Elijah muttered something under his breath, an oath perhaps. 'Why didn't you stop him?'

'Stop him?' Amos replied. 'Because I was not here when he did it. Why didn't you keep him under your supervision?' He had had enough of good manners in this house. 'Someone must have led him here.'

'Nonsense. Who would do such a thing? And why?'

'That I cannot answer.'

'Balderdash!'

Maurice lifted his hands in supplication. 'Please, gentlemen, let us just take the poor man to the hospital.'

Sir Elijah bent down and examined his patient. 'His wounds look far worse than they are. Superficial. I shall dress them myself.'

'Are you responsible for this, Elijah?' Gabriel asked darkly.

Sir Elijah grunted in annoyance at the suggestion. 'You presume to ask that, do you, sir?'

'I do.'

'Just help me, man,' Sir Elijah huffed angrily. He placed an arm under the shoulder of the mud-covered figure and attempted to pull him to his feet. Maurice rushed to lift the other side of him. Between them, they got him upright and began dragging him towards the chapterhouse. 'What in the name of God can it be? Whoever did this, I will tear him apart. *My work!*' Sir Elijah growled.

'We must call the police,' Amos told him.

Sir Elijah stopped. There was a long silence. 'We will not.'

Amos was outraged but quelled the reaction. 'This was an assault. The man is your patient but also has the rights of any man . . .'

'It is my house, damn you! I shall decide.'

'He is right. Any man—' Gabriel began.

'This is my domain, and I shall mete out any punishment. If you go against my wishes, I shall throw you both – you all – out of my house!'

At that, he flicked his hand at his brother and nephew, telling them both to depart. They took the instruction and returned to the house, stopping in the hallway to breathe and think over what had

passed in the last ten minutes that now felt like ten
hours.

'Where is the nearest police station?' Amos asked.

'There is a constable in the village. But if I am
wholly honest, I'm not convinced that any crime has
been committed.'

Gabriel was probably correct. No, an appeal to the
legal authorities would have to wait.

No dinner was taken that night, though they all gathered in the dining room. Sir Elijah scowled and paced,
eventually disappearing to his bed chamber. Gabriel
sat drinking steadily. Tears ran down Jessica's cheeks,
and Cleo subtly dabbed them away. Maurice was
utterly white in the corner of the room and gently
trembling. Amos, sick of the scene, bade them all good
evening and took himself outside to get some air.

He spent the better part of an hour sitting among
the broken stones and wondering at what had befallen
the priory and the house that had sprung up from its
ruins. An affair stranger than any other he had heard
of. Well, there was little to do now but sleep on it
– but sleep lightly.

He returned to his chamber. As he undressed, he
overheard voices from his uncle's room.

'We are under his examination.' Gabriel was
drawling even more slowly than usual.

'So? Let him examine. Let him!' Sir Elijah returned
hotly.

'Would it not be better, given what has happened,
if he found other lodgings?'

Amos was surprised. He had read no animosity towards him in Gabriel until now. The afternoon's unpleasant discovery had no doubt disturbed his younger uncle, but this was quite unexpected.

'I shall decide for myself who lodges in my own house,' Sir Elijah replied. 'And that goes for *everyone* here.'

At that, there was a moment's silence, and then the sound of Gabriel gently padding to his own room and shutting himself in. Amos sat at the small desk in his room and pondered. He would not stay if unwanted, but where to go? An hotel was possible, but he had little money and no job, so it could only be a short-term stay. He had one other friend in England, a former India correspondent for *The Daily Telegraph*, and he had planned to write to him suggesting that they attend the theatre in London together soon. Now it seemed he might have to beg a bed for a while. It might cripple his plans to court Cleo, but that was not to be helped. He would have to find another path there.

He took a pen and paper and began to write, saying that he was now in England. But he had barely finished his opening salutations when he was surprised to hear voices again from Sir Elijah's chamber. This time, it was his other uncle pleading with the head of the family.

'. . . beg you, Elijah, in the name of He who sits in Heaven to send that young man away,' Maurice was saying. 'What more reason do you need than that a good, loyal brother asks it?'

'Much more,' Amos heard his uncle growl.

'I . . . but . . . please, Elijah, I will be a happier man if he is gone.'

'Then you will remain an unhappy one. Get out.'

Amos sat for a while.

Then he tore the letter apart and dropped the pieces into the waste basket.

Chapter 8

Shaking off the strange events of the previous day, he worked steadily in the library the next morning, comparing Marlowe's language to Shakespeare's in *Romeo and Juliet* to see if there was an argument there that Marlowe had written some of it. At eleven, he went for a walk. When he returned, he was surprised to find Cleo at his desk, poring over the books that he was using. She spoke without looking up. '*Here's to my love! O true apothecary! Thy drugs are quick. Thus with a kiss I die.* It is blank verse.'

He took a seat opposite hers. 'Yes, it is.'

'Marlowe pioneered the form, it was a favourite style of his.' So she was helping him with his duty now. He took that as a positive sign of her disposition towards him. 'Not proof that he wrote this play, of course, not by a long shot. But an indication. As is Mercutio's line, *Laura to his lady was a kitchen-wench . . . Dido a dowdy; Cleopatra a gypsy; Helen and Hero hildings and harlots.*'

'How so?'

'Because Marlowe wrote of those classical beauties

in his other works. Dido in *Dido, Queen of Carthage*, Helen of Troy in *Faustus*, Hero in *Hero and Leander*. And what do we find when we read *Hero and Leander*?'

'Tell me.'

'Two lovers kept apart, consummating their violent love as dawn breaks. And rather tellingly, *Hero and Leander* was completed by another writer after Marlowe's death.'

'It is an argument.'

'It is.'

'So now you are a Shakespeare scholar?' he said.

'Perhaps I always was.'

'You are many things, Miss Woodleigh.'

'I am who I am right now.'

Luncheon that day was most notable for the moment when Gabriel asked Higgins to bring him a half-bottle of claret to go with his lamb. 'Drink enough and I won't have to eat any of this,' he informed the table as he lifted a lump of overcooked meat on his fork.

'Do not bring it,' Sir Elijah ordered the servant, who needed no more cue to shrug his shoulders and slope out of the room. 'You will take no drink today, tomorrow, or indeed the rest of the month. You are dry.'

Gabriel looked more panicked than outraged by the information. 'But why would—'

'Because you are a sot.'

'But—'

'And it is my position to stop you being a sot!' He pounded his fist down on the table. 'I will instruct Higgins to lock the wine cellar.'

Gabriel, quite ashen-faced, went quiet and pushed his untouched food away.

'Quite right, Elijah,' Maurice added.

'Be quiet, you pontificating fool,' the senior brother replied.

The meal proceeded in the same less-than-affable vein.

Afterwards, Amos went to the chapterhouse, unlocking it with the key secreted in the niche in the wall. The chapterhouse, the sleepers. There was much that was hidden at Kirchin Priory, and this building was surely at its secret heart. He stood before the image of Satan as a dragon and gazed at the somnambulist. The man was quite still, as if at perfect peace. But his bandaged eye sockets told a different story. Amos lifted his wrist. The pulse was slow and strong.

He glanced at the generator humming in the background, then to the wooden case attached to the wall above it. There was something there: the lock on its side had been forced open. Propriety would, of course, have been to immediately inform Sir Elijah. Instead, he opened the box.

As he had expected, it was the medicine cabinet, with three neat rows of vials and bottles. And a space where one bottle was clearly missing.

'Mandragora.' He spun around. Behind him stood Cleo Woodleigh, presumably there for her nursing rounds. She came over and examined all the medications in turn. 'You are wondering which bottle isn't there. *Mandragora officinarum* – mandrake root.'

'Did you take it?'

She ignored the question. '*Not poppy, nor
mandragora, / Nor all the drowsy syrups of the world,
/ Shall ever medicine thee to that sweet sleep / Which
thou owedst yesterday.* It's one that Shakespeare wrote
about, which makes it a candidate for the one that
he learnt of in Amsterdam.'

'And which play is that from?'

She finished checking the stock and seemed satisfied.
'*Othello, the Moor of Venice.*'

'Somebody took it, perhaps to try it on these men.'

He had once seen her, when she believed herself to
be unwatched, look upon Elijah Delpont as a surgeon
looked upon a severe case: ready to be opened up and
operated upon. This time, the dissecting gaze was upon
him, and she was quite open about it. He wondered if
it were curiosity, suspicion or perhaps a bluff to hide
guilt. Her complexity was very appealing to him.

'It seems so, doesn't it?' she said.

That night, after everyone had retired to their respective beds, Amos was in his chamber, taking some time
to reflect on what had passed. A creaking outside his
room made him peer out. He saw Cleo about to slip
into Gabriel's room with a bottle of red wine. She
spotted him and placed a finger over her lips with a
conspiratorial smile. 'It won't hurt him,' she mouthed.
He chuckled and closed his door. A minute later, he
thought he heard grateful sobbing.

It gave him an idea. Slipping silently out, he made
his way to the chapterhouse. There were the six men
scattered through the hexagonal room like so many

coffins. Each had his tube of ether hissing away to keep him in sleep. The sleepwalker lay under covers tainted with the mud of his night-time wanderings, his bandaged eyes turned to the wall. As Amos approached, a look of pain and confusion stole across the sleeping features.

The large canister of ether from which the rubber tube emerged was controlled by a blue lever. Amos turned the lever down and heard the hissing peter out. Almost immediately, the man in the bed began to stir a little, as if his being until then had been suspended by a thread of gas.

Amos gave him a few moments.

'Wake up,' he said.

The man stretched his shoulders, then lifted his head. His hands went to the bandages over his eyes and scrabbled at the dressing. Amos gently unwound the white gauze and slowly the man's swollen eyes emerged, flicking to and fro.

'Here,' he mumbled, dropping his head back to the pillow.

'You know where here is?'

'I sleepwalk.'

'You sleepwalk.'

'Put myself in danger,' he mumbled. 'Others, too.' The man's mind was still half-submerged.

'Have you woken when you have been here? Walked?'

The man looked all around again, then grasped at the air as if the memory were a fleet bird. 'I . . . can't remember.'

'Was someone here?'

A look of pain now twisted the man's mouth. 'Someone. Yes. Speaking to me.'

'What did they say?'

'I couldn't . . . It wasn't English. I . . . didn't want to do it.' His wounded eyes opened wider. 'It . . . It was horrible. They . . . They told me to do awful things. A terror! Please. Please!' He pointed to the canister of gas. Amos turned the lever back up, and the man's distress ended.

Chapter 9

The sullen butler Higgins served breakfast the next day with his usual aplomb, hesitating only at Cleo's chair, which remained empty – an absence that seemed to annoy Sir Elijah, who checked his pocket watch. 'Late! Bad manners,' he growled in the middle of the meal.

Outside for a smoke afterwards, Amos overheard Gabriel ask Higgins about the girl.

'Where is she? I fear she has angered your master,' he drawled. Had he abstained from the drink the previous night as Sir Elijah had ordered him, he might have sounded less seedy.

'My master is easily angered,' the servant replied.

'True, true.'

Amos sauntered away from his spot. He had half a mind to look for Cleo and ask if she knew anything about the somnambulist or the other patients. If Higgins didn't know her whereabouts, it was likely she wasn't in the house. He took himself, therefore, to the chapterhouse, only to encounter a new addition: a strong brass padlock on the door. There had been no warning from his host and employer of the sturdy lock. Was Sir Elijah trying to keep his patients in or enquiring eyes out?

A light drizzle came down as Amos retraced his steps and wandered the perimeter of the ancient estate.

There, at the rear of the house, was the green where they had played a damp form of croquet. And there the Poseidon fountain, trickling water into the basin at the god's feet. He wandered across the lawn, drawing on his cigarette until it had quite burned down. A yard or two away, he threw it into the water of the basin to leave a slick brown trail. But as he saw it sink, his heart stopped, for it was not the only dead thing in that water.

Looking up from below the glassy surface, her white palms up as if begging for forgiveness, Cleo Woodleigh floated. Her brown hair, streaming in all directions, shivered as a cold, invisible ripple flowed beneath the surface. All that she had been was drowned and gone. As Amos watched, his heart quite still, drops of rain began to fall on the surface of the water, distorting her image, bending her this way and that.

And as he stood looking at an empty image that had once been a woman with heat and thought, her right hand drifted upwards. Up it came, up and up through all the miles that divide the living from the dead, until it touched the surface and then broke through into the air, bloodless white, as if begging to be pulled from the grave. It struck him that he had never touched her fingers when they were warm, and he never would now.

A week here, a week in India. He barely knew her. And yet there was still a pang of loss. How can you lose what you have never had? It was a mystery, but still it was there.

'Is she gone?'

He knew the voice, young, female, perfectly horrified. And so, when he turned, it was with as much gentle sympathy as he could, to see Jessica, sat on the ground beneath a bush that had hidden her from his view.

'Yes, she's gone.'

At that, the young woman began to shake uncontrollably. Amos hugged her to him. She was shivering so much that, as she tried to speak again, there was only the chattering of her teeth.

But there was something else he noticed. His shirt was wet. It was more than the light rain falling could have made. He eased back. The damp was spreading from her dress. Her clothes were sodden.

'I t-tried to p-p-pull her out,' she sputtered. 'She's . . . she's dead.' And then words failed her, and she started to wail, beating at her own chest. Amos pulled her back into him, holding her wrists tight. She threw her head from side to side, trying to free herself, and yelled as best she could to the wind. Starlings in the trees scattered at the sound, and it echoed back sharper, sounding more like a bird of prey than a human in grief.

He felt suddenly purposeless. He had come to this place – to this country, in fact – in order to pursue Cleo Woodleigh, so as to know her better and perhaps build something upon that. And she would never know the truth. It was an unpleasant, dishonest feeling that lurked below the shock of finding her.

'Did you see anyone here?' he asked, gazing back at the stone basin, pregnant with the dead. She shook her head vigorously. 'Did you hear her call out?'

She managed a word. 'N-no.'

'Were you looking for her?' She nodded hard. 'What made you think she was here?'

'She . . . walked here s-sometimes. Who did it?'

'I don't know.'

'Why would they . . . ?'

'I don't know. When did you last see her?'

'Last night. Before b-bed.'

There was movement now at the edge of his vision. Maurice was walking quickly towards them. He stopped, amazed, when he saw Amos holding Jessica. 'Mr Sacher!' he said in an astonished tone. 'What on earth—!'

'Hold your tongue,' Amos ordered him. 'Look there.' He pointed to the fountain. Maurice did as he was told. At the sight therein, he fell to his knees and vomited.

Amos led Jessica towards the house, leaving Maurice on his knees. He took one last look at Cleo over his shoulder, deformed by the rain. It was a deep pity that it was of her in sorrow, not joy.

Sir Elijah was making his way up the stairs with a bundle of papers in his hand as Amos half-carried his cousin in.

'There you are. You will—' Sir Elijah began.

'Sir Elijah, would you come into the dining room?'
He saw that Gabriel was in there, a cigarette in one
hand, a glass of wine in the other, contemplating them
in turn.

'I follow no one in my own house!' Sir Elijah said
irritably.

Amos made no reply but led Jessica into the room.
Gabriel looked intrigued and took a last drag of his
cigarette before casting the butt into a huge fireplace
carved with cherubs.

A second later, Maurice burst in, looking wild. He
opened his mouth but found himself unable to form
words. Sir Elijah pushed him aside as he entered.

'Miss Woodleigh is dead,' Amos informed them all.
He remained as calm as he could, because as the shock
of her loss disappeared, the mystery of her death came
to the fore, and he wanted – needed – to get to the
truth of it. 'She has drowned in the fountain.'

'She . . . drowned?' Gabriel posed, his tone making
it clear that suspicion dripped from the event.

'Someone must have held her under,' Amos said
simply as Jessica sobbed. 'I can't see how else it could
have happened.' He saw Higgins in the doorway,
watching them. 'Jessica found her first. There was no
one else around.'

'Robbers!' Maurice yelled, having finally found his
voice. 'Brigands! They . . . they came here and . . .
and . . .'

Sir Elijah looked contemptuous. He didn't believe
it for a moment, his look announced. 'Calm yourself,'
he ordered Maurice darkly. 'Take me to her.'

She was as she had been, bloodlessly white, single strands of her hair moving gently in the water. Amos felt the skin of his hands and face run with rain, as if in sympathy with the woman before him.

In front of the others, he stepped forward and plunged his hands into the basin, slipping his palms behind her neck and back. Her head tilted back, stretching out her throat. He felt less emotion lifting the body than he had expected – it wasn't Cleo he was lifting, he knew, merely an effigy of her.

'She's dead, she's dead!' Jessica screamed, as pain, loss and terror overwhelmed her, jolting Amos with her cries.

'For God's sake, take her away!' Sir Elijah snapped. Immediately, Gabriel went to his niece and took her wrists, but she wrenched them away and slapped at his face, pushing him away and struggling, stumbling, towards Cleo's body.

'Leave her to me!' Sir Elijah barked. 'This way.' And he took strong hold of his daughter and near-dragged her towards the house.

'Amos.'

Two more hands were taking hold of his burden. Gabriel was by his side, placing his arm below Cleo's waist, so that between them they could carry her with something as close to dignity as they could.

'We can't put her in the house,' Amos said. 'Think of the effect on Jessica.'

'The mausoleum, then. It's what it's there for,' replied his uncle.

In dumb agreement, with Maurice behind, they conveyed her to the stone depository for the dead.

Between them, they laid her on the altar. Somehow that felt sadder to Amos than seeing her in the fountain, as if the last drop of humanity had now departed and she was nothing but a burden on the stone.

'The police,' Gabriel said darkly, for once lost for ironic words. 'No question.'

'Oh, yes, yes, we must!' replied Maurice. Well, that was settled.

They walked back to the house and into the parlour, where they stood with their hands in their pockets, contemplating what had befallen the household. A minute later, Sir Elijah came down the stairs. 'I have given her a sedative,' he said, this time with a pained expression that contrasted with his previous demeanour.

Amos was concerned at the idea that Jessica was better with drugs in her veins, but there was little point in protesting now that it was done. And he had an inkling that there would be fights ahead, so this dispute was one to let go.

Higgins was dispatched to call for the police, instructed that the family name should be used to ensure discretion. And for the rest of the daylight hours, the men remained smoking, drinking and watching each other. At one point, Gabriel went up to his niece's room. Then he came down, said she was sleeping and drank a bottle of port. He sent for another and glared defiance at his eldest brother. 'Hardly the time for clutching at your pearls, Elijah,' Gabriel replied to an unspoken comment.

'So there are no circumstances in which drunkenness

is not your preferred state? You are a disgrace to us all.'

Gabriel suppressed an incredulous laugh. Then it became a wracking fit of coughing that left him on all fours on the floor, tears leaking down his cheeks. Amos feared that he would cough until his mouth turned bloody. But like the other attacks, the fit slowly subsided, leaving him shaking. And in time he drew himself back onto his feet, wiped his face dry and tried to continue as if it had never happened. Amos recognized the need in a man to brush aside fragility that might well end his life. 'Are you aware, dear brother, what on earth we have just discovered in this, our own house? Are you aware that one of us is *guilty*?'

'Robbers!' Maurice insisted desperately.

'Oh, for God's sake,' his younger brother hissed. 'Even you . . .' But he discarded the end of the sentence, instead punctuating it with another draught of port.

'We should all leave,' Maurice said with determination but little force. 'Go our separate ways. Set up other homes.'

'Nobody is leaving this house,' the eldest of the three informed him decisively. 'Cowards flee. Men of substance remain.'

Gabriel howled a laugh at his brother's assertion. 'Men of substance indeed, Elijah. The three of us, Mr Sacher, Higgins or your daughter. Which of us has blood on his – or her – hands, eh?' And he lifted the neck of the decanter to his lips and poured the ruby drink freely down his throat.

When half of it was gone, he sat in a gilded chair

with a blue velvet seat and stared at the men around him.

They all waited for the police.

Some hours later, Inspector Lamass of the Newcastle force, a tall fellow with sallow, sagging cheeks and the air of a man who would never trust another soul, stood in the mausoleum with the gentlemen of the house behind him.

'Can't say it's murder yet, sir,' he said in response to Sir Elijah's question.

'Of course you can, you fool.'

'Just for the sake of the enquiry, it's best to keep an open mind.'

'Ah well, Elijah has never really had one of those at the best of times,' Gabriel replied. 'Let alone the current circumstances.'

'Oh, Gabriel, please!' the third brother exclaimed.

'There will be a coroner's inquest,' Lamass said. 'They will want the body of the deceased for that. I can send someone tomorrow to collect it.'

'I shall leave the house,' Maurice said with as much determination as he dared. 'I will put up at The Haywain.'

'Why?' Lamass asked with mild suspicion. 'You live here, do you not, sir?'

Maurice looked embarrassed. 'I do, yes, but the . . . the atmosphere.'

'Are you scared, Maurice?' Gabriel asked. His brother looked shiftily at his shoes.

For his part, Sir Elijah flicked his hands dismissively,

and Maurice, with some visible relief, went off to collect his things and head to the local pub.

Amos gazed at Gabriel.

'Hmm? Me? Oh no, I think I shall stay. It wouldn't do if we were all to depart, would it?'

Amos, Gabriel and Sir Elijah returned to the drawing room and remained there all night. Higgins was finally dismissed when the tawdry light of an autumnal dawn filtered through the windows. The embers in the grate were dying; the men who had fed and poked them all through the black hours were dead on their feet.

Gabriel was the first to leave, pushing himself out of his chair and staggering towards the stairs without comment. He stumbled noisily twice on the staircase as he made his way up. Amos tracked the sound of his feet. They creaked not to his bed, but to the chair in the oriel window that looked out towards the chapterhouse.

Instead of making his way directly to his own room, Amos looked into that of the deceased woman. He had not seen inside it before. It was spartan, almost a void. No pictures on the walls, no keepsakes on the dressing table. If she had any, they were all shut away somewhere in her press or her trunk, as if her whole character were a blank page.

The next chamber was Jessica's. He considered whether his presence would be welcome or helpful. In the end, he knocked gently on the door. There was no answer, but he opened it a little to see Jessica sitting up in her bed with the covers wrapped around her.

She had some magazines spread on the bed and watched blankly as he entered.

'How are you feeling?' he asked.

She looked at him. 'Numb.'

He sat beside her. 'It's a terrible, terrible thing.'

'What happened to her?'

'I'm sorry, I don't know.' He looked down at the magazines. They described buildings and statues in Italy and France. 'Is this where you were going to go?'

'Yes.'

He lifted one of the pages. It was a long poem about Venice. He laid it back down. 'How did you know Cleo?'

'We were at school together. In York.'

'If her family could afford the fees, why was she here as your paid companion?'

'She won a bursary. Her parents went to America to live, and she didn't see them again before they died.'

'That sounds harsh.'

'Yes, I think so. She became school captain, though. She could have gone to Cambridge if she had wanted.'

'She didn't want to?'

'She said she didn't. She wanted to stay with me.'

He paused to take that in.

'Which school was it?'

'The Grange.'

'Have you slept at all?'

'A little.' She put her head against his shoulder. 'I don't know how I'll cope without her. I won't. I can't.'

It was such a deep thing to say that he was unsure how to reply. 'I'm sure you will.'

'Will I? No, no, I can't. Everything I do is by her guidance.'

While her friend's death – that horrible death – would naturally devastate her and leave the girl shocked, was this not an excess of fear? Jessica was neither an invalid nor bedridden; she could have as full and normal a life ahead of her as any other. Cleo had been her companion – not her nurse, teacher, husband and priest in one.

'She meant so much to you,' he said, half to commiserate, but half also to probe and uncover.

'I adore her. We all do. Even my father.'

They talked for a few minutes more, but he realized that what his cousin needed was time alone, and so he left for his own room.

He did not cross the threshold, however, because there was something unexpected inside. Standing with his back to the landing, Higgins was gazing out the window, a smoking cigarette in his hand.

'Higgins?'

The surly butler did not turn but dropped the cigarette to the floor and slowly trod it into the carpet. 'You should leave.' Amos waited. 'You shouldn't have come in the first place.'

'Why?' He wanted to know what the butler knew. He wanted to know what deeds were happening behind closed doors in this house.

But Higgins turned and departed without another word.

Amos was in no mood for such games now and angrily stripped off his clothes, lay down in the bed and attempted sleep. For close to an hour, it was beaten away by thoughts of what had occurred at Kirchin Priory over the past week, how differently things looked from when he had first stood before the huge gatehouse. But eventually, exhaustion smothered his thoughts, and he fell into dark sleep.

Chapter 10

He woke in the late morning sun, rose, stretched and left the house. He would have to walk to the village – Maurice was there by now, in the pub, he presumed – to ask where the nearest telephone could be found.

There was one in the shop in the next village along, he was told. After another hour's tramp through country lanes, he found the shop and the phone – mercifully working. He paid the young woman behind a counter piled with tins and paper bags to make a call and eventually got through to one Miss Jenkins, headmistress of The Grange School in York.

'She is what? Oh!' There was an intake of breath, and the woman, who sounded as if she had seen many generations of pupils come and go, took a moment to speak again. 'From time to time, one hears of one's former pupils, and once in a while it is not good news. She would be, what, twenty-two now?'

'Twenty-three.'

'Yes, well, too young. Far too young. A pity. And you are calling simply to inform me as a courtesy?'

'I was hoping to understand a little about her.'

'Understand what about her?' The tone had a hint of suspicion.

'Miss Jenkins, I am afraid I have to tell you that her death was not an accident.'

There was a pause. 'I see,' she said gravely.

'I was wondering about her relationship with Jessica Delpont.'

'Were you now? And why should I tell you anything?'

'Because someone killed Cleo Woodleigh, and soon the police are going to accuse the person who was there when she was found. And that is Jessica. So if you want to see Jessica arrested, please, hang up the telephone.' There was a pause. The telephone was not dropped into its cradle. 'Thank you.'

The teacher spoke carefully, weighing her words. 'They were friends, yes, but not especially close as I remember. Woodleigh was an unusual girl. She didn't seem to have friends *per se*. I would say she had *followers*. Once in a while, you have a girl – and they invariably end up as the school captain – who has something about them that turns the other girls into acolytes.'

'I understand.'

There was another pause. 'Do you? Well, that power is something I've seen especially in girls who have a void as a home life. Woodleigh's parents were not around, you might be aware.'

'I was. They lived in America, I understand.'

'America?' She snorted a little. 'Well, they could have done, I suppose. She was abandoned to the parish as a baby. I doubt she ever knew who they were. I certainly didn't.'

Somehow, the revelation came as less of a surprise than it might have done. 'I was told she could have gone to Cambridge.'

'Cambridge? Yes, I'm sure she could. But then she would have had to be with girls as clever as she, wouldn't she now? How would she have done with a hundred girls who could calculate as she could?' There was a note of satisfaction in the woman's voice.

He asked one more question. 'Was there a girl in her year named Annalise?'

There was a long crackle through the line. 'Why do you want to know about her?'

'So there was.'

'Yes. I can't see how it is relevant, though.'

'I believe we – Cleo, Jessica and I – met her a few days ago.'

Another long crackle. 'One does not like to have low regard for one's girls, but that child was not one for whom I had high regard.'

'What was her surname?'

'Vigo. But if you want any more details, I am not prepared to supply them.'

He didn't need them. He knew where to find her.

He took a train from the little village station to Newcastle. Then a cab to the church mission by the docks. The verger was sitting behind a desk in his reception room, smoking a pipe of sweet-smelling apple tobacco while his feet rested on a pouffe. He jumped up, coughed and spluttered as Amos entered his chamber.

'I do beg your pardon, sir,' he managed to say between smoke-belching retches. 'I was taking a few moments to—'

'It is not my concern,' Amos informed him. 'You remember that I was here a few days ago with Miss Jessica Delpont and Miss Cleo Woodleigh?'

The verger looked like he remembered nothing of the sort, but neither did he want to seem impolite. 'Yes, yes, of course I do, Mr . . . ?'

'Sacher. Good. When we were here, there was a young lady who was one of your charity recipients. Her name was Annalise Vigo. Aged early twenties. Brown hair. Slim. I would like to find her.'

The verger's eyes narrowed slyly, as if a certain familiar thought had entered his head. 'Would you, sir?'

'I would.' Amos saw the cunning look and knew what was sliding about in the man's mind. For now, he would let it remain there.

'Well,' the verger said, sitting back down on his chair, more at ease now. 'I'm not sure I know the girl.'

Yes, now Amos understood the man well. And his misapprehension would probably be convenient. 'Well, we are both men of the world,' he said genially, sitting on the corner of the man's desk. 'A little help for another chap.'

'I would like to help, but if I don't remember the girl, I don't remember the girl,' he said, fiddling with his pipe stem.

Amos drew his wallet from inside his jacket and placed a half sovereign on the desk. The verger reached for it, and Amos snatched it away.

'But *do* you remember her?'

'Streetwalker. Stands about in Slipway Court most days.'

'Where is that?'

'Outside, turn right. Second on the left.'

Amos placed the coin back on the desk but held it down. 'If anyone asks, I was never here.'

'Course not, sir,' the man replied with a grin. The smoke on his breath only partly masked the reek of gin.

Along the way, there were cries and calls that told Amos this was a neighbourhood where no one was your neighbour.

He had come to this land to become intimate with a girl, using lies to gain his place. Now she was murdered and he – driven only by a desire to see justice done for her – was intruding on her past. What would he even do when all was settled one way or the other? He would return to India, he thought. England, a land where birthright seemed much if not all, had held little attraction for him before and held less now. Well, let it be, there was no turning back now.

Soon he was looking into Slipway Court, a dead-end no more than thirty yards long, enclosed by rookeries that must have housed those on the lowest rung of society. They had roofs over their heads, yes, but only just.

There she stood. In the same clothes he had seen her wearing before. The only change was the addition of a parasol of cheap imitation silk. She was walking – if you could call that slumped, slow death-march

walking – a few yards this way, then a few yards that,
until something, a cat-like primeval sense honed by
whatever hells she had been through over the past
years, made her look up and see him. A frightened
recognition showed on her face, and she bolted for
the nearest opening into one of those pits of human
misery. But she found it shut and barred to her, so
spun around and did her best to face him down, her
chest rising and falling.

'I am no danger to you,' he said calmly. 'I want to
speak. No more. No danger at all.'

Her chest began to slow. 'Why?' she demanded
hoarsely.

'You recognize me. I was a friend of Cleo Woodleigh.'

'*Was?*'

'Yes. No longer.'

She scoffed. 'She threw you over, too?'

'Not quite.'

Her suspicion returned. 'What do you want?'

For her, it was a sovereign. And it was handed over
without restriction. She bit it and sighed.

'You were at school together?'

'Yes.'

'What happened there?'

It was a question without an end, hardly even a
beginning. It left her to drift. 'I wasn't a good girl,'
she muttered. 'I wasn't nice.'

'How do you mean?'

'I made fun of people.' From one of the tenements
above them, the sound of breaking glass and shouting
rent the air.

'Did you make fun of Cleo?' She nodded. 'What did you say?'

'I said she didn't know who her parents were.'

He guessed that that was not the end of the tale. 'Did something happen after that?' No response. 'You can tell me. It was long ago.'

She was pained answering. 'One girl's hairbrush went missing. Our house mistress found it under my pillow.'

'And then?'

'I was warned. But a brooch went missing, too.'

'Blamed on you?'

'It was hidden in my trunk.'

'You didn't steal them, did you?' She shook her head. 'But you were expelled for it.'

She looked around at the brick towers of destitution around her. And he knew the answer to the question he was about to ask. 'Do you think Cleo took them?'

'Not her. She wouldn't. It was someone *for* her. I don't know who. There were girls who would do anything for her. They . . . adored her.'

On the train back to Kirchin, Amos gazed out the window at green fields and ancient barns. England. A land lush and beauteous, but one he would never understand. Such subtleties it had. Such intricate vices and jealousies. Its tragedy was written into the landscape and he pitied all those who suffered by it; all those who hoped for comfort and solace.

The wheels turned, and turned again, speeding over earth and rivers.

He descended from the train at the little village stop where he had arrived just five days earlier and walked until his feet touched the ground of Kirchin Priory. The late afternoon sun cast cold yellow light on the chapterhouse and long shadows all around. He walked past, to the Madman's Library.

Inside, he was the only waking man in the octagonal room, but not the only man walking. The somnambulist stood below the painting of God and his Son. Amos watched, strangely unworried, as the sleepwalker's head turned from side to side, sweeping the room, yet seeing nothing. Then the man began to walk, his left hand on the wall, a circuit of the room like the minute hand of a clock around its dial, creeping round, stumbling here and there, confused by the chaos in his path. He passed within a yard of Amos without seeing him. Past the mandolin on which the Italian composer Gesualdo had composed music after stabbing his wife and her lover; past a desk piled high with dictionaries of Farsi, Hebrew and Sanskrit that had proved useless in translating the mysterious mediaeval book that Sir Elijah had shown him; past the Shakespeare manuscript in its ebony box. How he had escaped the ether and the padlocked door of the chapterhouse, Amos neither knew nor cared right then. Something had led him here. Something had led them both here, to this library full of visions and dark history.

As the sleepwalker circled the room, Amos saw travel in his wake a cyclorama of images: Annalise in Slipway Court; Jessica's magazine pictures of escape;

Higgins sullen; Maurice falling apart at the sight of Cleo under the water; the somnambulist crying in pain and pulling a slip of paper with black symbols from his mouth.

And the weight of knowing fell on him like gold.

That slip of paper with its strange squarish symbols. So easy to overlook. But it was the key to all that had befallen them.

With triumph and despair, Amos opened the dictionary that rendered English words into Hebrew. All was in there. And the man kept walking around and around him.

He took the dictionary and an oil lamp and ran with them to the mausoleum.

Chapter 11

Between those dirty walls, he saw the caskets of a hundred years of Delponts rotting. Beyond them was the altar, turned orange in the light from the setting sun that fell through the skylight; and above it, the strange squarish symbols that had been drawn by whoever had taken the somnambulist from the chapterhouse. Letters. Hebrew letters.

He knew now what they spelled. Just a few days before, he had read of them in the Shakespeare manuscript. He found them now in the dictionary and traced them on the wall. And finally the truth was revealed, as if handed down by God.

'So it is true,' he said to himself, because it was madness throughout.

A noise behind him made him look around. Footsteps lightly crunching on the stones outside. Gabriel, perhaps, or the butler come to call him in to dinner. He waited for them to enter or speak. Nothing. 'Higgins?' he called. 'What is it?' Silence. And then a whining and grating: the sound of the door being pulled closed. Without a moment's hesitation, he charged for the entrance. But too late: the second before he touched it, it had slammed home and the key had turned with a metallic click.

'I'm in here!' he yelled, beating his fist on the wood. But even as he cried out, he knew it would do no good. It had been no accident. Whoever had closed him in wanted him out of the way. 'Open up or it will go hard with you!' he threatened.

He pressed his ear to the wood. He could just make out footsteps on the stones. One pace away. Two away. Then a pause. And one towards him.

'Who are you?' he demanded.

A pause, then a whisper through the timber, too light and muffled to tell if it was even a man or a woman speaking. 'The Devil take you.'

Amos put his face close and matched the whisper on the other side. 'I have spent a hundred nights out in the desert with no one but the Devil for company,' he said. 'We shall see who he takes!' And without even waiting for an answer, he retreated into the dank building.

Well, if his captor wanted to harm him, they clearly knew they were unable to do so in a fist fight. They had caged him because they feared him. But they might return with a weapon, it was true. Amos extinguished his lamp so he could hide better in one of the corners by the entrance, rolled up his sleeves and waited. The game might be a long one.

Minutes passed. No sign of whoever had gaoled him among the dead. It could have been any one of the residents of the house or none. For all he knew, it was someone he had never set eyes upon. He kicked his heel angrily into the wall.

What would he do if they entered? First, take their legs away, seize any weapon and then pin them down to use his fists. Be wary of a second weapon in reserve. But what if they never returned? Well, he could hardly be entombed here forever without discovery. In a matter of hours, people would come looking for him, and he could shout well enough to be heard. His captor must have a plan, and coming in to get him seemed the only one plausible.

He kept his limbs moving lightly so they would be ready the moment the key turned in the lock. His eyes adjusted to the gloom. His hearing changed, too. Now he could detect the birds outside, the wind whisking brass-coloured leaves in flurries, insects crawling across the stone floor and through cracks in the wooden coffins. Once ready, he—

There was a sound.

That slight crunching. He was sure it was the same step.

He tensed. His senses were so taut that he didn't hear the footsteps outside retreating, he felt them. Tiny tremors in the ground, miniature but full of omen, like earthquakes on the other side of the world. Amos moved around the wall, smoothing his palm over the bricks, feeling where his captor was now. He or she was walking slowly, stopping from time to time. Around the corner. Along the longest side. Stopping again. Amos mirrored their steps. Their breathing. Stopping to consider their plan? Or perhaps something else entirely.

More steps. One, two, three. Around the corner to the
rear of the cold mausoleum. Another stop. And now
something new: a tap and scrape on the outside of the
bricks. Something leant against them.

'Are you there?'

It was muttered this time, just loud enough to penetrate the wall.

'I'm here,' Amos replied.

'I warned you.'

And then no more words, no footsteps on the
ground.

Something was coming. He watched the lock as if
he might be able to see the key sliding in. Then something was breaking. He looked up sharply. An iron
bar was smashing through the skylight, turning the
glass into a rain of shards. By instinct, he put his arm
up to protect his face. The bar was pulled back out
of sight. The opening was slim, but a man could drop
through it, and Amos waited for that, ready to rush
them as they came down.

For a few moments, there was nothing but the twilight
sky through the opening. And then something fell
through: a dark mass like thick rain, no human. Heavy
and brown, then yellow, here and there red. Leaves.
All dropping down by the sackful. But they weren't
just falling, they were burning; smouldering at the edges
as they fell in a torrent, settling in a huge heap, smoking
like a damp bonfire. In seconds, acrid smoke had filled
the room. It was then that Amos realized his captor's
plan. He was not going to be attacked with a weapon
or fists, he was going to be suffocated. More leaves

fell. He kicked them apart as best he could to stop the burning, but more fell all around him and choking began to wrack his body. He bent over, coughing up lungfuls of blackened air. Still more came down, and now he could not stand, he was on his knees, crawling away, trying to find air that he could breathe.

Across the earthen floor, he dragged himself to the entrance. The bonfire was hissing and, as the heat began to dry the outer leaves, flames began to rise, making the smoke pour out faster and further, colonizing every corner, every crack in the bricks. Amos slumped to the floor. There were steps on the roof as his captor moved with him, then the sound of someone scrambling down to the ground.

'I said the Devil take you!'

'He'll have to come in here and get me!' Amos spat back with all the strength he had left. But his head was swimming. And then consciousness left him.

Chapter 12

He woke. His eyes struggled to open, fluttering before he forced the lids up. Immediately black smoke stung and scratched, threatening to close them again.

A mist of dark soot hung heavy in the air so that the walls could not be seen. They could have been four feet or a hundred miles away. But a sheet of smouldered leaves around him, visible in the light of an unseen lamp, told him that he was still in the mausoleum. He coughed heavily, and his body shook, expelling the smoke from his lungs.

He hauled himself to his knees but found his arms were on either side of the altar leg and his wrists tied tightly together with rough twine, so that he was bound to the altar. It must have been bolted to the floor too because he could not shift it. He shook his head, forcing the blood up, helping him to recover. The light, rippling in the smoke, was coming from his own oil lantern, which hung well out of his reach, from one of the iron hooks set into the wall.

Through the haze, Amos could see a figure, their back to him, stooped over, setting items on one of the coffins.

'Let me out or I'll kill you,' Amos growled.

At that, his captor stopped and straightened up. 'I am already bled dry,' they replied in a harsh whisper that became a choke as it struggled against the all-pervading smoke. Then whoever it was turned. But all Amos could see was a scarf tightly wrapped around their face and head to filter out the worst of the smoke.

The man or woman lifted a silver cup. From the cup, they took two small slips of paper. A thin hand almost disappeared in the mist but turned in the air to show what was drawn on the papers: two symbols in black ink. A rough square with curving sides and an inverted letter 'W'.

'I read the Shakespeare manuscript, too,' Amos said.

'You know?' It was spoken hoarsely through the smoke.

'The Book of Philip.' He let it hang in the air between them. Sir Elijah had said the ritual it described must have originated the belief that the name of God, written in Hebrew on paper and placed in the mouth of the dead, would raise and control a man to seek vengeance for the wronged. 'You wanted the Waterfall.'

'Yes. The Waterfall.'

'It's a folktale, that's all. No better than a child's story.'

'No, it's . . . Miracles take place.' Amos knew then who stood behind the wrapped scarf.

'Not in this age.' There was silence. 'I saw you turn food away, so tired in the mornings. You had barely eaten or slept for days.' The figure's head drooped. 'You wanted to believe it could be true.'

The figure put their hands over their eyes. 'I just wanted her gone. To leave us alone.'

Amos eased his feet towards the row of rusted hooks. 'You can come back from this. You can step back.'

The figure gently trembled. 'I . . .'

'You were provoked by the girl. I know now. I see how she led us to you.' It had been Cleo who had suggested a game of croquet despite the weather, to get them all outside. She had been the one to knock the ball over to the mausoleum so that they would all find the door unlocked. She had been the one who pointed to the living corpse of the sleepwalker. All the while, she had been taking them closer to her target. 'She had been watching you, hadn't she?'

'Oh, God in Heaven.'

'She knew what you had done here. And she led us close to it so that she could finally bend you to her will.' The figure slumped against the wall. 'Show me your face, Maurice.'

Slowly, the thin hand unfurled the scarf and let it fall to the ground. His collar turned from white to grey with the smoke. 'The Bible says: *Thine eyes did see mine golem unformed, and in thy book they were all written,*' he whispered.

The words had been hope for a desperate, unloved, mocked priest. When the Shakespeare manuscript, with its description of the supposed Kabbalah ceremony, arrived, it must have seemed to be a gift from God. Something to give him strength and dignity.

Maurice's tone changed. 'A scorpion. She was a

scorpion!' he said, with the purest hatred spilling from his lips. 'She wanted you gone, too.'

Confusion fell upon Amos. 'Why?'

'So you don't know all. It was because Elijah told us why you were here.'

'Elijah?'

'You were here to propose marriage.' Amos's mind rolled at the answer. 'You were here to propose marriage to Jessica.'

Surprise, then an inkling of comprehension began. 'No. I came for Cleo.'

Maurice lifted his head to the milky blade of moonlight. 'Oh,' he said. 'Oh. She thought you had come to take Jessica from her.'

'Maurice,' Amos pleaded. 'Let me go.'

For a moment, the other man hesitated. Then he moved towards his captive with a small bottle in his hand. In that moment, Amos twisted onto his back, lifted his heels and smashed them through the bowl of the lamp. The flame went blue in the draught from the skylight, turning everything in the mausoleum the colour of sapphires, then it fluttered out and all was black.

He heard his uncle, dazed, stumble against the altar, giving him precious seconds to kick the lamp from the hook. It fell to the floor with a crack.

He wound around, searching for it with his hands and feet. But he wasn't the only one. Maurice was on all fours too, scrabbling for it. Both knew it was vital – a weapon, a key to life. Then, as Amos's eyes became those of a nocturnal creature, glittering and attuned to the dim light filtering through the window above, he caught sight of it close to his side. He reached desperately for it with his bound hands. But so did his uncle. Their fingers grabbed it together, struggling for it. It wavered between them. But Amos was the younger, the stronger, and he wrenched it from Maurice's bony hands, then up and across so that the broken shards of the glass bowl found his uncle's neck. And again.

The priest crumpled; sucking horribly for air, unable to swallow any. It was the only sound as Amos watched him shake uncontrollably, dying; until the shaking stopped. He was glad to see it.

He gave himself a minute to rest. Then he used the broken glass to hack and saw at the twine around his wrists until it broke apart.

With his sleeve across his mouth and nose, he checked that the other man's heart was no longer beating. Yes, it was quite without life. He wiped some of the soot from his eyes, then got to his feet and went to the house, leaving the corpse of his uncle among his kin, like trash.

Gabriel was in his room, slumped at the oriel window with his hand on a bottle of red wine that was leaking its final drops onto the pink carpet.

'Cleo,' Amos said.

He wondered if Gabriel would be able to tell from his face that he had killed Maurice. He felt not the slightest pang of guilt or regret about it, so he doubted it.

Gabriel's eyelids fluttered, and he lifted his head an

inch to meet Amos's gaze, before it fell back. 'Oh, is it time? Yes. Yes. Now it comes.'

'Tell me.'

He rubbed his mouth and sighed. 'Oh Cleo. Unassuming little Cleo. She controlled us all. One by one. One by one, she took over.'

'Jessica?'

'Jessica didn't live in this house. She lived in Paris or Rome or wherever else Cleo said they would go together. The fantasy was far more real than this.' He waved his hand drunkenly around the room. 'And to Elijah she was the ideal of medical efficiency – almost his equal in that. Not quite, of course, no one could ever be such a thing. But if he had handed his practice to any of us it would have been her.'

'Higgins wanted me gone, I know. Was that her?'

'Good old Higgers.' Gabriel coughed hard. He didn't try to stifle it as he usually did, just let the ghost of an old disease wrack his body. 'He was doing her bidding. All it took was a bit of kindness cast his way, you know. A bit of empathy. A few words that weren't commands. The unseen people, that's what they both were, drudging away beneath our feet. Unseen until it mattered, anyhow.'

'What about you?'

Gabriel croaked a chuckle. 'Me. Ah yes, what about me, hmm? How did she get her claws into me? You must have seen her method, no? Her wicked magic? Well, it's like this: I think she just *understood*. Unlike everyone else, she didn't try to change me.' He gazed at his fingertips. 'I had been dead for years before she came here. She brought me back. Is it so wrong that I loved her for it?'

Amos said nothing. If anyone should have seen her, it should have been he, who had crossed an ocean in her wake. But then, of course, he had seen how her eyes had narrowed when examining Elijah Delpont, her gaze like a surgeon's taking her host apart limb by limb, when she had thought herself unobserved. And he had witnessed the subtle pleasure she had taken in humiliating her former schoolmate at the charity in Newcastle. And the way Jessica's personality had been subsumed into Cleo's. He had seen all that, so why had he not seen *her*?

'She even pointed you in the right direction, didn't she? To get you out of this house. Ah, I see the penny dropping.' The realization wound its way through Amos's flesh: yes, the hints she had given him regarding the authorship of the Shakespeare document, how she had found little nuggets to suggest that it was real, so that Amos's work would be complete and he would depart her realm.

'Oh, my friend,' said Gabriel, almost reading his thoughts. 'Cleo Woodleigh would place her hands on you and know everything about you. The book of your thoughts she knew by heart, and then whatever you wished for she would become. Let me guess. You wanted a soulmate who was witty and clever and vivacious. And then she was there, yes?' He took the silence as assent. 'Yes. And so there was only one soul in this house who was not her creature.'

'Maurice.'

'Maurice. Because his heart was already engaged with the Lord above.' Gabriel's index finger extended to point towards Heaven, and he laughed emptily.

Amos had killed Maurice. He briefly pondered whether or not to inform Gabriel of this fact. He decided not to, not because he wanted to keep it secret – it would hardly be a secret for very long – but because it seemed to carry little weight. There was no great importance to it. There was no moral mass against it and Maurice's presence or not in the world would make little difference to the swarms of men and beasts.

'Cleo being here drove him mad,' Amos said.

'As well it might. I truly am sorry for not informing you, but family secrets are best kept within the family, aren't they? It limits the damage, you know.'

Amos went to the window and gazed at the broken remains of buildings that had once stretched so high and now lay buried under mud.

'Why? Why did it all happen?'

Gabriel sighed. 'Elijah announced that you had come to take darling Jessica, and for once Cleo couldn't sway him. So she made me speak to him, to have you sent away. Yes, even she cared for someone. It just wasn't you.'

'She forced you how?'

Gabriel upended the bottle to his mouth. Nothing came out. He got down on his hands and knees and took a handkerchief from his pocket. He pressed the handkerchief into the damp puddle of wine in the carpet, soaking the drink into the fabric. Then he lifted the handkerchief into his mouth and sucked all that he could out of it.

'She said she would withhold her presence from me unless I did as she bade me,' he said. 'The cruelty of it.' He closed his eyes.

And so Maurice, who hated the power she held over the house – weak Maurice, who was half out of his mind – had read of a way to rid them all of her presence. He would make a creature stronger than he, who would cast her out of the house. But when he tried, she had witnessed it and exposed him.

'I was brilliant, you know,' Gabriel mumbled. 'Everyone said I would be the light of the age.' He began to laugh, then raised the empty bottle to his lips again. 'Oh, I forgot,' he said, looking at it. 'Empty.' For a moment, a confused look spread across his face. Then it drifted away, and he raised the bottle to his lips again.

Amos remembered something that Cleo had said to him. They had stood in the library, and she had told him who she was.

'I am who I am right now.'

Now he understood what those words truly meant: as the moment changed, so would she.

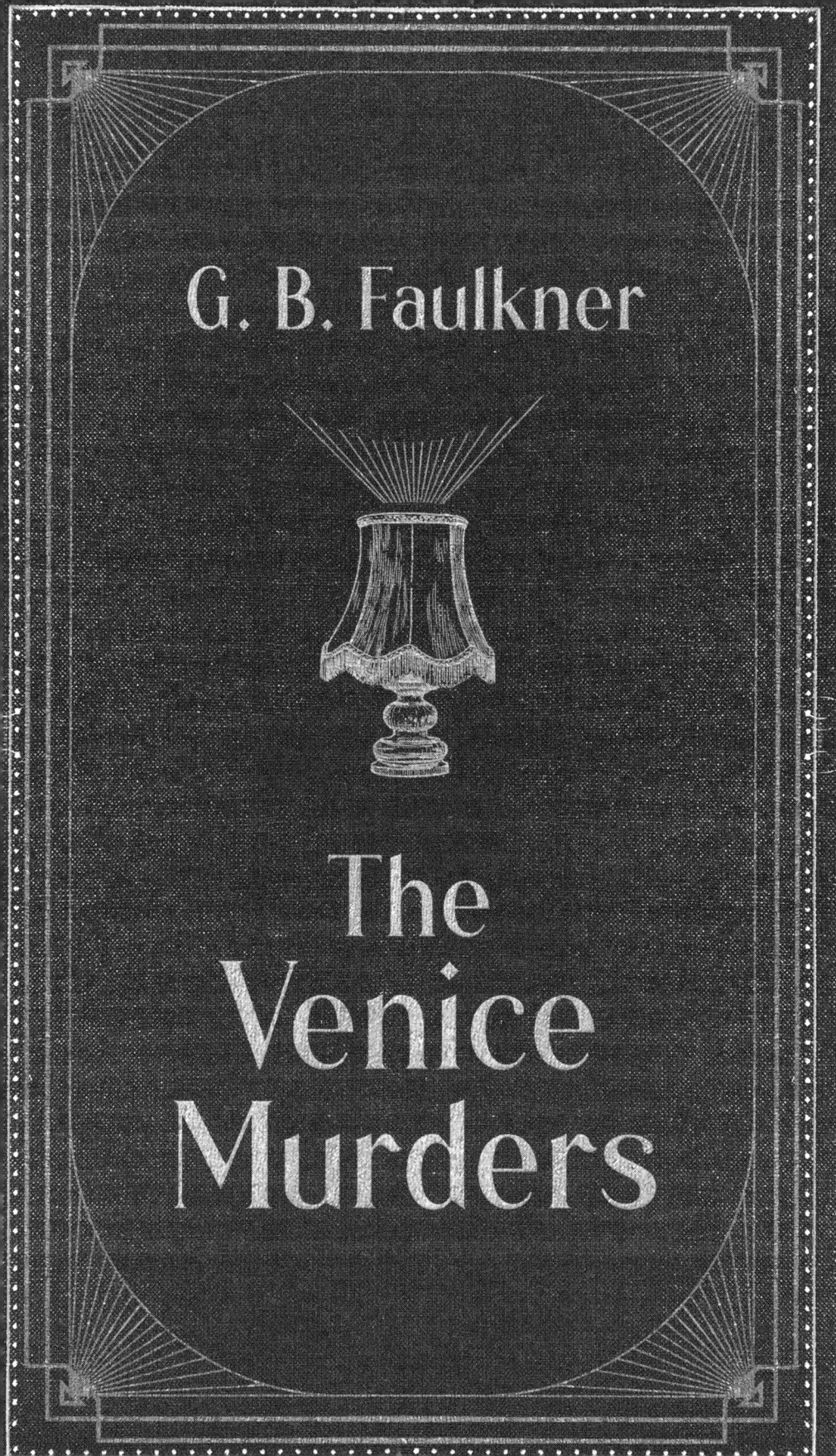

G. B. Faulkner

The
Venice
Murders

Chapter 1

Honora wasn't happy, I'll tell you that. I could just see her through the smoked glass of Dr Timcott's door. And when Honora isn't happy, she makes it plain.

'I am *not* run down, dear doctor, and I don't appreciate any man telling me that I am.'

'All I was saying, Mrs Feldman, is that you could do with a bit of a holiday. Some sun, perhaps.'

'Stuff and nonsense.'

'I've heard—'

'I don't care what you have heard.'

'As a doctor—'

'I've never seen your medical certification.'

'What?'

'For all I know, you're a quack.'

'I've been your physician for thirty years!'

'My mistake. I might as well have gone to a druid. He could have told me to take three sprigs of parsley and dance naked at midnight.'

'What good would that do?'

'How would I know? I'm not a druid. Now, I am leaving.'

And with that, she shoved the door open and strode out of the doctor's consulting room. And believe me, chum: no one can stride out of a doctor's consulting room like Honora Feldman. She was dressed in her best brown tweeds and the red felt hat that she had bullied out of a shopkeeper in Paris for half the price he had originally quoted.

'Pick yourself up, Pips, we're leaving,' she announced. So I jumped along behind her, out onto Harley Street, where she threatened to report a traffic policeman for being drunk on duty if he didn't tear up the ticket he was about to give us. Half a minute later, we were on our way up to the Highgate flat.

'Idiot thinks I'm run down,' she said, holding on to the felt hat. 'I'll show him run down.' I was driving, as always. 'Why are we dawdling? We're barely touching thirty.' She tapped at the speedometer. We were in the green Bentley that I had fixed up after finding it under a tarpaulin and some junk at a garage a couple of years ago. I put my foot down, and the motor – I could tell the carburettor was struggling and made a mental note to fix it later – took a good jump forward. 'That's better. A bit of wind in our sails. Now, I think the best thing would be a bit of a holiday. Don't stare, it's rude. Venice, I think. I have family roots there and I've been intending to visit ever since I read a monograph on the use of deadly poisons by the wives of Renaissance dukes. Stop here.' I stamped on the brake, and we lurched to a halt. She hopped out and into a branch of the Thomas Cook travel agency, where she grabbed a surprised young man in a shiny suit. Ten minutes later, she was out again with two tickets in her hand. 'Southampton tomorrow,' she said.

Chapter 2

You're going to laugh, but that spring of 1931 was my first time on a boat. Well, except for that time Ronnie McNee took me on the boating pond at Clapham Park and tried to get fresh until I told him I would push him in.

The ship Honora had booked us on was very posh, I must say. All stewards in white coats and dressing for dinner in pearls and twinsets. She said the chief steward was stealing some of the silver cutlery from the captain's table and she could tell because at every meal there would be a new fork or spoon that wasn't quite a match with the others. But she didn't tell on him because it was to pay for harp lessons for his son.

'I really can't understand how you don't see these things,' she said to me at luncheon one day. 'Too busy looking at that young man with the teeth, I suppose.'

He did have very nice teeth. And just then he smiled at me across the dining room. Honora tutted.

'Can't I let my hair down sometimes?' I asked.

'Of course. I have some excellent histories of the Medici clan that you could read.'

'No, that's all right.' I sighed. 'The other three were quite enough.' It's not that Honora doesn't understand, you see. There's hardly anything that she *doesn't* understand. It's just that she likes to razz me a bit.

'Was there enough about the poetry?'

'Quite enough, yes.'

'Oh well.' And she couldn't hide a bit of a smile. 'Then I shall retire to read them myself. Do be careful with that young man, though. He's very close to his mother, and we shouldn't want to give her another aneurysm.'

'Oh, Honora!'

'I shall meet you at dinner.'

Well, at dinner, there was someone new at our table. 'This is Penelope Batley,' Honora said. 'She lives in Venice and has invited us to stay with her.'

'What about the hotel?' I asked. I had been looking forward to it. It had looked top-drawer in the brochure that Honora had brought home from the Thomas Cook office.

'I've already sent a wire cancelling. Wonderful things you can do from ships these days.'

'You'll be staying with me at Villa Batley,' said the new woman. I guessed that she was in her fifties, like Honora – at least, I thought Honora was in her fifties, she would never let me know for sure – and looked quite glamorous. She had a permanent wave in her hair and very sharp red fingernails. Honora, of course, filed her nails down (I always bit mine to stumps), and her hair was usually tied back in a bun. I had tried that myself, but I suddenly looked like a ballerina and that didn't suit me when I was in overalls to work on the car or do odd jobs around the flat. I had also been experimenting with a bob, but that didn't suit me, either. Nothing did, really. 'It's all quite relaxed at Villa Batley. People drop in and out all the time. We're only there half the year when Aldrich's business allows him to leave London.'

'What business is he in?' I asked.

'Something to do with cats.'

'Oh. I like cats.'

'Do you?' She shivered. 'They don't like me.'

Penelope enjoyed two things best on board: a treble gin and tonic and a flutter at the roulette table, though she insisted that it was rigged. I think it was on the third night that she brought a man to dinner with us. I hadn't seen him before.

'This is Aldrich,' she said.

'Your husband?' I asked, surprised. I'd had no idea he was even on the boat. I'd thought he must have been away on business with the cats, whatever that meant.

He was significantly quieter than Penelope, well-fed with a big bald patch that he did his best to comb over, and generally looked a bit sheepish, as if he wanted to say a word or two but wasn't allowed. A few times he opened his mouth to break his silence, but Penelope would always talk over him. Poor chap would just shut up again and sigh a little sadly. He seemed a sweet old boy, and I don't think Penelope was deliberately trying to keep him schtum, it was just that she never really noticed when he was speaking. Maybe it was such a rare thing that she blotted it out.

Chapter 3

Well, a few days later our boat drifted through all these swish new cruise liners and little fishing boats towards the island city of Venice. Gosh, it did look utterly divine spread in front of us, shimmering in the sun. Ancient and decadent buildings everywhere, and I couldn't believe it wasn't a fairy tale we were sailing into.

We docked by St Mark's Square. Dear reader, how can I describe it? This big square *piazza* right beside the lagoon, with the huge cathedral, which has more gilt (and guilt?) than the Bank of England; and the Duke's Palace – which looks like something out of your school history primer, full of wicked noblemen and even more wicked noblewomen – around the corner. And there are two darling coffee shops on the square with tables and chairs out so you can listen to buskers, but they're not just any buskers, they're string quartets playing Vivaldi, Honora said. And the people! So beautiful in their Italian togs as they walk up and down for their afternoon strut in the sun. Honora was looking at her guidebook, but I ran up and down and then back to the waterfront and could have ripped off my blouse and trousers and dived in then and there. You could see all the way down, too, to the fishes. Not like the Thames, which looks like it's the run-off from a soup factory.

'Hat!' Honora ordered me. 'I don't want you burnt to a fritter before we even set foot in the Doge's Palace.' She stopped a costermonger passing by, haggled with him until he was hopping mad and handed me the headpiece that he gave up under protest.

'You look like a Hollywood doll,' Penelope twinkled at me.

'I would rather she looked like a driver,' Honora corrected her.

Aldrich just sighed.

Now, Venice isn't an island in a lake like I thought it was. It's actually lots of little islands in a lagoon. There's the main island, where almost all of the big buildings and people are, but also dozens of smaller ones with funny little populations. Some just have a few monks on, which must be a queer old life. Aldrich and Penelope lived on one called the Lido, which is very long and thin and serves as a breakwater for the main island, they said, so the sea doesn't wash it away. It has some nice sandy beaches, too. To get there, you have to go by boat. We could have got one from beside St Mark's Square, but Penelope said no, we had to see the splendour of Venice first, and I could have kissed her.

So they packed all our baggage off with a little man pulling a handcart, giving him instructions where to take it, and we set off through winding little lanes lined with even littler churches and statues to saints and magnificent tall houses and a grand opera house with columns and a fiery red-painted front and cafés everywhere with people spilling about kissing each other's cheeks. Everywhere was just fizzing! Wherever we went, there were hawkers trying to sell us all sorts because we must have looked like absolute rubes staring up open-mouthed at these gorgeous places – which are all on wooden stilts stuck into the seabed if you can believe that! We hopped across bridges that went over little canals until we came to the Grand Canal, and Penelope showed it to us like she had dug it out herself.

'Isn't it just wonderful?' she said. And the little punts they call *gondolas*, which are painted black and gold, nipping up and down like it's all quite normal, just left me wanting to dive in again. But no, Pips, you have to fly the British flag, and we don't do that sort of thing! More's the pity.

After a bit, we came to the edge of the island. So funny to have the streets just stop and there's a lagoon instead. We took the *vaporetto*, which is a sort of boat omnibus – a lovely steam-driven thing that toots as fifty of you crowd on and try not to overturn it. And then we were off, and I felt myself crushed up against some of the dishier Italians and I didn't have a single complaint.

Then we putted around the coastline (is 'coastline' right for a city island in a lagoon?) and sped up to the Lido, where we all jumped off at the northern tip, and the boat tooted away.

I liked the little street when we came ashore – it was full of tiny shops, and Penelope showed us all sorts of stuff that she said was typical of Venice. Honora, though, said it was tat for tourists who had more money than sense and she would biff me if I bought that plate painted with gondoliers. At one point, Aldrich disappeared, and we found him in a café around the corner, which had wicker chairs set out in front of a fountain, staring into his tiny, thick coffee like he was thinking of chucking it all in and drowning himself in it. I'm sure he really did love Penelope deep down, but she was just a bit much for him sometimes. And between her and Honora, he just seemed a bit defenceless. I still wondered about the cats.

Well, after Penelope dragged poor Aldrich away from his comfort coffee, with the owner saying 'Ciao, Signor Batley', we took a cab to the villa, where we would be staying for two weeks. It was a horse-drawn fly, but that was probably best on the cobbled streets – I can't think what all that bouncing around would have done to the suspension on our Bentley Sports Tourer (it had a 4.25l engine, which had raced us out of trouble more than once, but didn't like uneven surfaces). So off we clipped, out through the town – I was a bit sad to see it behind us, with all the chaos and shouting – and along the coast, where we could watch the fishing boats setting out or coming in. On we bashed, past rocky beaches and out to a brown, grassy headland about six miles away at the southern end. That was where we found Villa Batley – a big white place that could only have been five or ten years old and wouldn't have looked one bit out of place on the English coast. Opposite it was a smaller house built in the same modern style; and in front of that an absolute dish with jet black hair and a thin moustache was sat reading a newspaper. He had a bright, striped blazer thrown casually over the back of his chair and white slip-on shoes. As we drew up in the fly, he smiled at us.

'Ah,' Penelope said. 'I see Erwan's sunning himself.'

'Erwan?'

'He's French. Been here a couple of years. Lovely boy. Teaches at St Clara's.'

'Do they pay the teachers at St Clara's?' Honora asked.

'I expect so.'

'Then one would think he could afford a razor.'

'Moustaches are quite "in" right now,' I said.

'I'm not sure *what* they are in, but someone needs to take that boy to a good barber.'

Penelope's maid-of-all-work, Maria, opened up for us and in we trotted. It was so much cooler inside, with blinds on the windows and a white marble floor. I just wilted into a chair, and Penelope sent Maria off to prepare some mint juleps for us all.

'And what do you think?' Penelope said triumphantly.

'A very fine house indeed,' Honora said. She always finds people's homes fascinating. And not just from a professional point of view. I think she likes to look into people's souls, and their homes are the shortest route in.

Aldrich and Penelope threw back a couple of drinks

each. I think he needed one more than she did. I took a couple of gulps from mine, and it quite knocked me sideways, chum. They weren't scrimping on the firewater, that was for sure, and I was halfway to being quite squiffy. Honora drank hers down without raising an eyebrow but politely turned down a second.

'Yes, a very fine house,' she repeated. 'What is it that you do for a living, Aldrich?'

'Cats,' he said.

'Ah. Cats.'

'Now,' Penelope said, 'Maria will show you to your rooms. Do you have bathing costumes? We have spares.'

'Not a bit of it,' Honora said. 'I'm in the Hampstead ladies' pond by seven o'clock every morning of the year. They sometimes have to break the ice for me, but it's two laps before breakfast, rain or shine. I found a man in there last month skulking about in the bushes. He won't try that again!'

What rooms we had! Big and airy and with views right out to sea. There were a few more little islands in the lagoon, one or two of them with houses. It must have been smashing to live out on the water like that, your own little jetty to get to and from the mainland. Anyway, I jumped into the spiffy new red bathers I had bought at the Bon Marché and charged down the stairs. I'd been champing at the bit for a swim the whole time we were on the ship.

'You're a keen one!' Penelope said, finishing off yet another cocktail on the grey leather settee. And I'm pretty certain I heard a bit of a 'hic' at the end.

'I can't wait,' I told her.

'Out through the back and you're on the beach. It's quite safe.' She stood up, wobbled a bit and sat down again. 'Show her, Aldrich.'

Aldrich smiled at me like the uncle you always wish you had had and led me out to the garden room, which had French doors that opened straight onto the beach. Oh, it was ripper to jump about in the shallows and dive right into the deeper stuff while the sun beat down.

After about ten minutes splashing around, I was passed by someone powering through the waves like they were swimming to Australia. Well, I knew Honora's stroke well enough. She was wearing her black rubber bathing hat that makes her look like a torpedo coming towards you. I waded back to dry land just in case she knocked me down and flopped onto a big table-like rock to brown up as much as my English skin would allow. She did a couple of lengths of the beach, then shook herself dry and sat down beside me.

'Oh, look,' I said. There was a little sailing dinghy coming into sight, and I could see that it was being steered by the French teacher, Erwan. He did look the bee's knees in a white shirt and even whiter trousers, and he knew his way around the dinghy, taking it up into the face of the waves so that it flew over the top of them.

'Eyes are too close together,' Honora said, wiping her face with a towel.

'Oh, Honora!'

'Mark my words. Well, if you're determined to get yourself into trouble, then I understand he will be at a drinks party tonight that Penelope is taking us to.'

'Will he?' I tried to say nonchalantly.

'Oh, stop trying to sound like you're not bothered either way. It's at that house over there.' She pointed some way down the island, to another headland jutting out. I couldn't make it out very well, but it looked oodles old from where I stood, with a set of buildings and a church spire at the end of them. 'It's an old monastery. Owned by their old friend Dr Wetherby. Have you heard of him?'

'No.'

'Me neither. Apparently he writes adventure stories in his spare time when he's not practising medicine.'

'Like Arthur Conan Doyle.'

'I suppose so. Anyway, we're all over there for drinks at eight and back here for supper at ten. Of course, we might be carrying Penelope home at the rate she's going. I think she's already gone through half a bottle of something called bourbon, and she's just getting started.'

Chapter 4

That evening saw us all dressed up to the nines in a hotsy-totsy little power boat that Aldrich was steering round to Dr Wetherby's. I must say, his bolthole looked more romantic the closer we got. It really was jolly ancient and Penelope said it had been built for monks in the Middle Ages. It was like a little castle, with proper battlements and a gatehouse with a tower leading into the main two-storey house – all made out of stone that was going ruby-red in the sunset. We bounced out of the boat onto a wonky old jetty, catching a bit of sea spray into the bargain, and tied it up.

'It's a romantic old place,' said Penelope. 'Catholic monks lived here for five hundred years until they burnt their church down one night. Probably a little too much *vino*. Now, that gatehouse, oh, what was it that Matthew said it used to be? Oh yes, something called a chapterhouse.'

'It's where the monks used to have a meeting each day and be read books about saints,' Honora informed us.

Sounded dull, if you asked me, but each to his own.

We strutted on in through the arch under the chapterhouse. There were walkways overhead, where I imagined the monks pouring boiling oil on anyone coming without an invitation (though perhaps that's more the Knights Templar?), and on the other side there was a little courtyard with potted plants and a row of mulberry bushes. And a huge wooden door into the main house, which really was built like a little castle keep. Penelope was happy, because a butler was standing there with a salver of drinks, and she knocked one back before he had time to offer one to anyone else. She was just complimenting him on the strength of his moonshine when we all heard raised voices from behind the bushes.

'Tell me why!' some chap was insisting.

'It's over, Fred, that's all.' I knew a girl on the edge of tears when I heard one.

'For no reason?'

'There's . . . there's a reason.'

'I don't know what to say. Look, let's go for a walk.'

And without a word, they both emerged towards the lagoon. Fred clocked us and cast us a fuming look, as if we had been deliberately earwigging, and led her away out of our sight.

'Well, well,' Penelope said, trying to hold down a grin. 'I thought that pair were solid as a rock. And I've always had a bit of a soft spot for young Fred. He's Matthew Wetherby's junior partner in the practice. Works from here alongside Matthew. And Alice is Matthew's daughter.'

'Yes,' said Honora, with that I'm-all-ears sound to

her voice that you always hear when she's a bit intrigued. 'Interesting that she wouldn't explain why, isn't it? After all, if there's a reason, why not tell him so he can fix things?'

'I suppose so,' Penelope said, a bit doubtfully. 'Anyway, let's see who's here.'

Without further ado, she led us through the huge wooden door – big enough for a man to ride in on a horse, I'm sure. And as soon as we were in, I got the absolute heebie-jeebies. Proper creeps up my spine. Because we were in an honest-to-goodness medieval hall with suits of armour carrying maces, a fireplace big enough to roast a bally ox, coats of arms carved into the walls and a flight of stairs up to a gallery that ran around the upper part of the room, with doors to what must have been bedrooms opening off it. And the fact that everyone in the hall was in dapper modern evening dress and the radio was playing jive made it all look even more nutty.

'Oh no,' Penelope said, quite loudly. '*He* is here.' She nodded and tutted at the same time towards a skinny bloke. He was on his own and staring down into a port glass.

'Who is he?' Honora asked.

'William Glenn. Absolute blight on the community.' She looked to Aldrich.

'Blighter,' he confirmed.

'Fred's father, as it happens, though you can't blame Fred for that.'

'And how is he a blighter?' Honora enquired.

'How? I'll tell you how. We were supposed to be

living in his house. Wonderful place – takes up the whole of one of the little islands, Lazzaretto Vecchio. Stole it right out from under us, eight or nine years ago. We made the previous owners a good offer for it, they accepted, then right at the last minute in he jumps throwing cash at them. Well, they obviously cared more for funds than for honour and reneged on our deal. Shocking behaviour. Wasn't it?'

Aldrich said that it was.

'Did you have a contract in writing?'

'In writing? My dear, this is Italy. Nothing's in writing. It's all done on a nod. And then if you break your nod, it's blood money or a blood feud.'

Honora fixed her to the spot with her eye. 'Is it now?' She can do that when you're not expecting it, and it rattles you, I'll say.

Penelope looked jolly sheepish. 'Well, maybe not that much. But anyway. Let's introduce you to our host.'

She took Honora by the elbow and led her across the room. A slight haze of cigarette smoke – a rough old mixture of fine American and thick local brands – hung in the air, so it looked like everyone was just a little bit blue. I was in my short yellow number with the beading, while Honora looked quite glorious, really, in an ankle-length deep-blue affair, set off with a few sequins. Penelope steered us around all these people towards a chap who was giving a maid instructions about serving the drinks. The chap had a long, flat sort of phizog, with a long, flat Roman nose to go with it. Rectangular steel spectacles. Big bald patch and a truly frightful toupee that you would probably have set a dog on, thinking he was being attacked by a rat. Aged sixtyish, I expect.

'Matthew, this is my new friend.'

'Honora Feldman, Mrs,' Honora informed him forcefully, holding out her hand, which he shook.

'And her assistant, Pips . . . um . . .'

'Watkins,' I said.

'Hopkins. Yes, of course. Our host, Dr Matthew Wetherby.'

'Good evening, Mrs Feldman, Miss Watkins.' He had a stern sort of delivery, a bit like a Roman senator, to go with his Roman nose. 'Are you on holiday?'

'I am. I expect you know every British expat in Venice.'

'I should say that I am physician to every British expat in Venice.'

'Ah, then you are the man who knows all the secrets.'

'Many of them, yes.'

At that moment, I saw Honora's head cock to the side. And I knew the sign: something had caught her eye. It wasn't long before it was perfectly obvious what, because the young couple – Fred and Alice – that we'd seen arguing outside burst through the throng, him pursuing her and her in tears.

'For God's sake, just tell me!'

'I can't,' she said, casting him a glance over her shoulder. And at that, she pulled a ring from the fourth finger of her left hand and placed it on a table. 'I'm so sorry.' She stopped, almost with a look of horror, when she caught sight of us all.

'Alice, what's happened?' Dr Wetherby asked the girl, though he was staring at Fred.

'Leave me alone!' she sobbed, and hurried up the stairs and into one of the rooms above.

'Fred?'

The young man stopped beside us, holding his palms up as if asking the gods for manna.

'I . . . I don't know.'

He turned away and took a couple of steps back the way he had come, but flubbed it and just stood there like a landed trout, with his head drooping a bit.

'Well, well,' Penelope said, under her breath because he was still close by. 'Such a pity. A decent boy, young Fred.'

'A very reliable young man,' the doctor confirmed sadly. 'We shall see what develops.'

'I can't wait. Now, I was about to tell you that Honora is a celebrated private investigator.'

'Are you?' He looked interested.

'I'm not sure about the word "celebrated". It seems to promise too much.'

'But you undertake investigations? For money?'

'Sometimes for money. Sometimes for my own interest.'

'Indeed?'

'I suppose that means that, in one sense, you and I share a profession, doctor. Investigating the symptoms to find the underlying cause.'

'Yes, medicine can feel like a mystery. Not least because patients often fail to tell you the whole truth. Or any of it.'

'Do they often lie to you?'

'Frequently. Either because they are embarrassed to say what is wrong with them; or just the opposite:

because they feel they are making a fuss about nothing and therefore keep the severity of their condition to themselves. Either way, it makes my job twice as hard.'

'Luckily you have another string to your bow,' Penelope interjected, taking a tall glass of hooch from a salver. 'The most *wonderful* stories. All deliciously dark tales about even darker goings-on. "Who's to blame? How will she get her revenge?" In fact, we were having a bit of a tidy-up the other day and found this.' She held out her hand to Aldrich, who placed a book-sized package bound in brown wrapping into her palm. 'You brought us this years ago when I was laid up and feeling sorry for myself.'

He furrowed his brow and began pulling away the brown wrapping paper.

'Oh, it's *The Waterfall*!' he said, breaking out a big grin.

'Got it in one.'

'*The Waterfall*?' I burst out, ever so thrilled. 'I saw the talkie of it. It was utterly corking!' Crikey, but I was impressed. That film really had it all: Gary Cooper, who I would marry in a heartbeat, as Shakespeare; that creepy sleepwalker, who I still see sometimes when I close my eyes at night; and that poor girl who drowns but turns out to be a bit of a shifty sly-boot, though you never *really* know if it's her fault or not. 'So is the monastery based on this place?'

'Yes, partly,' he said with a bit of a chuckle. He held up the book that Penelope had handed him. It had a very beautiful cover with a golden key on a navy blue background. 'My best work, for certain.'

'Well, it got me through a tricky time. I was stuck in bed with some rotten dose of Delhi Belly,' Penelope said. 'We had just come back from India – Aldrich's business with the cats – and even before the boat had docked, I knew I wasn't match fit. So off to bed for yours truly, and Matthew came straight round with some really lovely drugs and a copy of his latest. Signed and dated it for us so we'll be able to sell it on when he's dead and collectors are snapping up his output like hot cakes.'

'You might have to wait a while for that,' he said.

She handed it to me, and I flicked through. There was a handwritten inscription thanking them for their friendship. I went back to the cover; it really was very spiffy.

For some reason I got the funniest feeling that someone was watching me and I glanced up – discreetly, I thought, but Honora says that discretion isn't my strong suit – at Fred. He caught my eye, a dead serious look on his face, then grabbed a glass of the hard stuff from the girl serving them and downed it in one.

'Tell him about your famous cases,' Penelope said.

'It's the least famous that are the most interesting,' Honora replied. 'We don't often go barrelling in after spies breaking into Downing Street.'

'Have you ever?' Penelope asked, wide-eyed.

'Of course not. And if I had to, I would send in young Pips. She's the one who sits through every afternoon feature with cowboys and Indians. It would be right up her alley.'

And I have to say, it probably would. The chance

to swing in through the window on a rope or something, kicking five rotters out the way and saving the secret plans – well, some nights I dream about such stuff and it's a bit of a disappointment to wake up and find myself back in Highgate with an electric fire in the corner of the room and not a single German spy within spitting distance. But still, life with Honora's ever so interesting, even without that.

Poor old Fred had decided it was time to slope off. He was heading through the doorway when another young man, obviously quite squiffy, and not in a pretty way, came through the other way. The new fellow was very tall and well-built, with daringly long blond hair, and he should have been a cracker but there was something a bit seedy about him. He had already lost his tie somewhere, and half his shirt studs were missing. Just as Fred was about to squeeze past, he shot out an arm and barred his way.

'Evening, old boy,' he said. 'I heard you having words with my sister.'

'Go to bed, Gabriel, you can barely stand,' Fred snapped back.

'Trouble between you two?' he asked with a lopsided smile.

'Nothing that concerns you. Now let me through or I'll chuck you out of the way.'

'Will you now?' Gabriel drew himself up to his full height and began shadow boxing. 'Shall we go at it with duelling pistols or good old-fashioned fisticuffs?'

'For God's sake!' And Fred shoved him out of his path.

'Father!' Gabriel yelled across the room. Dr Wetherby didn't let so much as a flicker of a reaction pass across his face. Sheer stone, it was. But I did notice – and Honora would have been chuffed, I'm sure – that his hand tightened its grip on his glass as Gabriel stumbled over, pushing a couple of revellers out the way. 'Father, Father, Father. Progenitor, paterfamilias.'

'You're drunk,' Dr Wetherby growled.

'You're right. Lovely, isn't it?'

'Come to my office.' And it wasn't a chummy sort of invitation, I'll tell you that.

'Your wish is my command.'

They went through a little wooden door (they were short people in the Middle Ages) that Dr Wetherby unlocked. I had a quick peek inside while they were stomping in. It was his office for medical consulting, but also must have been where he wrote his stories, because one side was lined with shelves full of all sorts of doctorish kit – bottles, a stethoscope, that sort of stuff – and the other was all bookshelves and a comfy-looking leather Chesterfield armchair and a typewriter.

Gabriel dropped himself into the chair, one leg slung over the armrest. And his dad shut the door very firmly in my kisser.

'Gabriel has been a real worry to his father,' Penelope said, watching the door. 'A tearaway in his youth, a drunkard now he's a young man. So . . . what are they talking about?' she asked me.

I made a show of pretending not to catch on to what she meant.

'Stuff and nonsense,' Honora said to me. 'Tell her what they're talking about. We're older than you, and our ears aren't as efficient.'

'Quite right,' Penelope added.

Aldrich nodded.

So I went to the door and pressed my cheek to it. Well, you didn't need to be a spy to guess what was going on on the other side.

'. . . what's more, you've had two thousand lire from me this month alone,' Dr Wetherby was barking.

'And I'll need another two thousand next month. But this month, Pop, it's a mere five hundred on top. You wouldn't want your only son to be a welsher on bets, would you?'

'Has it ever crossed your mind that you only ever lose them? That if you stopped, and maybe even stuck at a job, you wouldn't have to come crawling to me, month in, month out, to save your so-called honour?'

'To tell you the truth, Dad, my honour went a long time ago.' And his voice dropped a bit and started sounding more serious. 'No, it's my neck I want to save. You refused me last month, so I had to borrow the money.'

'Who from?' He sounded properly angry now.

'Andrea Gallo.'

'Gallo? That criminal! He's little more than a gangster. And he's friends with the Fascists.'

'I was let down.'

'By whom?'

'Someone I thought was a friend. His information was a dud. I lost it all.'

'You lost it all. That doesn't surprise me. You're an irresponsible little fool. Always have been. And I know what else you've been taking from me.'

'What do you mean?'

'I mean, it's not just money that's been going missing around here.'

'And who do we have to blame for that, eh?' Gabriel's voice was beginning to rise in anger; sneering, drunken anger at that. 'I blame the parents!'

'If you think you're getting another penny – or anything else – from me, you're mistaken, young man!'

'Of course I am. I thought you might just care about a threat to your child's life, but no! Couldn't care less, could you?' And then the door burst open. 'No, you only care about Alice!' He pointed up to the gallery. 'Sweet little Alice, who never puts a foot wrong. Well, I want to know why she's broken things off with Fred, don't you?' He knocked a chair flying as he stormed out of the main entrance, giving some chap a look like he'd biff him.

'I'm sorry you had to witness that,' Dr Wetherby said, leaving and locking up his office. 'I can't pretend things are easy between myself and my son.'

'Oh, Matthew, we all know how it is,' Penelope said, in what I guessed was her best 'comforting' voice, and putting her hand on his arm. It was obvious that she was in clover with all the gossip, though.

'I need to see to my secretary.' He plodded off across the room to talk to a very attractive young woman in her twenties standing at one of the tables with a glass of red wine in her hand. Her eyebrows were plucked very fine and she had the most perfect skin and long, curling black hair. I couldn't have touched that shade of lippy.

'I'll bet he does,' Penelope said, with a bit of a wink. Honora lifted an eyebrow but said nothing. And to be fair, the girl was a knockout. Penelope looked all around the room, then beckoned us in like witches around a cauldron. 'One thing I didn't mention about the good doctor's book is that there were always rumours about it, that the characters were disguised versions of some of the people on the island. Probably some of this lot here. It caused a bit of resentment, I can tell you.'

'Was one based on you?' Honora asked.

'Oh no, not at all. Matthew and I have always been on the best and most open of terms.'

It looked like Dr Wetherby was trying to convince the girl of something, but she was having none of it. She was barely even looking at him. Then she vamoosed without saying a word. 'All fun and games tonight!' Penelope said. 'Oh, there's our charming neighbour, Erwan. You're blushing, Pips.'

'I am not!' I said. But I might have been. He was looking ritzy in a short bolero jacket, leaning casually against the wall, blowing smoke and watching everyone mingling about. He lifted his cigarette to me.

Penelope gave me a shove towards him. I stumbled a bit but went over regardless.

'Hullo,' I said.

'*Bonsoir.*' Now, I don't know much French, but I could tell it wasn't a brush-off.

'Ripping place they have here.'

He looked around with two deep brown eyes that caught the light very well. 'It is nice.' I think that means 'swanky' if you're French. He fetched me a pink gin and told me that he was teaching for now, but his real passion was poetry and he'd had a small book of his work published in France, which was all quite impressive. And after a while, it was all getting so stuffy in there that he suggested we take a walk in the moonlight. And I was a bit nervy but said righty-ho.

Chapter 5

We slipped off out the front, and I could feel Honora's eyes boring into the back of my head but I didn't care. It had been more than a year since my last beau, Daniel, had emigrated to join the rubber industry in Brazil, and I had been pretty lonely at times.

Out in the moonlight, we wandered down to the jetty. Erwan pulled off his shoes and socks and dabbled his feet in the water, and I did the same. It was a lovely sort of feeling, just sitting there, kicking up a bit of spray, watching the moonlight on the waves. I could feel my lips getting closer to his, and he was saying, 'Pips, you look very beautiful in this light.'

'Do I?'

'I say that you . . .' He suddenly jumped up, pointed back above our heads and shouted something in French that I couldn't even spell if I wanted to. Then I looked where he was pointing.

'Bloody hell!' I yelped. 'Fire! Fire!'

The room in the upper storey of the chapterhouse was utterly blazing.

'Come on!' I said, yanking Erwan's hand, dragging

him back to the party. 'We have to tell people!' It was an awfully lucky thing that the chapterhouse was twenty-odd yards from the main house, or everyone at the bash might all have ended up smoked like kippers.

We sprinted back in, and the first person I saw was Penelope. She was about to open her trap, but we stopped it.

'Fire!' I yelled.

'There is a fire. Outside!' Erwan shouted, too. Though the way he said it probably confused people a bit.

'The chapterhouse!'

The radio was turned off, and Dr Wetherby forced his way through to us. Instead of explaining, Erwan shoved him out front to see for himself. Everyone else followed, pushing each other out of the way.

'Fetch water!' Dr Wetherby yelled as soon as we set foot outside.

And then there was utter bedlam, as some old dears started screaming, some of the young bucks tore off their dinner jackets and rushed around doing no good at all, and everyone else just gawped.

'Water, buckets of water!' someone cried.

'Here's the store,' shouted a young woman with a bit more gumption about her. She started rattling the door of a wooden shed. Well, the door was held fast with a padlock, but a few beefy kicks from Miss Gumption and the lock broke off. We found a handful of big buckets, a basin, even a sort of box made from rubber that we could press into service to douse the flames, though when the chapterhouse windows exploded and sent a shower of glass and sparks down, you might have thought we were in some sort of bust-up in Hell, and nothing would stop it.

At first, it was every man for himself, running down to the lagoon, then carrying the full buckets up to the fire, but after a minute we somehow came to a bit of order and formed a human chain from the sea, passing the buckets to the braver coves, who ran up inside to chuck them on the blaze. Some would come out choking and spluttering, their faces black with soot. Others were in and out in a second, looking like supermen who weren't affected by fire. I looked for Erwan, because he was so athletic he would have been prime choice for dashing up and down the stone steps, but he must have been at the lagoon end of the chain while I was at the other.

One poor fellow must have got a lungful, because when he came out, he sat down on the stones spluttering away and complaining about a splitting head. Honora helped him up and asked him about his bonce. He told her, and she nodded, then sent him off to wash his face in the lagoon and stop all that nonsense about choking.

Well, it wasn't too long until the blaze was out, and Dr Wetherby was one of the first inside when it was safe. Some poor young bloke tried to stop Honora following him and was lucky that she didn't box his ears. She shoved him out the way and told him she had lived through the Zeppelin raids, so a bit of a house fire hardly held any danger.

'Hmm,' she said when we got inside. It was a store-room by the looks of things, with a few bits of furniture burnt to a crisp and some crates that were just charred splinters by now. There were some empty tins on their sides beside the far wall with a huge black mark above them, and the floor was soaking from all the water chucked in. 'Thought so,' Honora said.

'What do you mean?' Dr Wetherby asked her. He had lost or thrown away his toupée during the kerfuffle and looked all the better for it.

'That boy's splitting head. It wasn't smoke inhalation – he was barely in here. No, it was from the burning paint.' I looked where she was pointing, the tins with the big black stain up the wall above them. 'Paint is an excellent fuel if you are an arsonist trying to start a fire.'

'Arsonist?' Dr Wetherby asked, his eyes widening behind his spectacles.

'The tops are off those paint pots.' She pointed. 'I presume you don't store them like that. And it's hardly likely that they would have been prised off by the young men throwing water in here. No, someone has gone to some effort to start a fire in an almost-empty box room. Which makes us ask: why?'

Dr Wetherby had lost his stony look now and was just bewildered. 'But . . . but I don't know.'

'I would say, Dr Wetherby,' Honora said, walking over to the blasted-out window that looked back at the house, 'that there is no reason to start a fire in an almost-empty box room unless you want everyone present to gather round it.' She looked back at him but pointed to the house. 'And leave wherever you don't want them to be.'

He rushed to the window. 'Are you saying . . . ?'

'I'm saying this was a diversion tactic. Quite a successful one, by the looks of things. I would get back to your house, Dr Wetherby, and find out what's what.' He looked horrified. The poor bloke was completely out of his depth. 'Come on,' Honora ordered him, hauling him towards the door.

As soon as we were back at the house, followed by a few partygoers and Dr Wetherby's children, Alice and Gabriel, Honora collared a maid and told her to check the silverware. 'Count it.' The girl looked at her master and he nodded urgently, so off she ran towards the kitchen.

'Here,' Dr Wetherby shouted, pointing to the little door to his office. 'Someone's forced it open. With this, by the looks of things.' He pointed to a poker on the floor by the doorway. It was certainly out of place without any explanation.

'Let me, Dad,' Gabriel said, easing himself in front of his father. He didn't seem so sozzled then. And he picked up the poker as a weapon. 'Empty!' he shouted a second later from inside the room.

'Let's have a look,' Honora said, striding in. 'Now, what's been disturbed?'

Dr Wetherby glanced around. 'Nothing. No, wait.' And he hurried over to a big green metal safe in the corner. 'It's open!'

He was right: the door was open half an inch and the key was in the lock. He was just about to take hold of the handle but Honora grabbed his hand. 'Fingerprints.'

'Oh . . . yes.' And I think that was the moment he realized this wasn't some sort of accident or prank, but a full-scale criminal case. I've seen it before with Honora, of course – someone comes into her consulting room at the Highgate flat with a strange little story that has left them perfectly flummoxed but not actually worried, and they leave two hours later white as a sheet and dashing to the police station at the bottom of the Archway Road as fast as their legs can carry them.

'Let me,' Honora said, gently pushing him out the way. She took a pen from the desk and used it to prise the safe fully open. 'Now, what do you keep in there, and what's missing?'

He peered in. 'The household cash – not a huge amount, enough for household expenses for a month or so. It's gone.'

'That must have been what they were looking for,' piped up Gabriel.

Honora shushed him. 'Not so hasty, young man. Do you keep anything else here?'

'The practice medical records.' He waved his hand at a stack of grey folders with tags on the edges that stated the year they were from. He looked next at the empty lower shelf in the safe. And then he gave Honora a glance that I can only call 'shifty', before dropping his eyes shamefacedly.

'Out with it.' He made no reply. 'Chop chop, Wetherby. What else is supposed to be here?'

He made a sound like he was in pain. Then he sighed. 'The restricted drugs.'

'Such as?'

'Morphine. Cocaine.'

'Thought so,' Honora said. 'Any idea who would have wanted them?'

'No.'

I wasn't altogether sure he was telling the truth.

'Is there a black market in them?'

'I expect so. Wherever you have drugs, you have people who want them.'

'Has anyone asked you for them, whom you refused?'

He broke away from the contents of the safe for the first time to face her. 'Not one of my patients has asked me for anything in there.'

'Well then, Dr Wetherby, you appear to be in a bit of a pickle. A pity the thief was clever enough to set the fire, or we would have had about a hundred witnesses. Now, the key. Where did the rascal get it?'

'I leave it in the desk. There's never been anything like this before.'

'There never is until it happens.' She tutted. 'Now. Three things to do.'

'Yes?'

'One: call the police. Two: search the house in case anything else is amiss. Three: search your guests for the missing items. All of them.'

'I am *not* going around accusing my guests of being thieves. The very idea!' he said, astonished.

'Then you will allow them to be thieves. One of them, at least.'

He paused to think it over. 'I'll take that chance. I will, however, call the police and search the house, as you say. Now, Gabriel, escort these ladies wherever they want to go.' And he picked up the telephone on his desk, dialled 0 for the operator and asked in Italian to be put through to the boys in blue – or whatever they were called in Italy.

'Dr Wetherby?' It was his secretary in the doorway. She had a nice voice, I have to say, quite deep and smooth. I wouldn't have minded sounding like her, especially when I laugh and Honora says I sound like a blocked drain. 'Would you like me to do anything?'

He rubbed his face. 'A brandy coffee, I think, Miss Grieves. Ladies?' We said no, ta. He didn't ask his son if he wanted anything.

'One moment, Miss Grieves,' Honora said, as the girl tried to leave. 'Were you in the house in the last thirty minutes?'

'No, I was outside, helping with the fire.' She was quite calm.

'Were you?'

'Yes.'

'Curious you don't show any sign of it. No soot on your face, clean hands.' Honora held up the secretary's palms. They were perfectly clean. I looked at my own. There was dirt encrusted in the wrinkles of the skin and under my fingernails. I rubbed my sleeve across my face, and the yellow cloth turned brown.

Cool as a cucumber, Miss Grieves reached into the little velvet clutch bag she was carrying and took out a packet of thin cigarettes and a red-and-gold book of matches. She lit one and blew smoke out of the side of her mouth.

'I just washed. I didn't want to get dirt in here. On top of everything else.'

'Yes. Of course you didn't.' And Honora smiled. The girl took that as her cue to sashay out. 'Right, then.' Honora tapped Gabriel Wetherby on the chest to tell him that he was now the subject of her interest. 'Show us the house. Everywhere a thief might raid or hide.'

Gabriel did as he was told and took us around the place. We looked everywhere, with his poker held up from time to time as a weapon, but Honora told him to put it down because he looked a proper chump. She was disappointed to find nothing of note.

I'm sure she would have demanded that the guests strip down to their undies while she rifled their clothes if the police hadn't turned up then and there, in a car that looked like it had been ready for the scrap heap for at least a decade.

Chapter 6

A big fellow with a bushy moustache and beard jumped out of the passenger side and started striding towards the group with his driver hopping along behind him. They were both in plain clothes, but it was obvious who they were.

'I am Commissario Ricci of the Polizia di Stato,' the big one said in good English. He was probably the one who always dealt with the expats. 'Where is Dr Wetherby?' he asked, quite cocksure of himself.

'Inside,' Honora replied before anyone else could. 'You may speak to me first.' Penelope, fizzing with all the excitement, joined our little group so she could be in on the wheeze.

'May I have your name, Signora?'

'Honora Feldman. Mrs.'

'Honora Feldman. Mrs.'

'That is correct, Sergeant.'

'Commissario,' he corrected.

'*Sergeant.* And I don't know what your wife's about, letting you out of the house with that face fungus.' He blinked. The other one, a youngish constable,

stifled a laugh. 'Yes, you heard me. Perhaps your Il
Duce could spend his time on his police's appearance,
though he doesn't seem very bright, does he? Well,
you might have time enough on your hands to spend
it gossiping like this, but one of us has a crime to
examine. So I will bid you goodbye.' And she turned
her back on him and went back to the crowd, where
she clapped her hands for attention. 'Now, everyone.
It would take too long to speak to you all one by
one. My name is . . .'

'Honora Feldman. Mrs,' I heard Ricci mutter.

'That's right, Sergeant.' He grunted in annoyance.
'And I am looking into this matter for Dr Wetherby.
It has been an upsetting evening, however I need to
know if any of you saw someone enter the house
while the rest of us were outside dousing the fire.'

'Wait,' the policeman piped up, cottoning on to the
fact that the investigation was already slipping out of
his paws.

'For what, Sergeant? The cows to come home? For
Kingdom Come?'

'I do not understand about the cows.'

'Perhaps that brush on your face is stifling your
brain.' He chucked up his hands in submission. 'So
speak up if you saw anything.' She waited; there were
a few shaken heads. 'Nothing that struck you as
strange?' Again, nothing. 'That is a pity. Well, if you
do suddenly remember any detail, I will be staying at
Villa Batley. Come this way, Sergeant, I have a job
for you.' She beckoned him towards the house. His
constable looked delighted by the turn of events.

'I have a job already, Mrs Feldman. It is Police Commissario.'

'Yes, yes, and I'm sure one day you will be perfectly competent in it. But for now, I will take you to the scene of the crime.' She began walking.

'How nice of you.'

'But straight after, you will want to put feelers out into the criminal fraternity – I presume you have one on Venice.'

'I am proud to say we have an excellent one.'

She stopped and glared at him. 'Don't be facetious. It's hardly becoming.'

'I am sorry.'

I'm not sure he knew what 'facetious' meant, but he understood that it wasn't a grand thing.

She started walking again. 'Now, as I said, feelers out into the Mob, there might be some illegal medical drugs on offer. You want to know about it if it happens.' The officer perked up at this point. Now he had something to get his teeth into. He nodded to his constable, who took out a notebook and wrote down a few words with a stubby pencil. She took him to the office, where Dr Wetherby was still sitting in his chair, his chin in his hands, looking quite defeated. 'Dr Wetherby, a sort of policeman for you.'

He looked up then.

'Good evening, Signor,' the officer began. 'I hear you have had some trouble this evening.'

Honora left them to it. We were planning on returning to Penelope's villa and were just crossing the great hall – it all looked very moody now, with the big crests on the wall and the suits of armour carrying maces – when someone spoke to us from above.

'Mrs Feldman!' It was William Glenn – Fred's dad – whom Penelope had pointed out to us earlier as a 'blight' on the community because he and his wife had jumped in and outbid Penelope and Aldrich on the house that they had intended to buy. I have to say, I think all's fair in love, war and house-buying, really. He came down to see us. He was a funny, wriggly little man, who always had one part of him moving, as if he had ants in his pants. 'I'm William Glenn.'

'I know.'

'Do you?' He wasn't sure how to take that. 'Well, it's . . . er, a little difficult.'

'Out with it, Mr Glenn.'

'No, no, yes. Well, the thing is . . .' He met her glance, and I swear he gulped. 'Are you official?'

'*Official?*'

'Yes. Official. In the investigation.'

'Tell me what is on your mind.'

'Yes. Yes. On my mind. Yes, indeed.' She rolled her eyes. 'Well, it's this. I did see something earlier. But I don't know if there's anything in it.' She lifted an eyebrow as an instruction that he continue. 'Oh. Yes. Well, it's that . . . I saw Dr Wetherby's secretary, Miss Grieves, out by the chapterhouse earlier. She was speaking to someone. I couldn't see who.'

'Why not?'

'I was in front of the arch, and they were in a bit of a nook.'

'Continue.'

'Well, yes, and the two of them seemed to be having an argument. Not a full-on yelling match, but Miss Grieves was refusing to do something, and whoever the other one was wasn't happy about it. Well, I didn't want to spy on them . . .'

'Of course you didn't,' Honora said.

He looked at her a bit huffily. 'No, I didn't. So I walked off.'

'And just what were you doing there at all?'

'I was feeling a bit hot and went out for some air. Simple as that.'

I could well believe a man in his fifties would be a bit taken with Miss Grieves, following her about. They can be creeps. I've had it myself. 'Where was your wife?' I asked.

He glared at me. 'My wife passed away six years ago – at Christmas, if you must know.'

'I'm sorry,' I said, feeling like a heel.

'Yes, everyone always is.' He was bitter. And I supposed he had a right to be. I guessed she would have been in her forties, which seems too young, really.

'Thank you for coming forward,' Honora said kindly (at least by her standards). 'This way, Pips. Back to Villa Batley. Nothing more to do here, so a good night's sleep is in order.'

We went out and collected Penelope and Aldrich, and took them back to the boat. Honora insisted that I be allowed to steer us home. She was wizard at knowing what you secretly wanted. Yes, she could be a very good egg at times.

*

Back at the house, we sat in the drawing room and recovered with a round of limoncellos, which Penelope insisted was 'just the thing' for a night like we had had. She was cock-a-hoop about the whole business. 'We haven't had anything quite so thrilling in donkey's years,' she said. 'You two are lucky. Dead bodies and jewel thefts must be ten-a-penny for you, but here we covet a single one a decade if we're lucky. Not like the good old days with the dukes, when you could have your head chopped off just for looking at a nun in the wrong way.'

'Is there a right way?' Aldrich asked.

'Be quiet, Aldrich. No one appreciates your sense of humour right now.'

'Sorry.'

'We saw William Glenn on the way out,' I said.

'Blackguard,' Aldrich mumbled.

'Quite right. What did he have to say for himself?'

'He saw Wetherby's secretary talking to someone outside the chapterhouse. Any idea who it could be?'

'Ha! No, it could be anyone. Let's just say I don't think Matthew employed that girl for her typing skills.'

'Typical,' Honora declared.

'As it happens, I think the son takes after the father,' Penelope added lightly, but expecting it to be a bombshell. 'And let's face it, Gabriel has rather more chance than Matthew. A tearaway, that boy, no doubt, but quite roguish with it. And us ladies do like a rogue, don't we?'

'Am I a rogue?' Aldrich asked.

'Hardly.'

'I see.'

'Glenn is a widower?'

'He is,' she softened. 'Poor man. I can't say we're bosom chums, but I wouldn't wish that on anyone. His wife died of typhoid fever. Dorothy, that was her name.'

'How horrid,' I said.

'Yes. She'd always been sickly, though. Anaemia, I think. Something that needed regular injections from the doctor, anyway.'

'Is typhoid endemic in Venice?' Honora asked.

'Heavens, no. It killed her, their gardener and the cook, but I've never heard of another case. Matthew quarantined their island, no one on or off for two months, and that seemed to work. He arranged for food to be brought over and left on their jetty for Glenn to collect. The chap had to bury those three himself, though.'

'That must have been hard on him,' Honora said. 'Digging his wife's grave, placing her in it. No man would come out of that unscathed. What about the boy?'

'Fred was away at medical school in England, as I remember.'

Honora was silent for a while, just thinking. 'Well, it's time for bed,' she declared at last. 'It's all quite interesting, but there seems little more I can do, and I do want to enjoy my holiday. So I shall leave it in the hands of that Italian policeman who is a stranger to shaving. My guidebook says that tomorrow is a great festival on another island, the Giudecca. The Feast of the Redeemer, correct?'

'Oh yes, it's quite wonderful,' said Penelope. 'They build a bridge of boats so one can walk across from the main island to a church that was built as thanks to God when the city survived the plague. A grand procession topped with fireworks at night.'

'I shall enjoy that spectacle.' We said goodnight and climbed the stairs. 'Has it occurred to you that the thief must have decided on the scheme at the last minute?' Honora said as we went up.

'I don't see.'

'Setting a diversionary fire, it's quite a lot of effort to go to. Quite a risk, too. There must have been easier times to get into the safe than when Wetherby was hosting a large party – late at night or when most of the household were out.'

'Drug fiends are desperate.'

'They certainly can be,' she admitted. 'But desperate without warning? They were at the party and *suddenly* desperate? No, I don't believe that, Pips. Something happened to force the thief's hand.'

Well, we said goodnight and went to our respective bedrooms. I was looking forward to seeing the city, so I went to bed in a bit of a tizzy that night and didn't get to sleep for hours.

Chapter 7

The morning came, and golly it was smashing. Eight o'clock and the sun was streaming in through the window, the sea glittering like it had been sprayed with gold dust. I wore my stripy blue sun dress and slingback sandals and took my wide-brimmed straw hat, because this English skin is prone to burn if the sun so much as peeps out from behind a cloud. Down to breakfast, and Honora strides in drying her hair after a morning dip on the beach. 'Ah, you're up finally,' she said. 'Thought I might see you on the sand, but here you are. Well, eat up, we're catching the vaporetto to St Mark's Square soon.'

I wolfed down some local pastries – all caked in honey – and threw on my hat. Honora was waiting by the front door, and we were just about to bash out when Penelope came in, arm in arm with Erwan.

'We did not have a chance for a nice conversation last night,' he said in that French way that makes you think he's suggesting something without saying a word of it.

Honora tutted.

'No, we didn't,' I replied.

'Then today I can take you for a drive? I will show you this island.'

'Oh.' I didn't look at Honora, because I could hear her rolling her eyes. 'Yes, I would like that.'

'Right,' Honora said. 'Then I will meet you at the Duke's Palace at noon. Penelope and Aldrich will meet us there, and we'll all go for a good lunch. Don't be late.' She marched out with dark glasses and a bag over her shoulder.

Erwan took me out to his car. It was a very dashing Alfa Romeo 6C with a double overhead camshaft engine on six inline cylinders. It knocked out 70 horsepower and could top out at almost 100 mph! We didn't get up to that, but my golly, we gave it a good try! Luckily the Lido island is long and thin, so we could put it through its paces.

Erwan let me take the wheel, and I scared the birds as we flew along the sea road. He was laughing his head off as I wound around the bends, lifting up onto two wheels and then thumping down again onto four. I don't think he thought a girl could drive like that. He even complained of a bit of whiplash as I spun us around one curve, and I told him to stop whining or I'd chuck him out and go off on my own. He laughed his bally head off again, so I stamped us to an emergency stop and he nearly cannoned right out over the bonnet.

'A final request!' he called out, holding up his hands to say sorry. 'A final request. Let me show you what is in the trunk.'

He jumped out and opened up the back, taking out a hamper. And that was that. We sat overlooking a sandy beach on the city side of the Lido and had blackberry cordial from a flask and salty local cheese on bread. Oh, it was smashing. We didn't say a word, we just ate, drank and looked out towards Venice.

After a while, we got up and sauntered along the sand. Buried under a few rocks, I found something. It was a rusted and bashed-about old metal sign that read: *Quarantena. Accesso vietato Lazzaretto Vecchio.*

I asked Erwan what it meant.

'It says: *Quarantine. Do not enter Lazzaretto Vecchio.*'

'Gosh,' I said to Erwan. 'That's the Glenn family's island. This is from when they had the outbreak there.'

'Outbreak?'

'Typhoid.' It was clearly before his time. 'Killed Fred's mum. It sounds awful.' I couldn't imagine being cooped up on that rock with nothing but disease and death, as Fred's dad had been, with no idea how the disease had come to your home. It was such a contrast to the warm, joyful Italy I was beginning to fall in love with. I suppose every island has something nasty in the soil.

'It is appropriate.'

'How so?' I asked, confused.

'The island Lazzaretto Vecchio. It is that one there.' He pointed to a small islet half a mile across the water towards the city, with a couple of buildings and some short trees. 'It was the quarantine island during the *Mort Noire*. The Black Death.'

Plague and disease throughout the ages. I stared out at the island. Such a sad place. I felt a bit of a chill, to tell you the truth.

Well, there wasn't time for moping about. It was time to meet Honora and the others, so I picked myself up, buried the quarantine sign back under the beach rocks – it was part of the island's history, even if it was a sad part, so burying it was more fitting than chucking the sign in a bin – and Erwan drove me to the vaporetto stop. He gave me a smooch on both cheeks, French-style – I can't pretend I wasn't willing for a bit more than that, but a girl can wait – and off I skedaddled to join the others. We had a glorious lunch of pasta and seafood and spent the day looking at the churches and galleries and what-have-you until dinner. Then, finally, it was time for the great procession over to the Giudecca island.

It was all in moonlight by the time everything kicked off. The city was just smashing as the gondoliers sang on the canals, which looked like great big silver snakes slithering their way through alongside the procession. The jamboree had been a big holy thing five hundred years back, but now it was an absolute blow-out of colour and dancing and sweets and drinking white wine that felt a little like a wallop to the old nut. Flowers everywhere made you think you were prancing about in the park, and the whole city smelled like the perfume counter in Selfridges. I was pulled into the procession for a dance so many times that I thought my legs would fall off, and I was glad to finally make it across the bridge of boats to the church on the

Giudecca. Perfect timing! I was just setting foot on dry land when the bells rang out for Midnight Mass and red, gold and green fireworks burst up into the sky. That was the signal that it was time to be a bit quieter and give thanks in the church. So we bowed out, leaving that bit to the locals.

Aldrich was the first in the house after we took a water taxi back to Villa Batley. We were all a bit pooped so I didn't think anything of it when he stopped as he hung his jacket on a coat stand in the hallway and looked a bit put out.

'Hullo,' he said. 'What's this?' He was flicking the light switch up and down, but nothing was happening.

'Must be a power cut,' Penelope said. 'They happen from time to time,' she explained to us.

'Must be. Well, it's late, so—' Aldrich was halted by Honora's hand gripping his arm.

'Don't say another word,' she hissed. And she pointed to the doorway into the drawing room.

It was dark through there, but I saw what she meant. In one corner, the beam from an electric torch twitched, then disappeared, as whoever was shining it turned it off ever so hastily. Whoever they were, they were up to no good, that was certain.

'Aldrich, go on,' Penelope whispered.

'Aldrich, my foot,' muttered Honora. 'Pips, you're up.'

I slipped off my own jacket. I'd been in a few icy situations with Honora, and I'd found the secret was to keep saying to yourself *Gosh, how thrilling!* because that way you didn't think about the fact that you might be about to get your block knocked off. I took up a heavy pewter vase and tipped out the flowers. It would give the bloke a jolly good thump on the head if it came to that. And I rushed in.

As soon as I crossed the threshold, it was utter chaos. Something flew right at me, and I had to duck or take it to the kisser. Aldrich and the others were on my heels, though Penelope tripped over and sent a side table flying. I looked up and saw the back of the burglar climbing out of the window and sprinting away through the garden, holding his torch in one gloved hand and something else I couldn't make out in the other.

'Out the front!' Honora shouted. 'Stop him at all costs!'

Well, I charged out, only to see whoever it was dashing along the road.

'After him!'

I did my best, but honestly, I wasn't dressed for it. I was in a sun dress and strappy sandals, and he (or she, I couldn't tell) was in a dark top, trousers and pumps that turned them into one big silhouette. When they jumped off the road and started off over some sand dunes in the pitch black, I threw in the towel.

'Blighter took the fuse out the box,' Aldrich said from behind us as the others caught up with me. 'That's why the lights didn't work.'

'How wonderful!' Penelope burst out. 'We're the victims of crime. Who shall we tell first?'

'How about the police?' Honora replied. 'Though I admit that you might as well tell the birds as that sergeant with the bush on his chin. Now, back to the house to see what they were after.'

We traipsed back. The drawing room was a total state, of course, but that was mostly our handiwork. 'Oh, that *is* disappointing,' Penelope said. 'I can't see a single thing missing. Is he saying we don't have anything worth "half-inching"?'

'We don't know that it was a he,' Honora corrected her. 'I've known plenty of female criminals – burglars, murderers and blackmailers. We shall keep an open mind at this time.'

Aldrich came down the stairs. 'Nothing out of place up there.'

'Do you keep any cash on the premises?' Honora asked.

'A little in the bedside drawer. It's all there still.'

'Caught in the act. Poor lamb,' Penelope said.

'I'm not sure,' I replied. 'They were holding something as they ran away.'

'Well, it's—' She broke off. 'Oh, now isn't that the strangest thing?'

'Clarify,' Honora ordered her.

Penelope went to the bookcase and pointed to the top shelf. There was a space about a third of the way along where one was clearly missing. 'It's where we keep our favourites, the ones we want to show off,' she said. 'But that one's not there.'

'Which is it?' Honora demanded.

'Well, isn't this odd? We showed it to you last night. It's Matthew Wetherby's book, *The Waterfall*.'

'That's all that was taken?'

'It seems so, yes. Do you think he *meant* to take it?'

'I'm certain of it. The question is why? Was it especially valuable in any way?'

'I can't see how,' Penelope shrugged. 'A perfectly ordinary copy, as far as I know.'

'Are first editions collectors' items? And he signed it, didn't he?'

'He wrote a little dedication, yes, and there was the film of it, of course, but Matthew's not exactly world-famous. It's hardly something someone would go to all the trouble of burglary for.'

Honora sat and mulled for a few moments, tapping her feet, which she does when she's frustrated that there's something she can't quite understand. 'You said that there were rumours that the characters were based on real people on the island.'

'Oh yes, yes, I did!' Penelope exclaimed, perking up. 'Do you think one of *them* took it as, you know, a terrible revenge?'

'Well, it's hardly a terrible revenge to take a single copy from someone who didn't even write the thing.'

'Oh yes, that's true.'

'Who are they? These people who appear in disguised form?'

Penelope patted down her hair. If you ask me, she was starting to feel a bit silly. 'Well, I don't actually know. I just heard there are some.'

Honora raised an eyebrow. 'That's hardly much help, is it? And yet, there *is* a reason it's immensely valuable to someone.'

'How do we find out what that is?'

'The first step should be clear to anyone.'

'Yes, of course. What is it?'

'To read it,' Honora told her.

'Oh. Oh yes! I see what you mean.'

We scrambled all around the house in case there was another copy hiding somewhere, then tried the neighbours, who looked at us as if we were mad for waking them up to borrow a book they had barely heard of.

'We'll sleep on it, and in the morning we'll track down a copy of that book,' Honora announced. 'Nothing's going to happen between now and then.'

But she was wrong.

Because something did happen. Something utterly awful.

Chapter 8

Not that I had the slightest idea of that the next morning when I woke, bathed in warm sunlight and a state of high excitement. I hurried down to the beach in my swimmers, ready to do some good exercise before breakfast, only to find that Honora had beaten me there again. But that wasn't the reason my morning swim was cancelled.

'Over there, Pips,' Honora said, pointing out to sea. She had her back to me and hadn't even seen me arrive; somehow she just had this sixth sense of my presence. 'You see?'

I followed where she was pointing. There was a little dinghy bobbing about on the water on the city side of the island, about eighty yards out. The sail was flapping loose in the wind, and no one was on the tiller, so it was drifting here and there with the waves.

'Funny,' I said, holding my hand up to shade my eyes.

'Not so funny when you look closer,' she said grimly.

It took me a few moments to make out what she

was talking about. Then I ran into the waves and started powering through to get to the boat, tasting the salt as the spray made its way into my mouth. Half a minute later I was at the little arrow-shaped craft and scrambling over the side. Sad to say, it had a cargo, that boat, and the cargo was a man dressed in a black shirt and trousers with dirty tennis shoes, slumped over the seat; his hands limp by his side.

Fred.

I looked into his face and I knew then and there that he was gone. Poor man.

I sat back, tipping the boat a little. I hadn't known him, but it was always sad when a young person's life ended. And I had to take him back to shore, so his father – a man who had already lost his wife to typhoid – could mourn his son.

A boat's not so hard to steer, really, and I quickly worked out how to bring it back to the shore. Honora looked in at what I had brought.

'Strangled,' she said.

'*What?*' Until then, I hadn't even thought about how the poor chap had died.

She pointed to a pink ring around his neck. The skin was rubbed hard, and I guessed it would have been redder if death hadn't drained all of his blood from his outer skin.

'Who did it?'

'That, Pips, we will have to find out,' she said gravely. 'Stay here.' And she went back towards the house.

While I waited for her to return, I looked across the lagoon towards Venice. Such a lovely town, such

swell people. It seemed so cruel to take someone's life
when everyone else was celebrating theirs.

Honora came back two minutes later with Penelope
and Aldrich. 'Oh God, oh God,' was all Penelope could
say.

For his part, Aldrich seemed surprisingly efficient
in a crisis. 'I'll go and telephone the police,' he said.
'I suppose they will know what arrangements to make.'

Honora bent down to the body. 'Where have you
been?' she asked. But he couldn't answer.

And then I realized something. 'Honora! He's
wearing all black.'

She glanced at me. And then she understood and
smiled proudly. 'Yes, you're right.'

'What?' asked Penelope.

'All black. Like your burglar last night,' Honora
said. 'And his pumps are dirty, as if he's run across
country, you see?'

'It was Fred?' She sounded incredulous.

'Why not? It was no common or garden house
burglary for cash and jewellery, was it?' She patted
down his clothes. 'But if he was the one who took
your copy of Wetherby's book, he doesn't have it now.'

'So whoever killed him . . .'

'Took it from him, yes. So long as Fred *was* the
original thief.'

'I never would have guessed,' Penelope said, shaking
her head.

'People mixed up in crimes often surprise you with
what they can do. So we have to surprise them with
what we can discover.'

We didn't say anything more until Aldrich came back, telling us that Commissario Ricci was on his way. Dr Wetherby was also coming, and he would stop off at William Glenn's home to break the news to Fred's father. Aldrich had brought a light blue sheet, which he laid over the body.

'That must be a beastly part of Matthew's job,' Penelope said. 'Death's messenger. It would make me want to find another profession entirely.'

'Thankfully, we have some, like him, who are prepared to do it, dear,' Aldrich said.

'Yes, yes, you're right.'

Bit by bit, we retreated and stood at a respectful distance. Honora and I took a few steps away from the others.

'Take note, Pips, how they all know each other. All in each other's pockets without escape. Even an English country village isn't quite like that – say Mr Johnson the baker is caught drunk and disorderly one night, well, he can catch the train to London for a month until all the tongues stop wagging. Not so easy when you're an expat in Venice. Here, there's no escape at all. That must send the temperature up.'

'Yes.'

We spent a long time there without speaking, until two people came up from the road: Dr Wetherby and William Glenn. Wetherby looked grim, while Glenn looked devastated. Penelope took them to Fred's body, and Dr Wetherby lifted the cover. Glenn took two steps back and lowered his head.

Just then, I spotted two more figures approaching us:

Ricci and his constable. Honora saw them, too. 'Come on,' she ordered me. And we hurried towards the two Britons. 'We want to speak to them before that sergeant.'

'Commissario,' I said.

'You can call a potato a fish, but it won't do in a soup.' Sometimes I think she just makes these sayings up on the spot. 'Would you come this way?' she said to Dr Wetherby and Glenn. She led them quickly towards the house. Over my shoulder, I saw the two policemen clock what was going on. Honora hurried everyone in, and we made it to the house before the officers could catch up with us. Honora locked the door. 'Mr Glenn, I can only say how sorry I am. To lose one's child must be the most painful thing imaginable.' He said nothing. There was a faraway look in his eyes, as if his mind had gone to another place and time. 'Mr Glenn?' She said it gently, and he seemed to come back to us. 'Mr Glenn, can you think of any reason someone would want to do this to your son?'

'No, no,' he said hoarsely, barely able to speak.

'Had he fallen out with anyone recently?'

He blinked and looked around as if he hadn't even noticed coming into the house. 'His engagement to Alice was off, I don't know why. I don't think he knew, either.'

There was a knock on the door. Honora ignored it and turned to Dr Wetherby. 'Fred worked for you, is that correct?'

'Yes. He qualified as a GP about two years ago and came back to the island to practise. I gave him a job – my plan was to sell the practice to him eventually so I could retire. It's not a goldmine, but it brings in a decent income.'

'And if he were married to Alice?'

'Well, maybe it would have been a wedding gift. I don't know. It all seems rather a painful thought now.'

'I'm sure. Have you informed Alice?'

He cleared his throat. 'Yes.'

'And how did she react?'

'React?' He seemed suspicious of the question. He was right to be. Honora's questions are never idle curiosity. 'I've never seen her so upset. Her brother's with her, doing his best to keep her calm.'

Glenn covered his face with his hands. Poor man.

'Do you think she regrets her decision to call the wedding off?'

'How on earth should I know?' he replied, piqued. 'What are you suggesting?'

She didn't answer his question.

'Dr Wetherby, something else very strange occurred here last night.'

'And what is that?' He didn't hide his contempt.

'There was a burglary. A book was stolen.'

'So?'

'It was the only thing stolen.'

'And how does that affect me?'

'It was your book. *The Waterfall.*'

He stopped, surprised. 'Well, I . . . That's strange,' he recovered. 'But I don't see why you bring it up now, of all times.'

The doorbell rang, and there was more knocking on the door. 'Don't answer that!' Honora bawled at the maid, who was hurrying to the door. She scuttled away, terrified.

'I bring it up now,' Honora said, 'because I have to, Dr Wetherby. I'm sorry to say, Mr Glenn, that it seems likely that Fred was the person who broke in and took it.'

'Fred?' Glenn didn't sound surprised so much as beaten down, as if this were just one more painful detail about his son's death.

'We came back last night to find someone in here. It was dark, so we couldn't really make out who it was. Then he turned tail and ran.'

'It can't be Fred,' Dr Wetherby said. 'Why would he?'

There was hammering at the door now, and the inspector's voice demanding to be let in. Well, unless he was going to kick the bally timber in, he was going to have to wait until Honora was good and ready.

'We couldn't see his face, but he was wearing black clothes and pumps, just like Fred is wearing now.'

'But that means nothing!' Dr Wetherby insisted. 'Black clothes? It could be anyone.'

At that, we heard the side door opening. Ricci burst in, red-faced, with his constable at his heels. Honora and I went to head him off in the hallway, leaving the two men in the drawing room.

'I represent the law, and you do not shut me out!' Ricci growled.

'Who shut you out, Sergeant? Point the finger,' Honora demanded.

'You, you did it!'

'Prove it. You can't, can you? Well then, you had better keep your accusations to yourself or I'll be registering a suit for slander. If you have that under your Duce.'

The Commissario shook himself like a dog in a right paddy. 'I'll—'

'No, you won't. Now, pull yourself together. Dr Wetherby and Mr Glenn are in the drawing room. You don't need me to remind you of what that poor gentleman is going through. And don't look at me like that, young man. Especially since I am doing your job for you.'

'I do not *want* you to do my job for me.'

'Too late.' She filled him in on the break-in and what Fred was wearing. He didn't thank her but strode into the drawing room, and we followed.

'And just for your information, Signora, some of us do not like Il Duce. Some of us do not like him one bit.' He glanced at his constable and said something in Italian that sounded like a warning to keep his gob shut about what he had just heard. 'Mr Glenn?' he said, more calmly. Glenn nodded. 'I am very sorry, sir. I am Commissario Ricci of the Polizia di Stato, I attended the incident two nights ago. I will be looking into the circumstances of your son's death.'

'Thank you,' the man said quietly.

'I looked at your son, Signor. We will have to wait for the police doctor, but I think we can say he was deliberately killed by means of a line around his neck. I am very sorry, it cannot be easy to hear that.' Glenn slowly shook his head. 'Do you know where he was last night?'

It was Dr Wetherby who answered that. 'My consulting rooms are in my house. There are two rooms; he has one, I have the other next door. He was there until five, our normal time to finish. He said goodbye and left then.'

'How was he?'

'Perfectly normal. Although he has been a bit down recently, because he was engaged to my daughter, Alice, and she called it off.'

I saw Ricci's eyebrows lift up at that. 'A broken engagement, you say, Signor?'

'But it was Alice who broke it off, not Fred. So if you're looking for some sort of revenge motive, you'll have to look elsewhere.' I saw Glenn look pained at the line of questioning.

Honora pushed into the conversation. 'Was he wearing the clothes he's in now?'

'No, no. A suit as usual.'

'Therefore, at some point, he got changed. So we must put aside any wild theory that he didn't intend to break in, that he followed someone else in or there was some unexpected emergency that meant he had to enter the premises. Dressed all in black and v ith a torch, he intended to break and enter.'

'Thank you, Mrs Feldman,' Ricci said stiffly. Poor man wasn't feeling too much in control, that was clear enough. 'He lives with you, Mr Glenn?'

'For now. Eventually he would have bought a place with . . . Alice,' he said. 'We're on the Lazzaretto Vecchio in the bay.'

'You live there alone?'

'Yes. My wife passed away some years ago.' Good Lord, it was a wonder the man could function. 'That's Fred's dinghy. The one he . . . was found in.' His voice cracked.

'So he left the surgery. Sailed back to your island, changed, came back here, broke in, was chased away.' Ricci glared at me, as if I had been the attacker instead of the one guarding the castle. 'And then at some point was either killed in the boat or placed in it afterwards and set adrift. But we know nothing of what happened in between.'

'There is one thing of which we can be near-certain,' Honora said. Everyone looked at her expectantly. 'Fred was willing to take huge risks to get hold of that book and, within hours of him doing so, he was murdered. Oh yes, that book of yours, Dr Wetherby, is at the very heart of this.'

'Good God,' he said under his breath.

Chapter 9

An hour later, Fred's body had been briefly examined at the scene by the police doctor and taken to the American hospital, in a rich area of the city they call the Rialto, for a post mortem. We weren't allowed to witness that – not that I was jumping up and down wanting to sit in on it. Instead, we had to twiddle our thumbs in the waiting room.

Like most of Venice, it was a whopper of a Renaissance building. It had been a hospital for expectant mothers a century ago, and you half-expected a nun to come charging around the corner.

'The Rialto,' Honora said. 'Where Shylock vowed revenge by Christian example.'

'Come again?'

'Just something that rings a bell.' She fell to thinking.

We had been there half an hour on ancient wooden benches when I looked up to see two people I recognized enter: Alice and Gabriel Wetherby. She looked like she had cried so much that there were no more tears.

'What do you want here?' Gabriel demanded, coming up to us.

'I can't tell you how sorry we are about Fred,' Honora told him.

'I said, *what do you want here?*' His tone was anything but chummy.

'Just leave them,' Alice said. 'What does it matter?' And fresh tears leaked down her cheeks, poor old thing.

Honora gave me a look, and sometimes she can say entire sentences like that. I knew what she wanted. 'Would you like to get some air?' I asked Alice. 'There's a nice little courtyard out there. It's got a pond and seats. You could breathe a bit.'

'Don't you try—' her brother began. But she cut him off.

'Yes. I . . . want a bit of space for a minute.'

'It's that way,' I said, pointing to a corridor. She went, wiping her cheeks.

'Now, Gabriel,' Honora said once she was out of earshot. 'A serious crime has occurred, and I'll brook no shilly-shallying.'

'Won't you, now? Well, isn't that nice?' And he sat on one of the wooden benches. 'All right, on you go. Might as well draw out the bad tooth.'

'Have you any idea why someone might want to kill Fred?'

'None. Next question.'

'We will stay with the same one. Did you get on with Fred yourself?'

'Couldn't stand him.'

'Why was that?'

'Oh, why does anyone like or dislike anyone? I

thought my sister could do better.' He leaned back against the wall.

'Where were you last night?'

'At home. All night. Alice and I were listening to the wireless.'

'I'm off to the ladies',' I said.

'Are you?' he asked with a bit of suspicion.

I ignored him and headed off down a corridor in the opposite direction to the one where Alice had gone. Once out of sight, I ducked out of an open doorway and nipped around to the rear of the courtyard garden where I had sent her.

There she was, beside the clear-as-day pond, with her hands over her face.

'Hello,' I said. We stood in silence for a while. 'I've lost people, too.' She looked at me. 'My parents when I was a kid.' She nodded and tossed a small pebble into the pond. It sent violent ripples through the water. 'I don't understand, though. You obviously loved him, but you broke off the engagement. Why?'

She tossed in another. 'I met someone else,' she said quietly.

'Oh. Gosh.' I didn't know what to say to that. It's not as if she was guilty of anything. Our hearts are all over the place, if you ask me, never quite singing from the same hymnbook. 'Who?'

'That's private.'

I wasn't going to push her. 'Can you think of anything that might help us find out who did this to Fred?'

'I don't think so.'

'Did you see him yesterday? Last night?'

She shook her head. 'I didn't see anyone last night. I went for a walk to clear my head. It's been so awfully full of things recently. None of them very nice.'

'No, I'm sure.' And this wasn't going to make it any better. 'Did Fred ever mention your dad's books?'

'Dad's books? He might have, but not that I remember. Why?'

'So he didn't ask if you could get him a copy of any of them?'

She looked surprised. 'No. If he wanted one, he could just buy it, I suppose, or ask Dad to lend him one. We have enough of them in the house.'

Well, that made sense. But it left open the question of why Fred would go as far as breaking and entering to get hold of one.

'I probably got the wrong end of the stick. Look, are you ready to go back in?'

She nodded, and we headed back to the waiting room. Honora had finished with Gabriel by then. He looked at me with rock-solid suspicion, and I had to give it to him: he was right. I *had* tricked him. He would have said something about it if Commissario Ricci hadn't appeared just then.

'Mrs Feldman,' the officer said, like he was sucking a lemon.

'Sergeant.'

He didn't rise to the bait, instead taking Gabriel and Alice aside to speak to them. And he made certain they were out of earshot.

'Gabriel said they were listening to the radio together all yesterday evening,' I said.

'Yes?'

'Alice says she went for a walk. Alone.'

'Does she now?' Honora replied, under her breath. 'We'll see about that.'

She marched straight over and inserted herself between the policeman and Gabriel. 'You just lied to me, young man, and I don't like it when people do that.'

'Don't you?' he said contemptuously.

'Mrs Feldman!' Ricci said, making no attempt to hide how cheesed off he was. 'I am speaking to Mr Wetherby. Wait until I have finished, and you can conduct your own amateur enquiries.'

At that, Gabriel changed his tune. 'Having considered the matter, Mrs Feldman, I will happily answer any questions that you have,' he said. 'Fire away.'

'You lied about your movements last night.' He waited. 'Don't try the silent treatment with me. You know exactly what I'm talking about. You claimed you spent the whole evening at home with your sister, listening to the wireless. She doesn't concur.'

'Gabriel?' Alice piped up.

'It's all right,' he said to her. 'Right then, better slap on the old handcuffs and break out the bread and water, eh? What is it I'm supposed to say now: "You've got me bang to rights, it's a fair cop." Yes?'

'Gabriel!' Alice blurted out, upset. And she walked away, back towards the courtyard.

He looked sheepish at that. 'Maybe this isn't the time for flippancy,' he admitted. 'All right, I wasn't at home all yesterday evening. I went out on a private matter that does not concern you.'

'Everything concerns us,' Ricci said, moving around Honora so she no longer blocked him. 'Murder is the most serious crime.'

'I suppose it is.'

'So where were you?'

'It is the most serious crime, but my whereabouts last night are unconnected to it. Ergo I'm not going to tell you.'

'Young man, you will.'

'You seem to be threatening me with something.' He reached into his jacket pocket, pulled out a steel cigarette case and a scarlet book of matches with writing picked out in gold letters and lit a fag. 'And it's not yet eleven.'

'Aha!' Honora burst out, grabbing hold of his wrist to hold it aloft. 'What do you say to that, Pips?'

'What?' I replied, at a loss for anything sensible to say.

She plucked the book of matches from his grasp and held it up. The gold writing said *Paolo's*, which must have been the name of a bar or restaurant. 'You must understand the significance of these?' Gabriel was also struck dumb by Honora's display.

'Well, I do not,' spluttered the Commissario. 'Do you want me to take you in for questioning, too?'

'Not at all, Sergeant. We have much better places to be. Come on, Pips.'

And off we bashed, out of the hospital and into the street.

'Honora?'

'Where have we seen a book of matches like this?'

'Um.'

'Miss Grieves had an identical book. The bar, I presume, where they like to meet.' She examined it. '*Paolo's*. Probably very seedy.'

'Oh yes,' I said, not fully cottoning on.

'I would lay ten pounds that Gabriel was the young chap that Glenn saw pleading with Miss Grieves in the arch of the chapterhouse at the party. Which makes us ask, what was he pleading for?'

'I have a bloody good idea.'

'Language! And no, despite what they say, young men don't just have one thing on their minds. We must find out. And we can only do that from the young lady herself.'

Chapter 10

We took a water taxi and zipped over to Dr Wetherby's house. The taxi was older than the hills, and I thought I was going to have to jump out and push. We just about made it to the Lido, and as we came in we saw a huge flock of little blue birds dipping about in the harbour, which reminded me what a corker of a day we were missing.

We arrived at the house, which looked a little less like a film set by day. Still not of this age, but at least it looked real. Honora told the taxi to wait for us and led the way. When we rang the bell – electric, because there had to be some surrender to the modern age, it seemed – it was Miss Grieves who answered, saying that the doctor was out on a house call and wouldn't be back until that evening.

'Well, isn't that convenient?' Honora said, pushing past the poor girl. I said before that I couldn't have worn her shade of deep red lipstick, but I had nothing against her. 'Where can we talk?'

Grieves knew fine well that there was no point trying to put Honora off, so she took us into the office, where we wouldn't be overheard by any of the other staff. It was quite odd being there now that everything was calm, unlike the last time, when there had been a theft, a fire and general bedlam all around. This time, the scene of the crime was far away – we didn't even know where – and the victim was lying in the hospital morgue.

'Miss Grieves,' Honora said, examining the room. 'May I ask your first name?'

'Deliah.'

'Thank you. What was it that Gabriel Wetherby was begging you for on the night of the party?'

She arched like a cat ready to strike. '*That* is none of your business. And whatever little spy you sent after us should have better things to do with their time.'

'No spy. Just someone who observed you by chance.'

'By *chance*?' she said, mocking the word. 'It was William Glenn, wasn't it? Oh yes, I saw him watching us like a proper little Peeping Tom. He's always staring at me. What? Not going to answer? Not going to deny it?' She snorted.

'Miss Grieves. You can be as irritated as you like. But the fact is, Fred Glenn has been murdered. And if you don't answer me, you will be answering to the Polizia di Stato in the cells. And they won't be as polite as I am.'

That caused her a bit of a chill, you could see. I wondered if she had been in trouble with the law before.

She actually stamped her foot before answering. 'Sleeping tablets. Opium derivatives. He needs them.'

'And you refused?'

'Of course I refused. I'm not a fool.'

No, Deliah Grieves might have been many things, but she wasn't a fool, anyone could see that.

'So he stole them from the safe,' I said, remembering how Dr Wetherby had said that they had been taken during the break-in at the party.

'From the safe? What are you talking about? They're locked up with all the other drugs, in the dispensary.' She reached into her clutch bag and took a small brass key from it. 'The key.' I reached out for it automatically. She snatched it back, dropped it in her purse and clipped it closed.

'Are you and Gabriel stepping out?' I asked.

'Hardly.'

'Are you stepping out with anyone?'

She cocked her head to one side. 'You know how it is, love, men are always *around*, aren't they? You just have to be choosy. And don't throw all your lot in with one, because when you do, they're straight out on the street again without a second look at you.'

'Dr Wetherby's book, *The Waterfall*,' said Honora, changing tack.

'What about it?'

'Have you read it?'

'Not much else to do around here, most nights, other than read books.'

'I shall take that as a yes.'

'Take it any way you like, madam.'

'I have been told that the characters in it were based on members of this community.'

'First I've heard of it.'

'Is that true? Or was one based on you?'

I caught my breath. In the story set in the creepy old monastery or what-have-you, one of the characters was a little schemer who looked like butter wouldn't melt in her mouth but had all the men twisted around her little finger. Could that have been Deliah Grieves?

'That would have been hard to pull off, given that I never even met Dr Wetherby until after the book was published. Never even set foot in this country, while we're at it.'

'I see.' Well, that was a bit of a disappointment. For a second, I'd thought we'd caught our fox – and a wily one at that. No such luck.

Miss Grieves stubbed her cigarette out and crossed her arms defiantly. 'And now that you've asked your questions, will there be anything else?'

'Yes, there will,' Honora said.

'No, there will not!' called out a man's voice behind us. I spun around to see Commissario Ricci striding in from the hall. 'Miss Grieves, I have some questions for you.'

'I've just answered hers.'

'She is not the police. I am. Now, do you know who wanted to kill Fred Glenn?'

'No.'

'Are you telling me the truth?'

'She's hardly going to admit she's lying, is she?' Honora huffed.

'Mrs Feldman. Do not—'

'How well did you know Fred?'

'Well enough. Or are you suggesting something improper?'

'I'm sure you have your own ideas about propriety.'

'Mrs Feldman!' Ricci blurted out. 'I have had enough of you putting your nose in. This stops now. Give me that telephone.' Miss Grieves, looking at first surprised, then pleased at the intervention, handed him the phone. Ricci picked up the receiver and asked the operator for the police station. 'I'm going to have you removed from here.'

'You can try.'

His call connected. '*Sono Ricci. Voglio che— Che cosa?*' He stopped and listened. '*Capisco.*' He hung up. 'Well, you have got another chance. I must go.' He clocked the glance that passed between us. 'Do not follow me.'

We followed him. He and the constable tore off in a motor launch, but we were able to stay behind them in our water taxi, which was still waiting for us. We pulled in to shore a bit up the coastline and could instantly see what we had come for.

There, in a ditch, was a man's body. A couple of police who had come on bikes were standing beside it and guiding in a white ambulance.

Ricci shot us daggers as we jumped out. And as we scrambled closer, I saw whose the body was: Dr Wetherby. He wasn't moving, and there was a huge patch of blood on his shirt.

'Stand back!' Ricci barked, as two ambulance men hopped out with a stretcher. I did as I was told. One of the medics checked his pulse and said something to Ricci. While Honora poked about in the bushes nearby I asked Ricci what the man had said. He grumbled but answered me. 'He says he is alive, but only just. His pulse is very slow. He has lost blood.'

'Will he live?'

Ricci asked the ambulance man, who shrugged.

'Here,' Honora said. 'The weapon.'

Ricci's constable went over and used a handkerchief to pull a large knife out of the undergrowth, while the Commissario tried to rouse Dr Wetherby.

'Dr Wetherby?' he said. There was no response. 'Wake up!' He waited. 'Dr Wetherby, you have been attacked.' He beckoned to the ambulance men, who brought over the stretcher. 'We are going to take you to hospital.' They gingerly lifted him and laid him on the stretcher. His eyelids remained closed. The men scampered with him up to the ambulance just as Honora tramped back with the constable in tow.

'Well, that puts a new hat on matters,' she said.

'Dr Wetherby knew there were no drugs missing, because there had never been any in the safe in the first place. They were all locked away in the dispensary, according to Miss Grieves,' Honora said as we strode up to the hospital reception.

'So why did he claim they were?'

'I presume it was because he knew what was really missing, and who had been desperate enough to break in and take it.'

'Why would he do that? Protecting someone?'

'No doubt,' she said. 'The question is who.'

'So what was really taken from the safe?'

'That is what we are here to discover.' She addressed a nurse in a white booth, who was wearing a uniform that looked a good deal more like a nun's than a nurse's. 'My client was just admitted after an accident. His name is Dr Matthew Wetherby. Where is he?'

'Your name, please?' She was a local.

'Honora Feldman. Mrs.'

The nurse consulted a clipboard. 'I cannot find—'

'I will,' Honora replied, striding off. I ran along in her wake. An ancient nurse tried to stall us, but Honora simply batted the old girl out the way. The sister stared open-mouthed as we marched along, double-time.

The stone walls had been scored with hundreds of years of graffiti and what looked like musket-ball holes. It had seen some action, that clinic. 'You might think they would take a bit more pride in their interior decor,' Honora said. 'Come on, this way.' And she shoved apart a pair of double doors. It was the emergency ward, with a dozen or so curtained cubicles and a few sisters buzzing about like grey flies. 'There!' she said, pointing to a cubicle in the far corner.

'How do you know?'

'Do use your eyes, Pips. The shoes.' And I looked down to where the curtain didn't quite reach the floor, allowing us a peep at two pairs of black shoes. 'Formal but cheap, Pips, the mark of the policeman, whether he's in Italy or Inverness. Ricci!' And I swear I saw the legs in those shoes stiffen. 'Out you come.'

The curtain pulled back a little, and the face of the Commissario glared out, looking like absolute thunder. 'Mrs Feldman,' he growled. 'Do not presume to—'

'I presume nothing. I work on facts,' she returned, taking hold of the other end of the curtain and whipping it back so we could enter.

Ricci maintained his unfriendly look at us. 'I did not give you permission.'

'Not your hospital, is it? Now.' She examined the patient. Dr Wetherby appeared to be asleep. 'Has he been like this since you brought him in?'

'Yes,' the Commissario replied, exasperated.

'Is it life-threatening?'

'The doctors said not. The wounds are in his side and did not penetrate any organs. But we have to let him rest.'

'Well, he's no good to us like that.' She bent down to his ear. 'Dr Wetherby!' she called. 'Dr Wetherby!'

A young nurse poked her nose into the cubicle. 'Please keep the noise down.' She spoke with an American accent.

Honora ignored her. 'Dr Wetherby!' She poked his arm. Hard.

'Please don't do that!' the nurse said, coming fully in.

'Dr Wetherby. Ah.' His eyelids were fluttering, attempting to lift. With some effort, they made it all the way up. She spoke more softly now. 'Dr Wetherby. You are in hospital.'

The nurse prepared a syringe. 'Morphine, Dr Wetherby,' she said, pulling up his sleeve to administer it.

'No!' he said forcefully. 'No morphine!'

She looked taken aback. 'But the pain . . .'

'No morphine. Not now or when I'm asleep.'

The nurse was flustered but put the syringe away and bustled out. We glanced at each other. Well, if the chap preferred to be in pain, it was his decision. Honora spoke again. 'Do you remember what happened?'

'Stabbed me,' he said hoarsely.

'That's right. Can you tell us anything about it?'

'A woman. I . . . don't remember.'

'A woman? Who?' she asked urgently. 'What did she look like?'

'I don't know.' He breathed deeply but slowly. It looked like it hurt him.

'You lied to us about what was missing from your safe.' I saw Ricci start at this. 'Who are you protecting?'

He opened his lips and licked them. 'Fred,' he groaned, as sleep took him once more.

Chapter 11

'Fred?' I said. 'Golly.'

'Not so surprising when you think about it.' The ward sister had put her foot down and harried us out with threats in Italian that sounded quite deadly. 'But it's not entirely straightforward. Does he mean that Fred broke into the safe or that someone else did and the truth would somehow expose Fred?' We were walking through the Rialto, where there were shops offering all sorts of pretty traditional goods such as the most beautifully blown glass and thick paper like ivory.

'Fred's past caring, surely.'

'The dead care about their memory, Pips. That's why we have so many churches,' she said, pointing to one where we could see inside to a huge ceiling fresco of the Heavens.

We happened to spot Penelope on a café terrace across the street, wearing a wide-brimmed sun hat and dark glasses. She was with Erwan. She waved at us, and he stood up politely when he saw who she was waving at. He really was a dreamboat.

'Hullo,' I said to him when we got close.

'*Bonjour.*'

I saw Penelope fight back a grin. Honora made a point of ignoring us and ordered a lemon tea, while Penelope's glass was full of fruit and bright red liquid. I asked if it was fruit juice.

'Hardly, darling. Campari spritz. And just a hint of vodka to give it some wallop.'

'We could go for another drive tomorrow morning,' Erwan suggested to me.

'That would be lovely,' I said.

'No. You have an errand to run,' Honora said.

'Have I?'

'I take it there are English-language bookshops in town?' Honora asked Penelope.

'Oh yes,' she replied. 'Four or five at least.'

'Good. Pips, you're off to buy two copies of Dr Wetherby's book. Buy them from different shops.'

'I can just go and get them now.'

'No, the shops are shutting,' she told me.

'They are not!' She pointed to one that was just closing up. 'Oh, all right, tomorrow morning. But why do you want them from different shops?' She just looked at me with a raised eyebrow. I sighed. It was one of those dratted times that Honora just wanted it done without having to explain.

'Now, Penelope, you claimed that some of the characters in Dr Wetherby's book were based on real people. How did you come to that conclusion?'

'Well, it was just *said*, really. People just *said* it.'

'Idle gossip and tittle-tattle, was it?'

'Well, when you put it like that . . .'

'That *is* how I put it. Would you like to put it another way?'

'N-no. I suppose that's what it was. But wouldn't it be so thrilling if it were true?' Her eyes got so big that I thought they might have popped off her face.

'Then I think we can discount that theory. The book, Pips – your mission tomorrow will be vital to unlocking this little mystery. You mark my words.'

Well, at least I got to chat to Erwan a little before Honora dragged me away.

'There's somewhere I want to visit,' she said after we'd marched through the streets, past the fish market, across two little bridges and into a little square at the north of the island. Honora pointed to a plain-looking three-storey building with tall windows and columns around the doorway. 'In there.'

'In there? What is it?'

'Family history.'

She went to the door and pulled a little chain. A bell tinkled, and a little man with thick glasses and thicker white eyebrows looked out. '*Buona sera*,' he said. Honora beamed at him and pointed inside as a sort of dumb request to come in. He looked a little confused but stood back and let her enter. We were in a tiny, very plain vestibule and could hear men singing quietly on the other side of a pair of white-painted doors. The little man watched as Honora gently pushed them apart. She didn't enter but stood still and watched as two dozen men and a few ladies sat at pews in a large rectangular room. A pulpit at the far end was occupied by a big fellow singing louder and more beautifully than the others.

'Hebrew with an Italian accent,' Honora said fondly. 'It adds a certain flavour, doesn't it?'

'Oh,' I said.

'This was my grandparents' synagogue. Just a little one.'

She sighed with what I think was contentment. The little chap with the white hair smiled at us. I think he understood.

Chapter 12

The next morning, instead of going for a lovely drive with Erwan, I was nipping back over to Venice in the steam vaporetto. Even though it wasn't my first choice for the morning, I couldn't tire of entering that town by St Mark's Square. I imagined myself back in the sixteenth century, and I swear I would have been one of those girls who cut their hair short, grabbed a sword and pretended to be a man to join the navy and get into sea battles. It would have been wizard thrills manning the cannons and sinking a few galleons. Well, you can't blame a girl for having a heart from an earlier age, can you?

The thing is, I think Honora thought it would be tricky to find that book of Dr Wetherby's, *The Waterfall*. But it was easy as pie. The first English-language bookshop I went into, a little place with a wonky door, had it in stock, and I snapped it up for ten lire. Admittedly, the next couple of shops didn't, but then the next one did.

Sad to say, I couldn't idle in the town all day, though, because Honora would want the results, and pronto. So back I hopped to Villa Batley. 'Oh, she's down on the beach,' Penelope told me through about a pint of gin and tonic. 'But don't go yet. All work and no play makes Pips a dull girl!' She just about held me down and poured two mint juleps down my throat. Crikey, they were strong, too. I got to my feet, staggered a bit, shook myself like a dog coming out of a lake and tried to focus on one of the three doors that were swimming about in my vision. 'Go for the middle one,' Penelope said, guessing my condition. 'It's usually that one. Pip-pip, Pips!'

I managed to step outside, trip over a rock, pick myself up fully anaesthetized so that I didn't feel a thing, giggle and make it down to the beach, where Honora was swimming lengths – if you can do that in the sea.

'Hon . . . ora,' I called out. She was about fifteen yards from the shore.

'Are you tight?' she asked.

'Mint julep.'

'Penelope.'

'That's the gal.'

She powered back to the shore and looked disapprovingly down on me. I realized I had sat down without noticing it. 'There's a time and a place, Pips. This is not it. Come on.' And she frogmarched me back to the house.

'Come for another mint julep?' Penelope asked.

'She's had quite enough,' Honora told her. 'Probably enough for a regiment of dragoon guards. Now, sit down, Pips, before you fall down.' I did as she said. 'Tell me if you found the book on sale.'

'Eas'ly,' I said, suppressing a bit of a hiccough that wouldn't have helped the situation. 'I've bought copies from two shups.'

'Shups?'

'Shops.'

'Good. That demonstrates that there was little reason for Fred to break in here for a copy. There was something special about that one. Now, our next task is to read the book thoroughly to see if there's anything in the text that can lead us to why he did it.'

'Is it all right if I go for a bit of a lie-down first?' The floor seemed to be rocking under my feet.

'No, it is *not* all right. Take a cold shower-bath and then read it standing up. At least if you drop off, the fall will wake you. I will commence with my copy.'

I wasn't too keen, but I did as she said, taking the other copy of the book up with me. The cold shower did perk me up a bit. But I couldn't find anything in the book that would make anyone desperate enough to steal it. And murder? Not a bit.

'Apparently Dr Wetherby's awake,' Honora told me when I came down the stairs. 'But that halfwit sergeant has said that if I go near him, I'll be clapped in irons and sent back to Blighty in an air mail package. So I'm going to take this little novel,' she slapped the back of it, 'and finish reading it on the beach.'

Top luck! As I saw her stride down to the waterline, I ran back upstairs, dolled myself up and dashed out the front, over to Erwan's house, jumping into his little runabout while his coffee cup was half-way to his lips.

'I just broke out of gaol,' I said. 'Drive!'

He laughed his head off, got in and hit the accelerator. We powered forward and were topping forty in seconds. We were going far too fast, really, but we didn't care as the wind flipped my hat off and carried it away down to the sea.

'Where are we going?' I shouted over the sound of the engine.

'There is a place that is beautiful. San Nicolò beach. It is very quiet. Sand dunes and trees. No people.'

'Spiffing!'

It was as wonderful a day as ever. And the picnic was just as lovely, with fresh bread and cheese dipped in honey. Erwan had a glint in his eye all the while, and it wasn't long before I worked out why. My golly, the French smooch like no one else.

Afterwards, he popped into a shop to buy us some cool drinks, and I hunted through my purse for something to tie my hair back. I couldn't find anything, so opened the glove compartment and felt about. Well, dear reader, I didn't find what I was looking for, but I did find something else. A lipstick in deep red. And I had seen that shade before, on the mouth of Deliah Grieves.

Oh, Pips, I told myself. *Not again. You are a fathead.*

So I sadly hauled myself out and stared after him. Then I opened the bonnet, drained out all the coolant and advanced the ignition timing, so that the next time Erwan gunned the motor to impress a girl, there would be an almighty bang and no more engine.

Buck up, old girl, I said to myself as I walked home. *Mr Right's out there somewhere. You only need to bump into him once.*

Chapter 13

Honora took one look at me as I walked in.

'Ah, you realized,' she said, a little quieter than usual.

'Yes.' I sighed.

'The lipstick?'

'You knew about that? I just found it in the glove box.'

'Glove box? No, I saw it on his shirt. He had washed it, but the stain was obvious.'

'You could have told me.'

'I did my best to keep you away from him. And I've always tried to tell you, Pips: it's better to see for oneself than have others tell us what they see. Now, come on, there's no point crying over spilt milk. We need to speak to Aldrich.'

'To Aldrich?'

'Well, how else are we going to get his side of the story?'

I didn't even ask which story we were getting his side of.

We sauntered out and took Aldrich's motor launch

to the little town at the north end of the island. We found him in the tiny café where he'd had his thick coffee the first day we'd arrived.

'However did you know I'd be here?' he asked, with a little jammy pastry in his hand.

'We have your boat, so you can't have left the Lido. And when we jumped off the vaporetto that first day, you were here looking utterly in your element. And the café owner called you "Signor Batley". So I presumed this is your usual haunt when you want to get away from Penelope.'

He looked cheekily sheepish. 'Other end of the island entirely.' And he dipped his pastry in his coffee. 'She says my waistline is expanding. Well, it is, and I don't care!'

'A blood feud.'

'Pardon?'

'Penelope said that in Italy, if there's a dispute between two parties, it's either blood money or a blood feud. Was that what happened when the Glenns bought the house you had set your hearts on?'

'Good Lord, no! Are you suggesting—'

'I never suggest. If I want to suggest, I come out and say it.' She did, that was true. 'Now, what happened with the house? The Glenns offered more money?'

That sheepish look again. 'Not exactly. It was . . . Look, will any of this get back to Penelope?'

'Not a word unless it is a criminal matter. Then things are out of my hands.'

'Oh, no, no, no. Not a criminal matter. It's just that . . . well, I didn't want to live there. Did you know it was a plague island in the sixteenth century? The Black Death. Whoever wants to live among those ghosts? But Penelope was set on it. Quite set on it.' He looked to the left and right. 'So I quietly told the lawyers that we'd changed our minds and didn't want it after all. William Glenn swooped in, and I informed Penelope that he must have outbid us. Now everyone's happy.' He plopped the pastry in his mouth and winked at me. I had to laugh. Honora rolled her eyes in that way that you can hear.

'We have two more calls to make,' she said as she led me back to the motor launch.

'Where to?' I asked with a bit of a sigh.

'First, to the main island.'

Well, any excuse to pop over and mingle with all those hotsy-totsy young things parading around. So it wasn't long before I was opening up the throttle to send us flying between gondolas and a big ocean liner with people lining the rail and taking photographs.

'*Riva degli Schiavoni!*' Honora yelled at a surprised gondolier close to St Mark's Square. Poor darling didn't know what she was talking about. '*Riva degli Schiavoni!* Where?' she tried again, miming looking about her. He pointed to the southern side of the island. So off we tootled, up a couple of small canals, docking outside an old palazzo with a sign that read *Questura di Venezia*. It was obviously the main police station, because there were cop launches coming and going. Honora marched us in and insisted on seeing Commissario Ricci.

A minute later, the Commissario came out to meet us, carrying a glass of steaming coffee. I could see him sigh inwardly when he saw who was asking for him.

'Have you identified the woman who stabbed Dr Wetherby?' she barked at him across the reception desk.

'Not yet.'

'That doesn't surprise me one bit. Consider Wetherby's morphine. The morphine, Sergeant!' And with that, she did an about-turn and marched away.

'Commissario,' he muttered.

'What's next?' I asked as we jumped into the motor launch.

'That book. We know Fred could have easily picked up a copy in a number of shops, so what was special about the one he stole? We need to find that copy. So we're heading over to the Glenns' island, Lazzaretto Vecchio.'

A few minutes later, we were back skipping over the waves in Aldrich's boat towards the lump of rock in the lagoon that held the Glenns' house.

It was an attractive white modern building, sprawling a bit here and there, with big expanses of steel-framed windows. We tied up on a little jetty and climbed a few stone steps to the house. William Glenn came out to meet us. He danced about a bit in the funny nervous way he had.

'I'm sorry, was I expecting you?' he asked. 'Only I've been a bit distracted lately.'

'Of course you have, Mr Glenn,' I said. 'You've been through a lot.'

'Yes. It's been . . . Oh,' he said, losing his train of thought. 'Did you want something?'

'We would like to see Fred's room,' Honora said. 'There's something of his that we are looking for, and it could be very important.'

'In his room? I don't know.' He gazed back at the house. 'It's *his* room. It's not mine.'

'Yes, I'm sure it is. But we must look into it. In order to find out the truth. About everything.'

'Everything?'

'There's a lot here that doesn't meet the eye. I intend to get to the bottom of it.'

'Oh, I see.' His hands wrapped around each other. 'Then yes, come in.'

He led us in. It was very modern and sleek inside, like a motor showroom. Glenn showed us to Fred's room but didn't enter.

'Mr Glenn, we need to take a look around. You might prefer to leave us to it.'

He looked unhappy for a moment, his feet tapping on the parquet floor. Then he wandered away, back downstairs. 'Right, get everything out of there for a start,' Honora said, pointing to a round black desk.

I did as I was told. There wasn't much there. A cheque book, a few keepsakes, a notebook (unused) and stationery. She looked elsewhere as I hunted.

'Well, that wasn't hard,' she said with triumph, holding up the book that we had been looking for. 'Hidden behind the wardrobe.' She flicked through it a bit, then sat thoughtfully for a while. 'Oho, yes, I see. Well now, isn't that a thing?'

'Honora?'

'Not yet, Pips. But I'll tell you one thing: that idea of Penelope's that it all had something to do with characters in the book being based on real people was poppycock from beginning to end. Now, off we trot.'

We found Mr Glenn outside, seemingly unsure if he was allowed in his own house, gazing at a clump of low trees fifty-odd yards away. 'Thank you, Mr Glenn. We have what we need.' She shaded her eyes, gazing where he had been looking. Among the trees was a row of three stone tablets on the ground. Honora lowered her voice. 'Is that where your wife and servants are buried?'

'Yes,' he said, his voice cracking a little.

'Six years ago, you said. And at Christmas, too. So very, very cruel.' He bit his lower lip. 'I am sorry. Would you be so good as to come to Villa Batley tonight at seven? I think we would all benefit from your presence.'

'If you wish.'

Honora was quiet as we climbed into the little launch. 'History is full of cruel echoes, isn't it?' she said eventually.

'Is it?'

'Yes, it is. Just look at how William Glenn's island was a quarantine site for the Plague, and a modern pestilence took his wife from him. So very cruel, history.'

Chapter 14

Seven o'clock in the drawing room at Villa Batley, and everyone had arrived. Aldrich and Penelope were in evening dress handing out cocktails, enjoying themselves; Gabriel and Alice Wetherby were on the sofa – him looking bored, her looking nervy. Their father, Dr Wetherby, newly discharged from hospital, was in an upright chair. He walked stiffly, but otherwise he was recovering well. William Glenn was fidgeting, of course, looking first at us, then at the bookshelves – those that his son had ransacked – then out of the window in a mad sort of dance routine. Deliah Grieves had sat herself at the back of the room – so she could watch us all like a hawk, if you ask me. Commissario Ricci, who had turned up and not said a word, was irritably checking his watch, though his constable beside the door looked a bit more intrigued.

In the centre of it all, there was a little lectern, the type you would get in school so the schoolmaster could read to you from some dry old text. Only this one had a book that we all suddenly cared about a good deal: the copy of *The Waterfall* that Fred had stolen from Penelope and Aldrich and stashed in his room. Everyone had been instructed not to touch the book: it was to be left looming over them like the bally Sword of Damocles.

'I expected to be here on holiday,' Honora said, striding into the room from the hallway. 'I expected Venice to be a serene location. Historical. Cultured.'

'I have work to do.' It was Deliah Grieves.

'What are you saying?'

'I'm saying that you can stand around gossiping like this, but I've got work to do. The monthly accounts need balancing.'

'Oh, Miss Grieves, the accounts will be balanced tonight. You mark my words.' And Honora allowed herself a little smile. She doesn't often do that. Only when she's very pleased with what she has said.

'Honora, really, I'm on tenterhooks,' Penelope said, actually raising her hand like she was in class. 'Could we . . .'

'For most of us, the whole affair began the night of the party at Dr Wetherby's,' Honora continued, ignoring her. 'A fire, started deliberately so that a thief could break into the doctor's safe. Which was made rather easy by the fact that he'd left the key in his desk.'

'I'm a fool for it,' Dr Wetherby said.

'Yes. And the fact that the thief was your junior partner in the practice soon became evident. What was it that he was after so urgently and secretly? What couldn't he wait, even until the next day, to procure?'

'Drugs?' Penelope volunteered.

'But there weren't any in there. Were there, Miss Grieves?'

'They're locked in the dispensary,' she confirmed.

'Which often leaves you high and dry, doesn't it, Gabriel?'

'What?' he said, looking shocked. Then his face melted back into nonchalance. 'Oh, if you will. Yes, I need certain chemicals to keep going these days. Nothing wrong with that. It doesn't hurt anyone but myself.'

'Doesn't it?' Honora replied.

'What do you mean by—'

'And then, of course, Fred was tragically killed, his body found in his boat. Such a fine-looking young man and a faithful lover, wasn't he, Alice?'

'Yes,' she said.

'And yet, you broke off your engagement because you'd met someone else. That's what you told Pips?'

'Yes, I met someone else.'

'You're lying.'

Gabriel stood up. 'Don't bully her at this time. She has a right—'

'Oh, sit down,' Honora snapped at him. He looked to Alice, and she gently pulled him back into his seat. 'There was no one else. There never has been. You made that up to disguise the real reason that you ended it, didn't you?'

Her eyes became the size of saucers. 'I'm sorry,' she replied. 'I couldn't tell him. I couldn't tell anyone.'

'No, you couldn't, could you? Because you never *wanted* to end things, you *had* to. Something had come between you and Fred. Something quite monstrous.'

Alice turned and buried her face in her brother's shoulder. 'Get on with it!' he ordered Honora. 'This is causing her pain, and I think you're enjoying it.'

'I am enjoying nothing of this.'

'Neither am I now,' Penelope muttered.

'No? Penelope, you and Aldrich had – what was it you called it, a blood feud? – with the Glenn family, all over ownership of their island home, which you thought was rightfully yours.'

'Oh, now,' Aldrich yelped out. 'Come, come!'

'A "blighter", you called William Glenn, didn't you?'

'In the heat of the moment! That's all.'

'The heat of the moment. That is true. Though a lot can happen in the heat of the moment. But it is his son's death we are here to examine, not his.' Aldrich settled down, though Penelope looked shaken. 'Gabriel, I can assure you that I am not enjoying causing anyone pain. Because this whole affair has been one unfortunate victim after another.' She paused. 'And Fred wasn't the first.'

'Wasn't the first?' Glenn asked, confusion written all over his face. 'Fred wasn't the first?'

I could see the confusion spreading. And I didn't understand, either. There had been another victim that we hadn't known about?

'The first, Mr Glenn, was your wife.' At that, Alice sobbed hard. 'Isn't that right, Alice?'

The girl struggled to control herself but managed to whisper an answer. 'Yes.'

'*Dorothy?*' Glenn stood, seemingly unable to understand anything around him.

'The reason that Alice broke things off with Fred was that she knew the secret behind your wife's – his mother's – death.'

'Tell me,' Glenn said, amazed.

'But you couldn't tell him, could you?' Honora continued to Alice.

'*No. No.*' The poor girl was being tortured, but I didn't understand how.

'Better to end things entirely than live with a man, a man you loved, but keep such a terrible secret from him.'

'What secret? What happened?' Glenn insisted.

'Your wife died in a local outbreak of typhoid, isn't that right?'

'Yes. Dorothy, our cook and our gardener.'

'In a sense, though you may not feel it, it was lucky that you live so remotely. The quarantine was easy – after all, your island had functioned that way during the Plague.'

'I suppose so. Matthew arranged for food to be sent over.'

'That's right, I did,' Dr Wetherby confirmed.

'But you had to bury those poor people yourself. You spent Christmas of 1925 digging graves for your beloved wife and your two servants.'

Glenn went to the window, looked out and wiped his hands over the top of his head. 'It was horrible. Horrible.'

'But you yourself survived, despite being exposed to it. Because typhoid doesn't affect everyone. Some people are naturally immune, some are carriers but have only mild symptoms. Is that correct, Dr Wetherby?'

'Yes, quite correct,' he confirmed, watching her hard.

'It was never established how your wife came to be infected at Christmas 1925, was it, Mr Glenn?'

'Oh, what did it matter? She was dead,' he replied, throwing up his hands.

'Yes, of course.' Honora went to the lectern and picked up the copy of the book that we had found in Fred's room. *The Waterfall.* 'A story within a story. Is there a term for that sort of book?'

'The term is *mise en abyme*,' Dr Wetherby said.

'*Mise en abyme*. And what does it mean?'

'It means "placed in the abyss."'

'Placed in the abyss. An abyss of stories. Yes, that seems appropriate. There's a lot about disease in this book of yours, too.'

'I suppose so.'

'This book. This little book. All this tragedy flowed from the existence of this book.'

'What? How?' Dr Wetherby asked.

'Yes, how?' Commissario Ricci added, annoyed. 'I read it from cover to cover. Every word. Nothing in it I could see.'

'No, you didn't read every word. You read every *printed* word,' said Honora. 'The secret is in those that weren't printed. The secret is in those that were written in this single copy by hand.'

And she opened the cover of the book to show the first page, with an inscription written by Dr Matthew Wetherby.

To Penelope and Aldrich, for your years of friendship.
Matthew Wetherby, 10 December 1925

'Oh God,' said Aldrich, standing up. His glass fell from his fingers. It hit the marble floor and broke into a thousand bits. He stared at the doctor.

'What is it?' Penelope said, staring at him.

'He understands,' Honora told her.

'Understands what?'

'At the party, you said Dr Wetherby signed this book to you when he came over to your house to treat you for a bout of gastric illness, what you called "Delhi Belly", after you had come back from a trip to India.'

'Oh!' she gasped. It was dawning on her too.

'It was rather more serious than that,' Honora said gravely. 'It was typhoid.' Penelope put her hand to her mouth, horrified. 'And two weeks later, it killed Dorothy Glenn.'

'B-but I never even saw her,' Penelope insisted. 'We hadn't spoken to them in years. It can't have been me who gave it to her.'

'It wasn't,' Honora said. 'It was someone else.' She turned to Alice. The girl had tears streaming down her face. 'Speak up now. It's time.'

'It was . . .' Alice started, struggling to talk.

'Don't say a word!' her father bellowed at her, leaping up. Ricci grabbed hold of him. 'Don't say a word!'

'Too late, Wetherby!' Honora barked at him. 'Say your piece, Alice.'

'It was him,' Alice said, pointing at her father

through her tears. 'He told me after I said I was going to marry Fred. He was drunk.'

'What did he say?' Glenn asked, barely able to comprehend what he was hearing.

'She's lying!' Wetherby shouted, trying to pull himself free, but the constable ran over and he and Ricci forced him to the floor. 'Can't you see she's lying?'

'He said it was his fault,' she bawled, turning away from him. 'He didn't recognize the symptoms. He should have sterilized all his equipment but didn't because he thought it was just a stomach bug.'

'No!' Wetherby shouted.

'He gave Fred's mum her anaemia injection.'

'ALICE!'

'Quiet!' Ricci ordered him.

'YOU!' Wetherby snarled at Honora.

'Quiet or I will put a gag on you!'

But Wetherby was a big man and threw him off. The others scrambled to their feet, but Wetherby was already leaping at Honora, threatening his own retribution against her. The constable had more about him than I'd thought, and chucked himself at Wetherby's legs, knocking them out; and then they were both down, grappling. By that time, though, good old Commissario Ricci had a pair of handcuffs out and was pinning the doctor down. On went the cuffs, and then it was all over. Wetherby lay there, seething like a tiger.

Poor Mr Glenn turned and stared out the window, and I saw him wiping away tears.

'At the party,' Honora explained, glaring at the captive but barely shaken, 'Fred overheard us speaking of Wetherby's visit to Penelope. He guessed the truth but needed to be certain. First, he started the fire so that he could steal the medical files from that year from the office. Thankfully, Miss Grieves revealed that you were lying about the restricted drugs being the target of the break-in.'

'You treacherous little tart!' Wetherby growled at Miss Grieves. She didn't reply but looked away with a sneer.

'But I presume those records didn't tell him what he needed to know – the date you'd visited the Batleys. Maybe you had destroyed the relevant notes to hide your mistake. He needed this book with its damning inscription.' She placed it back onto the little lectern. 'He stole it, took it home, found that the date tallied with the outbreak at his parents' home and went over to confront you.'

'And Wetherby strangled him?' Ricci asked.

'Yes.'

Alice sank her head into her lap. I simply couldn't guess what she had been through. Her loyalty to her father, her love for Fred, it must have added up to a dreadful storm inside her.

'But then, who tried to kill this one?' the Commissario asked, dragging his prisoner up to his knees.

'It's obvious now, surely,' Honora answered him.

'No one,' I said, realizing. 'He staged it.'

'Simple enough,' she explained. 'He stabbed himself in the side to produce a lot of blood, but away from any major organs. Digitalin or something similar would have slowed his pulse to look like he was close to death. That ruse took him off the suspect list. For a while.'

It was quite a revelation.

'What made you realize it was a ruse?' Penelope asked.

Honora turned to me. 'When we attended him in hospital, do you remember the very first words he spoke?'

I tried to think back. 'Something about the woman who attacked him, wasn't it?'

She tutted. 'His very first words were to refuse morphine. He was adamant. And why would a man who has been wounded and must be in severe pain refuse morphine?'

'Because he had already taken it!' I burst out, staring at him.

'Precisely. He had taken a large dose of it before he stabbed himself. And he knew that another dose so soon could be fatal. Yes, it was clear that it was all a blind.'

'*Alla stazione*,' Ricci told his constable. Between them, they wrestled Wetherby through the door. He wasn't shouting threats at us anymore, but the look in his eyes said he would have torn us limb from limb if he'd been able.

Gabriel rose then. 'You're a bully, Father. A coward and a bully.'

Wetherby took these words like stone. The police dragged him away.

'Horrible, horrible,' I heard Penelope say.

Mr Glenn wandered out in their wake, though I don't think he was following them. The poor man just wanted to be alone.

There was silence as we heard the house become quiet after the storm.

'What now?' Penelope asked, looking quite lost in her own home.

Honora took a deep breath. 'An evening dip, I think,' she replied. 'I'm here for my health. Doctor's orders.' She glanced at the door. 'Though we can't always trust them, can we?'

Chapter 1

Hollywood, 1944

Ken Kourian sat in a fold-up director's chair and watched himself strangle a German officer. The fake version of him – a hulking six foot four, with a jaw chiselled right off Mount Rushmore and muscles the size of the Chrysler Building – was a mute brute, punching his way through the German sentries to destroy an airplane parts factory outside Paris.

It was crazy to see how his countrymen wanted the war and his part in it depicted. On the screen, it was a thrilling boxing match out in the open, when the reality was a dirty street fight that no one would want to relive.

His eyes ranged over the set, on a huge sound stage in Burbank on the edge of Hollywood. There were real trees and fake soldiers.

'Here's your ticket to Hell!' the false-Ken snarled as he knocked a sentry unconscious with a single punch, before shooting another one sixty yards away with a stolen Luger. It would have been a hell of a shot if it had been real.

Ken had bribed and broken into German-run factories on sabotage operations, it was true – although it had been in occupied Romania, not France; and when he had done it, he had counted it a success if he was in and out without so much as the janitor seeing him.

But: Hollywood. This was a wartime propaganda film to lift the spirits of the American people in heavy 1944, and who was he to argue with that? No, he would let them have their hero.

The director called, 'Cut! Print it!', and everyone stopped what they were doing and breathed out. The huge lights dimmed, the actors drifted away, the studio doors were opened to let some of the heat from the lights and the sweat-drenched bodies blow out into the late morning.

The fake Ken – rebadged as Lieutenant Sam Walker – walked over to the real one. 'How'd I do?' he drawled.

'More like me than I know.' Ken was in good shape for a man who had been living on what he was sent by the British by airdrop and what he could scrounge from the partisans. He had pale green eyes that lit up when sunlight fell across them, and he was tall – six foot and an inch – but not so tall as to invite attention, which was important for his work. He had stood out enough already with his cover as a member of Romania's Armenian population. The Germans barely knew the difference, but the locals knew better. He had been living there for two years, watching the occupying troops, interfering with their supply lines, stirring up the native populace, and it would have been a damn sight harder to do that from inside a cell. He had once seen into one of those cells.

It was all a far cry from what he had expected when he had first come to California five years earlier. A youth in small town in Georgia, then college in Boston and a stint as a bit-player in Hollywood himself until the war had intervened. Now he was enjoying his leave before redeployment with the Office of Strategic Services – and a kind of fame organized by the War Department, even though his real name hadn't been revealed even to the producer of the movie.

'I want to get it right, Sam. I want my performance to be the truth,' the actor said, holding Ken's gaze hard like some kind of lunatic.

'Johnny, this *isn't* true,' Ken told him, waving a hand towards the set, where the production crew were taking a shed to pieces. 'It's not like that.'

'Why not? I mean, how?'

'Well, for one thing, you try not to kill people face to face, because they tend to fight back. You want to get in quietly, plant the charges and get the hell out of there before anyone sees you.'

Johnny looked distressed. 'But I need it to be true. If it's not, I can't . . . My acting coach says . . .'

'Johnny, trust me: you could bite those Germans in two and your acting coach won't know the difference. Just remember that the folks paying their dimes to see this are the only ones who matter. You're an American hero, Johnny, remember that.'

Johnny flashed teeth so white they could have lit

the set. 'Okay, Sam, okay. Yeah, I'll remember that. Hey, you sticking around for the party?'

At the edge of the stage, Ken could already see trestle tables being set up with drinks to celebrate the last shooting day before a two-day break. After the break, they would move to an exterior location for a scene where Ken's character commandeered an armoured car and blasted his way to freedom. Beyond the tables, making a half-hearted attempt to hide behind the props table, one of the actors and an extra had their heads down over something flat, before both jerking their heads up and rubbing their noses.

There had been a time when all Ken had wanted was to be in the movies. But when war had come, he had changed. Informed by what he had seen in the occupied nations of Europe, he had gained a sense of *what this is for* that he had never had before. The constant deception, though – that he wasn't so keen on.

'I'm not sure, Johnny.'

'Well, I hope you can. I need some more pointers.'

You sure do, Ken thought to himself. And then something – someone – else caught his eye. She was sitting in the shadows at the back, the red glow of a cigarette contrasting with her long dark hair. The smoke was a Nat Sherman, he knew, and it was held in an amber holder. He had no idea how long she had been there. 'I'll try to make it.'

'Okay.' And with that, Johnny left, pausing to tell a runner to send fresh iced water to his dressing room.

Ken watched him leave, then turned back to the woman at the rear of the sound stage. She didn't move as he walked back to her around mounds of discarded costumes and shooting scripts that lay like tombstones on the rubber-coated floor.

She dropped her cigarette and pressed it into the floor with her shoe.

'Where can we go?' she asked.

Chapter 2

The biographer carefully closed the door of his car and tried to read the house in front of him. He was occasionally called to the homes of wealthy businessmen who wanted their life stories set down in print, because that made them feel twice as important as their rivals without books. They usually had a few anecdotes and a lot of self-aggrandizing dross to tell, and he did all he could to turn it into a full book's worth. Sometimes, like now, he had no idea where they got his name from.

It looked like the family came from old money, though, because the house was a nineteenth-century Roman mansion some way out of the city, out towards San Miguel Mountain. Who had first owned it and why they had built it all the way out here were questions not on his mind as he crunched over the mix of gravel and tall weeds that made up the huge, sweeping driveway. The place was three storeys high and shaped like a bird of prey: a long, thin and muscular middle with classical pillars and a frieze of foreign animals around the entrance, and two wide wings that rose up at anyone arriving at the house. But the white stucco facades were now so broken up that there was more crack than surface. He had seen more welcoming cemeteries.

As he approached, two girls, neatly dressed in black skirts and white short-sleeved blouses, aged about ten and twelve, suddenly crawled out of the dense undergrowth to the side of the house, stopped in front of him and walked sedately to the entrance, a big double door, sporting a lion's-head knocker, that had been painted white but since turned to grey, like the rest of the building. He got the impression that the girls, who both had dark hair tied back with green ribbons, were the only escort he was going to get.

The older one twisted a black iron handle. No key needed; no one was going to rob this place. It swung back as the girl pushed with her full weight. The hinges whined like hell.

Inside proved to be an unusual oval-shaped hallway with a thin layer of dust and dirt on the wooden floor. Another layer coated the walls and the busts of Roman senators gathered together in groups of two or three like they had never stopped conspiring against Julius Caesar. One of the statues had become home to a bird's nest, constructed from bits of trash the bird had scavenged from the house. He wondered how the two girls were so neatly turned out, given the heap they lived in.

'What's that?' he asked. The younger girl looked at him inquisitively. 'The vibration in the floor. Like machinery operating. Young lady?' The girl just skipped on, approaching one of the doorways.

'Our brother's in here,' the older one said.

The visitor noticed some old bruises on her arm. She saw him looking and covered them with her hand.

'Allow me,' he said, pushing open the door. It ground over caked dirt to reveal a long, narrow room. Very long. So long, in fact, that it looked like he was staring right through to another house altogether. Strangely, though, it was bare except for at the very end, where French windows were letting bright sunlight stream in, forcing him to shield his eyes. The mechanical vibration was coming from the end of the room. As his vision focused, he could make out a large metal machine, the size of a small car, silhouetted by the harsh light. But it wasn't just a machine. Encased within it was a man, lying on his back with just his head exposed. And suspended above him was a mirror, tilted at forty-five degrees so that he could see around him even while he couldn't move. The writer had seen such machines before: iron lungs. A lifeline for victims of polio or botulism who couldn't breathe for themselves, it took over, expanding and compressing their chests. It was a coffin for the living.

'My agency said you were looking for a biographer.' His eyes met those of the man inside the machine. They were brown and soft, like the hair that hung down around the handsome face. He smiled.

Then there was a sound, a hollow metallic rapping, coming from within the iron lung. Three taps, then a pause. Three again. The man's reflected brown eyes didn't leave the writer's for a second. They seemed amused and curious. The girls went quickly to the machine, and the elder slowly lifted a handle, opening it up along its length, hinged at the far end so that both long sides lifted. The younger hurried to bring over a set of three steel steps. They stood beside a cart holding a large yellow gas canister with a rubber hose coming out of the top.

The metal steps screeched as she pulled them across the floor, while the upper half of the iron lung tilted up to expose the man's body. He shifted so he could look directly at the biographer through the dust swimming in the air. He was fully dressed in a powder-blue suit, with even a white handkerchief in his top pocket. And yet there was something strange about the clothes: they were almost rags, torn, stained and worn.

When the steps were in place, the younger girl ran to the canister and wheeled it next to her brother's head. He handed her the short wooden baton that he had used to bang on the inside of the iron lung; and in return she handed him the hose, which he took limply. She turned a lever on the canister and he placed the end of the hose between his lips. They waited for a few moments, then he languidly pulled an elasticated strap around his jaw to keep the tube in place. All the while, his eyes were locked on the other man's. His mouth closed tight around the hose, stayed for three seconds, then opened.

Even from a distance of ten yards, the writer could see his client's body bloat and then collapse as air from the canister first filled his lungs, then ebbed away as he let it go. Sometimes the subjects who paid him to write their life stories did it because they could feel the end closing in.

The man in the machine sucked in again, blew out again; only this time, there were words on the escaping air.

'I . . . am . . . Gabriel . . . Faulkner.'

He smiled around the tube in his mouth.

He looked about thirty years old, though he might have been younger. He banged twice on the inside of the iron lung, and the two girls rushed to either side of it, pushing and pulling his upper body upright and over, so that it flopped over the side of the machine. The girls hurried to support him under his shoulders. All the time, his breath was weak and rasping, his body bloating and then falling into itself. If he had muscles at all, they must have been like a baby's after a lifetime spent in that metal coffin. The biographer went to help, but his subject weakly waved him away.

Inch by inch, the two girls hauled Gabriel Faulkner over the side of the machine and down onto the steps. He managed to lower one foot and then the other unsteadily onto the metal. As he made it to the floor, held up by childish arms, he dropped forward to the frame of the cart holding the canister, using it as a new prop for his weight. With the girls holding him from the sides, he could wheel himself gradually towards his visitor. The wheels squeaked like mice running from a cat.

'This . . . way.'

And they all set off in procession over the gritty floor towards a door in the side of the room. The patient slowly, painfully, reached into his jacket and pulled out a ring of steel keys. He selected one, slid it into the lock and turned. It ground in the chamber. The ring was replaced, and the two girls ran to push the door open. Faulkner resumed his course, squeaking across the threshold, followed by his biographer.

The room beyond was in darkness until one of the girls flicked a light switch, leaving the visitor both agog and revolted at the sight before him.

The huge room, thirty yards in length and surely built for parties or balls with a hundred or more guests, was full of the tableware, the furniture, the decorations for a celebration. Elegant bottles crowded the tables, while upon a low stage two violins, a viola and a cello waited on chairs, seemingly ready to strike up at any moment. A microphone stood before them, ready for a compère to set the room a-roar.

Yet all were covered in dust, in cobwebs, in a layer of suspended life.

But far more offensive was an overpowering smell of rot. It was coming from mouldy piles of what had once been food set on dishes on the tablecloths. Food turned to grey mush covered in white mould, oozing putrid juices that stank like foul earth. Something on the ground scuttled away. Mice were the only diners at this party.

'What happened here?' the writer had to ask.

Faulkner stopped and laboriously turned his upper body a little to face his guest. 'Nothing . . . happened . . . here,' he said on breaths supplied by his machine. Then he started back on his slow track along the length of the room. The cart's wheels left long snake tracks in the dust.

At the other end, the ceremony of the keys was played out again, and then they were in a new room. Only this time, there was no need for electric light, because the California late afternoon sun was pouring in.

It was an octagonal room, obviously a library because the walls were lined with bookshelves and works of art. The centrepiece was something that took the biographer's breath away with its medieval intensity: a wooden panel painted with a huge red serpent that was chewing up what he took to be naked sinners and spitting them down to Hell.

And there was another obsession here: a single book. The room held hundreds of copies of it. Every shelf of every bookcase had copies of a single title with a dark blue cover. There were piles of the book on the floor and a ragged stack on a writing desk set before a floor-to-ceiling window.

Gabriel Faulkner staggered to the writing desk, and his sisters eased him down into a leather captain's chair. The older one tried to adjust the strap on his breathing tube, but he slapped her hand away, hard. The writer, surprised by the assault, started forward, but she shook her head.

'Yes . . . I . . . want . . . a . . . biographer.'

'Why?' He was not convinced he wanted any part of this man's life.

'Don't . . . we . . . all . . . want . . . to . . . explain . . . ourselves?'

'I guess that's true.'

'And . . . no . . . one . . . knows . . . when . . . we . . . will . . . have . . . to.' Something like a contracted smile formed. Then his eyes followed his guest's back to the chaotic shelves. 'You . . . want . . . to . . . see . . . my . . . book?' The visitor raised his eyebrows. For sure, he was curious about the volume that was in sight wherever he looked, and it must have some relevance to the biography that this weak – maybe dying – man wanted written about himself. 'Go . . . ahead.'

The writer reached to an overbalancing stack of the books by his side. He picked up the top one, not caring that it sent the rest of the pile toppling to the floor – it would make little difference. '*The Waterfall*. Haven't heard of it.' The older girl looked nervously at the man attached to the air canister.

'No,' hissed the patient. 'There . . . is . . . a . . . reason . . . for . . . that.'

'A reason?' He glanced at the book. The cover showed a golden key on the distressed blue background.

'Turn . . . it . . . over.' The man flipped the book head-to-tail. 'You . . . see?'

'I see another book.' It was another book, all right. This one was called *The Turnglass*, and the cover showed an hourglass with time running out. It had a different writer's name: Oliver Tooke. The name rang a distant bell – he was sure he had heard it someplace before. 'Who's the other author?'

'Dead.'

'I see.' Yes, he was sure he had heard the name.

'Died . . . before . . . my . . . party. The . . . launch.'

'The party was to be Gabriel's day of glory,' whispered the elder sister.

'My . . . day . . . of . . . glory.'

'What happened to the book?'

'Withdrawn.'

'Withdrawn? That must have been tough. Did you do anything about it? Sue the company?'

'I . . . tried. My . . . Hollywood . . . lawyer . . . tried.'

'I take it you had no luck.'

'Tooke . . . money . . . buried . . . the . . . case.'

'The Tookes are powerful,' said the girl.

Chapter 3

It was the last room in the hotel. The clerk told them they were lucky.

'What would Riley do if he knew?' Ken asked.

'I can't say.'

Los Angeles in the spring meant bright mornings and foggy afternoons that blotted out the mountains beyond the Hollywood hills. Now it was dusk, and the neon signs were flickering to life, promising movies set in far-off lands and endless whisky.

Ken lay back. The bed was comfortable but had been used too much. They had all been used too much. In the next room, a radio was turned on, then turned off again as the voice of a newscaster droned out of it. Everyone wanted to forget what was going on in the world. No horizons beyond what you could see. Just the room, the house, the tennis court, the forest. Living in the moment had become the greatest of all national pastimes.

'Coraline,' he said. She pushed herself up from the mattress. 'Where are you going?'

'You only use my name like that when you have

something hard to say. So I'm going to listen to it standing up.' She went over to the window, leaned against the frame and waited. The dusk light, turning grey, filtered in a haze around her. She had dark hair that reached her waist and seemed an extravagance in wartime. It looked black when it fell across her pale skin but was probably the deepest brown. Her clothes reeked of wealth, wealth that meant that even if it was wartime, she wasn't going to go without. She was thin, sure, but that was by choice and nature, not by deprivation. Her small chin and short, sharp nose completed the look.

'I'm going back,' he said.

'Of course you are,' she whispered. And she opened the window. The heat blew in. A bus honked low and long. A man on a bicycle screamed at the driver.

'We're making a difference. A small one.'

'"We."'

'Yes.'

'And you're not making any difference here.'

He placed his hands, fingers knit together, under his head. 'No,' he said. He could feel the sweat pooling under his back, seeping into the sheet. There was a long pause. 'Are you sure that . . .'

'I wasn't followed here?' She moved so that she stood bare before the open window. An old woman in an office building opposite glanced at her, then went back to mopping the floor. 'No, I can't be sure. I can never be sure. What are *you* sure of?'

'Not so much.'

She threw her smoke out the window. 'Was I

supposed to wait for you? Pine away? Keep a candle burning in my window?'

'The candle would have been a nice touch.'

'I'm a Tooke. We're not made like that.'

'Don't I know it.'

'How dare you go back,' she said under her breath, more to herself than to him. 'How dare you.'

Ken got out of bed and pulled on his clothes. 'It's a bigger world than the two of us.'

'I have an atlas.'

'Maybe you should use it.' She glowered at him. He relented but spoke his mind. 'Or maybe you should have had a little faith.'

'A little faith? And where's that got me in the past?' She lifted her powder-blue pencil skirt from the floor, examined it, then flung it across the room. It snagged on a chest of drawers by the bedside and hung limply like a flag on a still day.

Beside it, his tan suit looked cheap. It looked wartime. It looked like it was the suit of a man just like all the others on the street who weren't in uniform: the lucky, the unlucky, the maimed, the vital-to-the-nation's-ability-to-carry-on. *Which is he?* he could see people thinking as he passed them on the sidewalk. Well, none of those. He was just taking a break from a life that a hundred million souls couldn't take a break from. They'd had the bad luck to be born in Greece, France, Czechoslovakia, Yugoslavia.

'We're hosting a party tonight. The mayor's going to be there,' she said. Her voice was falling back into its natural softness that brought people in close.

'The mayor wants to be seen with your husband?'

'Riley's a respectable businessman. You know that.'

'I've met more respectable bums.'

'Well then, why don't you go hang around with them?'

'Maybe I will.'

A fly buzzed across the ceiling and settled on the glass lightshade. Ken went to the bathroom to wash his face. At least the faucet had good water pressure. LA had been going through a rough patch with the water supply, and the aqueduct that brought it from the Owens Valley had become a sort of cement god that the city's authorities prayed to every morning and every night and three times on a Sunday. *The Water Wars Are Heating Up!* one tabloid had shouted from the newsstand that morning.

From where he was, Ken heard a knock on the bedroom door and the itchy shuffling of feet that always announced a bell boy who wasn't too interested in his job. Ken waited until it became obvious that Coraline wasn't going to move from the window, then went to answer it himself.

A Mexican child, maybe fourteen, was outside, in a uniform that made him look like a wedding cake. He paused chewing gum just long enough to hand over a package wrapped in brown paper and white string. 'Thank you, sir,' he said mechanically, before staring past Ken to where Coraline remained by the window. Ken pushed him away, and the boy spun on his heels and ran towards the elevator, no doubt to tell the other bell boys that if they had a chance to attend Room 411, they should take it.

The package was rectangular and about the size of a dinner plate. A yellow address label on the front had Coraline's name on it. Ken tossed it onto the bed and sat with his back against the headrest.

'It's for you,' he said.

She took no notice of it. 'How many more years do we have of this?'

'Depends how lucky we get.'

'Sometimes I think about a giant tidal wave coming over and washing us all away.'

'Wait long enough, it'll arrive.'

'You know that's not a threat to me, it's a promise.'

'Do you want this?' He lifted the package.

'I don't know. What's in it?' she said.

'For all I know, it's a yacht folded in half forty times.'

'Open it.'

He untied the string and tore away the paper. In his hands was a book with a bright cover showing an hourglass. It was both incredibly familiar and incredibly strange at the same time. *The Turnglass*, the title blared in white text.

He stared at the door, then at her. 'Did you order this?'

'I didn't order anything.' She glared at it like it was an intruder.

The last novel written by her brother before he died. The cause of his death. It was a queer book. There were two separate stories, printed back-to-back and head-to-tail. Oliver's, *The Turnglass*, formed one side of the book. It had exposed deep family secrets, and someone had been so incensed and so afraid of them that they had killed him. The other story, which formed the other side, had been written by someone else and was a series of tales within tales.

'Okay, if you didn't order it, what the hell's it doing here?'

'How should *I* know?'

'It's addressed to you.' He turned it over in his hands. 'And if you didn't order it, the fact that it's addressed to you makes me think that it's a message to you.'

'From who?'

'Riley.'

'You really think Riley sent it?'

He put the book aside. 'I don't know. But even gangsters read books.'

'He's not a gangster,' she replied, side-eyeing him.

'Not exactly a nun, is he?'

'He hasn't broken the law since he was a kid on the streets.'

'Not himself, no. He's far too smart for that.'

She faced him fully now. 'And how do you know so much about my husband?'

'I know because I found out. It's not hard to find things out if you want to.'

The air stopped dead. There were things the two of them had found out in the past that they both wished they never had. They never spoke about them.

'He doesn't know about us,' she said.

'You sure about that?' he replied sceptically. He got up and went to the window. He couldn't see anyone loitering on the street.

'If he knew, he wouldn't be sending me gifts. Not even cryptic ones.'

Ken lifted the receiver on the telephone by the bed. He was connected to the reception desk.

'This is Room 411. Someone just sent us a package. Can you tell me where it came from?' An old and tired woman said that she would try and could he please hold the line.

'What *would* he do?' Ken asked, interested in what his immediate future might hold. She didn't answer. 'No, I guess I don't want to know.' He slid the book across the bed to her. She picked it up and opened the cover. He watched her read the ink on the pages, her hooded eyes sliding along the paper word by word.

'You haven't read it enough times?' She shut it hard. 'Only— Yes, hello? Okay, thanks.' He hung up. 'It came by hand a few minutes ago, delivered by a kid on a bike. They have no idea who he was. Some message.'

'I told you, it's not a message,' she insisted angrily.

'Keep telling yourself that.'

'He has no idea!'

'Then someone else has.'

'Why? Because a book gets sent to a room?'

She flung it across the room in the same direction as her skirt. Then she grabbed all her clothes, threw them on and stormed out of the room. Ken was left watching the air settle behind her.

The afternoon had been one of their more successful ones.

Chapter 4

The hotel was on Venice Beach. 'Venice': some property developer's idea to turn an empty beachfront in Los Angeles into an Italian town by digging a few canals, putting up some fake-Renaissance buildings and giving it an optimistic name.

They always met here because the first time they had arranged to meet at the pier for want of anywhere better, and the sight of miniature gondolas steaming up and down the canals had given them something to talk about.

Ken walked along the beach, stepping around families on their day out. His apartment was in East Hollywood, and he caught a streetcar heading that way; but as the sun slipped down to touch the top of the buildings, he jumped off and changed to one going to dried-out Elysian Park, where kids were packing up their ball games. The park meant something to him because an unintended stroll there five years earlier had been the first step on the path to meeting Coraline and her brother, Oliver. They had become his first real friends in LA, and suddenly things had looked promising. Then they had both lost Oliver and been thrown together like dice. They were betrayed by the people the world said they could trust the most, and it was all resolved to no one's happiness.

He walked on, past a clump of cacti that wouldn't care if there was never another drop of water brought by aqueduct, and rubbed his wide jaw. What bothered him was that she was right: he *had* let her down. They couldn't pin it down, but they'd had *something*. But then the war wasn't going to wait. No, like most of the world's history, it was just bad timing.

He stopped at a hot dog stand that was probably operating illegally and bought one that looked kind of okay. He put his hand in his coat pocket and realized that he had brought that damn book with him. Of all the reading material he had, this one would be bottom of the list. It represented too many harsh memories bound up in paper. He paid the hot dog seller and walked on through the park, back home.

Home was a one-room efficiency apartment in a block of thirty. The more expensive apartments had a big window that looked onto the street. The cheaper had a small one that looked onto the bare wall of the next building just three yards away. He was one of the guys who stared at bricks, which meant he had about a half-hour of daylight each day. The residents never spoke to each other and never expected to speak to each other. Single men all the way – divorced or bachelors – and a frustrated janitor, who mopped the floors with two lit cigarettes in his mouth.

Ken ate some bread and cheese, opened a can of peas and drank a beer. He was finishing up when there was a knock on the door. It was the first time anyone had ever knocked on his door. 'Yeah?' he called out.

'Phone call for you, pal.'

Ken wiped his mouth, took his keys and sauntered down to the lobby, where the telephone booth stood proud as the onset of modernity.

'Ken Kourian,' he said into the mouthpiece.

Heavy breathing. He knew the breath. 'I'm in trouble.'

'What sort of—'

'The club. Now.' And then the only sound was the buzzing of a disconnected line.

He knew which club. The Silver Waterfall on Sunset. It was Riley's place, of course, and that meant Ken was about to come face to face with the man himself.

The Silver Waterfall. It had been a late-night dive before Riley had bought it and transformed it into a later-night place that attracted actors looking to build a reputation and politicians who weren't too bothered about sinking theirs. At ground level, the hottest singers of the day warbled. Underground, the craps and roulette tables drew in the cash and supplemented the local police precinct's Christmas grocery expenses.

He didn't have to think it over. She had never called on him like this before. He grabbed his coat and billfold and ran out onto the street to hail a cab. One jerked to a halt right beside him, and he had jumped in, told the driver the address and slammed the door closed before the cabbie had had a chance to put the gears in neutral.

'Move it,' Ken said. And the guy moved it.

Sunset Strip. If there was a line of dreams waiting to be shattered, this was it. The brightest lights and the deepest pits LA had to offer. Glassy reverse-images of clubs, movie theatres, casinos and restaurants reflected in the car window. There was a queue to get into the Trocadero, which would make Mickey Cohen's heart glad. And that was Ginger Rogers just being shown in wearing a black fur stole, making the press photographers jump to it. But Ciro's was dead tonight by the looks of things. Bugsy Siegel wouldn't be happy, and that meant trouble for someone.

The Strip was outside the City of Los Angeles and beyond the jurisdiction of the LAPD. The LA County cops took a more countrified approach to the law, so it wasn't exactly 'anything goes' – but the strings got a lot looser out here, that was for sure.

Chapter 5

The cabbie was in a hurry, too, and it was just about ten minutes flat before the car ground against the kerb at the corner of the right block. The club's front was narrow, maybe twelve yards across, with two big windows of frosted glass that meant no one could look in or out. And it was shut – the doors wouldn't open for three or four hours, when the first of the hangers-on would arrive in paste diamonds and rented furs.

Never easy, Ken said to himself as he skirted the building to find a back way in. He stepped over a couple of men who might well have been last night's patrons and found a set of iron stairs up to the back entrance, which was hanging open. He walked into a kitchen – big steel pans on gas stoves, the door to a cold store, neat stacks of shining plates and bowls. Well, she wasn't in there. But there was the double doorway that must lead into the low-lit club itself. He glanced over his shoulder. He had picked up new habits living under the dead stares of a Fascist occupation. He eased his way through.

It was a dark, circular room surrounded by wallpaper the colour of old rubies. Moonbeams from circling spotlights overhead criss-crossed the room, flickering over tables and sliding to light the circular stage in the centre of it all, where they picked out a figure in burning gold. Coraline's eyes met his as the beams touched her. Then they slipped away, falling on something else. Someone else on the stage.

Behind her, a man in a dove-grey suit lay on his back on a velvet chaise longue. One arm was dangling to the floor, his forefinger touching the stage; the other was behind his head, as if cushioning it so he could sleep. But his right leg was crossed awkwardly over his left, and a patch of red covered half his face. Droplets of the red were falling one by one, through the moving beams of light, to stain the floor. Oh, he was dead all right.

And he wasn't alone. Three other figures were bending over his body: one pinning his waist to the couch, one with an arm across his throat, the third holding his head even as his mouth was open in a scream. But what made it all crazy as hell was that these three figures weren't made of flesh, they were smooth, dark, wooden mannequins, each with a blank wooden face and two eyes that had been violently gouged out.

Ken looked to Coraline. Then to the red-tipped knife in her hand.

Silently, she gazed back at the body of the man on the chaise longue. Then she walked to the edge of the stage, down black steps to a square table covered with a rumpled cloth. She placed the knife on the table. It smeared on the white cloth. She took out a long pink cigarette and lit it from a silver lighter.

Her hand was shaking.

'I need your help.'

'Yeah, you do,' he said under his breath. And then, finally, he went to the stage. The sliding spotlights glared in his face as he looked down at the corpse.

The blood was still oozing down the man's face in slow motion. It was coming from a deep, single stab wound above his right eye socket. The expression on his face was shock, amazement. Sure. What else would it be? He had been a plain-looking man. Clean-shaven, with mid-brown hair cut short and parted in the middle. Lacquer held it in place. Clean, nicely manicured fingernails. 'Well, I guess this is Riley.'

She paused. Smoke blew from her mouth. 'Is he dead?'

Ken glanced at her. 'Yeah, he's dead. Where did you get the knife?'

'I found it on the floor beside the couch.' She blew another line of smoke to the ceiling. 'You think *I* did this? You think I did this, then put these damn things all around him?'

For a moment, he paused. He knew her better than anyone had ever known her. But that didn't mean all that much. And when push came to shove, people were capable of anything. The tabloids would tell you that Riley Tithe had made a lifelong career out of pushing people to the edge. He could well have done the same to Coraline. There was no telling yet if this was the aftermath.

He felt through Riley's coat. It offered up a money clip fat with high-number bills, a set of keys and a linen handkerchief with the dead man's monogram. Well, they could rule out a robbery. The flow of blood was slowing as the reservoir in the deceased's head became tapped out.

Of course, if it wasn't her . . .

'Have you checked around to see if anyone's still here?'

'No,' she said thoughtfully, as if she hadn't considered that dangerous possibility.

He searched the room with his eyes. Nothing seemed out of place, and there weren't any obvious places to conceal a man. 'Stick behind me.' She followed as he went back to the kitchen. He took a steel chef's knife from a rack. There were places to hide in the kitchen – cupboards, the cold store, behind the line of ovens – but they were all clear. Without another word, they moved on to the bathrooms; then the storeroom full of booze and scuttling cockroaches; then the back office with a plush leather couch that made Ken speculate what Riley had used it for over the years. All empty, and no sign that anyone had been in them for a while. The safe in the office was built into the floor under Riley's desk and was locked and secure. 'You got a key to this?'

'No.'

'Pity.'

'If you want money, I can get you some.'

'That's not what I was looking for.'

'What *were* you looking for?'

'Evidence.'

'Of what?'

'How would I know?'

They returned to the show room. The dead man was still dead. Ken thought now that he could see the death ingrained in the walls; there was something about a killing that tainted everything around it. Maybe these wooden figures standing over Riley weren't mannequins, but witnesses. At least someone would know what happened. 'Okay, tell me,' he said.

'I was due to meet him here. We always meet here about this time on a Thursday. He likes to be here when the staff arrive so he can watch them set up. Then we'd be here for the night.'

'How'd he get here?'

'His driver would have brought him; he usually gets something to eat nearby, comes back and stays here until it's time to go home.'

'When's that?'

'Three or four in the morning, depending on the crowd.'

'Tell me what you found.'

'When I left you, I took a cab here. The front door was locked – it always is – so I came in the back. I saw him like that. I didn't touch him.'

'You touched the knife.'

'If you want to accuse me, Ken, come out and do it.' She sat and threw her cigarette into a cut-glass ashtray on the table. 'I made a mistake marrying him. But I didn't kill him.'

He stared at the sorry spectacle of a man whose

decisions had come back to haunt him. A lifestyle killing, that's what it probably was: Riley had lived a life that many desired without knowing just how many compromises on personal longevity it entailed.

'What the hell are these dummies?' Killing a man he could get, but setting these mannequins up as an execution squad, that took some work to understand.

'I have no idea. They're not from the club. Neither is that couch.'

He shook his head. It was queer, all right.

'You haven't said why you touched the knife.'

'No, I haven't,' she said bitterly.

'You want to or not?'

'Am I on the stand already?'

'I don't need to be a judge to want to know why you lifted a bloody knife at a murder scene.'

She placed her chin in her hands. Her exterior was shattering apart. 'I didn't do it. I wouldn't. Our marriage was shallow, but if I'd asked him for a divorce, he would have given it to me. He loved me. I loved him, in a way. And I didn't kill him.'

'Coraline . . .'

'I don't know why I picked it up, damn it! You see a knife, you pick it up! Maybe if you know what you're doing – if you've been there before – you don't, but I saw my husband dead on the floor and I picked up the knife.'

He took Riley's handkerchief and came over, stepping around the wooden models as if they were real people too shocked to move or speak. He used the handkerchief to lift the knife from the tablecloth. It was a switchblade with a brass-yellow blade and a mother of pearl handle that glowed like the moon in the low light. A woman's weapon, maybe, but for a very particular type of woman. Spots of Riley's blood seeped into the handkerchief.

She turned her milky blue irises to him. The spotlights were moving in them. 'Do you think I did this? Be open.'

'Then being open, I don't know what to think about what happened here. Except that Riley's dead, and the cops are going to have a lot more questions for you than I have. So you're best served if you call them.'

'Call the cops on myself. That's what it's come to?'

'It doesn't look good for you.' It didn't. There was no point coating it in honey.

'I understand.'

A sound made him look to the kitchen. A small Mexican woman was bustling in. She stopped on the threshold, dropped the leather bag that she was carrying and gasped at the sight of what the stage held.

'*Dios mío!*' she cried, staring first at Ken, then Coraline. He knew what was about to happen and he had to stop her. He moved, but she turned tail and ran before he could take three paces.

'Let her go,' Coraline called. 'What does it matter now?'

She was right. He cursed their luck. They could do nothing but wait.

It wasn't a long wait. A banging from the kitchen

ten or twelve minutes later announced the arrival of three plain-clothes men, two with bulges in their armpits, one with a bulge on his left hip.

The first officer was a whale of a man in a suit that had been made for someone two inches shorter and about a foot thinner. He had egg stains on his shirt and cuffs that would give a laundry owner a heart seizure. He entered the room, stopped, took in the sight of Riley as a bloody mess on the stage, whistled, then laughed. 'Boy, you two like to live dangerous!' he called out in a Jersey accent. A gold tooth flashed in his mouth. The other officers, a young black man with a long nose and a beefy white guy who also looked like he could afford to miss a few meals, stared at Ken like they were examining some kind of weird insect that had blown in through the window. 'Cuff 'em.' The black officer jumped to it. 'Now,' he turned to Ken, 'you wanna save us all the paperwork and tell me why you did the business on him? And while you're at it, why you stuck these dolls all around?'

He motioned to the heavier detective to look around the place. The cop walked away, poking in corners, then out of sight towards the office.

'We didn't do anything,' Ken said as the junior officer snapped the cuffs on.

'Yeah? Mercy slayin', was it? He had some terminal condition, so you put him out of his misery with a blade through the eyeball on a Thursday afternoon?'

'Officer, I'm his wife,' Coraline said, as her wrists went into the metal hoops.

'You think I don't know who you are? You think

I don't know who that piece of meat up there is? Now, I don't know who your friend is, but I don't really care right now. You're both in the frame for this. And just so you know, there's a bonus for whoever coughs first. The bonus is five years off the sentence. The bonus for whoever coughs second is death row. And every time I've pulled in a couple, one of them got the good bonus and one of them got the bad. Just so you both know.'

'I want you to take these off,' Coraline said, holding up her wrists.

'Santa Claus gives out gifts. I don't. Tell me what happened, and I'll think about it.'

'I came here and found him like this.'

There was a pause as the detective looked her up and down. The black plain-clothes man was moving his jaw like he was chewing gum, though the exaggerated motion seemed put-on. The other detective returned from his scouting mission and shook his head to say that he had found nothing of note. He went onto the stage and tilted one of the mannequins, letting it rock back into position.

'You found him like this, huh?'

'That's right, officer.'

'When?'

'About an hour ago.'

'And so you called the police, right?' he said in a mocking tone.

'I called Ken.'

'Why?'

'I knew you wouldn't believe me.'

At that, he belted out a genuine guffaw. 'You got that right, you got that right! Now, why don't you tell me what really went down? I mean, maybe it's not your fault. You find out about one of his side-girls? He slap you around?'

Coraline was unshaken.

'Officer, if you think I'm the sort to kill in a state of passionate rage, then you don't know who I am. I may not have been wholly in love with my husband, but he's always been good to me. The idea that I've ever wanted him dead is wrong.'

He sat at the table and leaned back in his chair to look up at them as they stood. 'You don't seem too cut up about it.'

The black detective knelt down to the body and pushed away the wooden hands that pinned the man to the couch. 'These things are creepy,' he said in a rasping voice.

Ken spoke now. He had seen Coraline fend off the cop's professional advances, not exactly putting him on the back foot but at least making him stop and think for a second. 'You never told us your name,' he said.

'Detective Sergeant Tadit.' He placed his palms on the tablecloth and pulled back, dragging the cloth across the table so that it rumpled into waves. 'Now, who the hell are you?'

'Ken Kourian.'

'Means nothin' to me. So you're not a hoodlum. Unless you're such a quiet hoodlum that we don't got you on our books.'

'I'm not a hoodlum.'

'So why you hangin' out with one and his girl?'

'*Wife*, Sergeant,' Coraline corrected him. 'If you're going to be disrespectful, at least do it respectfully.'

'Back to you, pal,' Tadit said, addressing Ken. 'So who are you?'

'I'm an old friend of Mrs Tithe.'

It took Ken almost a whole second to see that the policeman knew exactly what sort of old friend he was.

'Well, that's funny, Mr Koo . . . what was it?'

'Kourian.'

'*Kourian*. That's right. Well, it's funny, because people like Riley Tithe, their wives don't get to have *old friends*. Not if they wanna stay out the emergency room.'

'Riley was a businessman,' Coraline said.

'Sure. And my uncle's real big in bankin'. He mops the floor in New Jersey Provident.'

'My lawyer is Saul French – I expect you can find his number if you try.'

Tadit sighed. 'Okay, you wanna play it like that.' He motioned to his two colleagues to take Ken and Coraline from the scene. 'It's a lot colder at the station, I'll warn you.'

They began leading their two suspects to the rear exit.

'Real creepy,' the black officer muttered. 'Like some kinda Broadway show.'

Chapter 6

Gabriel Faulkner sat in an iron garden chair on what would have been a lawn if anyone had watered it in years. It was light-brown terracotta now, visible under electric arc lights attached to the side of his house. Before him was a typewriter. He wiped his face with a handkerchief that he took from his breast pocket.

The younger girl was sleeping. The elder girl was at her brother's side. She watched as the typewriter keys struck the black ribbon and glanced at him. They would be here until the dawn, spilling words onto the page. Sheet after sheet falling to the ground, blowing in the breeze, catching in the cracks between the bricks and in the branches of the camphor trees.

Chapter 7

They rode in separate cars to the station, just a few streets away on Palm Avenue – so they wouldn't have a chance to get their stories to match, Ken guessed. He was led into the low concrete building – more like a bunker than anything else – through a side entrance.

'Okay, Mr Kourian, we'll go over here, and you can tell me all about it,' said the white junior detective.

'Sure.'

And he did. He could have asked the cops to call the War Department, who might have bailed him out, but he wanted this kept low-key for now. So he told all about how he and Coraline had spent the afternoon in the hotel, how someone had sent her Oliver's last book as some kind of message. He pulled *The Turnglass* from his jacket pocket and slid it across the table. The cop ignored it.

'Riley Tithe's wife, huh? You got some kind of death wish?'

'I must have.'

Questions and more questions all night, until they were both hoarse and slumped back in their metal chairs.

'Riley's dead. But I had nothing to do with that. You know that, right?'

'Don't know nothing yet.'

'Yeah, you do. So it's about time I headed off home.'

The policeman snorted but let him walk. Just as he was heading out, Ken felt a meaty hand on his shoulder. Tadit.

'I said you can bounce. But I'm gonna ask you one last time. Those big dolls. Tailor's dummies, I guess, right? What they there for?'

'God's honest truth, I can't think why anyone would do that.'

Tadit looked right into him, then let his hand fall from Ken's shoulder. 'You come back when your memory is better.'

Ken stalked out of the station into the blazing morning and the parking lot. His ears were ringing with anger.

'Ken Kourian.'

It wasn't loud, it wasn't shouted, it was just placed in the air. Someone was confident that he would turn to see who was addressing him. Someone was right. A man coming up to sixty years old was leaning against the wall, one leg crossed in front of the other, wearing a cheap suit, a battered hat and a face Ken recognized.

'Expecting me?'

'I wasn't. Are you here on a friendly mission?'

The man laughed and held out his hand. Ken shook it. Detective Jakes was a sight for sore eyes. When Coraline's brother had been killed, it was Jakes who had proved an honest cop among a mass of dirty officers.

'Heard you got into a spot of trouble again, Kourian.' Ken checked the station doorway. No one around, but he was going to take no chances. 'Yeah, I hear you. Let's talk in my car.' They slid towards a Cadillac convertible on the other side of the lot, beside an open sewer that someone had forgotten to cover over. 'Hey, beat it!'

A uniformed officer was checking the licence plate.

'Y'got a permit to park here, Mac? This's for officers only,' the cop said without turning around.

'What does this look like to you?' Jakes said, flashing his badge. The other cop checked it.

'LAPD, huh? Outta your jurisdiction, ain't ya?'

'Ah, sue me.' The other cop snorted and ambled away. 'Car's not mine. The department's. I'm supposed to be watchin' some Louisiana Creoles runnin' a prostitution ring, if you can believe that. Gotta blend in.'

'I guess.'

'So all I heard was you and that hotsy-totsy got nabbed for killin' Riley Tithe. That right?'

'That's about right.'

'Y'do it?'

'Ah, come on!' Ken blew out, exasperated.

'Okay, okay. Just had to check. I mean, you had a hell of a good-lookin' motive.'

'She didn't do it, either.'

'Tell me everythin'.'

Ken did, and it didn't take too long. Then he got onto the cops' refusal to listen to anything about the book or any explanation of the murder that didn't involve Coraline plunging the knife into her husband's skull.

'Don't surprise me one bit. Only surprise is you're surprised.'

'How come?'

'Think about it: Tadit's on the mob squad. One minor hood gets knocked off. That's one file that gets closed. Good for him. Sunset gets just a little bit safer to walk down. Good for everyone. Now, what does he want to do 'bout it? Well, he can kick up a stink by pointin' the finger at one of the other hoods, but what does that get him? A cut in his squad's weekly take and maybe a bullet in the back some night. Way he sees it, what's done is done. Course, someone has to stand trial, so why not make it the beautiful widow who was found over the stiff with the actual knife in her hand? Only way it could be simpler is if she made a signed confession. And you know what?'

'What?' Ken said bitterly.

'Sooner or later, she will. He'll see to that.' There was a pause. 'Yeah, I believe you 'bout bein' innocent, but there's still a strong case against her. Strong enough for a court.'

'Circumstantial.'

'Wise up. That's enough. People round here have had enough of hoodlums takin' over. Most juries will be happy to trust whatever the cop says and put some mobster's moll on death row.'

Ken started at that. 'You really think she'll get the chair?'

Jakes's face was stoic. 'Gas chamber in Cali.'

'Jesus!' Ken's mind raced. On the turn of a dime, this had changed from a miscarriage of justice to Coraline's life hanging in the balance. 'We have to clear her!'

Jakes didn't look confident. 'I'll do what I can, but you saw how that uniform was with me. No love lost between City and County cops.'

'But it's a gangland killing. Has to be. You all want these people off the streets, right?'

Jakes shook his head. 'That's where you're wrong. There's a good number carryin' badges who like the status quo just as it is, thank you very much.' He rubbed his forefingers and thumb together beside his ear. Then he looked Ken up and down. 'I can see what you're plannin'.'

'Tell me what I'm planning.'

'You're plannin' on findin' who really did it and beatin' a confession out of them or somethin'.'

'That sounds like a good plan.'

'Well, it has its ups and downs.'

'Who am I looking for?'

'How would I know?' Ken stared at him without wavering. 'All right, all right. Maybe there's someone we can go see.'

He put the car in gear and gunned the engine.

Chapter 8

Yale Place, off Alpine Street in Chinatown, was the sort of street you could only find if you weren't looking for it. It looked like it had been closed down years ago – the whole street closed down for safety. The gaggle of old men sitting silently on shop doorsteps had all come to an arrangement that the first to twitch a muscle, let alone speak, would be cast out. Even the pigeons looked ashamed to be there.

Jakes jerked the handbrake up, and the car jolted to a stop. 'Gotta get the hang of that,' he muttered.

'More important things to deal with now,' Ken reminded him.

'Yeah, yeah. That's the one.' He pointed to a noodle bar at the end. A line of men with bad skin sat in the big front window shovelling steaming bowls of noodles into their faces.

'Get round the back. It's the red door.'

'Okay.'

Ken took the instruction and went around the back. He took off his jacket and hung it on a broken fence post to give himself more flexibility around the shoulders and waited. He didn't have to wait long. It was no more than twenty seconds before a Chinese man in his thirties came barrelling out of the building like he was trying to set a new world record. Ken stuck his leg out, making the guy stumble to the ground, and jumped on him, pinning him down with a knee in the small of his back.

'Hey, who you? Lee me alo'! I no do anysing!' the man yelped in a very heavy Chinese accent. 'You go' rong guy!'

'Cut it out, Charlie!' Jakes yelled as he emerged from the building.

'Goddamn it, Jakes, get this goon off of me,' the man on the ground grumbled, his voice suddenly changing to midtown LA.

'Now, Charlie,' Jakes said, casually sitting on the man's ankles, pulling out a pipe, stuffing and lighting it, 'it weren't so friendly of you to hit the track like that.'

'It weren't so friendly of you to show up without calling!' Charlie tried to push his chest from the ground but failed, collapsing back onto the dusty ground and getting a small shower of grit for his pains.

'If I'd called about this, I wouldn't have seen you 'til March at the earliest.'

Charlie sighed and gave up. 'Okay, what is it?'

'Riley Tithe.'

Ken wasn't expecting the reaction that came. 'Riley Tithe! You think I know who clipped him?' he laughed. 'If I knew, I wouldn't tell. I ain't rich, but I'm alive!'

Ken pulled Charlie's wrist up his back until the man yelped in pain.

'Y'see, Charlie,' Jakes continued. 'It ain't any of the mob boys you gotta be afraid of right now. It's my friend here, who's more'n ready to break all your limbs.'

'One by one,' Ken confirmed. 'I've done worse than that. Want to find out what I've learned along the way?'

A wrinkled black woman, leaning heavily on a pair of crutches, stumbled past. She stopped, slowly assessed the three of them, then casually resumed her journey without a word.

'Ow! Whaddya want to know?'

'Who did Tithe have beef with?' Jakes demanded.

'A lotta— Ow! Okay, I heard something!'

'Spill.'

'I heard Bugsy Siegel wanted to buy Tithe's place. Tithe wasn't biting. So Bugsy was spitting. He thought he was doing Tithe a solid by offering to buy it at all, instead of just taking it.'

Jakes looked thoughtful. 'Ain't many who say no to Bugsy Siegel,' he told Ken.

'More,' said Ken. 'You know more.'

'What m— Aiiiieee! Okay, okay! Jesus wept. That broad of Tithe's. She has admirers.'

'You mean Siegel?'

'I mean anyone who's seen her, right? An' Bugsy's seen her. We all seen her! That's all I know.'

Ken stood up and indicated to Jakes that the tree had given up all its fruit and it was time for them to leave. They walked back to the Caddy convertible. Gunned the engine and moved into traffic.

'I need to see Bugsy Siegel,' Ken said after a few moments' thought.

Jakes snorted. 'He don't take casual visitors.'

'Where does he live?' he asked as they steered around a bus.

'Knock 'em dead beautiful mansion on Beverly Boulevard in the Hills. You just gonna turn up and ask to be let in? If you're lucky, they'll let you walk away.'

'No, I know. I need . . . What the hell is that noise, anyway?'

'What noise?' Jakes asked.

'It's coming from the trunk. Is there something rolling about in there?' Jakes pulled over in front of a grocery store that seemed to have a rat problem. He jumped out and opened the trunk. 'I'm sorry,' Ken called back to him.

'For what?' Jakes said from behind the lid of the trunk.

'What I'm about to do.' He slid over to the driver's seat, released the handbrake and stepped on the accelerator.

'What the—!' Jakes yelled as the car roared away.

'I don't have time!' Ken shouted back.

Chapter 9

The Caddy sped in the direction of Beverly Hills. He took Santa Monica, because he was sure Jakes wouldn't want to call in the theft and make himself a laughing stock for the rest of his career. So no need to lie low on the back streets. No, he just had to keep to the speed limit and find his way to Bugsy Siegel's place.

It took about thirty minutes and just one paid enquiry of a teenage gang to find the right house. It was knock 'em dead beautiful, all right. A big Bauhaus-style place painted in white so clean and bright it gave you a headache. Even the gates were pretty. But the six guys standing in front of them, they weren't. Ken slowed to a halt and waited. One, the shortest, with olive skin and a waxed black moustache, stalked over and checked carefully inside the car.

'Help you?' he said with a faint Mexican accent.

'This is for Mr Siegel.'

'Never heard of him, chump.'

'He'll want to hear from me. The car's a gift.'

The guard snorted, but didn't send Ken on his way. 'Say I know a Mr Siegel. He sounds to me like a man who has enough auto-mobiles.' He took his time over the final word.

'Does Mr Siegel have a sense of humour?'

'So what if he does?'

'So I just stole this car from the Los Angeles Police Department.' The hood let out a bark of a laugh and pointed to Ken before ambling away to a telephone receiver beside the iron gates. He mumbled into it for a few moments. Ken heard: *Caddy. Convertible. Sweet ride.* And then a long pause as the guard waited for an answer. It came; he mumbled again and put his hand over the receiver. 'What's your name, pal?'

'Kourian. Ken Kourian.'

The hood mumbled into the phone again, then heard another instruction and hung up. 'Get out.' Ken did as he was told. He was patted down thoroughly, and the car was patted down even more thoroughly before it was driven away by another of the guards, who chuckled and nodded at Ken.

He was led up a long sweeping drive laid with yellow gravel that must have been scrubbed fresh that morning. It was probably cleaner than the cutlery he ate with. As the hood with the moustache led the way – and another, with his hand inside his jacket, followed – the house opened and a butler in full Regency English braids and livery stepped out.

'Good afternoon, sir,' he said. 'Mr Siegel is by the pool.'

They rounded the house to a garden big enough for a couple of armies to camp in. Within sight were a tennis court, a rose garden, a hedge maze, a putting green, some kind of rustic ruined church and a swimming pool where the Titanic could have sunk.

The rose garden was being used as a makeshift press gallery, Ken saw, as photographers and reporters crowded around a blonde woman, firing questions at her. She answered them slowly in turn. Ken caught a few words, spoken in a European accent, and a brief parting of the sea around her let the feline eyes of Ingrid Bergman meet his. In an instant, the bodies around her swallowed her again.

He passed the pool, where a young man with the body of a gymnast stood on the diving board pouring a bottle of Champagne over his crown, while a crowd of two or three dozen handsome young men with square jaws and girls with perfectly coiffed hair whooped and cheered. The diver threw the bottle into the water and bounced once on the tip of the board, flipped a tight somersault in the air and slipped perfectly vertically into the pool, barely leaving a ripple. Through the dancing bodies, Ken noticed a movie camera some yards away silently recording the scene like a Roman chronicler setting down the excesses of the Imperial court. And none of it looked like it could exist outside of some *LIFE* magazine fantasy of Hollywood.

Beyond them all, on a neatly trimmed lawn, tea was being served to a man watching like a hawk with time to spare. Bugsy Siegel – probably the only hood in town with the looks to match the stars who came to his clubs and his parties – was sipping from a peach-coloured cup. And as Ken came close, Siegel gave him a smile warm enough to melt an iceberg. 'Mr Kourian,' he said with a velvet voice.

'Mr Siegel. Thank you for seeing me.'

'I found your approach . . . amusing.'

'It's not quite ready for a live audience.'

Siegel's smile would have had the dead rise up just to bathe in it. He motioned towards a linen-covered couch on the grass. Ken sat.

'Tea?' He lifted a china pot.

'No, thanks. I don't like it.'

Bugsy Siegel, he guessed, was not the kind of guy who liked men to fawn.

The dapper gangster set the pot down and nodded to a bodyguard, who went to a cart stuffed with enough bottles to make an Irish seminary woozy. The goon fixed a couple of drinks and handed Ken a square glass of golden liquid and ice. 'But you like Scotch, right?' Siegel said.

'Sure, I like Scotch.' He poured half into his mouth. He wasn't an expert, but he could tell this was the best stuff money could buy. It was smooth and warm, and the punch it packed was perfectly cushioned in a glove.

'Do you like it?'

'I think it's the best I've drunk.'

'Would you like a bottle to take away? It seems a cheap exchange for the gift you brought me.'

'I was hoping for something else in return.'

'Were you?' Siegel put on a show of polite surprise and pretended to lose his train of thought. 'Do you like my party?'

Ken didn't turn to look at it. 'It's swell. You must be proud.'

'A lot of the people who come, well, no one would actually miss them if they stopped coming.'

'Here or anywhere?'

'Oh, anywhere, really.'

'What's with the movie cameras?'

'That's a sideline,' Siegel told him. 'I'm producing a talkie myself, you see. And there's a party scene at a house like mine. So why pay for actors and extras when I can just capture real life for the cost of a few bottles of cheap Champagne?'

'You make a compelling argument.'

'I try,' said Siegel.

'Riley Tithe.' The gangster just beamed. 'I know you heard.'

'Of his unfortunate demise? Well, yes, I had heard something.' Ken swirled the rest of the whisky around his glass. Siegel raised his own again as a toast before knocking it back. The ice cubes rattled. 'The thing is,' he said thoughtfully, 'Riley is – *was* – a businessman. Like me. Now, exactly what his business interests were, I can't say.'

Well, there was no point beating about the bush. Ken was here for answers, so he had to ask questions.

'You know the cops have taken in his widow on suspicion?'

'I heard that, too.'

'I know she didn't do it.'

'Then she has nothing to be worried about, I'm sure.'

'If only it were that simple. Mind if I ask you a question?'

'Not in the least.'

'Did you have Riley Tithe killed so you could take his club?'

Ken heard the goons behind him reach for their irons. But Siegel's reaction was unexpected. The mob boss burst into laughter and motioned to his men to relax. 'That's a hell of a question, Ken,' he said, raising his glass in salute for the last time. 'So I'm going to be honest with you. I don't mind Riley being dead. I don't mind one bit. But I had nothing to do with him getting that way.'

Bugsy Siegel wasn't afraid of the law. He certainly wasn't afraid of Ken Kourian. He didn't skulk in the corners and try to hide his tracks. He lived fearlessly out in the open. Flash. Daring all comers. If he had killed Riley, Ken was sure, he wouldn't deny it like a street punk. No, the LAPD detective bureau might disagree, but this gangster's word was enough for Ken.

'Can I ask you another question?'

'I think you're going to.'

'Have you ever read a book called *The Turnglass*?'

For the briefest moment, Siegel looked confused. Then his smile returned, and he shook his head. 'No, I haven't. But I'm always looking for a good story.' Ken looked into his glass and drained the dregs, leaving three melting lumps of ice. 'Now, you tell me something, Ken.'

'Okay.'

'Why are you interested? Any chance it's to do with the widow herself?'

'Maybe.'

'I'll take that as a yes.' Siegel gazed at the pool party, which had broken up into the men swimming lengths and the girls sitting by the side, sunning themselves. 'It's the ladies, Ken, they're always our downfall.'

'You might be on to something. Tell me one last thing. Who in your world had a reason to rub Riley out?'

Siegel gazed up at the lack of clouds, shading the bright sun with his hand. 'Riley wasn't worth that kind of trouble. The only thing he had was his club. He wasn't a real operator. And he knew better than to tread on anyone's toes. If I'd offered him enough dough, he would have signed the club over, so why go to all the trouble of knocking him off? No, if you ask me, you have to look somewhere else. You take a look at the man's personal life.'

Ken tossed the ice from his glass and stood. 'Good luck with your picture. What's it called, by the way?'

'I haven't decided yet. I like *Babylon*.'

'Catchy.'

'It is, isn't it?'

Chapter 10

Riley's personal life. Well, if it wasn't professional, it had to be personal, because it was hard to see how Riley could have stabbed himself in the head by accident. Ken thought it over as he tramped along Beverly Boulevard. A streetcar stopped, and three schoolgirls jumped out. He took their place and rode back to town. He would have to make it up to Jakes sooner or later, but he was in no hurry to make it sooner. He got out close to Elysian Park. Funny how he always seemed to end up there, as if it was his spiritual home in LA.

He sat down in the afternoon sun and took his shoes off. His feet hurt already. What did he have to go on? Not much. Whoever had done it had done it pretty clean. The only lasting effect was the one they'd wanted to leave: the shop dummies.

He bought a can of iced coffee that tasted of bad grit and walked home. Only he didn't make it all the way into his building, because there was someone waiting outside for him.

'Oh, hey, Kourian! Nice t'see you,' Jakes said, leaning in the doorway with his arms crossed.

'I was hoping you didn't have my address.'

'I bet.'

'Come up, I'll make you a glass of water.'

He walked towards the doorway. Jakes's arm shot out to bar his path. 'One Caddy convertible. If you *don't* mind.'

'I don't have it.'

'Then you better get it back.'

'I gave it to someone.'

'Then – at the risk of repeatin' myself – *you better get it back.*'

Ken sighed. 'You got a cigarette?' Jakes glared at him, reached into his pocket and pulled out a ragged pack of Camels. He stuck one in his own mouth and lit it with a match he struck on the wall. Then he tossed the rest of the pack to Ken, who took and lit one. Ken rarely smoked. He did it mostly to give himself time when he needed to work something out and there was someone waiting for his verdict. 'I gave it to Bugsy Siegel.'

Jakes, a man who would have displayed no surprise if a dinosaur had reared up from the gutter and danced a polka in front of him, looked close to astonished. 'Bugsy Siegel? You gave the LA City PD's car to *Bugsy Siegel?*'

'He had something I needed.'

'Was it to go boil your head, because that's what I'm thinkin' you need.'

'It was information.'

Jakes threw down his quarter-smoked coffin peg and ground it into the dirt. 'For your sakes, I hope it was somethin' so important, so goddamn earth-shakin', that the department will overlook grand theft auto on your part and dereliction of duty on mine. So spill.'

'He didn't kill Riley. He doesn't know who did.'

At that, Jakes's lips parted and stretched out into a grin. And he began to laugh. He laughed heartily, slapped Ken on the shoulder and then cracked his fist hard across Ken's jaw. Ken pulled himself back up and rubbed his face. It hurt, that was for sure. 'Well, you shoulda said! If I'd known you were gonna give a four-thousand-dollar car to one of the worst hoods in the state – any state – in return for him sayin' he has no idea about anythin', I woulda come, too, and thanked you both on the way out.'

'He says it's not mob-related.'

'Oh, well, if Bugsy Siegel says a murder's not mob-related, then why wouldn't we believe him?'

'I trust him on this. And just think: if it's not the mob, you can drop the corrupt, dirty cops of LA County into a DA-run investigation for why they wanted to lock up an innocent woman. Who knows what the DA will turn up when he gets going?'

Jakes paused. 'You trust him on this.' The cop shook his head as if telling off a child. 'Jesus, Mary an' Leon.' He stared at a diner across the street that was empty but for a gently crying waitress behind the steel counter. 'How's the coffee in that place?'

'Undrinkable.'

'Good.' And he started across the road, not waiting for the traffic to halt but glaring at the drivers in each lane, who hit the brakes and honked their horns at him. 'Come on, I'm not walkin' for my health.'

Ken followed him, angering the drivers more, to the cracked chequerboard tiles of Tina's Diner.

Ken hadn't been lying about the coffee. They each sat with a cup in front of them that they had taken two sips from and given up on. The waitress continued to sob to herself behind the counter.

'What makes you think he's tellin' the truth?'

'Why lie? Even if you were to arrest him on the basis of him confessing to me, it would hardly stand up in court. And he knows I'm not a cop, so he's not trying to take the heat away. I think he had nothing to do with it.' Jakes mumbled something to himself that Ken couldn't catch, but it sounded like foul language was employed. 'I even asked him about the book,' he said, more to himself than to Jakes. He didn't know why he'd gotten so hung up on the appearance of the novel. It could have been some kind of prank, after all.

'Oh yeah, that book. You still got it?'

Staring out of the window at the traffic, Ken took it from his coat pocket and pushed it across the table.

'Wait, I thought it was the one your pal Oliver wrote.'

'It is,' Ken said, confused.

'This one's by someone called G. B. Faulkner.'

'The other side. Remember, there are two books in one? Oliver wrote the other one, The Turnglass.'

'Oh, okay. I guess it's just a coincidence.'

'What is?' Ken asked, without much interest.

'The title.' He held up the book.

And it felt like a bolt of lightning in his head as Ken grabbed it out of the detective's hand and stared at the cover of the book written by G. B. Faulkner. *The Waterfall.* 'It's the name of Riley's club!' he said.

'Yeah. Must be a coincidence.'

'The hell it is,' Ken shot back. He pulled it open and thumbed the pages.

'You ever read it?' Jakes asked.

'No.'

'You should start.'

'That's what I'm doing.'

It is now the spring of the year of our Lord one thousand five hundred and ninety-three.

Jakes sighed. 'Well, I'm headin' home. An' I guess I'm catchin' the bus. Seein' as you gave my car to a hoodlum.'

'He says he's a businessman.'

'Yeah, an' I'm the Pope in a skirt.' He crossed himself, looking apologetically skyward.

Chapter 11

Ken stared down at the book on his apartment table. It was dawn, and he had finished reading it through. And then he had turned back to the passage he had already read four times.

Below the title was a poorly made woodcut print of the murder scene as described. Within an inn, a man labelled 'Marlow' was on his back on a settle, while another had an arm wrapped serpent-like around his throat, one had his waist and a third was plunging a knife into his forehead.

All in a book named *The Waterfall*. Not quite the same as Riley's club, but the name and the scene were far too close to what Ken had witnessed to be a coincidence.

He glanced out of the window. The sun was breaking over the horizon. Somewhere in the city, the light was falling onto someone else who had read – or written – those lines. Someone who had had an idea about them. Someone who wanted to recreate them and send them to Coraline. He knew what he had to do now.

He headed out and took the bus to Palm, then walked to the station, where he asked for Tadit. Yes, the detective was in, but he was busy, and Ken would have to wait. So he waited, watching a mouse dart back and forth, cleaning up the crumbs dropped by the homeless and hopeless. After an hour of the heat and dust blowing in from the street, he was shown to a bullpen full of detectives in cubicles. Tadit's desk was covered in a mix of stationery, full ashtrays and baseball cards so dog-eared it seemed he must have been chewing them.

'Mr Kourian. Nice to see you again,' he said, without cracking a smile. He had an egg stain on a different shirt today, and Ken had to wonder if he put it there deliberately each morning.

'I have something for you.'

'For *me?*' Ken ignored him, cleared a space on the desk by gently lifting away an open jotter covered in a series of shapeless doodles and placed the book on his desk. 'I don't read.'

'But you *can* read, right?'

Tadit laughed without mirth and picked up the copy of *The Waterfall*. He glanced at it and bent it double in one hand. 'I'm supposed to do *what* with this?'

Ken told him how it had been delivered to them in their hotel room, and that the murder of Riley Tithe matched the murder of Christopher Marlowe, right down to how the dummies had been positioned to mimic the men who had supposedly killed the playwright.

'You need to look into this book. Find the author. I've never heard of him.' He tapped the name 'G. B. Faulkner' on the cover page.

Tadit's face showed as much interest as a clock's. 'Then don't say another word, Mr Kourian. Let me just make one phone call. Don't you worry, I'll have your girlfriend, who was found with the knife in her hand standin' over the stiff just after the two of you spent the afternoon screwin', sent straight home. After all, you've brought me a book. And a book is a book, right? And I'm sure you got proof that this book was sent to your room like you say, and you couldn't, say, have sent it yourself in some cheap attempt to have us lookin' away from the fact that your *girlfriend* was found *standin' over the body* with *the goddamned knife in her hand.*' He tossed the book back to Ken.

'Were there any fingerprints on the knife?'

'Only hers. She got her prints on one of the dummies, too. Careless.'

'She must have pushed it out the way when she went to him.'

'Sure. Then we have some of the staff say they heard her and the vic arguin' a couple of days back.'

'All couples argue.'

'Sure. But we're chargin' her.'

'What with?'

'Murder one. What else? I mean, if you want to confess you were in it together, I'll listen. And so will the judge, I *ensure* you.'

Ken was going to get nowhere with this clown. In

fact, any more words could only harm Coraline. She would endure, he knew that. The best thing he could do would be to get out of there.

He did. Without bidding the cop a good day.

Chapter 12

He hauled himself up the stairs. It was another hot day. Just why America had decided that men had to wear full suits and hats in eighty-five-degree heat was beyond his understanding. Maybe one day they would all work out that what was right for Massachusetts wasn't necessarily right for California.

The stairs creaked as he went up. He couldn't shake the thought that there was someone out there he should be chasing after, but he just didn't know who they were or where to find them.

There was one other efficiency apartment on his floor. Two single men in single rooms with single prospects. He had seen his neighbour a few times, and they had shared a mutual understanding that there would be no warm friendship, only the briefest polite greeting and then a return to their single lives.

He had got used to things being how they were. Quiet. He liked quiet. The events of the past twenty-four hours had rocked that boat. But it was reaching his apartment and finding splintered wood around the lock that truly sank it.

It wasn't a good job. The lock had probably cost two bucks at most. He could have picked it in under a minute with a screwdriver, a pair of long-nosed pliers and a hairpin. Instead, some jackass had jemmied it. They might as well have got on the radio and announced to the world that they were breaking in.

He was tired, but not so tired that he was going to throw away his life, though neither was he going to run away from the confrontation. So instead of entering his apartment, he knocked softly at the one on the other side of the landing. No answer. He knocked again. After a few seconds of huffing on the other side of the wood, his neighbour appeared, frowning at the interruption to their unspoken routine.

'Hey. I'm Ken, we're neighbours,' he whispered, bringing his face in close. The other man, white-haired with huge jowls, nodded suspiciously. *Get to the point*, he seemed to be saying. *Tell me why you've broken the code.*

'Sorry, I've lost my voice. I'm making dinner, and I need a better knife than the one I have. Have you got one I could borrow?'

The jowls shimmied, then the man disappeared and returned with a carving knife. Its edge was sharp enough to do just what Ken thought he might need it to do.

He thanked his neighbour, waited until the guy had gone and turned to face his own doorway. Amateurs expecting a fight hold a knife with the point forward, like a sword. Guys who know what they're doing, guys who've been through this circus before, hold it with the blade along their forearm sharp edge outwards and the point towards their elbow, ready to slash, not stab.

He eased the door open, ready for someone to explode out. It opened with the whine of hinges crying out for oil. Gloomy inside. Little light forced its way through the postage-stamp-sized window that faced a blank wall close enough to reach out and touch.

He waited. Nothing. The plywood table in the centre of the room, the sink and the stove and the armchair waiting patiently. He stepped forward and scanned the shadows in the corners, just in case. Well, the one advantage of a home where if you swung a cat, the cat would try to swing you back, was that hiding places were limited. He left the light off while he crept across the cheap carpet.

The bathroom was the size of a normal person's closet, and the door folded along a vertical line in the middle. He wrenched it open. But it was empty as a grave before a funeral. No, whoever had jemmied his front door had cleared out. He retreated to the centre of the main room and pulled the cord to turn on the light. And then he spun in a full circle, amazed at what he saw.

Because what he saw was every wall daubed with blood-red paint. Not just mindless splatters, but words. Words that ran in an uneven line and had been painted with a heavy brush: *Few men have ever walked within half a mile of the whale blubber boileries of Greenland Dock in East London without retching. The stink of fat turned liquid by a thousand furnaces spreads through the air . . .*

It went on and around the room, dripping down the plaster. It was the result of a madman at work. But it wasn't all.

His eye fell on the table below the white-glowing bulb. There was something on it that hadn't been there before. A book. The same one that had been sent to their hotel room, the one whose first story had detailed the bloody method of murder that had taken Riley. *The Waterfall*. This new copy lay in the centre of the table with the pages open to the beginning of the book's second story, 'The Angel'.

Few men have ever walked within half a mile of the whale blubber boileries of Greenland Dock in East London without retching.

Ken tossed the borrowed knife onto the table. He wouldn't be needing it. *Okay*, he thought to himself. *I guess it's my move.*

And that move would begin with telling Jakes that he needed to come over.

Ken went downstairs and called the station. Detective Jakes was busy, they said. Well, he wasn't in the mood to wait around and see if the cop would return his call, so he would just have to turn up in person. He hadn't expected to be talking to the detective quite so soon after their head-to-head in the diner, but there it was.

Out on the street, a boy was selling the *Evening Herald and Express*, and Ken's eye was caught by the photograph on the front cover. It was Riley's club with a cop standing in front of it. Ken tossed the kid a coin and snatched up the paper. 'Stars Club Owner Slain' read the headline. 'The owner of the Silver Waterfall Club, known as the after-hours haunt of studio stars including Veronica Lake, was brutally murdered yesterday. Riley Tithe . . .' etc, etc. It was light on detail, heavy on brutality.

He learned nothing from the report except that Angelinos went wild for the news that their idols were mixed up in something dirty.

Chapter 13

Jakes's station was on San Pedro, right in the heart of Skid Row. The cabbie wasn't happy about even entering the grid of streets where more people lived on the sidewalk than in apartments, but Ken handed over twice the fee in bills and the man became happier with the views. Most of the population were from out of state, drawn by a promise of Hollywood everywhere, only to find Hollywood nowhere. Even the cockroaches were talking of moving out to a better neighbourhood.

Ken jumped out of the cab, which sped off the second his feet touched the asphalt, and sized up the station. He had seen more inviting Gestapo offices.

A junkie with wild hair and black teeth came up to Ken, panhandling. 'Brother, can I borrow a buck? I'll spend it on food.' He didn't care that he was right in front of the cop shop. Ken pressed a coin into his palm, and the man grinned amiably before shuffling off. Whether the money would go on food or dope was anybody's guess, but the way the man was, soon it wasn't going to matter.

Ken entered the station and approached the front

desk. He was about to speak when a voice stalled him. 'Kourian. You really are the bad penny who keeps turnin' up.' Jakes was striding through the reception area with a uniformed officer carrying a camera.

'Something's happened, and you're going to want to know about it.'

Jakes halted for a moment. 'It can wait. I've got an actual job to do. So you can take a seat, and I'll be back in a few hours.' He pointed to a row of wooden benches, most of them populated by people who looked like they had already died or wanted to.

'This can't wait hours, Jakes. Her time is ticking away, and I've got something.'

Jakes started heading for the exit again. 'Look, I can't just drop everything. Other crimes happen, you know. And this one's a murder. Frankie Angel deserves justice, too.'

Ken's hand flew out and took hold of Jakes's shoulder.

'What the—?' Jakes began angrily.

'Angel? You said his name is Frankie Angel?'

'Yeah, bit-part actor. Real name's Francisco Angelo. What of it?' He tore Ken's hand away.

'Angel.' Ken shook his head, shaking away the rueful laughter that he felt rising.

'What's got into you?'

'How'd he die?'

'I don't know yet, just got a call from a woman so cut up she could barely speak.'

Ken pulled his billfold from his jacket pocket. He took out a sawbuck. 'Ten says I know how he went.'

'What?' Jakes looked incredulous.

'Ten bucks.'

'Stop talkin' crazy.'

Ken pulled out another ten-spot, tucked the two
notes into Jakes's breast pocket and patted them in
there. 'You can keep them if I'm wrong.'

Jakes threw up his hands. 'Okay, I'll bite. How'd
he die?'

Ken went to the desk and asked the desk sergeant
for a pencil and paper. The officer looked at Jakes,
who nodded wearily. Ken wrote on the paper, folded
it and placed it alongside the bills in Jakes's pocket.
'Wait until we're there,' he instructed the cop.

Jake looked like he wanted to strangle Ken, but
gave in. 'Fine. Ride along. Keep us company.'

'That's all I need.'

They went out to the car lot at the back, which
was guarded by three officers with shotguns, and
jumped in a prowler. 'You gonna tell me why you're
so sure you know how the stiff got that way?'

'I'll wait.'

'You'll wait. Sure you will,' Jakes muttered to
himself.

'Where are we going?'

'What, you mean you don't know?' He rolled his
eyes. 'Imperial. Offa Sixth.'

They rolled at speed through the streets, steering
around piles of trash, some of them alight, and piles
of humanity, none of them conscious. They stopped
outside an apartment building that looked in a better
state than Ken's and a hell of a lot better than what

they'd left behind in central Skid Row. There was even a worried concierge behind a desk in the lobby, who directed them to the fifth-floor penthouse.

'Penthouse? We got penthouses round here now? Jeez,' Jakes muttered as they entered the elevator, which had a potted plant on a stool in the corner. 'Don't know what the place is comin' to.'

The elevator, operated by a tiny white boy who could have disappeared inside his hat, opened with a ding, and Ken, Jakes and the uniformed officer found themselves facing the entrance to Frankie Angel's penthouse. To the side of the elevator was a service door that must have led to the stairs. It was bolted closed from their side. They pushed open the door to the apartment to reveal a plush two-storey affair, all open with a lounge area that sported sky-blue leather furniture, a kitchen zone with chrome breakfast bar and a drinks bar that would have been lit by a neon sign saying 'Serving' had it been serving. It was all surrounded by huge windows that gave out onto a roof terrace and the skyline of Los Angeles. Everything about it looked like a movie star's haunt. They stepped through a barrage of bags that sported the names of upmarket boutiques.

'Bit-part actor, you say?' Ken said.

'I mighta over-underestimated him.'

'He was a star!' howled a voice from above them. They gazed to the top of a glass staircase that wound up to a mezzanine level. 'You must have heard of Frankie Angel!' It was a once-majestic redhead, now with streaked mascara, sobbing on her knees. 'He's famous!'

'I'm sorry, ma'am,' Jakes said, climbing the stairs. 'I'm not up with the latest.'

'Everyone loved him. He was the racing driver in *Gasoline*. And he was in *Who Drew First?*'

'Were you the one who called?'

'Y-yes,' she said.

He reached her, the other two treading in his wake. 'Can I ask your name?'

'Diane Angelo. We're married.'

Jakes placed a hand on her arm to steady her. 'Can you show us where he is?' She picked herself up and stumbled along the mezzanine to a white doorway. She pointed at it, then turned her face away and fell back to her knees, tears streaming down her cheeks.

Jakes glanced at Ken, then, taking his hat off, stepped in.

They were staring into a huge bathroom. There were two identical sinks, a shower enclosure and a partly sunken porcelain bath. But the bath had burst its banks onto the pink marble floor, creating an indoor lake an inch deep. And there was something in the tub. Something staring up at them. Jakes, Ken and the cop were looking at the distorted rippling image of a man on his back, his eyes and mouth open in a silent scream. Beside the bath, its hands inside the water and holding the dead body under the surface, was a wooden clothes dummy with its eyes gouged out.

Ken tapped Jakes's breast pocket. His eyes still locked on the bath, the detective took out the slip of paper that Ken had placed there.

He unfolded it. It had one word written in grey pencil: *Drowning*.

Without shifting his gaze, Jakes spoke. 'Looks like I owe you twenty bucks.'

'Keep it.'

A draft from somewhere sent waves drifting across the surface of the water. Jakes motioned to the uniformed cop, who took a flashbulb-lit photograph.

'Let's get the poor bastard up,' Jakes said. He took off his jacket and reached in, soaking his shirt cuffs, and hauled the body to the edge. A face emerged. An exceptionally handsome face with Mediterranean colouring, matched by jet-black hair on the head and toned chest. 'Guy worked on his body.' He lifted an arm with strong, rounded biceps. Ken joined the detective, the uniformed officer remaining where he was, looking a little queasy. 'Tell me how you knew it would be drownin'.'

'You don't see, do you?'

The detective sounded exasperated to the point of anger. 'No, that's why I'm askin'!'

'The book I showed you. *The Waterfall*. The one that was printed with Oliver's last book.'

'Jeez, that damn thing again?'

'Yeah, that damn thing again. But look.' He pulled his copy from his jacket pocket. 'Riley Tithe was killed like the victim in the first story, stabbed above the eye and held down by three men. The first story's also called "The Waterfall", kind of like Riley's club. Now, the second story in the book is "The Angel" and the victim is drowned by one man. And this here is Frankie Angel, drowned by one man.'

Jakes narrowed his eyes as if it was the craziest thing he had heard in a long time. 'So the perp is offin' people in line with this book?'

'That's about the size of it.'

'Goddamn.'

'Well, just wait. There's more.'

'What are you, a game-show host? Get on with it.'

'I came to see you at the station because someone got into my apartment.'

'A thief?'

'I wish it were that simple. They left another copy of the book.'

'Jeez.'

'It was open at the beginning of the "Angel" story. And to top it all, they'd painted the first lines of the story on the walls of my apartment. It was a message. That this was coming.'

A vein on Jakes's temple bulged out, and he stared at the corpse before them. 'Well, I seen it all now. We got a madman on the loose. An' a madman with some kinda obsession with this book. And you, or your girlfriend.'

'It looks that way, doesn't it?'

'This place is gonna be locked down as soon as the science boys get here and an ambulance comes for the sti—' He glanced towards the open doorway. 'The deceased. I wanna talk to the widow before then, while she's still somewhere close to calm.'

Ken followed him out. The grieving woman – who looked about thirty-five, like the late Frankie Angel, RIP – was sitting on a bed that could have slept a football team. Her knees were drawn up to her chest, and she was no longer crying but wiping her red-raw face with her sleeve.

'I'm Detective Jakes, ma'am.' She squinted at him, then at Ken. 'And this is my associate, Mr Kourian.'

'You're not an officer?'

'Not in the police.' Well, it wasn't lying, and she could read into it what she liked.

'Can you tell us what happened?' He took out a notebook. Ken remembered it from the first time they had ever met, when Coraline's brother had been the victim and Ken the first suspect.

'I came home a half-hour ago.'

'Is that a precise timing?'

'I-I guess so. Maybe twenty minutes. But not more.'

'Okay.'

'I'd been shopping.' She pointed over the edge of the mezzanine to the forest of retail bags. 'I came back, and I called out for Frankie but couldn't find him, then I found him. With that *thing* in there.' She descended into sobs again.

At the edge of his vision, Ken saw two medical orderlies carrying a stretcher step out of the elevator and look around. The uniformed officer went down to quietly tell them to stay out of the picture for now.

'Mrs Angelo, is there any way up here 'xcept through the lobby?'

'No.'

Ken saw a flicker of satisfaction on the cop's face. So the concierge or elevator boy must have seen whoever came up – and anyone carrying a shop dummy, or a bag big enough to hold it, wouldn't be forgotten in a hurry. 'And can you think of any reason someone would target your husband like this?' Jakes asked.

'No. Of course not. He didn't have any enemies. He—' And she began breathing in short, sharp breaths like she was about to faint. Jakes helped her to a leather seat that was a cross between a chair and a bed. She lay back in it, her eyelids fluttering.

'Jus' try to breathe,' he said gently.

'I am . . . I can't . . .'

'You bitch! You filthy whore!' It was yelled from the floor below. Ken stared over the edge of the mezzanine. A short, thick man with a full beard was rushing towards the stairs. Ken and Jakes both moved to head him off, but Ken was there first, intercepting him like a linebacker and thudding him against the chrome banister. 'She killed him! She did it. She did it!' the man continued to shout, even as Ken pinned him to the metal.

'Who the hell are you?' Jakes snarled in the man's face.

'Tell him, and tell him quickly,' Ken added, his fist full of the man's pin-striped shirt. He was a foot shorter than Ken, and the padding around his midriff meant there would be no long fight if the man refused.

'Keep him away from me!' the widow cried, burying her face in her hands.

'She killed my brother. Bitch.' He spat on the glass step at his feet. 'She's a gold-digger.'

Ken softened his grip just a little to give the man the benefit of the doubt. 'So you are?'

'Carlos Angelo. Francisco's my little brother.' He stopped, and the rage seemed to pour away. He folded in the middle. 'Can I see him?'

Jakes met Ken's glance. 'You should wait,' the cop said.

'For what?'

'For us to take him somewhere else. You don't want to see him where he is. It'll just upset you.'

'Is he a . . . mess?'

'No. He drowned. He looks okay.'

Ken made a quick calculation. The family were Italian or maybe Mexican. Catholic, either way. They'd want an open casket, so they'd want him to look okay. They'd surely all been proud of their handsome son, stealing his way into people's hearts on the silver screen with only a bit of a name change to soften his background.

Ken eased the brother back down the stairs. 'You keep talking to Mrs Angelo,' he said to Jakes. 'I'll take him aside.'

'Okay, but you don't ask him any questions. We're the cops, and that's our job, got it?'

'Loud and clear.'

Ken took the man into the lounge area and onto a couch. 'Mr Angelo,' he began.

'Call me Carlos,' he mumbled. 'Everyone does.'

'Okay, Carlos. I have to tell you something. It's going to be strange to hear. First, have you ever heard of a man called Riley Tithe?'

'Who? No.'

'Your brother never mentioned him?' Carlos Angelo

shook his head. 'Okay. He owned a nightclub named the Silver Waterfall on Sunset. Ever been there?'

Angelo frowned. 'I've heard of it. Never been there. I've had Francisco snapped by the press at a number of clubs, never that one.'

'You got him photographed?'

'I'm his manager. Have been for years – I was a lawyer for MGM Studios before that – and it suited us both. And before you say anything, we were both very happy with the arrangement. My brother was born to be a star. I was born to be nicely off. We both got what we wanted. Until *she* came along.' He stared up through the ceiling. 'Got her claws into him. She wants his cash, nothing more. I'd check if she took out an insurance policy on him in the last week if I was you.'

'I'm sure we'll get to that. But here's the thing I need to tell you that's strange. Riley Tithe was murdered two days ago.' Angelo shrugged to say that meant nothing to him. 'There's a book called *The Waterfall*. Like the club. Ever read it?' Angelo looked increasingly confused by what he was hearing. 'And Riley was killed in a way that makes reference to the first story in it. The second story is called "The Angel", a bit like your brother. And *he* was killed in the same way that someone is killed in *that* story.'

Carlos stared at Ken for a full ten seconds. 'I don't understand.'

Well, it was a lot of information, and it didn't seem to make a cake of sense.

'Neither do we.'

'You mean it wasn't her?' He pointed upwards.

'No, it wasn't. For one thing, your brother was in the bath. He must have been held under, and I doubt your sister-in-law could have done that.'

'She could have drugged him.'

'I think the police will check for that.'

The short man's brow furrowed. 'So you're not the police?'

'I'm what you'd call an "interested party".'

He saw that the two medical orderlies – sent by the coroner, probably – had now been called up to the mezzanine. Ken and Carlos went to the bottom of the glass stairs and watched as the two men, accompanied by the uniformed policeman, entered the bathroom and came out a minute later with the body on the stretcher, covered by a blue sheet. They descended the staircase and left the apartment.

Ken heard Carlos sigh. 'Never thought it would be like this. You hear of the kids getting into dope or drink and that killing them, but nothing like this.' He shot an ice-cold look at the widow, who was hanging over the banister, snivelling, and pointed at her. 'Crazy guy out there, okay, but she's still a gold-digger. First sniff of the inheritance and she's off to Acapulco, you listen to what I'm telling you. Probably won't even stay for the funeral. Ah God, the funeral. I bet she'll want it to be Episcopalian. Stupid mixed marriages never work.'

Ken left him to whine about which funeral rites his little brother would receive. More officers were coming in now, setting up for the crime scene report. Jakes ordered a couple of them to take Diane and Carlos

Angelo to the station to make formal statements. 'Check with the neighbours, anyone else, if anyone's been seen hanging around. Though it looks like he's a careful guy.' One of the officers muttered something to him. Jakes looked annoyed.

'What is it?' Ken asked.

'Somethin' don't . . . The guy on the desk in the lobby.'

'The concierge.'

'If you say so. He says they got a signin'-in register. Anyone not a resident has to be registered in advance; or if they turn up without him bein' notified in advance, he calls up to the apartment for approval. If they're allowed in, they're recorded in the book.'

'Don't tell me. No one came up in the past few days.'

'No. An' I don't think the vic voluntarily dropped to the bottom of the bath and filled his lungs with water. There's the stairs by the elevator, someone coulda come up from one of the other floors,' the detective suggested.

'That would make sense if the door to those stairs weren't bolted from this side. It's just about possible that someone could have come up the stairs from another floor, been let in by Angel and then killed him – but our man couldn't get out again and bolt the door behind him, could he? He . . .' A realization struck Ken. 'Hey, wait!' he shouted to one of the policemen about to lead the widow out of the apartment. He went over to her. 'You said there's no way up here except through the lobby, right?'

'Right.'

'Then what do you do if there's a fire?'

'A fire? The fire escape.'

'Show us,' Jakes said.

She led them to the balcony, where a door constructed from a rectangular metal frame with a wire mesh across it gave access to a metal fire escape. Only the mesh had been cut away and dropped onto the balcony's concrete floor.

'That's not . . . it's not meant to be like that.'

'Y'don't say,' Jakes muttered.

Ken examined it. 'Bolt cutter. Wouldn't even take much strength.'

'Well, now we know.'

Chapter 14

The biographer closed his car door. There was a problem with the catch mechanism, and he had to put his weight against it. He noticed, as he did so, a set of wheel marks in the gravel.

'Have you had visitors?' he asked as the two sisters appeared to escort him inside. The younger one shook her head. 'A car? Someone been and gone?' The elder one glanced at her, and she shook her head again. Something about the way she was lying made him uneasy.

He was led into the octagonal library. The brother was there in his threadbare suit, wheezing into the rubber tube. The writer put down the satchel he was carrying and took out his notebook and pen. 'Who built this place?' he asked while he was setting things up to take down this man's life story, such as it was.

'Father.' His gaze travelled up the wall to a life-size portrait in oils of a man on a chestnut horse galloping across a dry field. The rider was glaring at the artist. The painting was so large that it took up an entire wall. Below it was a brass plaque that read 'George Faulkner'.

'Is he still with us?'

The rubber tube swished from side to side. 'If . . .
he . . . was . . . I . . . would . . . never . . . have . . .
written . . . at . . . all.'

'Why? He wasn't a big reader?'

Gabriel shook in silent laughter. 'You . . . could . . .
say . . . that.'

Something glinted on the writing desk. A blue glass
letter-opener. 'Attractive piece,' he said as he sat where
he was directed.

'Venetian.'

'I love Venice. I went once on an assignment. Just
unforgettable.'

His subject closed his eyes. 'I . . . have . . . only . . .
been . . . in . . . my . . . mind.'

The writer paused to pluck up courage. 'May I ask
a question? It's a little personal.' There was no immediate objection, just the sound of the breath in the
machine. 'Can you get out? Leave the house? Drive?'

There was a pause. 'My . . . time . . . is . . . limited.'

Chapter 15

Ken and Jakes left the apartment block and drove back to the station. The smarter streets soon gave way to the old Skid Row, where bums swayed across the road, shops sold liquor through the windows and cops never got out of their cars. When they got to the precinct house, it looked to Ken more like an island than anything else.

'What now?' he asked, as Jakes sat at his desk with a coffee he had been given by a secretary. She hadn't offered Ken one.

'What now?' He sounded tired. 'Now we start callin' all the nut houses and askin' if one of their guests with a thing for literature's been discharged or escaped in the past month. Hey, Klinghoffer! Ring round all the booby hatches. See if any of them can shine a light on this guy. Must have a history of serious violence an' maybe likes books.'

'Novels,' Ken added.

'Yeah, novels. Make sure y'say novels. We don' want them talkin' about any other kinda books, do we now?' He looked contemptuous.

'You should tell the press,' Ken said. 'People need to be warned. And someone knows something.'

'The press. Jeez. Just let me handle it from here.'

Ken thought it over. Well, he had got into this to clear Coraline's name. And unless the LA County detectives were going to open themselves up to a hell of a lawsuit, even they had to admit that Coraline couldn't have had anything to do with the murder of Frankie Angel and would have to let her go. 'Call LA County. Get them to release Coraline, and I'm gone.'

'Consider it done.' Jakes picked up the phone. 'Put me through to County.'

Ken left him to it and discreetly wandered away. He watched the officers as word spread about what they had found that afternoon. Some of them looked grim, others amused, as if a good slaying only came along once a year and here it was. And a two-time killer who maybe had more in store? Well, that was overtime and then some.

There was a wooden tray in the corner of the room that had once held pastries of some kind and now held only crumbs. He was hungry, he realized, having eaten nothing all day. He casually opened a cupboard above the pastry tray in the hope that there might be some food in there.

'Kourian!' It was Jakes, of course. He looked over. The detective had the telephone receiver wedged under his chin while he was writing on a pad. He looked pained. He looked that way a lot. He beckoned irritably to Ken.

'Yeah?'

Jakes rolled his eyes and muttered 'Right' into the phone and 'You serious? What's that gonna do?' Finally he said, 'Okay, okay, I'll call you back.' And he rammed the receiver down with about ten times the force needed to place it in its cradle. There was a pause.

'Jakes?'

'I heard you the first time.' He tapped his pen on the pad, where he had made a series of scribbles that looked like a child learning to write. 'Some idiot's told the mayor.'

'Told him what?'

Jakes glared up. 'What d'you think they told him? They told him some nutjob is out rippin' up actors an' nightclub owners.'

Ken couldn't help but poke the bear. 'And how does he feel about that?'

'He's against it.' He looked through the blotches of ink on his pad.

'I think we agree on that. But all I want right now is for you to tell me that Coraline is being released.'

'She'll be released.'

'Okay, then. Have a nice day, won't you?' And he turned to leave.

'But they want her t'make a public appeal for information. Alongside Frankie Angel's girl.' Ken knew how Coraline would react to the request. Especially when she would be required to play a weeping widow, while all the cops around her knew exactly what she had been doing while Riley was being shivved. 'It's all about *people power*. The mayor's big thing now is *people power*. Don't trust us to do our job, wants the public to do it for us.'

'She probably hasn't slept for forty-eight hours.'

'She can have a nap. They want t'run it on the news shows tonight.'

'Just get her out. We'll take it from there.'

Jakes picked the phone up again. 'I'll have her at your place in two hours.'

Ken looked at the cover of *The Waterfall*. 'We need to track down the guy who wrote this.' He tapped the name. 'G. B. Faulkner.'

'You think he's in the frame?'

'Could be. Could be he knows who else should be.'

'Could be he knows nothin'.'

'One way to find out.'

She knocked on his door. He knew it was her because it wouldn't be anyone else. It was six o'clock, and her skin was pale through lack of sleep, and her hair was tied back underneath her pink pillbox hat, but her milky blue eyes pierced like they always had. 'Aren't you going to invite me in?'

'You've never needed an invitation with me.'

'That's true,' she said softly as she stepped in. She turned slowly to gaze at the words painted on the walls. 'Jakes told me about this.'

'You should try sitting with it for an hour. It makes you think God's telling you to be better.'

'We could hardly be worse.'

'I don't know, we could be whoever did it.'

'I suppose that's true,' she replied.

'I made a deal with Jakes. You're going on the TV and radio to appeal to the public for any information about Riley's death. Frankie Angel's widow is going to do the same.'

She took the deal. 'Let's hope no one calls in with information about where we were when it happened to Riley.'

'Yes, let's,' he said tersely. 'It's something to do with Oliver's book.' He held up a copy. 'But the other side to it. *The Waterfall*.' He explained the murders and their links to the work by the obscure G. B. Faulkner.

'Who is he?'

'I have no idea. We're trying to find him.'

He stood and went to her. She lifted her mouth to him, and he pressed his lips to hers. Her skin was cold, but her mouth was warm.

Chapter 16

An hour later, they sat on opposite sides of the bed. The air smelled of what they had done. He knew what it meant to him, but not to her, and they had gone past the point where he could ask, for fear that the very act of asking would end it all.

He watched over his shoulder as she pulled on her pantyhose and then her brassiere, all black. It was time for him to dress, too. Neither spoke. Soon they were both ready to head to the station, where the press conference would take place at eight, in time to be live on the nightly news. Neither wanted to do it, but the consequences of not doing it – the renewed suspicions and whispers of guilt – outweighed the pain of Coraline having to play-act the weeping widow who'd loved her husband to the exclusion of all others.

'I'm always playing a part, aren't I?' she said, almost to herself, as he drew a glass of water from the faucet, thirsty in the hot night. 'Why do you think that is?'

'Just destined for it.'

She paused for a long time. 'I guess that's it.'

She straightened her hat on her head and went out.

The station was besieged, not by the homeless masses of Skid Row, but by a crush of press men who had got word that something big and brutal was happening, and they all wanted a slice of the action to sell.

'If it bleeds, it leads,' Ken said under his breath as he and Coraline slipped in a side entrance to avoid the flashbulbs and notepads at the ready.

'What did you say?'

'Just something reporters tell each other.'

One of those reporters, a thin man wearing dark glasses, had strayed from the rest of the pack and was hanging around in the corridor. 'Hey, are you part of this? Can I get a picture?' he asked, shoving a Kodak 35 in Ken's face.

'Get that away from me or it won't be usable for much longer,' Ken growled back, pushing him away.

'Hey, no need for that!' the guy protested. 'Anyhow, we'll get you soon enough. Freedom of the press. What made this country great.' And there was the click of a camera shutter. Ken stopped, turned around and began to walk back. The reporter shrank into a corner. Ken didn't stop. He walked up to the man, grabbed his camera, tore the film out and dropped it on the floor. 'S-sorry,' the man stuttered.

Around a corner Ken found a junior officer, who escorted them to a large meeting room, where a number of journalists were huddled in a corner, sharing cigarettes and laughter. A couple glanced at

Coraline and whispered to each other without trying to hide it. At the other end of the room, a platform with a table, four chairs and heavy microphones had been set up. People were scurrying about, setting out rows of Bakelite seats.

'Kourian.' Jakes was looking harassed in the centre of the room with a clipboard and a pen that he was trying to get to work. He threw it aside and snatched another from a passing uniform.

'Jakes. Did your men find anything at the Angel house? Prints?'

'A few unidentified around the place, but they could be any visitors'. Only ones on the bathtub were the wife's. Dummy was wiped clean. We checked Mrs Angelo's story. About half of Los Angeles saw her that day. She bought a truckload of clothes from the kinda boutique where they charge in gold bars, then had lunch with some girlfriends who are so above board they might as well be nuns.'

'What about the author of the book?'

'G. B. Faulkner? No one we spoke to has heard of him. Publishin' house closed down a couple of years back. We're tryin' to track him down through public records.'

There was a second ripple of interest as Frankie Angel's widow, Diane, was guided in by a female cop, followed a few moments later by her husband's brother. She was already dabbing away tears, while he was glaring at her back.

'Mrs Angelo,' Jakes said. 'Thanks for comin'.'

'I hope it does something,' she sniffed, attempting

a smile. 'Frankie's not coming back, but I want whoever did it locked away.'

Carlos shook his head in contempt and barged her aside. 'Are we going through with this goddamn charade? Whatever happened, she's only ever wanted his money,' he growled, jerking a thumb at his sister-in-law.

At that, the tears started to flow again, and Diane Angelo ran out of the room. Jakes looked to Coraline, apparently expecting her to show some sisterly instinct and hurry after her to sympathize. Coraline only met his glance and shrugged. She didn't know this woman. Jakes instead pushed the female officer towards the doorway. 'Try to get her to come back, will you?' he ordered. 'And you,' he stabbed a finger in the face of Carlos Angelo, 'keep it buttoned!'

'Fun and games already,' Ken muttered. From the beginning, he had been sceptical that any useful information would come from this public appeal, but now he was doubting it would even happen.

'I'm telling you—' Carlos piped up again.

'Oh, for Chrissake!' Jakes shoved the man into one of the seats. 'Sit there, keep it shut until I call you up.' He lowered his voice. 'You say what I want you to say an' nothin' else. Got it?'

'Yeah, yeah, okay,' Carlos muttered.

Jakes stomped back to Ken and Coraline. 'Like dealin' with street kids.'

'He's angry. His brother was murdered,' Ken said. 'How would you feel?'

Jakes relented. 'I got a brother. Someone rubbed him out, I wouldn't rest 'til I'd broke their neck myself.'

He sniffed. 'We're not gonna mention anythin' 'bout the book here, by the way.'

'Why's that?' Coraline asked.

'It's a test,' Ken said. 'Five hundred people are going to call in and say they're the killer or the killer's their neighbour or some guy they passed on the street. But if they mention the book, the cops know it's someone with good information.'

'You always gotta keep somethin' back,' Jakes confirmed. 'And besides, we don't want to start a total panic. It's bad enough sayin' we got some guy killed two people. We throw in that he's doin' it outta some book, an' for all we know he's gonna keep doin' it, then the whole city goes nuts.'

Diane reappeared, led in by the female cop. Her brother-in-law caught Jakes's glance and stared at the floor. 'What do you want me to say, Detective?' she asked in a fragile voice.

'Truth be told, we want you to tug at people's heart strings. Someone knows somethin', but they don't remember it or don't wanna come to us with it. You can make them remember and come forward.'

'I presume it's the same for me,' Coraline said.

'Yeah.'

Coraline flashed Ken a look that said *Playing a part again.*

The room was full now, and the reporters, from some unseen signal, were taking their seats. Jakes looked at his wristwatch. 'All right. Let's get this goin'.' He clicked his fingers at Carlos to tell him that he was wanted, but on a short leash.

Diane and Carlos Angelo studiously avoided looking at each other as Jakes showed them to their seats and subtly separated their chairs. The sound of joshing from the journalists gave way to a degree of hush as Jakes tapped his microphone to make sure it was on. It was.

'Gentlemen.' He peered into the audience and seemed to pick out a couple of faces. 'Tonight we're askin' for the public's help to track down a killer.' A few flash-bulbs went off. He outlined what he could about the crimes and then introduced Coraline.

'Riley Tithe was a fine man,' she said. 'If anyone has any information at all, please call the station.'

A few reporters called out questions that she answered calmly, batting away snide enquiries about his line of work.

'Do you miss him?' one more shouted. It was the one they'd had the set-to with a few minutes earlier.

'Every day.'

Ken caught a look in the pressman's eye. He was one journalist who wasn't convinced by Coraline's performance. Maybe she was just too beautiful to credit with honesty.

Then it was Frankie Angel's wife's turn. There were a lot more waterworks there, and Jakes had to move it on to the dead man's brother or she would have cried all night about her loss. Carlos spoke about how people should keep an open mind about who might have committed the crime and if they suspected anyone at all they should speak up. Jakes reiterated that it looked like the work of someone who had brutally targeted two complete strangers.

This sparked a chaos of yelled questions.

'He done it before?'

'Who knows?'

'Do you have any leads?'

'That's why we need help.'

'You need *our* help? What's the police for if it needs our help?'

'*We got a madman on the loose?*'

Jakes didn't like the new direction the show was taking and tried to shut it off. 'That's speculation!' he yelled from the stage.

'Speculation? It's a front page!' one of the reporters, a one-legged example of the species, cried out to the delight of his pals. Ken could see that the event was getting away from Jakes. Well, he hadn't wanted to do this in the first place.

'That's the end of the meeting, gentleman!' And Jakes gestured to the attendant cops to hustle all the reporters, thrilled that a really juicy case had come their way, from the room.

Diane, appearing lost, wandered away, looking for someone to guide her but not finding any help at all.

Ken stepped in. 'The way out is this way,' he said, showing her the path.

'Thank you.'

He could barely credit the difference between her and Coraline, who was still in her seat, impassive, while here was Diane Angelo, wet handkerchief in hand, barely able to leave the room on her own. 'You need someone to call you a cab?' he asked, accompanying her along the corridor, which was lined with

bills alerting the reader to wanted individuals, the
dangers of leaving your gun unattended and options
for medical cover.

'A cab!' She laughed, her laughter turning into a sob.

'I didn't know I was such a comedian.'

'Oh, Mr Kourian, you're not. It's just that . . . I
can't even afford a cab.'

He slowed.

'Aren't you the beneficiary of your husband's will?'

She stopped and dried her eyes. 'Yes, I am. But
there's nothing there. Frankie was living beyond his
means for years. He wasn't getting the work like he
used to. And we owe the IRS more than we have.'

'The apartment?'

'Rent paid until the end of the month.'

'Then what?' She shrugged. Something occurred to
him. 'You'd spent a lot on shopping when I saw you.'

'It was on credit. I'm going to take it all back. It
was so when my girlfriends saw me at lunch, they
thought everything was swell.'

'I see.'

She gazed along the corridor. 'Frankie had a good
heart. But he was no accountant.' She fanned her face
rapidly, as if trying to waft away the sadness. Ken
watched her leave and returned to the room where
the press call had taken place.

Carlos was sitting alone. 'Mind if I sit here?' Ken
asked. The dead man's brother vaguely indicated that
he had no objection. 'How are you, Carlos?'

'Ah, okay. Okay,' he sighed, staring at the floor. He
hesitated. 'I'm ashamed.'

Somehow, this didn't come as a surprise. 'What of?'

'My behaviour. I loved Francisco. I raised him when Mom and Dad were working in the bakery every hour that God sent.' He silently signed a crucifix over his chest. 'I got angry at her because I never liked her. I thought he could do better. She's . . .' He broke off.

'What?'

Carlos met his gaze. 'I just always thought there was nothing to her.' He shook his head. 'But I guess she loved him.' He paused. 'Tell me you'll find who did it? Help my brother rest in peace. He didn't deserve what they did to him.'

'We'll find the guy,' Ken said.

He didn't know if he was lying.

Chapter 17

Gabriel Faulkner looked up into the tilted mirror above his face to watch his biographer's reflection. 'So now we come to *The Waterfall*.'

'Do we?'

'We have been coming to it since you first set foot on my driveway. And the telling of it will also answer the question you have been dying to ask since that morning. Three days in, and you haven't asked. Oh, what patience you have.'

The author waited. He *had* been patient. Now he was being invited to pose the question. 'Why are you in that thing?'

'It was a gift from my father.'

'Hell of a gift.'

'In a sense.' He paused for a few seconds. 'Have you ever felt hunger?'

'Sure,' the writer answered, without thinking too much about the question.

'Have you? Really? I don't think you have. What you have felt is a desire to eat. I have felt hunger. True hunger.'

'Tell me about it.'

Gabriel Faulkner's gaze ranged around the room, sliding over his sisters' faces as they waited patiently beside the machine that encased him. 'My father never understood why as a child I only wanted to read. I couldn't tell him that it was so that I wouldn't remain ignorant like him. Water.' One of the girls hurried to collect a short bottle of water. A paper straw was folded over its side. The end went into her brother's mouth, and he sucked until he let the straw fall from his lips and his sibling took the bottle away. 'Cattle prices, that was what he knew, and no more than that. I baffled him. He didn't know where he'd gone wrong with me. And my mother wasn't the type to tell him. Did you ever hear of one William McKie?'

'I don't think so.'

'Some people called him "McKie of the North". He was known for living hundreds of miles from humanity in the barren wastelands of northern Canada. Every few years, he would return to civilization and be lauded by those who praised the human spirit of defiance. My father heard of him. It gave him an idea. Possibly the first he'd had in his life.' The biographer could guess what the idea had been. 'He paid McKie to take me into the wilderness. To make a man of me.' Of course he did. 'I was seventeen years old.'

'What did he think it would do?'

'My father? He truly believed it would do me good. That I would enjoy the outdoor life, the nature. I wanted to believe him, so I agreed to go.'

'For how long?'

'Two months. We would hunt the migrating caribou for food. In the end, it didn't matter how long we'd planned, because the plan fell to pieces. But I'll come to that. I only met McKie once before we left. He was more bear than man. He stood like one and had the manners of one. He was from Glasgow and spoke in a dialect of English that I barely understood. And I remember him rooting through what I had brought for the journey. He picked up every item, one by one, sniffed them like a dog and threw half of them out on the street. But I had hidden three books in the lining of my bag: a volume of Shakespeare's tragedies and two mystery novels.' The biographer noted down the words. 'We set off in May, travelling to Vancouver and then east to Calgary and Edmonton. We only took what we could carry. From Calgary, we rode to the Thelon River, where we set the horses free. From there, we had to paddle upstream in an Indian canoe he had brought. It dawned on me then that he was mad. It became clearer every second that he forced me to fight our way against the flow through the freezing waters. Even as we spent ten hours each day in this hard exercise, I shivered with the cold. Can you believe that the daytime high temperature was fourteen or fifteen degrees? Man can't live in that. And I realized something else too.'

'And what was that?'

'That McKie's plan to live off the caribou was flawed. He kept insisting that the next day we would see them. But we never did. We'd missed their migration.'

'By how long?'

'Days, weeks, months. It made no difference. No, it wasn't the cold that would kill us, it was hunger.'

'You must have had some supplies.'

'Some pickled fruit and beef he had canned himself. Enough for a couple of weeks, no more. I begged him to turn around. To go downstream, to hope to come across trappers or prospectors who could help us return to civilization.'

'He refused.'

'Of course he refused. And as I grew hungrier, I grew weaker. I could paddle less. He started to look like an animal when he turned to watch me. The cold, the lack of food, didn't seem to affect him.'

'What then?'

'More days of hunger, of pain and exhaustion. Of McKie's madness and the empty sky overhead. And finally, sickness.'

'Sickness how?'

'A week in, I realized that the reason I'd stopped saying anything at all to McKie wasn't that I hated and feared him. It was that my mouth could no longer form sounds. My entire face was frozen. The muscles were paralyzed. I could turn my head, but I couldn't speak or lick my lips. It wasn't the hunger that had left my arms too weak to paddle and my eyelids drooping, it was something worse than that. One day, I collapsed in the bilge at the bottom of the canoe, unable to push myself up or call out to McKie. For hours I lay there, hoping first that he would turn around and lift me up, and then that I would die and not have to put up with this world of cold and hunger anymore. Hours and hours. And then, finally, he did turn, to snarl at me to paddle harder. But when he saw me folded up, he looked strangely at me for a while. He shook me, but I could only see him in double vision and couldn't drink the water he offered me. After that, I sank into unconsciousness.'

'And then?'

'Few men have ever fallen through books. I am one of them.'

'What do you mean?'

'You've read my book, *The Waterfall*. What do you note most about it?'

It was something the biographer had kept back from saying.

'That you're in every story. There's always a Gabriel.' He had kept back from saying it because it made the man sound as insane as the hunter who had escorted him into a windswept hell.

'In my dreams, in the unconscious state when I was on the edge of death, I found myself falling through the books I had brought with me. The stories were pouring down, one into another. The Shakespeare. The mystery novels. It was a cascade, a waterfall of characters and vistas. As we plunged down I thought I was dead.'

'Looks to me like you weren't.'

'No. The human body will eat itself to stay alive. And one day I woke up. I woke up in the Edmonton general hospital. I was raving, they said, about a bear trying to kill me. I knew what that meant, though I didn't say it. The doctor told me that fur trappers had brought me in. Men of a local Eskimo tribe had taken me to their camp. One of them spoke English and said that I had been found on an island they used to quarantine members of the tribe who had diseases. Of course, the disease I had wasn't one that I caught from another living soul.'

The biographer had guessed the origin of the sickness. The iron lung, Faulkner said, had been 'a gift from his father'; and there was the detail that the few provisions they had taken had been preserved by McKie himself. 'It was botulism. From the canned beef.'

Faulkner nodded in the mirror. He drank more water and let the paper straw fall again. 'I spent a month in that hospital, by turns raving and writing in a fever the work you hold in your hands. I wrote day and night, breathing through tubes, eating nothing, bathed in sweat, as mad as chaos. I poured my whole self into it; it was my blood, not ink, on the pages.'

'I see.' He weighed the book in his hand. 'What did your father do?'

'He arranged for my return. I came back with the manuscript that was half my existence and the clothes that I stood up in. And this.' He struck the inside of the iron lung. 'The present that my father bought me.'

At that, Gabriel Faulkner banged three times on the inside of the metal coffin that encased him. His two young sisters ran to open it and help him out, to the cart with the canister of compressed air that inflated his lungs. They secured the rubber tube to his face with elastic straps. Then he trundled out through the vast room where the feast for a book's celebration stayed mouldering and rotting on grey cloths, into the octagonal study where copies of *The Waterfall* lined every surface and poked out from every crevice. The invalid hauled himself to one of the bookcases, and his guest noticed for the first time that one shelf of it was fronted by iron-framed glass, which should have made it beautiful but instead made it look like a see-through casket at a Catholic funeral.

Faulkner stumbled a little, breathing hard through his tube, then made to lift away the glass cover. He struggled, and his elder sister hurried to help. He batted her away and tried again, this time pulling it away.

Inside was a neat stack of handwritten papers, bound in red ribbon like legal papers.

'I . . . read . . . my . . . own . . . words . . . night . . . after . . . night,' he huffed on each breath from the rubber tube. 'Full . . . of . . . anger . . . for . . . what . . . had . . . been . . . taken . . . from . . . me. But . . . I . . . had . . . to . . . bide . . . my . . . time. My . . . father . . . still . . . had . . . little . . . but . . . contempt . . . for . . . me. And . . . then, two . . . years . . . later, his . . . death . . . left . . . me . . . free.' His eyes focused scornfully on the portrait of his father. 'Finally, I . . . could . . . have . . . my . . . book . . . published. My . . . day . . . of . . . glory.' He paused and reached a trembling hand to a copy of the book on a table.

'And then?'

He sent the book tumbling to the floor. He sent a wooden globe crashing after it. 'And . . . then . . . it . . . crumbled . . . before . . . the . . . corrupt . . . power . . . of . . . the . . . Tookes. Their . . . lies. Their . . . family . . . secrets. Their . . . wickedness . . . smothered . . . me.'

'What did you say happened? This guy Oliver Tooke wrote the other side of the book, exposed some scandal and died for it?'

'It . . . was . . . withdrawn . . . from . . . sale . . . ten . . . days . . . later. Now . . . it . . . moulders . . . in . . . my . . . house.'

'I understand.'

'You . . . do . . . not!' Faulkner cried as best he could. 'Now . . . that . . . wickedness . . . has . . . rebounded . . . on . . . them.'

'How so?'

Faulkner's eyes brightened with laughter. 'I . . . had . . . a . . . visit . . . from . . . the . . . police! They . . . told . . . me . . . the . . . strangest . . . thing . . . is . . . happening.'

Chapter 18

Ken and Coraline weren't in the mood to return just then to his apartment. They took a cab to Beverly Hills, where there were one or two bars that weren't run by hoodlums and wouldn't recognize Coraline as Riley Tithe's widow. She didn't want to start more talk about how she was running around with another man even before her husband was cold.

They chose one in a hotel that catered to wealthy visitors to the motion picture studios, with recent movie bills on the wall. There was *Cat People*, which Ken had seen, a creepier-and-sexier-than-you-think film about humans turning into animals when they got aroused. *Saboteur*, directed by the limey who was making a name for himself in Hollywood, got a lot wrong about what it was like to sneak into factories and put them out of action for a while; but given Ken's own part in turning that lonely, shadowy pursuit into entertainment for young men giving their best girls a Friday night out, he could hardly complain. There was a television set screwed to the wall across the bar, showing a cowboy slowly riding across a blurry plain, joking with his friend. The sound was turned off, so it could have been a comedy or a tragedy for all Ken knew.

He thought through what was happening to them from every angle. It could, just about, be something to do with his work for the OSS, but that seemed a stretch. Was it connected with his previous scrape with the law, when Coraline's brother Oliver had been killed over his book *The Turnglass*? But apart from the repeated appearance of the book itself, nothing pointed to that. He was lost.

They sat drinking sidecars, watching the silent screen for an hour before either spoke. In the end, it was Coraline who broke the silence.

'If Riley hadn't been killed, what would you have done?' she asked.

'About what?'

'You and me, Ken. Always you and me.'

He shook the ice around his empty glass. It wasted four seconds, giving him time to come up with an answer that revealed nothing. 'I would have thought about what you want, what I want, and then done nothing about it.'

'Then you and I really are the same, after all. I guess—'

'Wait.' He pointed to the television. The cowboys had been suspended for the local nightly news, the last edition of the evening. Ken's face was at the edge of the picture, surrounded by flashing bulbs and reporters asking questions that the viewers in the hotel bar couldn't hear. A passing drinker, an old woman who looked like she'd had enough and then ordered some more, glanced at it, then at Ken.

'Yeah, yeah, it's me,' he muttered.

'You're finally famous,' Coraline said.

The report changed to show a newsreader looking stern. She could have been telling those with the sound on that there was a madman in the city. Or she could have been reading out the football play-by-play. No way of telling now.

They paid the check and walked along the sidewalk to get some air. On the opposite side of the street, a heavy black man in overalls was pasting a huge bill onto the front of a movie theatre. 'FRANKIE ANGEL IN *WHO DREW FIRST?*' the poster screamed. There was a picture of a hand holding an old-fashioned revolver below the words.

'This any good?' Ken asked, walking over.

'I seen it. Wish I had the time back instead.' He packed up his paste and brush.

'That bad, huh? Why are they showing it, then?'

'Ain't you heard? This guy got bumped off by some nutcase. Now every picture house is yelling for a print of anything he made. Can't sell the tickets fast enough. Honest, he's in this movie for about five minutes.'

'The biggest star who never was.'

'You got that right.' The man spat on the ground. 'Hollywood.'

Chapter 19

The next day, Ken was called again to the movie studio to oversee the film about the OSS's exploits in occupied Europe. There was more ludicrous exaggeration of the risks the American agents took and how blasé they were about them. If he and the rest of his network had stomped about in front of the Germans as much as they seemed to in this picture, they would have lasted about a half-hour before being captured. And shooting their way out of an SS prison wasn't as easy as it was being depicted on the studio lot in Burbank.

At the end of the morning, during which he made a number of observations and the movie director listened to about a tenth of them, lunch was called. The extras were sent off to a pen where they were doled out hamburgers on paper plates, while the actors were led to an open-air dining area with a limited menu to choose from, but a menu all the same. Having had no instructions against it, Ken took himself into this area but went for the burger anyway. At least here, in the bubble that enclosed Hollywood and pictures, no one seemed to watch or read the news, and he was only recognized as the expert imposed on them by the War Department to nix the script's few good parts in the name of 'accuracy'.

When the day closed and the producer had thanked Ken for yet another well-made point that would go nowhere, he was sent home in a studio car. The driver stopped off at a drugstore, where Ken bought a quart bottle of rye and a cup of ice and poured one into the other on the back seat, taking the edge off the day.

He was passing the payphone in the lobby of his apartment block when it rang. He swallowed what remained in his cup and lifted the receiver.

Point Dume, a headland on the coast some miles west of LA, was the site of one home and one home only. Turnglass House was a unique building, two storeys constructed almost entirely from glass and steel by Coraline's grandfather, who had established the family fortune. He had come from England with money from a dubious source and founded a glass-manufacturing company that soon became a near-monopoly in the state. The house was perfectly see-through – a bitter irony, considering the grim family secrets that it held. But when you approached it from the road and you could see right to the waves of the blue ocean behind, it was like a jewel box inviting you in.

Ken hadn't been back here in years. Truth be told,

even though it was the home where Coraline had grown up and into a beautiful young woman, he couldn't understand why she had wanted to live here with Riley. It had been the scene of two terrible deaths that had just about wrenched her heart out. Maybe she thought that by living there in a new life, she would exorcize the ghosts of the past. How had that worked out for her? He had no idea.

She was beside him in the cab as it came to a stop but he wasn't going to ask how it felt to be home.

Right now, at night, the house was dark inside, so the glass walls reflected the moon overhead and the car's headlights. 'We don't have staff at night,' she said as she fished in her purse for keys. Their feet crunched on the driveway gravel as the car turned around and left them to the Pacific Ocean. Reaching the house, they found something waiting for her on the doorstep: a wicker basket of white flowers with yellow stamens. 'Gardenias,' Coraline said, picking one up. 'Riley liked to fill the club with them.' There was an ivory envelope among the blooms, too. She opened it and read the card inside. '"With great sadness on your bereavement, Humphrey Bogart."'

'Riley knew interesting people.'

'I hope it makes him happy now.'

The black-and-white chequer tiles and the sweeping marble staircase in the hallway were just as Ken remembered them: cold, clinical, lifeless. Coraline's heels clicked on them like a clock as they made their way into the main living space, what had always been called the ballroom, where the parties of the young, gorgeous and abandoned had once filled the night air with music.

Coraline stopped to turn on the lights that hung in crystal chandeliers. Then she dropped the flowers, which exploded across the marble. Ken spun around, staring at what the shimmering lights had illuminated. On the glass walls, a hand had painted words, the same words over and over again: *Honora wasn't happy, I'll tell you that. Honora wasn't happy, I'll tell you that. Honora wasn't happy, I'll tell you that.*

Coraline inhaled, controlling herself with her breath. Then she turned her hooded eyes to Ken. 'You know what this is, don't you?'

He did. And he guessed there would be something else in that wide room. His vision scanned over it, until it fell on the white grand piano that had entertained those parties of youth and insincerity. On top of it was a copy of the book.

'*Honora wasn't happy, I'll tell you that*' proclaimed the start of the third and final story of *The Waterfall*.

'Stay behind me.' He proceeded to check the whole house. The kitchen, the library and bedrooms upstairs. No, whoever it was, they had gone. And a smashed window at the side of the house was obviously how they had gotten in. 'Whoever they are, they've latched on to us and they're not letting go,' he said.

'I can see that.' She screwed a Nat Sherman into her amber holder and lit it. Then she went to one of the windows and stared out. The moonlight left the warped shadow of painted words on her skin. 'Do you think he's coming for us?'

'No. I think he's taunting us.' Yeah, it had been a hell of a day, and Ken had just discovered that it wasn't over. He glanced at the book and noticed something unusual. The paper was thinner and cheaper than usual. He examined it. On the bottom of the cover, below the author's name, G. B. Faulkner, were the words 'PROOF COPY'.

'This is a proof,' he said thoughtfully.

'What's that?'

'They're early prints sent out to journalists for review, or to writers and editors to check for mistakes. Not for sale.' He stared at the painted words again. 'I'll call Jakes.' She made the tip of her cigarette glow in reply. He went to the telephone and dialled the station.

He heard a cop on the other end call out, 'Jakes, hey, Jakes. For you.'

'Tell them to call back in the morning. I'm clocking off.'

But before the cop on the line could relay the message, Ken spoke. 'Tell him it's Ken Kourian. I'm at Turnglass House. We've had another message from our friend.' And he hung up.

Thirty minutes was what it took for Detective Jakes to stumble wearily into the house rubbing the five o'clock shadow on his chin and complaining about how hungry he was. He clocked the painted words on the windows and shrugged as if he was past caring.

'What now?' Ken asked.

'Get some turpentine.'

'I'm not talking home maintenance, Detective. This means he's going after another victim.'

'So you're his messenger boy now?' He sat down. 'Got a drink?'

'On the job?' Coraline asked.

'Best time for it.' Ken made him one. 'I don't usually get to drink stuff this good.'

'It was my husband's favourite. A thirty-year-old Dalmore.'

Jakes looked her up and down. 'He had good taste.'

'Careful, Detective.'

'Yeah, yeah, I'll be careful. Jus' let me take the weight off for ten minutes.' He took off his shoes and loosened the faded blue tie that wound around his neck. 'You two, you always bring me a headache. Jus' when I think I'm havin' a nice quiet day, up you pop again.' He upended his glass. 'All right, all right. So we got another warnin'. This one's about the last story in the book, I presume.'

'You presume correctly.'

'Yeah, I got a talent for it. An' what's this one called?'

'The Venice Murders.'

'Okay, hand it over.'

Ken gave the detective the proof copy. He glanced at it, went to make a call to the station, returned and settled down with the book and another expensive Scotch. An hour later, he had skimmed through the story and the boys in blue had arrived to take photographs, flick fingerprint dust around and generally make a mess for nothing.

It was midnight, and they had all had enough of the circus around them.

'Stay at my place tonight,' Ken told Coraline. 'I'll get some clothes.'

Chapter 20

The next morning, he left her asleep in his bed and walked to the streetcar stop. He wanted to collar Jakes at the station before the detective went out and couldn't be found.

'Mr Kourian?' It was a big man with a small head and a huge hat. His check suit was wearing him.

'It depends who's asking.'

'Mr Siegel is askin'. You Mr Kourian for Mr Siegel?'

'Yes, I am.'

'Then that is to the good.' He spoke like his nostrils had been sealed with glue. 'Would you be so kind as to get in the automobile?' He waved his hand at a sleek Chrysler on the other side of the road.

Ken didn't need asking twice. And neither did he bother asking how the junior gangster had known where to find him. After all, it didn't matter; they had found him. Bugsy Siegel probably always found you. The chauffeur tapped his cap and put the car in gear.

'Mind telling me where we're heading?'

'To see Mr Siegel. I would have thought that was obvious.'

The car swung up Western, but then onto the Hollywood Freeway. 'This isn't the way to Mr Siegel's house,' said Ken. His instinct was kicking in. And it was kicking hard.

'We'll go where—'

'Ah, save it.' He had a hard time being scared of a man who sounded like he'd misunderstood the point of sniffing glue.

Off the Freeway and into Hollywood itself. Ken knew the patch. He had spent years trying to get onto it, then months trying to get out.

Hello, RKO, he said to himself as the car slowed and turned through the studio gates. It came to a stop in the parking lot, and a beautiful girl with a clipboard and dreams of making it big that she had just about pinned to her shirt for all to see escorted him and glue-nose past the shooting lots and over to a corner office in the main building. Bugsy Siegel was sitting on a modern couch that was made of chrome tubes, smoking a cigar and looking delighted.

'Ken, good of you to come,' he said. Ken shook his hand. 'This is Terence Zoot.' It had to be a made-up name. 'We're in partnership on a couple of projects. We have a proposal for you.'

'Already? Not even flowers first?'

Zoot, a nervous-looking midget sitting on a raised-up chair behind a smoked glass desk, laughed more heartily than any man would have done if he had meant it. 'No, Mr Kourian, Mr Siegel—'

'Bugsy, please.'

'Bugsy.' The producer inclined his head, taking the

benediction of a Catholic saint who also happened to be a Jewish hoodlum. 'Bugsy says you would be perfect for fronting a television show we have on the slate.'

Well, that took the cake.

'Really? I'm sorry if I sound sceptical, but I am.'

'I understand that you have a prestigious acting career already.'

'Prestigious? I once had two lines in a third-rate picture, if that's what you mean.'

'But you have presence. *Presence!*' Zoot might have been announcing the second coming of Jesus Christ.

Ken supposed there was no harm in stringing them along.

'So, what's the show?'

'Crimes. Killings, shootings, bank jobs. We reconstruct them, interview the witnesses – and if we're lucky, the perpetrators.'

'That would make for quite a night's entertainment.'

'I can see you comprehend its potential.'

'Yeah, I think I do.'

'We would want to start right away. On the investigation you're working on right now. Mr— uh, Bugsy has filled me in. It sounds like a cracker.'

'It sure is. Tell me, what's the name of this show?'

'That's the best part. *Murder Tonight.* Unforgettable, right?'

'For certain.'

'Good.'

'Just like a burst appendix.' The small man looked confused, then crestfallen, like Ken had taken away his favourite toy. 'I'm going to say no. And it's not a "no, thank you", it's just a "no".'

The room was filled with a slow clapping.

'Bravo, Ken, I had a feeling you wouldn't go for it,' said the handsome Bugsy Siegel. 'But it was worth a spin.'

'I'm sure it was. Now, it's been brief, but you gentlemen are very busy so I won't take up another minute of your time. Would you be so kind as to arrange for your pet gorilla to take me back to where he found me?'

He smiled. 'Of course. And Ken?'

'Yes.'

'I'll be seeing you.'

'I'm sure you will.'

Two buses and an hour later, he was striding towards Jakes's desk. The detective was attempting to speak at the same time as lifting a coffee mug that read STAY THE DISTANCE to his lips. Every time it came close, he had to lower it as he growled more words of wisdom to a junior officer, who was struggling to take down the main points. 'Look, just get onto it, will you? We don't have the whole year!' He caught sight of Ken. 'What, you just walk straight in these days? The boys on the front desk—'

'Said it would be okay. Don't get all twisted over this.'

'Twisted over this? Over *this*? You kiddin' me? You don't know what's happenin' in the city?' Ken tossed some papers from the seat of an office chair. He noticed a copy of *The Waterfall* on Jakes's desk, half-hidden by a diary. 'Tell me.'

'Okay, big shot, I'll tell you. Chaos. It's jus' 'bout chaos out there. Since the press call last night an' then reports 'bout what we found at your girl's house, we got a switchboard lightin' up with people askin' if they need to get outta the city or tellin' us it's their neighbour or the Communists or the Japs.' He sipped his coffee angrily. 'I got called into the Chief of Police's office at six in the morning – six! – to be told that he wants this man caught. As if I was just sittin' 'bout an' waitin' for him to hand himself in.'

'It must be someone with a grudge against Coraline or me.'

'Y'don't say. I mean, right now that only narrows it down to all'a these guys.' He swept his arm across the office. 'But sure, thanks for the tip.'

'Do you have anything?'

'Yeah, we got somethin'. We found your G. B. Faulkner.'

'Where?'

'You're not gonna believe.'

Chapter 21

As Ken and Coraline pulled into the parking lot for the Hollywood Cemetery, they saw Jakes emerging from his car – this one was a Chevrolet Deluxe 5, a long way from the Caddy that Ken had taken from him and handed to Bugsy Siegel. A couple more uniformed cops emerged from a prowler behind him.

'What's that about?' Ken pointed to a bus, painted flamingo pink but now faded in the California sun, which was pouring out excited families with leaflets, brown paper bags and cameras.

'Tour group,' Coraline told him. 'They come to see the stars' graves.' Sometimes LA still had the power to surprise Ken.

'Who's buried here?'

'Ask them.'

'Okay.' And he went over. 'Good afternoon, sir, you have a lovely family,' he told one sweating middle-aged man with an apple in his mouth. 'May I have a brief look at your guide?' The man couldn't speak through the apple but offered up a folded pamphlet. It had a map of the graveyard, with circles marked

'Rudolph Valentino', 'Douglas Fairbanks' and 'Tragic Peggy Shannon' among graves hosting the unremembered dead. Each grave had a number.

Ken gazed at the open gates. *You should let the dead sleep*, he thought.

'Let's get this over with!' Jakes called over.

'Sure.'

Guided by the numbers on the pamphlet, Jakes led the way through the cemetery's Jewish section, where small headstones decorated with Stars of David, menorahs and Hebrew script lined the way, then into the Episcopalian section with more ornate headstones showing crucifixes. In the distance, a group of mourners stood at a graveside scattering soil on a newly interred coffin.

'Over there, where that woman is,' he said. There was a woman dressed in a black outfit kneeling at a grave, her back to them.

They picked their way across neatly cut grass towards the grave. The woman seemed lost in her thoughts, bent over in apparent prayer, not turning to face them as they drew close. She had thin grey hair drawn back into a tight bun.

'Ma'am, police. Could I ask you to step away from the grave?' Jakes said as he reached her. She didn't respond. He put his hand on her shoulder and moved around to face her. 'Christ Almighty,' he growled, staring into her face.

At the same moment, Ken reached them and looked down at what the cop had seen. The woman's face was pale and wrinkled. So was the skin on her neck, except for a livid red ring around her throat. And she was bent over because her chest was resting on something wooden: an eyeless shop mannequin, with its hands on her throat, kneeling in a mirror image of her. Take it away and her dead body would collapse onto the grave.

Ken looked all around. Nothing and no one looking back. The mourners at the other grave, which was at least fifty or sixty yards away, were engrossed in their prayers. The bus party of people looking for the graves of dead actors was at the far side of the park.

The headstone at the woman's feet read: *George Berwick Faulkner. Born 19th February 1889. Passed into the presence of God 2nd September 1937.*

'Who is she?' Coraline asked nobody in particular.

'If I knew that, I'd be at least some way to knowin' what the hell is happenin' here,' Jakes replied. 'Jesus, Mary an' Leon.' He narrowed his eyes at Ken. 'Were you expectin' this?'

'Hardly. Tell your men to sniff around the place. Maybe whoever did it is still here.'

'Ah, you know as well as I do that he ain't.'

'Just do it, Jakes.'

The detective huffed in annoyance but directed the uniforms to quickly check the perimeter of the cemetery and shake down any suspicious characters. The officers dragged their attention away from the old woman. The midday heat would slow them down soon enough.

Ken sized her up. Aged in her sixties. Medium height and weight. Suntanned complexion. Black woollen dress, equally black shoes with neatly tied laces. There was a black soft hat like a beret on the ground in front of her and a white purse beside it. Jakes opened the purse and took out a little money, a bunch of house keys, a membership card for a bath house, a flyer for a shoe store and a brown paper bag with crumbs in it.

'So now what do we do?' Ken asked.

Jakes wiped the sweat from his forehead with his sleeve. 'I'm outta my jurisdiction. Gotta call it in to LA County.'

'I could do without their help.'

'Yeah. Me, too.'

Three hours later, they were leaning on a stone grave nearby watching the County police swarm around, shooting angry glances their way. Coraline had moved to a weatherbeaten bench some way off to watch from a distance. The body had been respectfully placed on a stretcher and taken a few yards away, where it was being examined by a police pathologist.

'You haven't made any friends here, Jakes.'

'I got you to thank for that. Again. What is it with you an' pissin' people off?'

'Everyone needs a hobby.'

Jakes lifted his hat from the lichen-covered stone, placed it unevenly on his head and walked over to the local detective captain. 'So what we got here?' he asked.

'What we got?' repeated the local guy in a voice deeper than Ken would have expected, given that he was about five foot six. 'What we got is you bozos way outta your area!' He sounded as exasperated as

Jakes looked, and Ken thought they must teach them that at cop school.

Ken pushed himself away from the grave and approached. He was tired of watching cops bicker. 'Look, tell us what you know, and we'll be on our way,' he said.

'Vic is Maria Spiteri. We got that from this bath house ticket. We called her husband. He doesn't speak great English. Seems they're—'

'Italian,' Ken interjected.

'Yeah. How'd you . . .'

'I'll tell you when I've got a month to explain.'

The local officer accepted this. He would have been happy if none of this had ended up on his plate at all. 'Well, the husband said – we think he said – that his wife was offered a job. All she had to do was bring flowers to the cemetery. This grave, I guess.'

They all looked down at the rectangular mound of earth, grass and weeds and the carved stone that spelled out George Berwick Faulkner's name, the dates he came into and left the world. Nothing about what he had done, who he really was. Or that he had written a book, it seemed.

'Poor bastard,' Ken muttered.

'The vic?' Jakes asked.

'Her. Him. Frankie Angel. Riley Tithe, while we're at it. Whatever's going on, this guy's not behind it.'

'That's for certain.'

The police medical officer, a bearded Irishman with a heavy accent and nervously fluttering hands, was finishing up. 'It's just as it looks, officers. Strangled with a ligature. From behind, I would say. No other marks on her body that I can see. Between two and four hours ago.'

The local cop nodded his thanks, and the body was removed.

'*Go away! Go away!*' It was a female voice, screaming from a distance.

Ken turned to see two young girls dressed in white blouses and black skirts running towards them.

'Who're they?' Jakes asked, sounding mystified.

'I'll bet anything you want they're George Berwick Faulkner's daughters.'

'Ah, jeez. That's all we need.'

'*Go away!*'

Jakes and the local cop went to intercept the two girls, taking gentle but firm hold of the children.

'Girls, we're cops,' Jakes said.

'*Get off his grave!*' shrieked the taller of the two.

'I'm sorry, miss, but we have to do this.' The girl bit him on the hand. '*Ow!*'

'You need to brush up on your restraint technique,' Ken called over.

'Ah, shove it!' He loosened his grip on the girl but stayed blocking her path and squatted down to speak to her. 'Who told you to come here?'

'Our brother. He said you were taking Dad out of his grave.'

'No, sweetheart,' Jakes said, struggling for a reply. 'We just came lookin' for him.'

'Why?'

'Why? Well.' He hesitated. 'We just did.' The younger

girl began to cry, and Jakes looked ashamed. 'I'm sorry. Look.' He beckoned over a couple of uniforms. 'Go with these gentlemen, okay?'

'Or what?' demanded the older girl defiantly.

'Or we'll arrest you. You want that?' His tone was harder now, though Ken knew that Jakes would just as likely turn backflips as arrest a couple of young girls. 'Okay, then jus' . . . let us do our job.'

'Gabriel . . .'

'Gabriel what?'

'He said we had to stop you.'

And Ken realized that their search had been directed to the wrong member of the family. 'Your brother's called Gabriel?' he asked quickly.

'Yes.'

'Is he a writer?'

'Yes.'

Ken stopped to work out how their brother knew they were at the grave. He must have been keeping tabs on them in one way or another. 'He told you to come here?'

'We have to do as he says.'

There was something in her face that made Ken concerned. 'What if you don't?' he asked. The girl looked at the ground and rubbed her left arm. Ken stooped and gingerly pulled up her white blouse sleeve. She tried to stop him, but he gently moved her hand away. As the cotton lifted up, it revealed a number of bruises. Some brown and old, some red and new. Ken slipped the sleeve back down and stood up, looking into the distance and wondering.

Jakes told the uniforms to take the kids away, and muttered something under his breath.

'The brother,' Ken said. 'He's the G. B. Faulkner we're looking for.'

'I guess he is.'

'Hello, ladies!' It was shouted from a distance. Ken wasn't happy to see Detective Tadit flanked by his usual two subordinates. 'We heard you screwed up again. Oh, look, another deceased! You girls really know your jobs, right?' He came over and stood smirking by the grave.

'Go back t'your precinct, Tadit,' Jakes snarled. 'You got no reason t'be here.'

'And you have? What, to make sure more people die?'

'Don't tempt me.'

Chapter 22

The Faulkners – those still alive – resided in San Diego. He kept it to himself, but Ken enjoyed the drive down along the Pacific Highway in the convertible Rolls-Royce Phantom III that Coraline had inherited from Riley. His arm over the side of the car, the radio playing honky-tonk, the sun beating down to sparkle on the waves beside the road, he could almost forget where they were heading and why. There had been times like that even when he was in Romania, when he could see trees and mountains and birds and nothing of what was going on around him. It would only last an hour, maybe two, of course, but that time was golden.

The two sisters, who were riding in Jakes's car, directed the short motorcade to the family home, while the local cops had returned to their station to fill out the paperwork necessary for finding someone dead in a cemetery.

And then there was the house: a fallen-on-hard-times mansion built for a man who'd read too many books about ancient Rome. Jakes stepped out of his car and sceptically checked it out. He looked like his journey hadn't been as pleasant as Ken's: he had torn his tie off, his hat was nowhere to be seen and he was sweating hard.

'The hell is this place? A mausoleum?' asked the cop.

'You worried about ghosts?'

'Maybe I am.'

The girls led them in, past the busts of emperors, over the broken plaster on the floor. To the room where a man lay encased in a machine that breathed for him.

'Gabriel Faulkner,' Ken said, his eyes meeting those of the man inside the machine. The man smiled.

'Are you Ken Kourian?' The voice was slow and graceful.

'Yeah.'

'I thought you might favour me with a visit.' He banged on the inside of the machine, and his sister scuttled forward to open it and bring his air canister. 'And . . . who . . . might . . . you . . . be?' he rasped, the effort contorting his face.

'Detective Sergeant Jakes, LAPD.'

Faulkner waited for Coraline to speak, too. Eventually she did.

'Mind if I smoke?' she said.

'Yes . . . I . . . do.'

In response, she opened her purse, took out her silver cigarette case and screwed a Nat Sherman into her amber holder. She took half a step back before lighting it. 'Is that better?'

He smiled around the tube in his mouth.

'You can drop the act. You know who she is,' Ken said.

'I . . . know . . . who . . . she . . . is.'

'You've been watching us. Or your sisters have. It's flattering, but why?'

Gabriel haltingly turned himself and the cart a quarter turn to his left. The girls looked up expectantly. 'The . . . Chapterhouse,' he told them. And the three of them made a gradual trip across the dusty floor, heading for a doorway flanked by dead potted plants.

Ken followed, then Jakes, with Coraline's heels clipping on the dry boards. 'Hey,' Jakes muttered to Ken. 'Guy looks like he died ten years ago an' someone forgot to tell him.'

'You're not exactly a Greek god yourself, Detective.'

'Yeah, yeah.' They stopped talking when they entered a long room full of rotting food and abandoned chairs. The only sounds then were their own breaths. 'What's this for, Mr Faulkner?' Jakes asked, his voice aggressive with suspicion.

Faulkner moved on without an answer, the wheels of his cart squeaking like rodents.

And then they were in an octagonal library, with the art of salvation on the walls alongside a portrait of Faulkner's father galloping past on a chestnut horse and copies of a book with a blue cover that read *The Waterfall* stuffed into every space. With an effort, Gabriel drew one from the nearest shelf and thrust it at Ken.

'You . . . can . . . read . . . it . . . if . . . you . . . want,' he rasped.

'I've read it before,' Ken said. 'Both sides.'

He couldn't drag his gaze from the oil painting of the senior Faulkner. He went nearer and looked closely at it. Invisible from any more than two feet away, there were a series of little scores in the canvas, where it had been mended. Hairline slashes of a few inches or more. The repairs had been expertly done, but the marks couldn't be hidden entirely.

'But . . . I . . . want . . . you . . . to!' Faulkner smacked his palm down on the book.

'The Tookes are powerful,' whispered the elder girl. 'They caused our difficulties.'

'What difficulties?' Ken said.

'It was to be Gabriel's day of glory. A night of splendour.'

'Be . . . quiet!' her brother snapped, then had to grab hold of her to catch his breath. When he had taken three lungfuls, he pushed her aside and she fell hard against a bookcase. Jakes tried to help her up, but she pushed him away. 'You are . . . here . . . to . . . gloat. That . . . her . . . brother . . . destroyed . . . my . . . book.' His eyes burned into Coraline's.

'We're here because someone is committing a series of crimes.'

His face lit up. 'What . . . crimes? Tell . . . me.' His hand shot out and gripped Ken's shirt. It was forcefully knocked away.

'Murders. You know anything about them?'

Gabriel's face contorted. Then his chest panted.

'Are you *laughin'*?' Jakes demanded.

'I'm . . . I'm . . . so . . . sorry . . . Detective. Do . . . you . . . want . . . me . . . to . . . confess?'

'You need a lawyer?' Jakes said.

'My . . . lawyer . . . handles . . . movie . . . studios . . . not . . . murder.'

'Maybe we'll just set a watch on you.'

'Beyond . . . your . . . jurisdiction . . . Detective.' And he fell to his knees, shaking and panting, his face contorting with airless laughter.

Coraline spoke. 'Enjoy this while you can. It won't last.' She dropped her cigarette to the floor, where it burned itself out.

'The . . . Tookes.' He thrust a finger at her. Pulled it back and thrust it again. 'Damn . . . the . . . Tookes!'

They stopped the Rolls-Royce in front of Coraline's glass home. Ken helped her out of the car.

'Hey, Mr Kourian!' He turned and immediately something flashed in his face. A Kodak 35 clicked. The reporter he had taught some manners at the press call was sitting in a Ford Tudor.

'What do you want?' Ken said. He wasn't in the mood for a dust-up.

'Anthony Willis. The *Examiner*. We met before.'

'I know.'

'Yeah. Well, I heard he's hit again. In a cemetery, right?'

'You tell me.'

'Okay, I'll tell you. And I'll tell you something else: we're calling him the Mannequin Killer on account of—'

'How his nails are cut?'

The reporter looked confused. 'No, manne . . .' But then his face cracked into a smile, and he wagged his finger. 'Okay, okay, you got me. You're not some dumb flatfoot. Our readers have a right to know what's going on. Can you fill them in? You might save a life.'

'I'll save one right now by telling you to get off this property before I shoot you dead.'

'Okay, Mr Kourian. Mrs Tithe: a little birdie tells me the killer is a fan of your brother's writing. Leaves his books at the scene. That so? You a fan of it yourself?' She walked away without a word. 'How about you, Mr Kourian?'

Ken thrust his hand inside his jacket, the reporter hit the gas pedal and the Ford was out of sight in seconds.

Chapter 23

The morning light bounced drunkenly off the iron lung as Gabriel Faulkner lay inside watching his younger sister read from the *Examiner*. Her face showed the concentration of someone who doesn't want to get a word wrong. She had shown him the front-page headline: *City in Terror of Mannequin Killer!* Below it were police photographs of the murder scene at the Silver Waterfall Club. Someone on the force had been making a little money on the sly, by the looks of things. And below those pictures was one of Ken snapped the evening before outside Turnglass House.

Mr Ken Kourian with Mrs Coraline Tithe at the Tooke family seat, known as Turnglass. What is their connection to the crimes? read the caption.

Faulkner closed his eyes in pain. 'Call for the car,' he said.

A Caddy came, driven by a black man in a peaked cap. He looked like his natural character was to be jolly, but the atmosphere at the Faulkner residence had drained all the spirit from him. He didn't look back as his three passengers crawled onto the cracked leather seats.

The elder girl gave him directions. He consulted a map, then put the car in gear and rolled over the threadbare gravel.

It was a long journey out to Point Dume. A hot day – a day like any other – and the two girls pressed their faces to the shut windows. They passed other children playing with balloons, riding bikes, tripping and grazing their knees. 'I hate the Tookes,' the twelve-year-old said. The other glanced at her, then back out to where an ice-cream shop had a line of people waiting. It disappeared behind them.

Three hours later, they stopped outside a house made of glass. Faulkner trundled to the entrance, gripping the cart that held his gas canister for support. He pressed the electric bell button, and a Mexican maid answered.

'I . . . am . . . an . . . old . . . friend . . . of . . . Mr . . . Oliver . . . Tooke. I . . . have . . . been . . . out . . . of . . . the . . . country . . . for . . . some . . . years . . . and . . . have . . . only . . . recently . . . learned . . . of . . . his . . . death. I . . . understand . . . his . . . grave . . . is . . . here.' The maid nodded. 'May . . . I . . . pay . . . my . . . respects?' The woman blinked three times like she had never been asked such a strange question in all her life. But when Faulkner reached into his pocket and pulled out a sawbuck, the maid checked over her shoulder, snatched it away and hurried out, leading them around to the back of the house. She pointed out into the ocean. About a hundred yards from the shore, there was a mound of rock rising up from the water as if it was trying to get dry. Something like a little white lighthouse had been built on it. 'Ah . . . that . . . was . . . his . . . writing . . . tower.'

The servant checked again that there was no one from the house within earshot. 'Yes. He wrote there every day,' she confirmed. 'They buried him there.' The waves were breaking on the foot of the tower.

'Fitting.' He drew from his own pocket a copy of the book that was titled *The Waterfall* on one side and *The Turnglass* on the other. 'We . . . wrote . . . this . . . book. He . . . and . . . I.' He threw it limply in the direction of the tower. It fell to the ground no more than a yard from his shoes. The wind pulled a few pages up, then they flicked back into place. The maid looked nervous and backed away, slipping back into the house through the rear entrance and watching from a distance.

Jakes stood on the circular stage of the Silver Waterfall Club. It was ten in the morning, but all the lights were on. A few uniformed cops were standing around, poking around.

When the call had come in an hour earlier, he had taken the details wearily, no longer angry or amazed. '*Another one,*' he had muttered to himself.

'This like how it was before?' he asked Coraline gruffly.

She gazed around at the walls. They had been painted with words, '*had to bury those three himself*' over and over. A copy of the book they came from was open at Jakes's feet. And this time an extra gift had been folded into its pages: an empty hypodermic needle.

'No,' she said. 'Last time, the body of my husband was where you are standing.'

'Yeah, okay,' Jakes said quietly. 'I guess he wanted to send a message again. But your house an' his apartment are probably too hot right now. Too many people would ask questions. So he comes back here.'

'Makes sense, I guess,' Ken said, though he wasn't a hundred per cent convinced.

'Thing is, what the hell's this for? Three stories in your book. Three murders. He's done them all. What now? Do them again? An' what's with the syringe?'

The book showed a fine spray of grey dust. 'You've checked this for prints, right?' Ken asked.

'Right. All wiped off, as usual.'

'I'll tell you what it's for. Three stories, three murders. But those aren't the only deaths in the book.'

'What?'

Ken's finger traced the red words on the wall: *had to bury those three himself.*

'In "The Venice Murders", three more people died before the story even began.'

Jakes looked ready for rage. 'You sayin' there's gonna be three more? *Three?*'

'That's what it means.'

Jakes unbuttoned his collar. 'Jesus. What the hell do we do?'

'I'm pretty sure I know who's behind it all. And

they're picking victims based on the names of the stories.'

'So . . .'

'We've got a shot to catch them. But you need to lock down Venice. Our Venice. Venice Beach.'

Jakes stared hard at the paint running down the wall. 'You sure that's where he's gonna kill next?'

'I didn't say that. I said we have to lock down Venice.'

Jakes moved so that he stood face to face with Ken. His eyes narrowed. 'What is it?'

'What's what?'

'What you're keepin' to yourself.'

Ken didn't answer the question, not directly. 'Jakes, you have to ask yourself a question: do you *want* to trust me on this?'

The cop stood rock-still for half a minute before he breathed out. 'How long do you think we have?'

Ken was relieved that Jakes was giving him the leeway he needed. 'Going by previous attacks, anywhere from two days to half an hour ago. We go and see Faulkner, and the next day this. It's a message: we're not in control, they are. So let's do something about that.'

The press circus this time was in the square parking lot of the police station on Clune Avenue in Venice. Someone in the Chief of Police's office had chosen that precinct for no good reason, and the station learnt it was going to play host to fifty or more reporters, a few bereaved family members, some cops from the

City detective bureau and who-knows-how-many hangers-on about two hours before the curtain went up on the afternoon show.

'Why are we doing it out here?' Ken asked Jakes as he kicked stones away, a couple of yards from where a microphone had been set up.

'Told us somethin' 'bout the only room big enough being closed for decoratin',' Jakes grunted back. 'Total bull. Truth is they just don't like that we're on their patch. Now we look like idiots out on a picnic.'

At least the police prowlers had been taken out and left on the roads outside. Now they just had the midday heat to battle. A light breeze lifted a mist of dust into their faces, making them cough. In front of them, groups of journalists stood laughing, sharing cigarettes, pushing each other around as jokes or warnings. A radio broadcast crew was fixing the antenna on the roof of their van. On the other side of the road, kids were filtering back into a middle school after lunch.

'Detective, are you going to tell us what's going on?'

It was Anthony Willis of the *Examiner*, of course. He was accompanied this time by a photographer, who stood behind him, framing shots.

'Just wait.'

'What for? Are you going to catch him in the next ten minutes?' The photographer laughed so hard that he shook.

'Fine,' Jakes muttered. He walked to the microphone and didn't wait for the chatter to stop. 'We believe the man some people are calling the "Mannequin Killer" is goin' to strike again soon.'

The reporters ran to record him on tape and film. 'Where?' yelled one.

'Here in Venice.'

Ken was irritated to see an unmarked car pull up and Tadit get out and lean against the hood with his arms crossed, watching the show. But Ken's mood changed when he saw the reporter Willis also notice the cop and give him a nod on the down-low. Well, that cleared up the little mystery of how the journalist always knew the state of the investigation.

'So you know who he is?' a radio presenter with a microphone asked Jakes.

'I didn't say that.'

'But do you? Don't play games, Detective.'

Ken saw Frankie Angel's brother and wife arrive in a taxi and hurry over.

'I'm not playin' games. We got leads, we got information. I can't reveal all of it.'

Out of the corner of his eye, Ken could see that Willis wasn't paying full attention to what Jakes was saying. He was staring in the other direction, across the road to the middle school.

'Then reveal some of it. We have to—'

The man was interrupted by Willis. 'Hey, Detective, are you holding this here because it's opposite the school?' They all turned their heads to look across the street like him.

'The school?' Jakes said.

'Yeah. Is the school the target? Are *all* schools

targets?' The press men suddenly stopped moving.
They could sense something happening.

Get out of there, Jakes, Ken thought.

'The schools are . . . I mean, we haven't identified
the target . . .' He was beginning to lose control of
what was happening.

Get out of there.

'So it could be *any* school? *Any* school in Venice?'

'I . . . we don't know.'

'Any school in Venice!' The cameras rolled or
clicked, the pens took down his words and made them
more shocking for the evening newspapers.

'What should people do?'

Jakes had prepared a few comments for this question. 'Stay with other people. Lock your doors.'

'Get a gun?'

'I'm not sayin' that.'

'You're not saying *not* to.'

'I'm sayin'—'

'What about the schools? If parents are worried,
should they take their kids out of school?'

'I guess, if they're worried . . .'

Should have gotten out of there, Ken thought. He
knew exactly where this was going.

'So what are you going to do about it?'

'We're floodin' the area with officers. We're sendin'
a message to this man: not in our city. If he's out
there, we'll catch him.'

'You sure about that?' It wasn't shouted by a journalist, it was shouted by Detective Tadit, leaning
against the hood of his car. There were a few sniggers.

'Yeah, I'm sure 'bout that.'

'Ah, well, if you're *sure*. You know who he is?'

'We got a damn good idea.'

'Give us a name,' shouted a female reporter in a loud pantsuit.

'You'll get it when the handcuffs are on. You'll get everything then!' Visibly angry, he threw up his hands and stalked away from the podium as some of the journalists ran off to file their stories and others hung around to josh each other.

'Mr Kourian.' It was Carlos Angelo, Frankie's brother, keeping his voice low. 'What's going on? I got a message to come here with . . . her.' He chewed over the final word as he glared at his sister-in-law.

'We think the man who killed your brother is going to hit Venice tonight.' Carlos's mouth opened and closed a couple of times without sound. Diane Angelo clutched her purse to her chest.

'Venice? Why here?'

'He's choosing the locations and victims from the book. The final story is called "The Venice Murders".'

'Oh!' Diane gasped.

'You heard Jakes say the cops are going to flood the town. He wants everyone to stay in their homes. That way, we'll be able to spot him.'

'But won't he just not do it?' she replied. 'He'll see all the police.'

Ken looked her straight in the eye. 'I know this man. I know he won't back down. He's obsessed. He's been taunting us, taunting me, from the beginning. If he didn't want a showdown, he would have stayed in the shadows. No, he wants that showdown. We'll be there for it.'

'I see.'

'And we need you out with the cops tonight. You'll be spotters.'

'What?' gasped Diane.

'This man doesn't leave things to chance. He's cased your home. He's watched the two of you. You've seen him, even if you don't know it. And you might recognize him.'

'But it's dangerous!' Diane yelped. 'I don't want to. I want to stay at home.'

Ken put a hand on her shoulder. 'You'll be in a police car with at least two armed officers and a radio link to a hundred more. You'll be safer there than at home, I'll tell you that.'

'All right, all right,' she whispered. 'Can I go home now?'

'I've got something to take care of first. Jakes?' He took the cop, who looked like he wanted to break something, over to where Willis was smoking and laughing about something with his photographer. 'Ha-ha, what's the joke?' Ken asked with a smile.

'Mr Kourian,' Willis said through his cigarette, a bad-smelling Chesterfield. 'Want to make a statement to the press? You didn't last night.'

'Yeah, I want to make a statement. It's this. You're about to be arrested for paying off a police officer.' The reporter's jaw fell an inch. 'And that's a very serious offence, right?' he asked Jakes.

Jakes stared at the reporter, who looked desperately

at his photographer for support. He didn't get any. 'Very serious.'

'How long could he get?'

'Eight years. Thing is,' the cop said, 'it's not how long the jolt is, it's *where* it is. Corruptin' a cop, you're seen as a big risk. So you're in the Rock.'

'You mean fucking *Alcatraz*?' Willis said, spitting his cigarette to the ground and wafting smoke out of his eyes.

'I mean fuckin' Alcatraz.'

Willis stared again at his photographer and back to the two men in front of him, then relaxed. 'No, you have nothing on me.'

'Your big mistake was the photo,' Ken said. 'Of the crime scene at the Silver Waterfall. You see, the information in your story, well, that could have come from anywhere. Hard to trace. But the photo, that came from Detective Tadit. And we can trace a photograph.' He pointed to where the arrogant, big cop was back sitting in his car, eating a hamburger. 'Eight years in the Rock. Man, I hear they got a murder rate inside that's a hundred times what it is outside.'

'At least,' said Jakes.

Willis winced in pain. 'How do I make this go away?' he muttered.

'Rat out Tadit – before he rats you out. And to make the deal a little sweeter, when we catch the killer, we'll give you a head start on the facts.'

'What do you mean, rat him out?'

Jakes moved in closer to the man. 'Right now, you an' me go into the station here, you sign an affidavit.

The affidavit will give dates and sums that you paid Tadit for information an' those cute pictures you got in the paper. Don't worry, we'll write all the dates an' sums for you.' Willis tried to work his jaw into speech, but Jakes didn't give him the chance. 'You will also attest that he was the source of the information in your rag last year that the Commissioner's son had been caught in a dope house.'

He managed words now. 'That . . . He wasn't.'

'But you'll say that he was. And then you go home nice an' free. An' what we do with that signed statement is our business. But you won't be seein' Detective Tadit around so much after that.'

Willis hesitated, looking from one to the other. His voice turned sly. There was, after all, an upside. 'And I get an exclusive on the arrest?'

'You have my word. Wait for us in the lobby. We'll be there in less than a minute. And don't even think of changin' your mind.'

'I won't.'

Now looking smug with the deal, he and his photographer walked towards the station entrance.

'Have you got any intention of keeping your word about that exclusive?' Ken asked.

'Sure I have. So long as Jesus Christ himself appears in the next five minutes an' tells me to.'

They approached Tadit's car. He was in the driving seat, spilling hamburger ketchup down his shirt.

'You enjoyin' that?' Jakes asked through the window.

'It's kinda cold,' the other cop mumbled through a mouthful of ground beef.

'Well, way I see it, we're 'bout to do you a favour.'

'Watcha mean?'

'We're givin' you a lot of time off to work on your cookery skills.' He laughed, slapped the top of the car twice and they walked towards the station to drive a stake through Tadit's career.

They had more important things to get onto right then, but truth be told, there was nothing Ken wanted to do more than settle the score with Tadit. He walked away from that car ten pounds lighter than when he'd walked towards it.

Gabriel Faulkner laboriously stood up from his chair and stretched over to turn off the radio, which had carried the press conference live. He looked at his biographer, who had taken the opportunity to write up some notes.

'Did . . . you . . . read . . . my . . . book?'

'I did. I liked it. Very innovative format.'

'*Mise en abyme.*'

The writer gazed up from his notebook. 'Oh yeah, *mise en abyme.*'

'Did . . . you . . . hear . . . the . . . news . . . broadcast?'

'I wasn't really listening. This will all turn out to be nothing, if you ask me.'

'You . . . think . . . so?' He paused. 'I . . . am . . . a . . . little . . . tired. I . . . think . . . that . . . is . . . all . . . for . . . today.'

After the biographer left, Faulkner made his way to the garden and began tapping at his typewriter again. A minute later, the biographer returned.

'I forgot my hat,' he said. He looked at the typewriter. 'You're writing again?'

'Yes.'

'I didn't realize.'

'I . . . feel . . . inspired.'

Chapter 24

It was the radio broadcast that set the animals running. Within half an hour, Ken watched as cars – first a few, then more, came to sharp halts in front of the school. Parents dashed in, fighting each other and coming out a few minutes later dragging upset kids.

After two more hours, the school was empty and Ken settled. Perspiration soaked through his shirt as they sat, baking in the canteen of the Venice second precinct police station. Half the ceiling of the major operations room had collapsed the day before due to a water leak in an upstairs bathroom and the other half was on its way, they had been told. So tonight's operation would have to be run from the only other large room in the two-storey concrete bunker. There was no food in the refrigerators, they couldn't work out how to activate the air conditioning and the water had been turned off.

Ken, Diane, Carlos and Jakes had been there for long enough to want to kick through the wall for a breeze. The sweat was so heavy in the air that it dripped down the walls and collected into reservoirs in the dented floor.

Two rows of trestle tables had been set up with telephones and radios, operated by female officers, all with their hair twisted back into neat buns. They spoke on one, then another, rapidly taking down details. Some of the notes went straight in the trash, some were discussed with their head officer, a few were sent over to Jakes.

His mood had started black and turned blacker. After the schools had been evacuated, a storm of fear and suspicion had hit the city. It had been no more than two hours after the first reports hit the airwaves that stores had closed and hospitals had posted security guards at every entrance.

Local residents had been interviewed on the radio and even the TV news, saying first that they were worried for their kids' lives, then that they were furious with the police department for leaving this killer on the streets and finally that they and their neighbours had formed safety groups to protect their families.

By seven, the first reports were coming in of men on the street blocking off roads, demanding to know who was who.

'This isn't America,' Jakes muttered as he was handed another note telling him that a cop car had been turned around and sent back to where it came from.

'It is now.' But Ken wasn't any happier with that being true.

'Detective!' one of the women called over, a radio headset pressed hard to her ear. Jakes looked over; it was the first time one of them had spoken directly to him.

'Yeah.'

'Mobile reports one of the vigilance committees has taken a man on Windward. They're saying he's the perp.'

'Who is he?' Jakes demanded, striding over.

'No more details. Just that.'

Jakes flashed a look to Ken and the other two. 'Could be nothin'. Could be somethin'.'

'Whatever it is, it's something.'

'Yeah, I guess it is. Let's go.'

And that was it. All four barrelled out to Jakes's car with little idea of what they were heading for. It was hot inside and somehow got hotter when they rolled the windows down and sped along Pacific, which was deserted in the dark, then onto Ocean Front Walk, narrower but still empty, running alongside the waves rolling onto the beach. One stretch still had people – men – on it, sitting around a campfire. Not speaking, just sitting with their backs to the sea, watching the road.

'Muscle Beach,' Jakes muttered. 'Those guys welcome trouble.'

He kept the gas coming until they were close to the corner with Windward Avenue, then stamped on the brake. Ken, in the front passenger seat, felt Carlos slam into the back of his seat. The reason for Jakes's emergency stop was obvious: the headlights lit up a barricade in the road made from a pile of metal poles that must have been ripped from a construction site.

There were three men standing beside it wearing white undershirts. One, the tallest and meanest-looking, held a baseball bat that waved in the headlight beams. Few of the houses and businesses had their lights on, and the streetlights were so underpowered that they might as well have given up.

'You plannin' on playin' ball?' Jakes demanded, getting out of the car and marching up.

'Who's askin'?' the guy replied in an Italian accent.

'Police.' Jakes showed him the badge folded over his belt.

'You can't keep us safe. So we keep us safe.'

Out of the corner of his eye, Ken saw the hotel where he used to meet Coraline in the afternoons. It seemed like a hundred years ago. It was five days.

Jakes grabbed hold of the bat and threw it across the street. The owner didn't try to stop him. It cracked onto the asphalt and rolled a yard or two before dropping into the gutter.

'You wanna be safe? Go back to your homes an' lock your doors. 'Cause if I see you out here again, I'm takin' all three of you in. An' you won't be safe in Folsom, I tell you that.'

The tall one smirked. 'I know why you came.'

'Oh, you do?'

'It's 'cause of who we got. We got your man.'

'Yeah? Where is he?'

'So now you want us to help you?'

'Listen,' Jakes said, stabbing the man in the chest with his finger, 'I'm tired of playin' third-grade games with you. Tell me where you have him or you're all comin' with him to the station. An' you won't be walkin'.'

One of the other guys put his hand on the tall man's back as a signal to give in and talk. He shrugged as if he couldn't care less. He pointed up the street past a grocery shop with wooden shutters over the windows. 'Back of the movie theatre.'

'All right. Now beat it.' He stood strong while the three men looked at each other and silently agreed to stalk away. One of the two mutes picked up the bat on the way.

Jakes went back to the car.

'They say he's in there.'

The front of the Venice Theatre, a stone's throw from the pier, was a lavish building with white tiles and yellow moulded flowers. Red bulbs blazed its name above the entrance. Tickets were a quarter, or ten cents on Tuesdays.

Ken and Coraline had paid their ten cents once. They'd watched a comedy and laughed for a while. Now, underneath letters spelling out '*Double Indemnity*', were more announcing '*Who Drew First?* starring Frankie Angel'. He saw that Diane had clocked the sign and bitten her lip.

A prowler passed with a cop hanging out of the window yelling through a loudhailer: '*Stay in your homes. Do not go out on the street. Stay in your homes. Do not go out on the street. Stay in . . .*'

'Is it safe around here?' Diane squawked. 'It doesn't look safe. Can we go back?'

'We need you,' Jakes told her while watching the theatre. 'We're goin' in there. You can wait outside.'

'You're going to leave us here alone?'

'Only if you want.'

'No, no, take us!' She sounded distraught.

'Okay, then.'

Jakes took a snub-nosed .38 revolver from a hip holster, opened the cylinder to check it was loaded, snapped it closed and put it back in the holster.

'Shouldn't you have that in your hand?' Diane insisted.

'Not necessary. Better like this. Safer. You go in with a piece in your hand and everyone gets jumpy real quick.'

She turned to Ken. 'What about you, do you have a gun?' she asked desperately.

'No.'

'Then . . . But . . .'

'Jus' get outta the car,' Jakes demanded, his temper slipping away.

They all climbed out onto the crumbling asphalt. Ken looked up and down the street. Piano jazz was drifting out from the window above a carpet store. It was the only sound, except for a *tap-tap-tap* as the leader of the barricade men dragged his baseball bat over the uneven sidewalk and through puddles of light from the streetlamps.

'We shouldn't—' Diane began.

'Christ, Diane, just follow them,' Carlos growled as Ken and Jakes walked carefully towards the cinema, watching for movement. She took his advice.

They reached the front doors, which were covered in weather-beaten posters for movies that had come and gone. There were no lights on inside the lobby, so it was the street lamps that picked out a couple of blue velvet-covered seats and the ticket booth in the centre of the room, standing desolate and open, its cash register empty. A strange, fast popping sound took Ken's attention, and he made out a bar in the dark corner where a glass cabinet was spilling popcorn across the floor like an invasion of cockroaches. A rubber tube stretched from the bottom of the cabinet to a large orange gas canister. Ken's feet crunched over the popcorn as he went to turn the lever and choke off the gas. The popping stopped, and they could make out the sound of voices on the other side of the double doors into the auditorium. The voices were arguing. One was a man's deep voice, the other female, shrill and furious.

Jakes glanced back to Diane and Carlos. Ken threw his coat and hat aside.

'Let us go!' Diane whispered.

'You're safer here where I can see you.' Jakes pushed the door but found it locked. He thumped hard on it. 'Police,' he yelled. 'We want to see who you got. Might be someone we know!'

Mumbling from the other side. '. . . *Cops* . . .' '. . . *sure they are* . . .' '. . . *not what we need* . . .'

Jakes slammed the bottom of his fist harder on the wood. 'Open up, or we're comin' in!' And he shooed his two guests a few yards away, as if the place might explode any second. 'Last chance!' He checked the revolver cylinder again. Ken could see that, behind the bravado, the detective was nervous.

'Have you ever pulled that trigger?' Ken asked.

'Once. Hit a dog.'

'How did it do?'

'Died.'

'Well, that's what's meant to happen.'

The sound of footsteps told them the door was being opened. They stood back.

What emerged was a face that looked like it had erupted and never healed. Volcanoes and deep caverns had ripped apart the flesh. Two deep eyes and a sunken nose confirmed a diagnosis of syphilis.

'We don't need you,' the broken-up face drawled through a three-inch gap between the double doors.

'Where you from, friend?' Jakes asked.

'T'nnessee,' it replied, clipping the first syllable.

'A long way from home.'

'What?' it started, confused, then looked angry. 'Can I help you with something?'

'We heard you had someone in there. Someone who might be the man we want.'

'We got this one, Sheriff,' the ruptured face laughed. And he tried to shut the door. The barrel of Jakes's gun wedged it open.

'I heard you folks from Tennessee had better manners.' The barrel was pointing down, but Jakes slowly tilted it up.

The ruptured face cracked into a sneering smile. 'Okay, okay. You got it. You come on in and see what we got.' He stood back. Jakes shoved him aside and entered, followed by Ken. Diane and Carlos scuttled in behind them.

As he stepped into the darkened chamber, blueish-white

light shone in Ken's eyes, blinding him for a second. Then he focused. On the screen, Fred MacMurray and Barbara Stanwyck were tearing strips off each other, their shadows moving, warped, across the seats.

All those seats were empty except for three in the centre of the front row, which were occupied by men looking up towards the screen. But it wasn't the movie they were watching; it was what was happening on the stage in front of the screen itself. An obese man with his wrists and ankles bound by rope was trying to crawl into the wings while the three in the stalls laughed. His face was covered in red welts and blood trickled from his nose. Another man, stripped to the waist and shining with sweat, stood over him, with cloth wrapped around his knuckles to protect them as they pounded down. He looked up as Jakes entered and wiped his arms across his forehead. Not worried, just hot.

'Come in, officers!' called the middle of the three men in the front row seats. 'Watch the show. We've been doing your job for you.' He turned around. He was tall and black, with a lot of gold jewellery that glinted like an eye when the light from the movie fell on it. The two white men on either side were laughing like gurgling drains.

Ken caught Jakes's glance and bounced it back to Diane and Carlos. She looked ready to vomit from fear, while he was edging himself squarely behind Jakes.

Jakes lowered his gun but kept it in his hand. Mr Tennessee smiled and went to the front, leaning nonchalantly against the stage as the fat man above him tried again to crawl away.

'You know who he is, don't you?' Ken said to Jakes, studying the policeman's face.

'I know who he is.' He raised his voice to the fat man. 'Didn't know you were out, Arnie.'

Arnie's mouth moved, but the sound was only a moan. He did his best to get to his knees until the man standing over him kicked him hard in the ribs.

'My God!' Diane burst out. And she turned tail and ran.

'You better go after her,' Jakes told Carlos.

'Her look-out if she leaves us,' he replied.

Jakes didn't care.

'He confess to anythin'?'

'Give us time,' the black man called back with confidence.

'Time. Time,' Jakes said, walking slowly towards the front, his gun out of sight but not out of his grip. Ken checked where the exits were as he followed. 'Time won't be enough. You think Arnie's the Mannequin Killer? Don't make me laugh.'

'Caught him snooping about an old lady's house, Sheriff,' said Mr Tennessee.

'Probably after her underwear. I wouldn't trust him alone with my wife, but the Mannequin killings? Not a chance. He couldn't stage that. He don't have two brain cells to rub together.'

'Another ten minutes, and we'll have him confess.'

'Oh, I'm sure you will. He'll confess to shootin' President Lincoln if you beat him enough.' He got close to the stage. 'Problem is, that still leaves the real killer out there. An' I can't have that.'

Ken spun around and grabbed the hand of the man from Tennessee, twisting it over while rocketing his left fist up and under the man's chin to punch him so hard that it lifted him from the ground. The man fell back into an upturned seat, dropping a black-gripped Colt .38 Super Automatic. Ken caught it in mid-air.

'Safety's off,' he said. 'My friend's a cop. I'm not.' Mr Tennessee tried to pull himself up from the chair, but Ken kicked his legs away. Out of the corner of his eye, he saw Carlos sink down into one of the rows of seats.

'Now, Kourian,' Jakes began.

'Enough of that. Who is he?'

'Arnie Holman. Lowlife. Not a killer.'

'Then we're leaving.'

'You're leaving him to us?' asked the black man.

'We've got more important things to deal with.' Ken ejected the round from the chamber, released the magazine and flung it to one side of the auditorium and the gun to the other.

'I guess we're leavin',' Jakes said. 'You ladies have a good night. He confesses to anythin' he *might* have done, call the station. Ask for anyone 'xcept me.'

Chapter 25

Diane was huddled in the back seat of the car, flitting from one window to another as if she could see killers in every direction.

'Where to now?' Ken said.

'Ah hell, why ask me? I know as much as you. Back to the station, I guess. As good as anywhere.' Jakes put the car in gear and started driving. But even in the ten minutes they had been in the movie theatre, things had begun to change on the street. The barricades had grown bigger. There were more men on them.

'You ain't comin' down here!' one yelled at the car from fifty yards away. And he and his eight or ten buddies started walking towards them to make the point. Jakes slowed the car to a crawl.

'What, you've got a gun, haven't you?' Carlos burst out nervously.

'I'm not gonna start shootin' just 'cause they got ants in their pants,' Jakes snapped back. He put the car in reverse, then pulled a fast U-turn and went back the way they'd come. They all watched the men behind them begin to trot after them in the half-light.

'Be careful,' Ken said. He could feel the atmosphere turning ugly.

'I get you, I get you.'

They hung a right onto Pacific, which would take them towards Clune. At least it would if another group of men, half a dozen of them, weren't doing their best to build another barrier across the road. They were different to the others. These guys looked Chinese, though it was hard to tell because they had caps pulled down and neckerchiefs pulled up. They checked quickly back as the car approached. A couple started shouting. Ken caught a few words and guessed they weren't friendly. This time, Jakes hit the gas and threw the car towards a gap in the mass of crates they had roped together. The men scattered, waving their fists at the car as it whipped past.

Suddenly something hard and heavy smacked onto the car roof. Looking up, Ken could make out a dent in it. Another on the hood. A stone or brick. They were being thrown down from the apartment buildings along the road. A bottle, a child's wooden doll, a broken stick all fell like hard rain. And then there was an explosion on the side of the car, swerving it across the road.

'They're shooting!' screamed Diane.

'Blow-out,' Ken told her. 'We drove over broken glass.' He turned to Jakes. 'Can we make it in this heap?'

'We'll see.' He pumped the gas pedal again, and the car shook but kept moving. As they reached the end of the block, the falling trash disappeared and was replaced by a few whoops and shouted cusses.

Jakes drove them past a burning car and a clothes store where the windows were smashed and empty. The mannequins that had modelled the shop's goods were on the sidewalk, broken to pieces. 'Crazy kinda retribution,' Jakes said.

'Let's hope they stick to dummies.'

'Ain't that the truth?'

They rolled unevenly on, passing a boarded-up gas station. *No money left here* said paint across the front of it. That wasn't stopping three men and a dirty-haired girl from breaking in. Ken checked Jakes. No, he wasn't going to stop. The girl watched with a sullen glare as they drove on past. Ken was struck by how young and hungry she looked.

Onto West Washington. The car rocked and swerved as the wheel rim cut the burst rubber to pieces. They were a hundred yards from the precinct house, but they weren't driving that last hundred. A small mob was marching up the street, shouting. Jakes asked a straggler, a young woman with her hair in a net, what their business was.

'Cops doin' nothin'!' came the answer. 'They doin' nothing, we gonna give 'em no peace!'

'What you got in mind?'

The woman grinned knowingly. 'You gonna come 'long?'

'Maybe I will. Maybe I won't.' He let her stride away and told everyone in the car to get out and stick behind him. They hurried up the side of the street, but only made it about twenty paces before the mob started pointing at them. 'Let's go!' Jakes said.

At that, they ran.

The entrance opened at the last second, held by a uniform with his hip holster unclasped. 'You got about a hundred angry people comin' this way,' Jakes told him as they fell into the lobby.

'Yeah, we saw.'

The waiting room was full of families in a fury, in tears, telling of property broken into, of fights with their neighbours, of cars stolen. They hadn't come to the cops because they thought the cops could do something about it, they'd come because they were afraid and had nowhere else to go. Jakes pushed his way to the desk and tore the desk sergeant away from taking down the details of a white-haired old woman.

'What the hell's goin' on?' Jakes demanded.

'We're swamped, Detective. We asked for backup, but the Chief said we had to deal with it ourselves.'

'We need to get you out of here,' Ken said to Carlos.

'Yeah, yeah, let's do that.'

'Deal with it?' Jakes said. 'Hell, the next—'

He spun around to see the entrance crashing open and the cop on sentry duty knocked back by the mob spewing in, turning over benches and trash cans.

'The apartment!' Ken shouted to him.

Jakes grabbed Diane and Carlos, dragging them to the side entrance. Ken kept up with them and they burst out into the parking lot just as a prowler was backing in. Jakes threw the driver out and commandeered the car, pushing Diane, who was red-faced with shock, into the back.

'Let me go!' she cried. But the detective wasn't listening. He gunned the car, and they swept out through the gates.

'Look out!' Ken said. A body bounced off the passenger-side fender. A very tall man dressed in dusty and torn clothes shook himself and came urgently to the driver's open window. Ken saw Jakes's hand drift down to the gun on his hip.

'You a cop?' the man rasped through a hole where his front teeth should have been. Some kind of bug fell out of his hair.

'I'm a cop,' Jakes said warily.

'I need to talk to you.'

'Then talk.' He didn't say it in a friendly way.

'It's me,' he said with a lisp through his teeth. Jakes waited. 'I told you, it's me.'

'Okay, pal. What's you?'

'I'm the killer. The Mannequin Killer. I did it.'

'Oh yeah? Okay, well, you go straight in there and tell the desk officer what you did. And don't leave nothin' out, you hear?'

The man seemed to shake all over, like a dog. Then his lips stretched back to bare his remaining teeth. And his head burst right through the open window, winding his shoulders through, grappling with Jakes, trying to force himself into the car. Ken went for the revolver on Jakes's hip, but just as his fingers closed on it, Jakes hit the gas pedal and the car lurched forward. The dirty man was thrown clear, smacking down onto the road and rolling a couple of yards. Within seconds, the car was doing twenty.

'You want to go back and check he's okay?' Ken asked, watching him in the rearview mirror. The car jumped forward again. 'Thought not.'

They came to a sharp halt in front of the apartment building where Diane and her husband had shared a home until someone decided that Frankie Angel's life had run its course.

There was something very different about it today, though. Most streets in Los Angeles were deserted. This one had a small crowd gathered in front. At first Ken thought they were about to face down another mob. But it wasn't that. These people, mostly young women, had sad faces, not angry ones, and they were gathered around a small patch beside the entrance. Ken eased a few aside and looked down. A framed photograph of Frankie Angel – autographed, maybe by him but more likely by a press agent – was surrounded by candles and cheap paper flowers. A makeshift shrine to a second-rate actor.

Through the lobby, then into the elevator. Diane was gently shaking, and tears were smearing lines through her rouge. Carlos had a grim, stony face. The moment the car opened at the penthouse floor, Diane burst through between Jakes and Carlos, running to her front door with her keys in her hand, scrabbling at the lock and throwing it open. She rushed in and flicked the light switch. Nothing happened. And yet there was a glow in the room. A line of candles was burning on the floor.

'What the hell?' Carlos said.

'I . . . This isn't . . .' Diane stammered. The candles led from where they all stood towards the staircase, up the stairs and along the mezzanine to the bathroom. She stared at Jakes, looking for direction.

'I guess you'd better follow them,' Ken said.

She looked dumbly from the candles to him and back. Her mouth tried forming words but failed. Then her feet began to move.

The four of them moved like a single animal, slowly drawn pace by pace to the bathroom. And then Ken began to hear the sound. A light rushing sound of water pouring into water. Diane looked back at him, but he pointed to the door, and she took the order. They had to go on.

Through the door they saw the source of the crazy sound. In the wide bathroom, the tiles were awash with cold water. Low waves drifted through a flood an inch deep. It was spilling in a waterfall over the sides of the bath, reflecting the sheen of light from a ring of candles around the tub. They couldn't help but look inside the bath, and when they did they saw, at the bottom, a mannequin with its eyes gouged out. Drowned just like Frankie Angel.

Still the water streamed out from the faucet, pouring into the tub, rising over the sides, spreading towards the doorway to swell around those watching. Diane let out a scream.

'Remind you of anything?'

The words were spoken from behind them. They spun around. Coraline stood in the doorway, watching them all. 'Does it?'

'You!' yelled Carlos, and he lunged at her. She moved aside as Ken's arm shot out, pinning him by the neck against the wall.

'Detective!' Carlos cried, looking desperately to the cop.

Jakes took the gun from his holster and handed it to Ken. Diane fell to her knees in sobs.

'Shut up,' Ken told her out of the side of his mouth. She instantly stopped and her eyes darkened. 'It all started with Francisco Angelo, who became Frankie Angel. A good son but a second-rate actor. And you two had had enough of him, hadn't you?'

'What? I have no idea—' Carlos cried. Ken pistol-whipped him in the stomach, then pressed the barrel under his ribs. Carlos coughed and wheezed, the wind knocked from his lungs, then tried to climb the wall as he felt the gun pushing up into him.

'We'll listen,' Diane said coldly.

'And where better to hide your tracks than in an entire wood full of them? The book that we've all been running around after. *The Waterfall.* We never asked if you knew Gabriel Faulkner, did we?'

'I've never heard of him,' Diane said.

'Don't lie now, Diane. You knew about him, and you read his book. And you noticed that one of the stories is called "The Angel". That gave you the idea: kill Frankie in a way ripped straight out of the book; but before and after, kill two more poor saps in crimes that shouted they were from the book, too. You must have known Gabriel Faulkner was a recluse and you wanted us to think it was him.'

'Tell me.'

'Your fingerprints. We found them on the bath where you drowned Frankie.'

'I live here! Of course my fingerprints are on the bath.'

'Sure. But the killer would have wiped them away. If he had existed. The other scenes were meticulously wiped clean and you said you never entered the bathroom, you only saw him from the doorway, so you couldn't have laid them down after the killer had wiped the tub clean. But Frankie was the first to die, because you wanted to make sure he was dead before you started killing the others to lay a false trail. And because he was the first, you hadn't thought of the fact that you'd have to start wiping away any prints from then on.'

But her voice dripped defiance. 'Oh, he was the first, was he? Then how come the autopsy said he died the day I called you?'

'The water slopping all over the floor.'

'What are you talking about?'

'It was like a lake in there. Totally flooded. Like tonight.'

Carlos found his voice. 'What does that prove? Frankie fought back against whoever did that to him! The water splashed out of the bath, that's all.'

'Then how come, when we found him, the water level was right up to the top of the tub?'

'What? I don't know,' he said dismissively.

'But I do.' He shoved the gun barrel up hard, making Carlos gasp. 'You needed to make it look like he'd died as the second victim to avoid suspicion. So you spent two days pouring bag after bag of ice into the bath to keep him cold and fake his time of death. But each time you did that, the water rose over the sides. And there's your little bathroom lake.'

Carlos regained some of his lawyer bravado. 'You think any of this will stand up in court?' he sputtered. 'It's all circumstantial.'

'Sure. But we'll find how you knew about Faulkner. He was going to have a party when his book was published. A bunch of actors on the guest list. I'll bet Frankie was one of them, poor sap. It's all still there, you know; rotting away in that big mausoleum of his.'

Diane began to laugh hysterically, then she threw herself on Ken, tearing at his face and grabbing at the gun.

The sound of it firing made the room shake. And when she fell to the floor, she sent a wave of red surging through the cold water. For a moment, they were all still. Then Carlos fell to his knees and pulled her towards him. He bent over her face and kissed her lips, but they didn't kiss him back.

The air was dead still. 'What are you going to do now?' Ken asked.

As an answer, Carlos jumped up, knocking Ken aside, and dashed for the door, through the darkened living quarters and out onto the balcony. The lights of Los Angeles lay spread before him. Car horns sounded, and the drawled shouts of strangers pierced the night. Ken ran after him. He was three or four paces behind when Carlos sprawled his body across the waist-high concrete wall around the veranda, balancing on the parapet. A plane passed low enough to see the undercarriage in its housing.

Ken wasn't sure whether Carlos would do it or not. But he wanted to find out. 'It's the gas chamber in Cali,' he said. He didn't give a damn if he saw Carlos die in a prison execution room or broken up on the sidewalk. Which would it be? It was like a gameshow host showing the prize, but keeping it back until enough points had been scored. Carlos twisted his head to look back at Ken, then he stared down to the ground three storeys below. 'Make your choice. Make it soon. I don't care which it is.'

The cars rumbled past. The horns sounded. And Carlos Angelo slumped back from the parapet and to his knees on the balcony floor, wiping the night sweat from his face.

'Gas chamber, then,' Ken said. He paused, looking into Carlos's face, and then at the city before them. The fumes from the cars below drifted up. He could taste them on his tongue. 'One thing I don't understand,' he said. 'Why did you try to implicate Coraline? What did she ever do to you?'

The only reply was Carlos's eyes, as empty as if he were already dead, turning to Ken's and then to the apartment where everything – all that treachery, all that lying, all that abandonment – had taken place.

Ken glanced back over the cityscape, where the skyscrapers were pointing up into the night sky like bones. He didn't understand people like this, they might as well be dumb animals. Then he walked back into the apartment and left Carlos Angelo on the floor of his dead brother's balcony, for Jakes to clear up.

Chapter 26

It was eight days later that Ken Kourian was driving along the coastal road to Turnglass House, the family seat of the Tooke family at Point Dume, where he was to pick up Coraline. They were going for dinner at a beachside restaurant, where the conversation would begin light. Then, by degrees, he would make it more serious until he worked it round to the point: things between him and her had a future. He was thinking of telling the War Department that he had to stay home, at least for a while. As he drove, his arm bare below the elbow and hanging out over the side of Coraline's Rolls-Royce, he wondered how she would take it. He thought he knew: she would initially give little indication that she had even heard what he'd said, then she would lightly shrug her curving shoulders and suggest that it was his business what he did. He would tell her that that wasn't true, that it was their joint business. Then, and only then, would she say what was on her mind. She would want him in California. They both knew it. It was just a matter of them both admitting it.

He brooded again over the book that had started it all, *The Turnglass/The Waterfall,* and over the proof copy they had found in her house. Sent out to journalists and the book's authors. It was, perhaps, the only one of those left in the world. He wondered how Carlos and Diane had procured at least two other copies of a book that had been withdrawn from sale within a fortnight of its publication.

He stopped the car by the roadside and got out. He stared at the sea for half an hour, as gears in his mind fell into place. He drove to a payphone and called Jakes.

'You ever hear of people coming together to commit murder?' he asked, as the orange sun dipped in the sky.

'Comin' together? All the time.'

'I mean strangers. Or near strangers.'

'Like mob hitters?'

'No, like two parties who realize their aims can work together. Like someone wants someone dead, and another party wants someone else blamed for it, out of some grudge for revenge that's eating away at them. And if these two parties do it together, it makes it a damn sight harder for you or me to work out what's really going on.'

'Ain't heard anythin' like that. What you talkin' 'bout?'

'One thing I couldn't understand: why Carlos and Diane targeted me and Coraline. Why, of all the books that are out there, did they pick the one written by Oliver Tooke and Gabriel Faulkner?'

'An' the answer is?'

'The answer is *they* didn't. Someone else did. Someone who had a grievance against us and wanted retribution, but also wanted to taunt us along the way. Someone who came up with an idea that would get them all what they wanted. Someone who once had need of a Hollywood lawyer. And Carlos was the one he hired.'

'Kourian, you got somethin' on your—'

Ken hung up the phone. It had been so clever. Blind on blind. But if he and Coraline hadn't been so wrapped up in themselves, would he have seen it before?

The biographer closed his car door. Another vehicle was parked on the weed-strewn gravel in front of the Faulkner house. It was an expensive car, a Rolls-Royce of all things, and a man was standing beside it with his hands in his pockets, gazing at the house. He was a big guy, well built, but wearing a cheap suit. He turned two penetrating eyes on the writer.

The biographer went to the solid oak double doors and rapped home the lion's head knocker. It opened instantly and a girl, the younger one, stood in the doorway, dressed in a neat black skirt and white blouse. She peeped out at the man in their overgrown driveway, before standing back to let the writer in and shutting the house again after him. The bottom of the door scraped over the uneven tiles.

There was no need this time to stalk through the house in search of Gabriel Faulkner. He was there in the hallway, propped up on a metal walking stick, the tube in his mouth to inflate his botulism-wracked lungs. He stood in profile, peering through a narrow gap in the window shutters at the man outside. The hallway was dark, but something beside his left hip, shielded from the writer's view by Faulkner's body, was glowing yellow.

'Who is he?' the visitor asked.

'He . . . thinks . . . I . . . am . . . guilty . . . of . . . a . . . crime,' came the rasped reply.

'A crime?' Faulkner nodded slowly. 'Are you?'

Gabriel Faulkner haltingly and painfully turned his body. In his left hand was a copy of a book. *The Waterfall.* It was alight, and flames had devoured half of it already, turning the pages to fluttering ash. The fire was enveloping his fingers, burning them black.

'I . . . will . . . tell . . . you . . . the . . . story,' he said. And he stretched his mouth, around the rubber tube, into a smile.

If you enjoyed *The Waterfall*, discover
more mind-bending mysteries from Gareth Rubin,
the master of ingenious crime fiction . . .

The TURNGLASS

GARETH RUBIN

'Vivid, resonant, melancholy and beautiful' Janice Hallett

1880s England.

Idealistic young doctor Simeon Lee arrives on the bleak island of Ray, off the Essex coast, to treat his cousin, Parson Oliver Hawes, who is dying. Parson Hawes, who lives on the only house on the island – Turnglass House – believes he is being poisoned and he points the finger at his sister-in-law, Florence. Florence was declared insane after killing Oliver's brother in a jealous rage and is now kept in a glass-walled apartment in Oliver's library. And the secret to how she came to be there can be found in Oliver's tête-bêche journal, where one side tells a very different story from the other.

1930s California.

Celebrated author Oliver Tooke, the son of the state governor, is found dead in his writing hut behind the family residence, Turnglass House. His friend Ken Kourian doesn't believe that Oliver would take his own life. His investigations lead him to the mysterious kidnapping of Oliver's brother when they were children, and the subsequent secret incarceration of his mother, Florence, in an asylum. But to discover the truth, Ken must decipher clues hidden in Oliver's final book, a tête-bêche novel – which is about a young doctor called Simeon Lee . . .

'A stunning, ingenious, truly immersive mystery.
The Turnglass is a thrilling delight' Chris Whitaker

Available in paperback, ebook & audio

SIMON &
SCHUSTER

London · New York · Amsterdam/Antwerp · Sydney/Melbourne · Toronto · New Delhi

MURDER A̅T̅ CHRISTMAS

A cosy crime mystery in the style of a Choose
Your Own Adventure.

It is 1932. You are Dr Kim Tenor, a Scotland Yard pathologist
with a sideline in private detection when the boys in blue are
stumped. You're celebrated in the newspapers, but you tend to
get the official police's backs up. You attend the opening night
of your friend Johnny MacAlister's ritzy new nightclub, the Silver
Star. While you're there, Johnny says something a bit odd has
been happening and can you come back tomorrow and look
into it for him?

But you have also promised Algy Hurley to go down to the
family seat, Hurley Court, where some strange events have been
occurring.

If you return to the Silver Star, you're caught up in a mystery
that turns out to be a thrilling spy caper where you have to foil
the plot; if it's Hurley Court, it's a Christmas-set country house
murder involving an old family ritual and a silver dagger.

What would you choose?

Available for preorder now

SIMON &
SCHUSTER

London · New York · Amsterdam/Antwerp · Sydney/Melbourne · Toronto · New Delhi